PRAISE
TO SCOTLAND WITH LOVE

"A magnificent triple-hankie read that goes straight to the heart, by turns tender, funny, heart-wrenching, and wise. Prepare to smile through your tears at this deft, brave, and deeply gratifying love story."

—Grace Burrowes, *New York Times* bestselling author of the Lonely Lords and the Windham series

"Griffin has quilted together a wonderful, heartwarming story that will convince you of the power of love."

—*New York Times* bestselling author Janet Chapman

"Griffin's style is as warm and comfortable as a cherished heirloom quilt."

—*New York Times* bestselling author Lori Wilde

"A life-affirming story of love, loss, and redemption. Patience Griffin seamlessly pieces compelling characters, a spectacular setting, and a poignant romance into a story as warm and beautiful as an heirloom quilt. Both heartrending and heartwarming, *To Scotland with Love* is a must-read romance and so much more. The story will touch your soul with its depth, engage you with its cast of endearing characters, and delight you with touches of humor."

—Diane Kelly, author of the Tara Holloway series

continued . . .

Some Like It Scottish

A Kilts and Quilts Novel

Patience Griffin

A SIGNET ECLIPSE BOOK

SIGNET ECLIPSE
Published by the Penguin Group
Penguin Group (USA) LLC, 375 Hudson Street,
New York, New York 10014

USA | Canada | UK | Ireland | Australia | New Zealand | India | South Africa | China
penguin.com
A Penguin Random House Company

First published by Signet Eclipse, an imprint of New American Library,
a division of Penguin Group (USA) LLC

First Printing, July 2015

ISBN 978-0-451-46831-4

Printed in the United States of America
10 9 8 7 6 5 4 3 2 1

Acknowledgments

To Cagney

The most wonderful daughter in the world, who shares my obsession with fabric and my love of quilts. Thank you for being my girl.

A big thank-you goes to Lori and Lisa for sharing their childhood game with me.

PRONUNCIATION GUIDE

Aileen (AY-leen)
Ailsa (AIL-sa)
Bethia (BEE-thee-a)
Buchanan (byoo-KAN-uhn)
Cait (KATE)
Deydie (DI-dee)
Lochie (LAW-kee)
Macleod (muh-KLOUD)
mo chridhe (mo hree) my heart
Moira (MOY-ra)
shite (shite) expletive

DEFINITIONS

burn—small river or large stream
céilidh (KAY-lee)—a party/dance
fash—trouble
Gandiegow—squall
Ghillie (GIL-ee)—an attendant or guide for hunting or fishing
ken—understanding
selkie—mythological creatures who live as seals in the ocean but shed their skin and become human on land

Quilters of Gandiegow

Rule #2
Quilt with all yere heart.
It's the best investment ye'll ever make.

Chapter One

Twenty-six-year-old Ramsay Armstrong pulled the fishing boat alongside the dock and hollered to his oldest brother, John. "What's so important that ye've called me back? I haven't checked the north nets yet." He threw the rope to his brother.

"I'll take care of the damned nets." John tied off the boat. "I have a job for you, and it can't wait."

"Do it yereself!" More often than not, Ramsay got stuck with the crap jobs in the family.

"I had planned to." John ducked his head and, stepping aboard, muttered, "Maggie won't let me."

Ramsay grinned. "Yere wife telling you what you can and can't do." He pounded John on the back. "There's the reason I'm still single, brother."

"Nay." John shook his head. "Ye're an arse, Ramsay. That's why ye're still single. No woman would have ye."

"So what's this job you need done?"

John didn't meet his eye. "It has to do with the maintenance we scheduled for the boat."

"I thought we set enough money aside for that."

"I thought so, too, but a revised quote came in. The price has gone up. Way up."

"By how much?"

John shook his head.

Ramsay frowned. John never shared the actual numbers with him, always keeping him in the dark, always treating him like the babe in the family. "So what's this have to do with the favor you want?"

"Ross and I'll take care of the boat while ye're doing it," John hedged.

"Spit it out, man." Ramsay was about to knock his brother into the drink. "What is it?"

John pulled a sheet of paper from his pocket and thrust it at him. "It's all there. Her itinerary."

Ramsay took it and opened the crumpled paper. The letterhead read:

Kit Woodhouse Matchmaking, Inc.
Kit Woodhouse, CEO

Real Men of Alaska   *Real Men of Scotland*

Ramsay snapped his head up and glared at his brother. "What the crank is this? Matchmaker? From the U.S.?"

"Read on." John busied himself with two empty buckets, but really he was avoiding Ramsay's glare. He should be chagrined.

It was indeed a detailed itinerary—beginning with when this woman would land and her schedule for each day.

"For the next three cranking months?" Ramsay yelled. "Surely, you don't expect me to play nursemaid *for three months* to some sappy matchmaker!" The word made him feel like he could breathe fire.

John hung his head. "I saw her ad for a driver on the Internet. We need the money. I thought you and Ross could run the boat for the summer and I'd put up with driving Ms. Woodhouse around. But when Maggie found out, she nearly chopped off my balls."

"It would serve you right." Ramsay ran his eyes down the length of the paper. "Did you never think to consult Ross and me in your scheme?"

"I'm the oldest; I make the decisions." John acted like he had decades on Ramsay, but he was only thirty-five, nine years older than Ramsay.

Ramsay huffed. "Well, ye've screwed up this time. You better call it off and tell this woman we can't do it."

"But I signed a contract." John's brow furrowed as he ran a hand through his hair. "Ms. Woodhouse doesn't care who lives up to the contract, as long as somebody does."

Ramsay wadded the paper in his fist. "So you volunteered me."

"Ye better get back to the house and clean up." John started the motor. "You'll have just enough time to get a shower, *and shave*, before you have to rush off to the airport."

Ramsay considered cramming the itinerary down his brother's throat. He stepped off the boat instead, too angry to speak. On autopilot, he loosened the line and pushed the boat away with his foot.

John shouted above the motor. "Be on your best behavior and don't screw this up. We need the money."

Ramsay flipped him off, and then, shaking his head, trudged off the dock.

He sure as hell wasn't going to let John's asinine matchmaker interfere with his own plans. In one month Ramsay intended to have enough money to buy ole man Martin's boat. Between the odd jobs at the North Sea Valve Company and helping the surrounding farmers after he was done fishing for the day, he would have enough. *One month.*

And dammit, if he didn't get the old codger the money by then, the boat would be put up for auction and go for twice what Martin had agreed to.

Well, Ramsay had no intention of losing his chance to get out from under his brothers' thumbs. He wasn't born the youngest for nothing. He'd learned early on there's more than one way to wiggle out of a chore. He would make short work of the matchmaker, he decided. Three days with him and the interfering ole biddy would be paying him to go back to her nice cushy life in the States, where she belonged.

Kit's plane landed late—way late. Of course she couldn't control the weather, but she prided herself on being prompt. She'd learned a thing or two about how to come into a remote area and set up shop. First and foremost, she had to gain the locals' trust. Getting off on the wrong foot wouldn't do.

After Kit deplaned and made it to the other side of the gate, there was no one there holding a sign with her name on it, no one to pick her up. She waited around a few minutes, in case whoever it was had run to the bathroom. But no one came.

"Dammit." She marched off to baggage claim to get her luggage. After filling up a trolley, she checked one more time at the gate—no one. She pulled out her folder and found the phone number for John Armstrong. When he answered, the background noise of an engine was loud and obnoxious.

"Mr. Armstrong, I thought we agreed that someone would be here for me."

"Och, I sent my brother Ramsay to fetch you. He left eons ago. Is he not there waiting?"

Kit looked around in vain, trying to keep her cool. "No." She started walking, heading for the parking lot. "Do you think he might be waiting outside?"

"Hold on, lassie. I'll give him a call." John seemed to be struggling with something on his end, wherever he was.

Kit stopped and snatched a pen from her pocket. "Why don't you give me his number and I'll call him?"

"Sure." John rattled it off. "I'm sorry about this, Ms. Woodhouse. It's a hell of a way to start out in Scotland."

Tell me about it. "It's okay."

They said goodbye and hung up.

Kit pulled her trolley outside to see if the brother waited at the curb. There wasn't anyone. She dialed the number. As it rang, a phone in the parking lot played the song "Kryptonite." She hung up and dialed again—"Kryptonite" played once more. Exasperated, she dragged the trolley out into the lot to hunt for the owner of the phone.

She dialed once more and followed the song to a muddy Mitsubishi Outlander SUV where the door was open and a sleeping man sat inside. He had earplugs in, an iPod on his knee, and the cell blasting "Kryptonite" beside him. She hung up and stared at him for a long minute.

He was the same type of man she'd fixed up with her East Coast socialite clients through her Alaskan operation. *A real man.* He wore a red plaid shirt, jeans, and black wellies. The boots were awful and she couldn't imagine anyone wearing them anywhere beyond a fishing boat. His dark hair was long and wavy, and framed a handsome, rugged face that also sported a day-old beard. Very attractive. But definitely not her type.

She dialed again, but this time as the phone rang, she nudged him. "You've got a call."

He came awake on a slow inhalation and focused a heavenly groggy smile on her. "What?"

She pointed to the seat. "Your phone is ringing. It might be important."

"Oh." He picked it up. "Hallo."

She put her phone to her ear, frowning, while maintaining eye contact with him. "I've arrived in Inverness. I'd like to go to Gandiegow now."

The place between his eyebrows squinched together. "Fine," he said into the phone, a quick flush of pink on his neck. He hung up.

She gave him a curt nod, pleased she'd embarrassed him.

He frowned at her. "They said your flight wouldn't be in until eight p.m. I came out here to rest my eyes."

"It's eight thirty."

He glanced at his phone and his brows knit together again. He unfolded his tall frame from the SUV. Scrutinizing her, he leaned against the side and crossed his arms over his massive chest. The puppy-dog sweetness was gone now, replaced by a mutt who didn't like the smell of what had been dropped in his dish. "So ye're the matchmaker."

She slapped a smile on her face and stuck out her hand, determined not to let this skeptic get to her. After all, he was obviously not one of the wealthy Scottish bachelors she needed to win over. "Kit Woodhouse at your service."

He considered her hand, and for a moment, she wondered if he might not take it. Just as she was about to abandon her effort at being civil, his hand enveloped hers. It was callused and firm. Normally, she had a good read on a person in the first five seconds, male or female. But she wasn't clear on this guy. He was gorgeous if you liked rough-hewn and unpolished, which she didn't, but that dark gleam he gave her hinted at more.

He held her eyes hostage while he gripped her hand. "Ramsay Armstrong. Unfortunate brother to John Armstrong, who contracted services with ye."

She dropped his hand and shifted her eyes away from his gray ones. "Why are you the *unfortunate brother*?" She glanced up at his face again. "Or maybe I don't want to know."

He shrugged. "I'm a sea lover, not a land dweller. I understand that I'm to take ye all over the Highlands by auto. *To do yere job.*" He was indeed unhappy with her.

"Yes, I need to fill my stables."

"Yere what? Is it man or beast ye're after?"

"*Stables.* It's an expression. I'm after men." *Great!* That hadn't come out right. Her delayed flight had her rattled. "I need to find eligible bachelors to fill my database."

Her phone rang; it was Donna, her office manager in Alaska. "Excuse me."

"We've got a problem," Donna yelled into the phone. "Morgan has arrived from Connecticut, but Greg, her date, can't be found. He isn't answering his phone, either."

Kit's stomach dropped. "*Son of a bitch.* Greg assured me he'd show up to meet her, but I had a feeling he'd go MIA. *Damned bachelor.*" She'd been in Scotland all of three seconds and everything was going to hell back home. And here was this Scottish brute listening in on her conversation. She turned her back to him for privacy.

"What do I tell Morgan?" Donna said, fretting. "That's a long way to come here for nothing."

"Tell her not to worry. She just needs to hang on. I'll find her a man in Scotland. Tell her that I'll take care of her flight, everything." It would cost a pretty penny, but Kit prided herself on customer satisfaction. It took another couple of minutes, but Kit was able to calm down Donna; then she hung up.

When she turned around, Ramsay was assessing her. "Ye know, don't ye, that what you want to do here won't work." He lifted one of his smug eyebrows.

"What?" She couldn't believe her ears; he'd given voice to her biggest fear—that she wouldn't be able to make things work here in Scotland.

Kit had gone with her gut and gotten lucky with her operation in Alaska. The single women she'd known from the country club set—before her family had been forced to exchange caviar for bologna sandwiches—tended to be quiet and romantic; she sensed that what they wanted was a "real man" with a traditional approach to relationships. So she'd foregone the lower forty-eight entirely, bypassing not just the financiers and tech millionaires but the ranchers and oilmen who sounded rugged but who were just business tycoons, and sought out men from Alaska. And she was right. Real Men had proven to be what her clients' hearts desired.

But when it came time to expand, Kit didn't go solely on instincts this time. She'd hired a team of consultants to figure out her next move. The consulting firm's recommendation: Expand her Real Men operation into Scotland. The firm had a great track record, but Kit had been worried ever since that they'd gotten it wrong. She worried whether her clients really yearned for a bigger adventure in a foreign location. She worried about the Scots and their compatibility. And she worried whether her East Coast socialite clients really longed for a Highland romance like the consulting firm said they did.

Kit's father used to say *never let them see you sweat*. But right now, she could use more Arrid Extra Dry. She went on the defensive with the Scot before her. "You don't even know what I do."

Ramsay crossed his arms over his massive chest again, a man relaxed and sure of himself. "I have a pretty clear idea. If ye think your Alaskan *boys* don't like to be told what to do, what makes ye think we Scottish *men* will?"

The *Scottish man* standing in front of her may have a lot going on in the looks department, but he had a lot to learn when it came to Kit and her tenacity. "I'm very good at what I do, Mr. Armstrong." She had a high marriage rate to prove it.

"Why are you even here?" he questioned. "If you wanted to fill yere *stables*, as you say, you could've done that with yere computer from the Hamptons or Martha's Vineyard or wherever ye call home."

She took a cleansing breath. The Martha's Vineyard house had been auctioned off with their other homes to pay their creditors. But she wasn't telling this brute about her family's plunge into poverty.

She straightened her shoulders and stood as tall as her five-foot-two frame would allow. She'd endured some stubborn men before and now it looked like she would have her hands full with this one. She stood her ground with the Scotsman. "For your information, Mr. Armstrong, I do things the old-fashioned way. I interview my clients and their prospective dates in person." It was the best way to get an accurate assessment of them. "Skype or FaceTime might be considered the face-to-face of the twenty-first century, but I believe in the personal touch."

He raised his eyebrows as if a crude comment was forthcoming.

She put her hand up to stop him. "Computers are for storing databases, not for getting to know one another." It was bugging her that she still hadn't pinned down this Ramsay Armstrong. She decided it must be because he was all brawn and no brains.

He had been leaning nonchalantly against the vehicle but pushed away from it, standing to his full height. He skimmed his eyes over her, from her summer sweater to her Lee jeans, right down to her new Doc Martens.

She wasn't intimidated. She'd learned from her Alaskan adventure to dress properly. For the weather and the culture. *And the natives*. It was best to try to fit in, but not to try too hard.

When he was done with his perusal, he gestured at her person like she was nothing more than a mannequin. "You don't look like an old-fashioned kind of lass. You look to me like you saw this outfit in an outdoor magazine and ordered it online."

"Are you trying to provoke me, Mr. Armstrong?"

He shrugged. "I think what you want to do here is a crock of . . ." He stopped himself as if he'd thought better of it and stepped forward. "I don't believe in matchmakers. People should come together naturally without the help of a third party, unless it's the Almighty. Haven't ye ever heard *three's a crowd*?"

"All brawn, no brains," she murmured. She wished she was taller, but her feminine stature was no match for him. He had to be six-two at least. She made sure her attitude made up for the difference. "You're arguing against history. Matchmaking has been around since the beginning of time. Look it up."

"If ye're so good at this, then how would you match me?" he challenged.

She maintained eye contact. She was going to enjoy putting this arrogant cave dweller in his place.

"First, we'd have to discuss your assets. Do you own a manor house or an estate?"

"Not exactly."

"What do you mean *not exactly*?" It felt good to wipe that smirk off his face.

"I live in a cottage."

She raised her eyebrows. "Is it at least a nice-sized cottage?"

"It's the house I grew up in."

"You still live with your parents?" He didn't look like he'd *failed to launch*.

"I live with my brother Ross. And of course John, and his wife, Maggie, and their boy, Dand."

Good grief. "That's quite a crew." She bet they were stepping all over one another. But back to the business at hand. She tilted her head back, trying to stare him down. "What about other property? A ranch? Any sheep? Cattle?"

He looked riled, his neck and chest creeping with red. "My brothers and I own a fishing boat."

She shook her head. "Maybe if you owned *a fleet of boats*. Sorry, Mr. Armstrong. I won't find you a bride."

His eyes narrowed. Brawn looked like he was barely holding back a few choice obscenities.

In Alaska, she didn't require the bachelors to possess major assets, just a decent job, but she was changing it up here in the Highlands. She was tired of running interference between her socialite clients and their parents. It had been a monumental task, trying to prove to the girls' families that a man's substance didn't lie in his wallet. Kit was done with that hassle. She couldn't change the paradigm for Alaska, but she sure as hell could require her bachelors here in Scotland to have money, or property, or both. *Mummy and Daddy* would feel better about losing their daughters to the wilds of Scotland if their offspring were matched with millionaires.

The great hulk of a Scotsman before her stood rodstraight, a warrior ready to make a scene here in the parking lot.

He could bluster all he wanted. Tough guys like him needed to be brought down a notch. Especially if they were attacking how she made her living.

She'd gone on the offensive; now, it was time to help the poor lout out. "I have a list of *Marriageable Attributes.* You should check out my website." She reached in her bag, pulled out a business card, and slid it into the front pocket of his flannel shirt, patting it. She couldn't help but notice he was rock solid, all muscle under her hand. She had the urge to pat a little longer. "Maybe after you review the list on my site, you can work at being a better catch."

He caught her hand before she'd fully withdrawn it, turning the tables on her. He oozed with latent sexuality. "I do fine all on my own. I don't need help to find a mate," he drawled.

The word *mate* hung in the air. He let go of her hand. *Gads.* Her imagination raced into overdrive. She was either extremely jet-lagged or she needed a date herself. She hadn't been out in ages; she was too busy bringing other couples together. From the beginning, she'd drawn a clear line. She chose rugged men for her clients and picked Wall Street suits for herself. That way she was never tempted to mix business with pleasure. She hadn't found a man with the qualities she wanted, but one day she would. As it turned out, her greatest gift—reading people—was also her biggest impediment to finding some-one for herself. The stockbrokers and bankers she'd dated so far had only had money and sex on their minds, and little else.

Ramsay grabbed her bags. "Let's get going."

She glanced up and saw his muscles ripple under his shirt. Her breath caught. *Yeah, I need a date.*

He opened the back and threw in her luggage with brute force. She started to protest, but inhaled deeply instead. It would be best to choose her battles with this one. Otherwise, it would be a long, long summer.

She slid into the passenger seat and chewed her lower lip. There was a subject she had to broach with him and he wouldn't like it. But it was important. She turned toward him in the seat.

"Mr. Armstrong—"

"Ramsay," he corrected.

"Ramsay, then." She paused. "We need to talk about my expectations." She scanned his person one more time, really hating those black wellies of his. She steeled herself for what had to be said. "The bachelors I've selected to interview are men of substance."

Almost imperceptibly, he shook his head as if he was barely tolerating her. "Don't confuse substance with worldly goods; they're two different things, lassie. Ye mean men of wealth, power, and standing."

It wouldn't do any good to try to convince him that she knew the difference. Hell, she'd put it in her business plan. "Yes, I'm speaking of wealth, power, and standing, as you put it."

"Then what's the rub?" he asked.

"I was wondering if you might reconsider your attire. Wear something a bit more upscale."

He glanced at her with raised eyebrows. "Ye have a problem with me being a fisherman?"

"No, of course not. It's an honorable profession." She meant it but hurried on. "There's nothing wrong with being casual and comfortable." She gestured toward her own clothing. "But when I interview these men, I'll be dressed professionally."

"I see. And since I'll be with ye, ye'll be wanting me to convey the right image as well." He put his eyes back on the road and jammed the gearshift into drive. "Don't worry, lassie. I'll be dressed the part."

"Thank you, Ramsay. I appreciate your cooperation."

She didn't tell him that everything was riding on this trip. Every dime she'd made and saved. Her sister Harper's fall tuition for graduate school. The cost of community college for her younger sister, Bridget. Kit expected she'd have to help her mother with her living expenses now that Bridget had graduated high school and her social security survivor benefits from Daddy had run out. Even Kit's self-worth and ego were on the line. *Everything.* She had to make a go of it in Scotland or lose it all.

As silence filled the car, Kit gazed out the window. It was late and the sun still hung in the sky. The summer days were long in the north of Scotland, the view desolate and beautiful. The mountainous hills rose out of the earth like giants. There were few trees and she couldn't help but compare it to the Alaskan bush with its vast forests of green. The stark landscape around her had a soothing quality, but Kit couldn't tamp down the fear rising within her. Fear of the future and the unknown. In the past, she had never let the fear overtake her. She'd always made it through the tough times and she would again this time, too, wouldn't she?

She must've dozed off because she came awake abruptly as Ramsay brought the vehicle to a stop.

"Are we here?" She looked out and saw the road-block in front of them.

"Nay. But we'll be there shortly." He shifted into four-wheel drive and drove the car down an embankment.

Warning bells should've gone off, but the man in the seat next to her must've instilled a walloping dollop of trust. Or she was too exhausted to be concerned at his sudden foray into off-road four-wheeling. "So do you want to share with me what's going on?"

"The road into Gandiegow is being repaved. We'll have to go in by boat."

Dread swamped Kit and she twisted her hands in her lap. She hadn't been on a boat since her father died. "Is there another way?" She hated how weak her voice sounded.

He glanced over at her. "Ye have my word that ye'll be safe."

She nodded. He couldn't know what this did to her. As they rose over the last dune, the water appeared. *Her father's grave.*

Ramsay pulled the SUV to the edge. "There it is."

A wooden dinghy was tied to a post with a long rope that drooped in the mud. "Low tide, I presume?" She looked down at her new Doc Martens, not happy to have to break them in this way. But more importantly, did Ramsay have a life vest?

Her father used to call her *trout* because she was a born swimmer. But that was before.

Ramsay turned off the car and shoved the keys in the glove box. He jumped out and retrieved her bags.

They walked through the grass to the edge of the mud. There Kit hesitated.

Ramsay shook his head and muttered, "New shoes." He dropped her bags, scooped her up, and began trudging toward the boat like she was nothing more than a piece of luggage.

She gasped. "What are you doing?" She clung to him for dear life as he walked her toward the water. "Stop!"

"Ye're lucky I don't sling you over my shoulder." His wellies hit the water and he held her higher, making sure she didn't get wet.

She could only stare into his determined face, forcing herself to calm down, focusing on his chiseled features, weathered from the sun and wind. His solid arms and shoulders made her feel safe, reassured he wouldn't drop her.

She relaxed just enough to get why he wore the wellies.

Whatever lingering thought she'd had that he'd behaved gallantly slipped away as he none too gently deposited her in the boat. She had to grab the gunwale to keep from falling on her butt.

As he waded back to shore for her bags, she scrambled for the life jacket stored under her seat and quickly secured it around her, buckling it into place. She ignored that it was wet.

He frowned at her in the life vest for a long second before putting her bags in the boat. She didn't care if he thought she was a chicken or not.

He untied the rope from the post and looped it to the front of the dinghy before climbing in next to the motor. "You better hold on." He pulled the rip cord and they were off.

Thank God the ocean was calm tonight or else she might've flung herself at him for a stronghold as they bounced through the water. She'd never been afraid of the ocean as a little girl on her father's yacht. How times had changed. How she'd changed. Just another example of what she'd been reduced to.

As the boat zipped through the water, spray shot up, lightly misting her face. She turned back to look at the Scot.

He was the picture of serenity, his face gazing toward the setting sun. He looked like he owned the ocean around him, as if perhaps he were a relative of Horatio Hornblower or the nephew of Poseidon. He did look like a Greek god—well, a Scottish god anyway.

Even though it was after ten at night, the orange sky filled the expanse. A fishing boat was anchored just to the right of the white sun that rested on the edge of the earth. Everything shimmered with color. As they rounded the corner, she caught her first sight of the village. For a second, she forgot how unforgiving the sea could be as the scene before her stole her breath away. Arcing around the cove, idyllic cottages painted blue, red, and white nestled like a row of children's blocks. The town glowed from the setting sun, making Gandiegow look alive, a beautiful sleeping beast, nestled under the ancient bluffs.

Ramsay steered toward the dock, dropping the motor into idle. "Are you ready for Gandiegow?" He cut the power and tied them off.

She stood and climbed out on her own, proving she didn't need or want his help this time. She removed the life vest and set it on the seat.

He grabbed the suitcases but stopped. "Oh, ye won't be staying at the Thistle Glen Lodge, the quilting dormitory." He looked as if he was baiting her. "Your arrangements have changed. Ye're now at The Fisherman."

"What?"

He had a gleam in his eye.

She didn't know what he was up to, if anything. But she could give as good as she got. She turned the tables on him. "But I thought I was staying at your place. That's what your brother John told me."

And as expected, Ramsay's eyes bugged, looking horrified to have her shacked up with him and his family.

She smiled at him sweetly. "You do have room for me at your spacious cottage, don't you?"

"I— I . . ." The poor guy's mouth opened and shut like a fish out of water.

She had mercy on him. "Breathe, Ramsay. The Fisherman will be fine. I'm up for anything." She'd even slept a few nights in a tent in Alaska.

"Aye. Right." Relief spread across his face. He stopped in front of a two-story stone building reverberating with noise and turned to her, that glint in his eyes restored. "You do know, don't ye, that The Fisherman is a pub?"

"Sure." She hadn't known until that moment, but she certainly wasn't going to let on now. She walked ahead of him, worrying if she'd get any sleep with it being so loud. The Alaskan bush had been quiet, and once she'd gotten over the worry of being mauled by a bear, she'd slept like a baby. *A baby with one eye open all night.*

Before going in, she glanced up at the building one more time. Hopefully, there was a separate bedroom upstairs and she wouldn't be relegated to sleeping behind the bar. She opened the door to the establishment and went inside.

The place was packed with wall-to-wall Scots, mostly men. There were all different sizes of them, from the tall, lean types, to the boxy weightlifters, to a few beer guts.

But every one of them was as rugged as the bluffs that hung over the town.

Ramsay put his hand on her shoulder and shouted to her. "The steps leading upstairs are over there behind the bar." He pointed to where a very buxom blond woman was pouring shots. "That's Bonnie."

Bonnie had a lot going for her—a tight T-shirt stretched over double-Ds, red gloss on full lips, and men gathered around her like flies to bait.

"I'll introduce you," he said.

But when they stood before Bonnie, Kit could see the other woman's hackles go up and her talons come out. She sneered while Ramsay made the introductions; the man didn't have a clue. Ramsay stood so close to Kit that she could feel the heat coming off him. And whenever anyone tried to squeeze by, he bumped into her back. None of which Bonnie missed. She looked ready to start a catfight, but this kitten wasn't interested in making trouble.

"It's nice to meet you." Kit presented her hand.

"I don't think so." Bonnie grabbed a bottle, poured a dram, and shoved it toward Ramsay, all the while keeping her eyes on Kit. "I hear from Maggie that ye've come to steal away all of our men." The other barmaid gave a commiserating nod.

Hell. Kit had hoped to head off some of this posturing. She had planned to offer her services pro bono to a few local women, to build up goodwill in the community. *Too late now.* Even the sweet-faced young woman nursing a Coke at the end of the bar was giving her the evil eye.

Ramsay leaned down and spoke in Kit's ear. "Just so ye know, Maggie's my sister-in-law. John's wife. She has two younger sisters. *Unmarried* sisters, Sinnie and Rowena."

Kit got it. Gandiegow wasn't going to turn out to be smooth sailing—by any stretch of the imagination.

Kit hollered back to Ramsay. "I'm ready to go to bed."

There was a sudden hush, her declaration hanging in the air. Bonnie set the bottle down so hard on the bar that the drinks in front of the two customers in either direction shook.

With her face hot, Kit stammered, "I mean, I'm tired. I want to get settled in."

Ramsay, unfortunately, rested his hand on the small of her back and guided her. Was he crazy? Bonnie looked ready to dive over the bar after her.

As they made their way to the narrow steps leading up, Kit wondered if it was too late to call John and get the other brother to drive Kit around Scotland. Ramsay was clueless. And his warm hand on her back wasn't helping.

Bonnie's eyes followed them and her scowl deepened. "Watch yereself, Ramsay," she said.

But Kit was pretty sure it was directed as much at her as it was at him. She felt certain it'd only been her first glimpse of the summer to come. Gandiegow might look beautiful from the sea, but she was going to be a bitch to deal with.

Chapter Two

Ramsay followed Kit behind the bar, toting her bags for her. Hell, Bonnie was right. He'd better watch himself. The matchmaker hadn't turned out to be the battle-ax that he thought she'd be. She was young, spirited as a colt in spring, *and gawd help him*, beautiful. He tried to focus on her flaws and not her arse as he followed her up the stairs.

Kit Woodhouse believed in all that bull she was trying to sell, too. *Matchmaking.* Complete bollocks. But he had come up with a surefire plan to get out of this misbegotten scheme of hers. He'd surely given more forethought to his plan than the ruddy matchmaker had given to hers.

His first idea hadn't worked—trying to talk her out of this crazy notion of hers of *matchmaking here in Scotland*. Of course, she hadn't listened. But camping over the rambunctious pub would certainly change her mind. He needed her gone. Sooner rather than later.

He glanced up. *Aw, hell.* Those jeans. Her bum. Her hips swaying from side to side. Gawd, he had no right to enjoy her backside as much as he did. The matchmaker had fit nicely in his arms, too, as he carried her to the dinghy, her clinging to him like a barnacle. He liked that he was bigger and stronger than she was. The tough guy. The man.

Aye, he'd better watch himself.

And he'd better remember that Kit Woodhouse Matchmaker was out to ruin Ramsay's plans. Before he'd been saddled with her, he'd been confident that he'd be able to come up with the final bit of money to buy ole man Martin's boat in time. Ramsay could and would bust his arse to make it happen. But if he didn't get rid of the matchmaker, his dream would be postponed once again. He resented the hell out of being stuck *driving Miss Daisy*. He would just have to make her miserable enough to get her to leave.

At the top of the stairs, he reached around her and opened the door to the room. "The loo is down the hall." He dropped her bags inside and turned to leave.

She was right there, her five-foot-barely-nothing blocking his path.

He tried to step around her.

"Wait." She dropped a hand to his chest like that would stop him.

The earnestness in her eyes did, though.

"We need to go over my itinerary first. Before we do anything."

"I'll come for ye at eight."

A skirl of a bagpipe broke out downstairs. *Right on time, just as arranged.*

She slumped. "Can you make it nine?"

"At nine the day's half gone to us fishermen."

She rolled her eyes. But then a roar of laughter drifted up the stairs as well.

He grinned. *The plan is working.* "Suit yereself on the

time we leave." He didn't say good night but left her to settle in on her own. On the way downstairs he tried to put her worried eyes out of his mind. He had to, or else he wouldn't be able to do what needed to be done next.

As he hit the bottom step, Bonnie gave him a look. She'd probably been counting the seconds he'd been upstairs with the intruder.

Ramsay motioned to Coll, who had just stepped out of the kitchen. "Pour me a dram, will ye?" He sure as hell didn't want Bonnie fixing him a drink. It would give her another chance to rag on him. The bagpiper ended his tune, which gave Ramsay an opportunity to shout to the room, "How about a dance contest?"

Everyone whooped and hollered, exactly as he'd hoped.

Ross, his brother, pounded him on the back and yelled over the noise. "Ye'll not beat me at the sword dance."

"No," Ramsay said. The sword dance didn't make enough noise. "I was thinking more along the lines of clogging." He pulled Thomas, one of the fishermen, from his barstool and set him on his feet. "Show them how it's done."

Thomas yanked up his brother, Lochie, as the bagpipes came to life again. The brothers stomped and shuffled to the beat as the rest of the bar patrons clapped.

Ramsay looked up at the ceiling and hoped their upstairs guest was getting an earful *and a clue*. He didn't care if she wasn't the old crone he'd expected. The matchmaker wasn't wanted here, and the sooner she realized that and left, the better.

Kit lay in the dark with her pillow clamped on her head as the noise reverberated through her overexhausted body and traveled up until it banged against her temples.

If she didn't know any better, she would've sworn that the later it got, the noisier it became downstairs. Didn't these people sleep?

Something else bugged her. Ramsay's presence remained in the room, although he'd only stepped in far enough and long enough to drop her bags and run. But he was still here all the same.

It wasn't easy being a sex-deprived matchmaker.

He wasn't her type anyway. She wanted smooth, sophisticated security from a man. She didn't need sexy and rugged. She had plans. Big plans. In ten years' time, she'd be done paying for her sisters' educations and would've bought back their home, the sprawling estate that had been in her father's family for generations. Kit would not veer from her goals, not even for a little self-indulgent fun. Like having a fling with her red-blooded polar opposite — Ramsay. Besides, he was her chauffeur. The number-one rule in matchmaking: *Never mix business with pleasure.*

The phone beside her vibrated. She shoved the pillow off her face and checked her e-mail.

"Crap." Something had come up with Art MacKay, one of her potential bachelors. He could only meet first thing tomorrow morning, and then he was going to be away for a while. She'd have to rearrange her schedule, but she'd make this work; Art was one of the wealthiest men on her list.

She wrote him back with a time to meet and hoped Ramsay was a go-with-the-flow type of person. If he wasn't, he'd better learn to be. Matchmaking was a fluid business, and they'd be stuck together for the next three months.

The noise downstairs thundered on. She climbed out of bed, dug an eye mask out of her carry-on bag, and then wrapped the pillow around her ears. After she snuggled under the quilt and right before she drifted off to sleep, she had the strangest thought: She couldn't have a fling with Ramsay—this bed wasn't big enough for the both of them.

Kit heard knocking and her name. But everything was black. She heard the door open.

"Wake up, Your Majesty," a very male voice said. Then a prolonged, "Ummm."

She pulled the mask from her eyes. Ramsay stood in the doorway, holding a tray. But his eyes weren't on her face. He was focusing on her chest.

"What?" She glanced down. "Ohmigod." She snatched the edge of the sheet and yanked it over herself. Her night-gown had shifted to the side and one breast was nearly exposed.

"What are you doing in my room?" Her pitch sounded close to a wail.

The rogue leaned in the doorway and shrugged, grinning at her embarrassment. "It's ten. In my defense, I did knock and call out first. Then I tried to call you. Did you shut your phone off? It went straight to voice mail."

"Crap. My battery. I should've plugged in the phone last night."

He smiled at her expletive and walked toward her with the tray. "Breakfast?"

She pulled the sheet up farther. "Out."

He set the tray on the nightstand.

"What is that smell?" She glared at the offending tray.

"Dig in. It's pickled herring and haggis. A right proper Scottish breakfast." He took one of the mugs from her tray and sipped.

Her stomach came close to revolting. "Can you take

the tray out of here? And can you leave, too?" She grabbed the other mug with her free hand.

Ramsay leaned back against the wall again, as if he was just settling in. "I looked at your detailed itinerary. There's one appointment you don't have on there."

She took a drink of tea, then set the mug back down. The food looked inedible. "The plans for today have changed anyway."

"Aye, they have."

What was he talking about? He didn't know about Art and the rearranged schedule.

Ramsay smirked at her. "The quilting ladies are gathered at Quilting Central. They want to meet you right away."

"I'd like to, but there's no time. We have more pressing matters. This morning is our only chance to catch Art MacKay before he leaves."

Ramsay didn't look happy to *catch* anyone. "Lass, have you not heard the storm raging outside?"

No, she hadn't. She was barely awake. *She'd hardly gotten any sleep.* She swung toward the window, still clutching the sheet to her breasts. Rain and wind battered the window. "So?"

"It's not safe to take the dinghy to the SUV."

"Oh." She'd been reduced to monosyllables.

"Now, get dressed." He eyed her like he expected her to climb from the bed and dress while he watched. "Ye don't want to get on the wrong side of the quilters." He gave her a devilish grin like he definitely knew something that she didn't. He remained there.

"I'm not getting out of this bed until you vacate the premises." She clutched the sheet like a lifeline.

"Oh. Aye. Yes." He turned for the door, but then spun

back around like he remembered something. He stopped and scanned down the length of her sheet. By the smile on his face he looked as if he was imagining all sorts of wicked things.

"What is it, Ramsay?" she said with exaggerated patience.

He lazily brought his gaze back up to her face. "That sheet won't do. Ye'll give the *wrong impression.* Make sure ye're dressed appropriately. Something more professional than what you have on now."

That's when it registered what *he* was wearing and she dropped her death grip on her sheet. Up top, he had on a crisp white long-sleeved T-shirt pushed up to the elbows. Down below, he sported a khaki-colored utility kilt. *A kilt.* She looked farther down to a nice set of knees and heavenly muscular calves. On his feet he wore army boots and thick black socks. *Holy smokes.* He looked even more masculine today than yesterday. How could that be possible? If she was being honest with herself, it kind of took her breath away.

Maybe *kilt* should be added to her must-have list for the Scottish bachelors. Hell, all of her bachelors.

She straightened her shoulders, feeling vulnerable while he towered over her. "That's not exactly what I had in mind when I asked you to ratchet up your attire."

"Oh?" He looked down at himself, seeming perfectly puzzled and looking as innocent as the mug in his hand.

She knew he was messing with her.

Then understanding dawned on his rugged features. "I know the problem. I forgot the best part." He set the mug on the floor and pulled a cap from his back waistband, slipping it on his head. It was a chauffeur's hat. And he looked absolutely ridiculous in it.

She laughed. "Lose the hat and you'll be fine."

He smiled back, and she liked it. Maybe a little too much.

"Now, shoo, so I can get dressed."

For a second he stood there, grinning, like he wouldn't leave for all the sheep in Scotland.

"Out," she commanded again.

"Okay, okay. Whatever you say, boss. You American lasses sure like to tell men what to do." Ramsay pulled the door closed behind him.

"You forgot this blasted tray."

But he was gone. She took the tray and set it outside her door. She found her adapter, plugged in her phone, and wrote Art MacKay an explanation and an apology. She grabbed a quick shower and did exactly what Ramsay suggested—dressed professionally for the village quilters in a black tailored pantsuit. She grabbed her day planner, shoved it into her waterproof carrying case, and headed downstairs with the awful tray.

Ramsay stood when she came out of the kitchen—her breakfast now deposited in the trash. He picked up his rain slicker and headed toward the door.

"Wait." She grabbed his arm—one of the strong arms that had carried her over the water last night. "Is there a store in town where I can buy a pair of wellies, too?" She shivered—with what might have been regret. With her own wellies, she would have no excuse to cling to him again.

"Aye, ye're right. I can't be lugging ye back and forth from the boat. I think ye hurt my back." He rubbed his backside like he was in terrible pain.

She rolled her eyes. "Poor, fragile, wee man."

He shoved his arms into his slicker. "You don't have

time right now to shop, but the General Store has them. I'll point it out on the way."

She pulled the hood up on her trench coat. From the sound of the storm, they were going to get wet.

When she stepped outside, she found she was wrong. She wasn't going to get wet; she was going to get drenched. A gust of wind hit her and she fell back into Ramsay.

"Whoa." His arms came around her and he spoke in her ear—loud enough to be heard over the storm and close enough that it made her shiver. "I've got you. But ye have to be careful, lass."

"I can see that." The town sat right on the water's edge with the retaining wall serving as the boardwalk. With the sea churning violently, the waves crashed onto the walkway. One misstep or rogue wave, and a girl could be pulled out to sea before she had the chance to say *Ramsay, save me.*

He righted her but held on to her arms as he guided her down the boardwalk through the village. She wanted to ask him about the quilting ladies, to prepare herself, but the gale-force wind prevented it. They passed several buildings, but she didn't get a good look at their facades. Her whole focus was set on getting to safety. It would've been smarter to have stayed at the pub.

Ramsay stopped her in front of a building. "Here." Still holding her arm, he reached around and opened the door. The wind caught it and it flew open. Ramsay pulled her back into his hard chest again. She felt a little like a ragdoll, the way he manhandled her. But for some reason, she really didn't mind. He guided her inside, pulling the door closed behind him.

Relief swept over her that they'd made it through that harrowing experience. She pushed her hood back, expecting to see a few elderly women waiting. But in the very large open room filled with tables and sewing machines was a crowd, both young and old, men and women alike. Was the whole damned town here? The room went silent. She turned to Ramsay, questioning him with her eyes.

He shrugged, looking too innocent. He reminded her of Bridget, her youngest sister, when she was up to no good. Kit wondered if he'd arranged for all these people to be here. And by the scowls on their faces, this wasn't a pleasant meet-and-greet.

Ramsay pushed her toward them with a light shove, but she felt like he was throwing her to the Scottish wolves. She could've sworn she heard him say *good luck* under his breath.

Stalling, she unzipped her coat and slipped out of it, trying to buoy herself before speaking. She smiled at the crowd. "That's some storm, huh?"

They didn't say a word but looked at her as if she were a caged creature for them to gawk at before they started poking her with sticks.

"Hi, everyone." She put her hand up in salutation. "I'm Kit Woodhouse."

Bonnie stood and slammed her hands on her hips. "We all know who you are."

Not you again.

Ms. Big Boobs stuck out her chest. "They all know, too, and why you've come. To steal our men."

"Aye," said an anonymous female voice from the crowd.

"Steal them *and* give them away to American lasses," Bonnie corrected.

The crowd grumbled.

An old woman, a few inches shorter than Kit, and

older than Old Mother Hubbard, stood up and lumbered over to her. "I'm Deydie McCracken. A quilter here." And apparently one of the town's elders. By the scowl on the old woman's face, she wasn't here to welcome Kit. She looked ready to forcibly pitch Kit back out into the storm.

Deydie positioned herself in Kit's space, delivering the fiercest glare she'd ever experienced. *Up close and too personal.* "We want to know what your intentions are with the lads of Gandiegow."

Kit opened her mouth but didn't get to answer.

Deydie shifted to address the group. "We all know that our village is male-heavy. There aren't enough lasses to go around."

Another woman stood. She had piercing blue eyes and long dark hair, which was plaited into a braid slung over her shoulder. "But we still have single women here. Good girls like my sisters." She motioned to the two beet-red women beside her. "Why should we let *her* bring more women to our town?" She pointed at Kit.

Ramsay leaned over her shoulder and whispered into her ear. "That's Maggie, John's wife. My sister by marriage."

Deydie cleared her throat. "It wouldn't hurt to bring fresh blood into the village."

"Aye," said several male voices from the back of the room. They had to be the fishermen of the town, gathered at the back wall, all wearing those ugly, but necessary, black wellies.

Deydie spun on Kit but kept her voice loud enough for everyone to hear. "But if ye bring these lasses to Gandiegow, and I remind ye that you haven't been given permission to do such a thing, then those girls would be expected to raise their bairns here amongst us. We'll not be letting ye take our lads away to America with you. Do ye hear?"

Several of the older women nodded their heads in agreement. Bonnie gave a loud harrumph. Maggie looked nonplussed and her sisters looked defeated.

This is a nightmare. Kit moved closer to the crowd, though facing the storm outside seemed the safer choice.

As alienated as she felt, she wanted to tell them she'd come in peace. Nothing like this had happened in Alaska. There had been a few hardheaded bachelors, but never a community ready to crucify her for just pulling into town. She better do something before the lynching began.

She nodded to Deydie and put her hand up to get their attention. "I assure you, your concerns are unfounded." She made certain to give Bonnie and Maggie eye contact. "I have no plans to take any of your men away from Gandiegow. In fact, I won't be pairing them with any of my clients from the U.S."

"What?" said one of the fishermen from the back wall. Indeed, the fishermen looked ready to rebel. There was a low-pitched rumble as they groused among themselves.

Kit held her hand up for silence. "I only want to base my operation out of Gandiegow because the town is centrally located for my recruitment needs."

"Why?" Deydie said. "Our lads aren't good enough for ye?"

More rumbles rolled out from the back. Even the females were getting into the heat of it. Kit wondered whether they would pull out the tar and feathers next.

A brilliant idea popped into her brain. One that should

appease the majority of the crowd. She'd planned to host her mixers in either Edinburgh or Glasgow. But desperate times called for desperate measures.

Kit put her hand up once again. "But what I would like to do is to have my mixers right here in your town."

"What's a mixing?" asked Deydie.

"A *mixer* is where I bring the men and the women together. That is if Gandiegow can accommodate such an event." This would be Kit's out.

Deydie's eyes took on a shrewd gleam. Kit got the feeling that the negotiations were just beginning. "Ye would have to make it worth our while."

And Kit felt her checkbook being cleared of its balance as well. "What do you propose?" Reward never came without risk.

"Aye, we can accommodate this mixing thing, as ye say. We have the restaurant's grand dining room. Right, Dominic and Claire?"

A couple in the middle of the room waved. "There's plenty of room," the strawberry blonde said.

"We'd be happy to cater it," the dark-haired man beside her agreed.

"Yere American lasses can stay in one of the quilting dorms," Deydie said.

"For a fee, of course," Kit mumbled under her breath.

Deydie proved her wrong, though. "The lasses can stay free on one condition."

"And that would be?"

The old woman grinned. "They would all have to sign up for a quilting retreat."

Chapter Three

W*hat?* Kit valued quilts—especially the one that had been her grandmother's—but she doubted her clients knew very much about the craft. "I don't know if any of them can sew."

Deydie bobbed her head up and down. "We'll teach them. Won't we, ladies?"

Several *ayes* went up from the crowd.

What had Kit gotten herself into? Even more pressing, what had she gotten her socialite clients into?

Kit knew the rich well, having grown up wealthy. She had been setting up her friends on dates since boarding school, because she had a knack for seeing who belonged with whom. Up until her father died, she had matched people for free. But to finish college and to help support her family, she began charging for her services. And her friends willingly paid. Word spread and Kit's reputation as a reliable matchmaker had grown, as did her client base. But what would her clients think now? *Quilting?*

"You sign up all your lasses for a retreat and we'll make sure they have the *mixing* of their life." Deydie stuck out her hand. "Do we have a deal?"

For some unknown reason, Kit turned around to get

Ramsay's reaction. Or maybe it was his approval. But what she found was that he was frowning, looking extremely unhappy at how this had turned out.

So he's no help.

Kit glanced at the crowd, wishing for at least one friendly face, but the only face not glowering at her was Deydie's, so she took the old woman's hand. "We have a deal." Her checkbook, though, would be hurting after paying for all her clients to come to the retreat.

Deydie gave her a snaggletoothed grin. "In twelve days' time."

"What?" Kit dropped her hand, realizing the other shoe had fallen.

"Yup, that's the deal. The first retreat is in twelve days. And every time you bring your lasses over the pond, we'll give them a quilting retreat."

Kit sighed. "What else?"

Deydie grinned at her. "Those bachelors yc're rustling up? They'll need to stay at the other dorm. Of course, we'll have to charge ye for them. Heatin' that dorm don't come cheap."

"It's summer," Kit argued for the sake of reason.

"Then call it overhead."

"Fine. Let me know how much." Kit had already made the other concessions; why not this, too? "You drive a hard bargain, Ms. McCracken."

"Call me Deydie, or I'll take my broom to ye."

Kit thought she might be serious. "*Deydie* it is."

The old woman motioned to the room. "We better get cracking if we're going to make this happen. Caitie, draw up the contract and get it to the matchmaker."

"Yes, Gran," said a woman with an American-Scots accent who had a young boy beside her.

As if the meeting had been adjourned, everyone stood and cleared out. The fishermen grabbed a couple of scones before they huffed to the door, looking angry and disappointed.

Ramsay nudged her from behind. "A friendly bunch, aren't they? Are ye ready to leave Scotland yet?"

Kit spun around. "So it's you that I have to thank for this ambush. You certainly didn't warn me."

He definitely had a glint in his eye. *The devil.* "I don't know what ye're talking about."

"Sure you don't."

Ramsay left her without another word, heading for the refreshment table, acting almost as if she'd ceased to exist.

He was the only person she knew in town, and he was treating her like a pariah. That little voice in the back of her mind said, *I told you so. You should've thought twice before coming to the land where warriors were invented.*

Kit glanced over at the head *warrioress* as she spoke with a group of women. Deydie looked as happy as a seal who'd caught a thrown fish. And why shouldn't she? She'd taken Kit to the cleaners and had gotten exactly what she wanted for her town. This whole debacle had only added to Kit's workload and troubles.

Deydie broke away and came back over to Kit, towing the woman who had the American-Scots accent. "Ye need to meet my granddaughter, Caitie Buchanan." The old woman gazed over at her proudly. "The Kilts and Quilts retreat was her idea. She's a smart one, my Caitie."

"You can call me Cait." She extended her hand. "It's nice to meet you." She seemed truly friendly, with no hidden agenda. "This is my son, Mattie." The two restaurateurs joined them, plus another couple. "This is Claire and Dominic Russo, and Emma and Doc MacGregor."

Kit shook their hands one by one, putting names to faces and noticing that Emma was well into her pregnancy, her belly filling out her maternity blouse. The two couples looked to be close friends.

"We'll get together soon to discuss menus for the quilt retreat," Claire said, smiling and glancing at her husband. "Come by the restaurant anytime." The four of them wandered off together.

As if she couldn't help herself, Kit glanced over, searching for Ramsay, and found him pouring himself a cup of coffee. He caught her staring and his eyes locked with hers. She saw a hint of something—craftiness? *Surely not.* She'd pegged him as the brawny bear, not the fox with cunning and intellect. Then he plastered a smile on his face.

Cait turned to where she looked. "What do you think of our Ramsay?"

Not willing to curse in front of this seemingly nice woman, Kit flipped open her day planner. "I'll need a few details about the retreat."

Inside her planner was a laminated photo of her grandmother's antique quilt, the picture she kept with her at all times, her talisman. Usually, it centered her, but out of the corner of her eye, she saw Ramsay join two other men—fishermen by their wellies, and undoubtedly his brothers by their outward similarities. Ramsay crossed his arms and glared at the one who looked to be lecturing him. The other brother stood by and grinned. If she had to guess, Ramsay was doing his damnedest to get out of transporting her all over Scotland, but he wasn't succeeding.

At that moment, he speared her with a glower. She

wasn't intimidated. She responded with a sweet smile and a curt wave. He clenched his teeth and turned away. You're stuck with me, buddy, she thought to herself.

Cait cleared her throat. "Yes, the retreat."

Deydie leaned into Kit and peered over her day planner. "What's this? Did you make this quilt?" She snatched the photo away, examining the picture.

"It was a family heirloom." But it was no longer in her family. It had been promised to Kit as a little girl and displayed in a glass case in her bedroom while she was away at college. But then, when everything had gone to auction to pay the creditors, her grandmother's quilt had been tagged, numbered, and sold, leaving Kit heartbroken. It had been the only thing in their family home that had held any real value for her. Their house was gone. The quilt was gone. But the memories remained.

The old woman handed the photo to Cait.

"It's beautiful." Cait returned it to Kit.

The subject wasn't closed yet to Deydie. She openly scrutinized her. "Do you sew or do you just matchmake?"

Kit smiled at her. She liked this direct and bossy woman. "I know how to sew." Kit had been roped into learning. When Bridget, the youngest of them, needed costumes for *The Sound of Music*, all three of the sisters had worked together with the rest of the drama club. By the time Bridget was singing "My Favorite Things," they had mastered the basics of laying out patterns, cutting fabric, and using a sewing machine.

"But can ye quilt?" Deydie asked eagerly.

Cait put her hand on her grandmother's shoulder. "Ye're badgering."

Kit smiled and shook her head. "No, it's fine. I've never quilted, but I'd love to learn."

Deydie smacked the table nearby. "Well, damned if I won't teach ye." She hopped up and went to the bookshelf.

Ramsay sauntered over to Kit. "The storm has let up. If you want to get on the road today, now's your chance. I'll come to the pub and get you when I'm ready."

Kit checked her watch. It was too late to meet up with Art. But they could get started with the other bachelors on her list.

Cait wrote down her phone number for Kit. "Call me when you get time so we can discuss the details of the retreat."

Deydie was still thumbing through pattern books when Kit told her goodbye. She grabbed her trench coat and left.

Ramsay was right; the storm had blown over. Kit stopped at the General Store and met the clerk, Amy, who had a sleeping baby in a playpen behind the counter. The young woman was friendly and helped Kit pick out and buy her own pair of ugly black wellies. She hurried to the pub.

Twelve days wasn't much time to convince a group of bachelors that they needed her. And it wasn't much time to plan the mixer and make all the travel arrangements for her clients to come to this quiet corner of Scotland. Kit thought about the raucous scene at the pub the night before. *Maybe not so quiet.*

While in her room, she packed her notes and readied her suitcases. She thought about making a few phone calls while she waited for Ramsay to arrive, but stretched out on the bed instead to rest her eyes. It had been a long, noisy night and a trying experience at Quilting Central with the Gandiegowans.

Next thing she knew, there was someone pounding on

her door. She felt disoriented and couldn't quite lift her eyelids. She heard the door open.

"Are you sleeping again? I leave ye alone for one minute and you pass out. Are you a narcoleptic?" Ramsay was too perky for her right now. "What's wrong? Didn't ye get enough shut-eye last night?"

Kit groaned, feeling half dead. She rolled onto her side and opened one lid. "I know we have to go, but can't I rest for one more minute?"

"Nay. Another storm is preparing to roll in. It's now or never." Ramsay picked up her brush and tossed it onto the bed with her. "Fix yere mane. I can't take you out with you looking like a wild sprite."

His comment was probably justifiable, but couldn't he have mercy on her and leave the *near dead* alone?

She clutched the brush to her and sat up. "Give me a second."

He looked down at her business pantsuit. "I personally like the rumpled look." He scanned the length of her again, stopping this time at her breasts. "But don't you have something a little less masculine?"

She examined her wrinkled clothes. She was disheveled from the rainstorm and her forty winks. "I'll change into another suit."

He shook his head and *tsk*ed. "It won't do. Don't ye own a dress? The *lairds* you want to sign up for yere database will be turned off by this." He motioned to her person. "Don't take offense, lass, but ye look like a wee boy. If we were stopping at my cottage, I'm afraid my nephew would think I'd brought home a lad for him to play with." His eyes danced with mischief.

It wasn't professional of her, but she threw the brush at him and barely missed his gorgeous head. She'd feel bad later for her behavior. Right now, she looked for something else to lob at him.

He didn't even blink. "Och, are ye sure ye don't have a wee bit of Scot in ye?" He'd poured on the brogue extra thick. "Ye're sure acting like a spoiled Scottish brat."

"Out." She barreled toward him and bulldozed him from the room.

Ramsay stood outside her door, grinning. He'd had a rotten day so far, but baiting the matchmaker and getting a reaction relieved some of the disappointment he felt toward his village and his kin.

He still couldn't believe that Gandiegow hadn't run her out of town. Especially after he'd worked them up into a frenzy. But he had to hand it to Kit; she had pulled that mixer idea out of her backside and saved herself. If he wasn't determined to dislike her so much, he no doubt would feel a smidgen of respect for her fast thinking. And her business savvy.

He knocked on her door. "How old are you anyway?"

She swung the door open. "None of your business."

He stared at her, captivated. Her summer dress was yellow—the top half hugging her breasts with the bottom half flaring at her hips. How could it both show a little cleavage and be modest at the same time? he wondered.

He took a step back and grabbed his chest. "Oh. My. Gawd. Ye *are* female."

The straps on the yellow dress were the width of his kilt belt and the length of the dress came down to the tops of her kneecaps. He had the urge to bend down and worship those nice little knobs for knees, maybe with his hands, even better with his mouth. She looked sweet with her shoulder-length hair barely touching the skin of her shoulders. Her heart-shaped face and soft smile drew him in. She didn't look like the shrewd businesswoman he knew her to be; she could be the lass from the cottage next door. His chest beat hard, but he sure as hell couldn't let her know he was affected.

She put her hands on her hips and blinded him with a withering scowl. "You really need to brush up on your etiquette, Mr. Armstrong. A compliment was in order. Go to my website; I'm saying this with all seriousness. If you don't work on your manners, you'll never find a woman who will have you."

Yep. There she was. The matchmaking shrew was back.

"Ye better bring a jacket. Yere breasties will get cold here in the Highlands without one."

She huffed and turned, muttering to herself, "A girl gets all dolled up and nothing. *Nothing*." She came back with a white sweater and a forced smile on her face.

He took the sweater from her and opened it.

She gaped.

"I can be a gentleman when it's called for. Come now, step inside."

She slipped her arms in and his world shifted. Suddenly, he felt like he was doing more than helping her with her sweater. This wasn't his granny or his aunt before him. Dressing Kit didn't feel innocent in the least. With her back to his chest, it felt cozy, plain and simple. Though "cozy" didn't come near to describing the lust-filled waves crashing through him. Since he had met her, they seemed to be having a lot of these intimate moments. He thought about how nice it'd been earlier when he'd pulled her to his chest, when she'd almost gotten blown away with the storm.

He pointed toward the steps, picking up her luggage. "Shall we?"

"We shall." She walked past him as if she were the flagship of the fleet.

And he got a whiff of something girly, citrusy.

The sprite must've used some spritz. She smelled damned good, and he didn't mind following her down the stairs. She glanced back and caught him taking her in with his eyes, and his nose. He was male and weak when it came to damned attractive females who smelled good enough to devour.

But she better enjoy these few moments of glory, besting him and his raging hormones, because he planned to wipe that uppity smirk off her cute little face. She wouldn't be the one in control for too much longer. Because when they got on the road, he'd make sure to let her know that all of her plans were about to unravel.

Kit stopped and turned. "Oh. I almost forgot." She ran up the stairs. Seconds later, she was back with her wellies, grinning like she'd caught the largest fish.

He shook his head. "Those'll look nice with yere pretty dress."

"Was that almost a compliment I heard?" She patted his arm. "I didn't take you for a fast learner, Ramsay."

"Ah, lass, haven't ye heard? A blind squirrel comes across a nut every now and then. Even in Scotland."

Amusement danced through her eyes. He felt satisfied that he was the one who had put it there. Then she went and did it—shot him a genuine smile. *Aw, hell.*

"Are you going to put on those boots or are we going to stand around here all day yabbering?" he groused.

She frowned.

That's better.

Fascinated, he watched as she used her opposite foot to slip out of her flimsy slipperlike shoes. *Shoes not fit for the wilds of Scotland.* She glanced up and caught him watching. He turned away and busied himself with the luggage.

They walked to the dock in silence. When they got to the dinghy, he pulled the dry life vest off his seat and handed it to her. He wouldn't ask why she feared the water. Or poke fun at it, either. Fear of the water was wise. A healthy respect for the sea was a good thing.

Kit looked surprised at his gesture. "Thanks." She didn't say any more but put the vest on. She motioned to the packed boat. "What's all this?"

"Supplies," he said. "In the Highlands, you have to be prepared for anything." He'd added a sleeping bag, extra blankets, and food. "Maggie fixed some sandwiches for the road, in case we get hungry."

"That was nice of her. I'll have to thank her when I get back."

"You do that." Ramsay couldn't tell Kit the crap Maggie had spewed at him while she'd piled food in the ice chest. *The matchmaker is ruining everything for Sinnie and Rowena. They'll never get a husband with her around.* The truth was that Sinnie and Rowena probably needed to quit listening to Maggie and start leading their own lives. He loved Maggie because he had to, but damn, she was a pitbull, thinking every unattached person in town had to be married. But he was happy as a clam with his freedom. And he suspected if left alone, Sinnie and Rowena would be, too. Sinnie was quiet, but Rowena had a mouth on her. Maybe Kit should take them back to the States with her when she left and find them husbands there so Maggie would shut the hell up and quit talking him to death about it. He was pretty sure Maggie was still holding out hope that he'd take one of her sisters off her hands. Hell would freeze over first.

Kit went to step into the boat herself. He reached out and grabbed her hand, steadying her. Her eyes widened, looking like two full moons on her pretty face.

"Don't look so surprised, Ms. Woodhouse," he said. "Fishing you out of the water is more work than I'm willing to do today."

Her cheeks turned pink. "Well, thank goodness for your lazy tendency."

"Here." He took one of her hands and placed it on the gunwale. "Grab the seat with yere other hand for a smoother ride." He glanced out to the ocean; it was choppy. He wasn't going to worry like an old woman, but he knew this short trip would be rough on the matchmaker. "Hang on, okay?"

She nodded.

He stowed the rest of her luggage and climbed into the boat, too. She stared out at the sea and then back to him with a leery expression, her eyes almost pleading with him to not make her go. Her white knuckles gripping the boat backed up his suspicions. For her sake, maybe they should've waited until the ocean was less angry.

He shot her a wink, following it up with a calming smile. "Try to enjoy yereself."

She guffawed as he started the motor and pulled away from the dock.

She kept her eyes glued on him. He couldn't help himself—he gave her a soft smile to let her know all would be okay. Infinitesimally, she relaxed—not completely, but at least he didn't worry that she would have a nervous breakdown before they reached the SUV. Her gaze didn't leave him the whole time, which, surprisingly, was fine with him.

It didn't take long to get to the tie-off post and the SUV. He jumped out and secured the boat. Even though she had her wellies on, he snatched her out and held her in his arms.

She latched her arms around his neck as if he were her anchor. But her words said otherwise. "What are you doing?" She wiggled her boots. "I bought wellies."

"It's rocky here. I would hate for you to lose your footing and get yere pretty dress wet." Aye, he was acting the sappy fool, but he blamed it on how good she smelled. "I'll let you down on the mud so you can get your boots all dirty. Would that make you happy?"

"Yes." But the frown on her face suggested using her boots wasn't the problem. Perhaps he frazzled her the way she did him.

He put her on the grass instead and went back to unload the dinghy. While he packed the SUV, she changed back into her girly slippers, plugged in her smartphone, and then pulled out her map. He took a page from her book and changed from his wellies back into his army boots.

"Are we headed to McGillivray's sheep farm?" he asked as he stowed the sleeping bag on top of their things.

"Yes, the sheep farm is our first stop. It looks like it should take us an hour or so to get there."

Now that he wasn't holding her in his arms and close enough to take in her damned perfume, or wherever her good smell came from, he realigned his brain and focused on his plan. He climbed in the SUV and they were off.

He wondered if she would be talkative on the road, now that they knew each other a little better. But when he glanced over at her, her eyelids were drooping. For a moment, his convictions wavered. But he couldn't allow her to keep him from taking on extra jobs so he could buy his boat. He waited until she looked fast asleep, her head back, resting on the seat, her eyes closed. Then he steered into the first pothole he saw.

She jumped. "What the—"

He hit the next one.

"Oh!"

"Sorry. The road's a bit bumpy." He gave her his most innocent smile.

"Bumpy, my ass," she murmured, pinning him with a murderous glare.

For a second, he visualized that lovely arse of hers and how it had filled out her jeans to nigh on perfection. But he banished the thought. He had plans to see through to the bitter end. No matter what.

He toyed with enlightening her with how it was going to be. He wasn't going to make it only a bumpy ride; he was going to make this a ride she'd never forget.

Kit forced herself to stay awake the rest of the way to Here Again Farm. Two statues of multicolored sheep sat on either side of the sign. The sheep and the wrought-iron gateway made for whimsical guardians to the farm.

"Well, this is quaint." She imagined that any one of her clients might think so, too.

Ramsay gave a noncommittal grunt and drove through the entryway.

On either side of the lane, sheep grazed in lush pastures. The fence corralling the ewes and the rams was a crisp white as if newly painted. So far, the sheep farmer was scoring well in her eyes. They rounded the top of the hill and on the other side sat a castle. *A castle!*

"Oh, my!"

"It's just a ruddy old estate. It's nothing to write home about." When he said *about*, it came out like *aboot*. For some reason that had her smiling as much as the castle did. She noticed that the more she smiled, the more Ramsay frowned.

They pulled in next to the other vehicles—three identical Range Rovers with the Here Again logo on the sides. As she was storing the map, she saw out of the corner of her eye a man come out to greet them. She had to take a second look. He had on plaid knickers and a matching wool cap. His black short-sleeved T-shirt was pulled tight over bulging muscles. She glanced over to get Ramsay's reaction.

"The bluidy lord of the manor ought to be on the golf course instead of a sheep farm. What a fool." Her chauffeur got out, leaving the door open, and stood there, peering over the top at the man.

She stepped out and her potential client lit up, grinning from one big ear to the other.

He quickened his pace and reached out to her. "Sir Ewan McGillivray." He grabbed her hand and held on. "And ye're the lovely Ms. Woodhouse." The man put an arm around her and pulled her to his side like a newly acquired possession.

Kit would've sworn she heard a feral growl from the Scot leaning over the top of the SUV. She leaned away from McGillivray and confirmed Ramsay's scowl.

She carefully unlatched herself from the wealthy bachelor and introduced her chauffeur. She had to hand it to

Ramsay; he recovered quickly, walking over to shake the man's hand, too, with a pleasant smile plastered on his face.

"Come inside and we'll have tea," McGillivray said.

"Nay." Ramsay pointed toward the sheep they'd just passed. "*Ms. Woodhouse* here is anxious to inspect yere flock. She wants to go directly to your fields."

That made McGillivray beam. "Aye, right. I adore a woman who can appreciate sheep." He grabbed her upper arm and squeezed it.

Ramsay growled again.

She extracted herself from McGillivray and forced a smile for the both of them. "I'll need my day planner so I can take notes. Ramsay? Can I see you for a moment by the SUV?"

He gave her a cheeky grin. "Why, of course, *boss.*" He sauntered to the passenger side and opened her door for her.

As she leaned into the car, she hissed at him. "I don't need to see his sheep."

"Would ye rather have him undressing you with his eyes or talking about his flock?" Ramsay gave her a matter-of-fact eyebrow-raised expression.

"I— I . . ." Well, he had her there.

"Besides, you must make sure the sheep farmer knows his stuff and is good enough for yere money-lovin' debutantes." Ramsay, *the cad*, reached in, pulled out her day planner, and dropped it in her hands.

"My clients are not—"

He cut her off, nodding toward McGillivray. "And if I were you, I'd make certain straightaway that this one knows ye're not up for sale. By the way he's checking out yere arse, I'm afraid he's already trying to size you for an outfit that matches his own." Ramsay pushed her toward the fashion-challenged bachelor.

"Come." McGillivray pointed to the gate. "You'll see our sheep. Then we'll go to the barns so ye can witness the operation from there, too."

Kit hurried to catch up with McGillivray, knowing Ramsay was right. She would have to set this potential client straight. "Mr. McGillivray?"

"Ye must call me Ewan." He scanned her body, as if he were indeed taking her measurements.

"Ewan. I wanted to tell you about my clients, *your prospective brides*." She glanced back. Ramsay and his long legs were catching up with them.

"It's too early to be talking about matrimony. Don't you think, McGillivray?" Ramsay's tone held the perfect mixture of camaraderie, authority, and persuasiveness.

Ewan's eyebrows crashed together in thought. Finally, he nodded in agreement. "Aye. You haven't even seen my prize ewes and rams yet."

He opened the gate and they all went through. Not even three feet into the field and something squished under Kit's Bella-Vita flats.

She looked down at her once yellow footwear. "Oh, shoot."

"No, that's shit," Ramsay corrected, straight-faced, those eyes of his dancing.

She glared at him, but he didn't waver.

McGillivray beamed unapologetically. "Ye get used to it. It's all part of being a sheep farmer."

Kit would have to warn her clientele about the perils of the pasture.

McGillivray rattled on about his acreage, heads of sheep, and every detail of the operation. He was a sweet man and Kit could think of two of her clients who would be perfect for him.

"Ah, now, there's my prize ram." McGillivray pointed. "He's one hell of a stud with a pizzle the size of a hammer. Look at that scrotal circumference. It's greater than forty centimeters." Suddenly, the man looked up at Ramsay and guffawed. "We call him Ramsay. That's your name, isn't it?"

Kit laughed—not only because of the coincidence, but because Ramsay looked more horrified than angry.

McGillivray turned. "Come, I'll show you the others."

As she walked by, she couldn't help but rub it in. "Come on, stud." She patted Ramsay's arm. "Be grateful he didn't ask to compare your pizzles."

Next, they went into the sheep shed. If she thought the sheep poo was thick in the pasture, that had been nothing. The shed was a carpet of excrement. The farmer explained how the shed was on skids. Every year, they'd pull the sheep shed to a different area, leaving that naturally manured spot for their garden. It was all interesting, but she hadn't come here to get Old McDonald's tour. She gazed down at her shoes. They were ruined. The smell of damp wool, sheep bodies, and poo was almost too much for her nose to bear.

"That's some smell." She thought if she pointed it out, that it would move him along. She was wrong.

McGillivray inhaled deeply. "I only smell money."

She looked to Ramsay, pleading with her eyes to get her out of there.

But Ramsay, the lug, pretended not to notice. "Ms. Woodhouse, wouldn't you like to have a go with a sheep and a pair of shears?"

McGillivray clapped his hands. "What enthusiasm. What a fine addition ye'd make to the farm."

This was her opportunity. Whether she could breathe past the horrid stench or not, she would make herself perfectly clear with McGillivray. *Ramsay* she'd deal with later. "Ewan, I wouldn't make a fine addition to your magnificent farm." She was laying it on as thick as she was standing in it. "I'm in the business of setting up other couples. We matchmakers have a strict code of honor. We *never* mix business with pleasure." She made sure she sounded terribly disappointed. "I'm so sorry, but I'm just not available for matrimony."

McGillivray's face fell. "Oh."

Kit laid a hand on his arm. "But I promise you that my clients are far better catches than I. All of them are bright women who can appreciate a man with livestock. In fact, all of my current clients own horses."

His face lit up again. "I have a horse barn with a few nags in it. Plenty of room for more."

"If ye marry, you could add one more nag to yere collection," Ramsay drawled.

If she'd had duct tape, she would've used it on her chauffeur's mouth. Thank goodness the double entendre sailed over McGillivray's head.

"How about that tea now?" Kit had derailed her chauffeur, and hopefully, tripped up McGillivray enough that he wouldn't remember the shears.

"Yes, tea. That would be good," the sheep farmer said.

If she could've sighed without breathing, she would've done so with relief. "Do you have somewhere for me to clean up?" She gestured toward her shoes, which would go straight into the garbage.

"Aye, plenty of space for a pretty lady to get gussied up."

She saw Ramsay roll his eyes.

"I'll need to get a few things out of the SUV. Ramsay, could you join me?" She gave him a pointed look.

He didn't take the hint. "Nay. I'd like to speak further with McGillivray about his sheep, if he doesn't mind." He produced the keys from the folds of his kilt and tossed them to Kit.

She walked off alone to the Outlander, thinking of tossing her ruined shoes at Ramsay's perfect head. Out of the corner of her eye, she saw Ramsay lay a hand on the sheep farmer's shoulder as they walked toward the side entrance of the castle, their heads bent together. It seemed weird.

It was only innocent conversation between Scotsmen, she reassured herself. But then Ramsay turned and gave her a look. *A strange look.* One that said he was setting her up again for more shenanigans, perhaps more traipsing through the minefield of sheep dung.

At the SUV, she dug out her Mary Janes from her bag and slipped them on. Just to be safe, she grabbed her wellies, too. From the front, she retrieved her messenger bag with a stack of contracts for her potential bachelors. It was time to get down to business and close the deal.

But a sinking feeling came over her. Intuition told her that Ramsay's little chat with the sheep farmer wasn't only a few questions about his livestock and their habits. Ramsay was up to something. And that *something* felt like a sheep load of no-good.

Ramsay glanced back at Kit, wondering if she was watching while he sabotaged her plans. Her eyes widened, and even from this distance, he could see the worry spread across her face, kind of like the sheep crap that had taken over her shoes.

He turned back around and gave McGillivray an earful. "As I was saying, you don't need the matchmaker's services, now, do ye?"

"Well—"

"If ye're after a wifey, why take on an American shrew? Wouldn't a pretty little Scottish lass do just as well to tell you what to wear, what to say, and how to act every waking hour of the day?" Ramsay motioned to the expanse of his home. "A Scottish lass could do a right fine job of nagging ye from one end of the castle to the other."

McGillivray stopped and peered up at him with a perplexed look on his face. "When Ms. Woodhouse contacted me she said an upper-class American woman would be good for Here Again Farm, give our brand an international appeal." The man dropped his gaze. "And I thought it would be grand to have a woman at the dinner table to share my meals and a warm body in my bed to share the nights."

Ramsay patted his shoulder. "Och, ye don't need an American woman to help ye with your business. Look at what ye've done all on yere own." He gestured once again at the grandeur of the house. "Ye're doing a fine job. Besides, I say it's best to get another dog for the dining room and a warm quilt for the bed than to take on a wife." He felt victorious as he saw McGillivray cave under his argument.

"Aye, ye're right. I don't have the time or the inclination to have a woman tell me what to do."

Ramsay pounded him on the back. "Good man. It's

best to make up yere mind before she tries to talk you out of it."

The door to the SUV slammed. Ramsay turned around and shot Miss Matchmaker a genuine smile.

One down.

The rest of the bachelors to go.

Chapter Four

Kit sat across from the sheep farmer, wondering if she'd lost her touch. No amount of persuasive argument or reason could convince Ewan to sign her contract.

"I'm sorry, lassie. I shouldn't have said you could come. I'm not in a mind to take a wife at the present." McGillivray glanced over at Ramsay.

Her chauffeur gave her an *oh, that's too bad* look.

She didn't believe his bullshit expression, not for a second. *Rascal. Cad.*

"May I get you another biscuit?" McGillivray said. "Ye're such a bonny lass." His cheeks turned red. "I know what ye said before, but I might reconsider my position on marriage if ye were to fix me up with yereself."

Ramsay stood abruptly. "We better get on the road." He reached down, took Kit's hand, and hoisted her to her feet.

Before she knew what was going on, he was ushering her toward the exit.

He opened one of the huge front doors and shoved her through while talking over his shoulder. "We've a long stretch of road ahead of us tonight."

It was a good thing she had her messenger bag looped

around her arm or it might've been left behind. As it was she didn't get a chance to tell Ewan goodbye. Ramsay had her in the SUV before she found her voice.

She glared over at him. "What was that all about?"

"You're looking haggard. I thought we should get ye to the inn to get yere rest."

Bullshit. "I think if I'd had more time with McGillivray, I could've convinced him."

"Lass, he wasn't interested in looking at the pretty pictures of the American girls in yere briefcase." With disgust, he glanced down at her messenger bag as if it offended him. "The only briefs he was interested in are the ones under yere dress."

"Ha. Ha. Very clever of you. Well, don't do that again. Next time, we'll leave when I say we leave, and not a moment before."

"Whatever ye say, *boss.*" He gave her a cocky grin.

She rolled her eyes. This man was a handful. It would take a Herculean effort on some woman's part to tame this one. Certainly no one in her database would be up to the task.

She dropped her head back on the headrest and closed her eyes. "Mind the potholes. I'm going to rest for a minute."

But after a few moments of near whiplash, she gave up. She saw that he'd negotiated the SUV onto a road that was little more than a dirt track with grass down the middle.

"I hope you know where you're going."

"Aye."

She turned toward him, keeping her head lying on the headrest. "Entertain me. Tell me a story about yourself. Preferably an embarrassing one."

"There's too many to pick from," he deadpanned.

"Give it a try," she insisted.

"Okay. But I'm only going to tell you this because I'm confident in my manhood."

She glanced at him and smiled. He had every right to be confident. He was big and imposing. The only problem she saw with him was that he was never serious. *Never*.

"It's about my mother, Grace. She always wanted a girl. You know, a lass to dress up and fuss over." He paused for a second. "Mind now, that this happened when I was a wee lad, younger than my nephew, Dand, is now."

"Come on, you're hedging."

"As I said, I was a wee one, four or five years old. It was Mothering Sunday and John and Ross decided the best gift they could give Ma was to find her a girl. At least for the day."

"No." Kit already saw the end of the story.

"Ross borrowed a pink frilly dress from Pippa—ye haven't met her yet, but she's like one of the family. Besides Ross scrounging up the dress, John got ahold of Ma's makeup and pearls."

Kit was all-out laughing now.

"They dressed me up bonny and presented me to Ma with her tea." Ramsay shrugged. "It's what my mum wanted more than anything else in the world."

"And then what happened?"

"Da came home. He yelled the roof off the cottage. Sent me in the other room to change. John and Ross were stuck doing dishes for a month. My mother laughed for years that I had been pretty in pink—the prettiest daughter she'd ever had."

Kit wiped tears from her eyes, unable to imagine Ramsay in a dress now. But how sweet it was that Ramsay, the tough little boy, would go along with such a thing because he loved his mother so much.

Straight-faced, Kit said, "You are kind of pretty."

"Handsome," he corrected with a grin. "Ruggedly handsome."

She agreed with him, but she wouldn't say it out loud. His ego was already too big for the SUV.

"So where are your parents now? Gandiegow?"

"Da passed three years ago."

"I'm sorry," she said, feeling bad for asking.

"His heart gave out."

"Your mother?" Kit prayed she was well.

"Ma is in Glasgow with her sister. My aunt Glynnis has been sick and Ma moved in to care for her."

"Does your mother get back often?"

"We go and see her once a month. To take Dand."

Kit thought about her own family, how she'd left them for long periods of time to set up her business in Alaska. And now here in Scotland.

She studied her map instead of thinking about how she missed her mother and sisters. She and Ramsay had been on the dirt track for a long time. She was beginning to wonder if they weren't lost when Ramsay pulled onto a road with actual pavement. After a few miles, he pulled into a micro-village—a few houses and a pub. The pub turned out to be the inn they were staying at for the night and the place was packed. She wondered how far the patrons had to drive to get here.

Ramsay spoke to the pub owner and brought back two keys—one for her and one for him. "The sandwiches will be ready soon."

"Please tell me it's not anything like what you brought me this morning." The smell was still in her nose.

"Ham and Swiss on rye," he said.

"Can it be brought to my room? I'm bushed." She clutched her messenger bag to her chest.

He wrapped his hand around her arm. "Why don't you stay and have a dram? A dart tournament will be starting any minute."

She gave him a weak smile and had the urge to lean in to him for support. "I'm about to drop. Seriously, I need my sleep." Even though she'd seen Ramsay talking with Ewan McGillivray and believed him the culprit, she wondered if her exhaustion wasn't the real reason she'd failed to close the deal. "Good night, Ramsay."

He let go of her. "Aye. Get some rest."

Like I'll let you. Ramsay watched Kit drag herself to the stairway.

The pub owner slapped him on the back. "The teams are forming right now. Yere idea to have a dart-throwing tournament was a grand one. The bets are already being placed."

Ramsay had a twinge of guilt, but he ignored it. Kit would have done the same thing if she were in his place. Business was business, and it was every person for himself. Right? "Are the sandwiches ready yet?"

The pub owner tilted his head. "They're on the counter."

Ramsay left to take the tray of food up to her himself. At the top of the stairs, he found her room and knocked with his elbow. He expected a *come in* or for her to appear, but neither happened. He set the tray down and was surprised when he turned the knob and the door opened.

Inside, Kit lay curled up, passed out on the single bed. Guilt pricked him hard, no passing twinge this time. She looked so peaceful, a veritable angel, slumbering away, not realizing that he'd requested the noisiest room for her. Soon she'd be pulled from her sleep by the racket he'd arranged downstairs.

He retrieved her plate and laid it on the little table, using the napkin to cover her sandwich, in case she woke up and was hungry.

He felt like a cranking nursemaid, and conflicted as hell, as he gently slipped off her shoes and arranged them under the bed. Then he covered her petite body with the light quilt lying across the foot. Quietly he pulled the door behind him as the first *whoop* of the crowd resounded from below. The tournament must've started.

He trudged downstairs to join them. To drink. To be merry. To make enough noise to raise the roof . . . and the dead. But most of all he hoped Kit took the hint soon and figured out that her matchmaking gig wasn't going to work. He needed her to get the hell out of Scotland. Now.

The next morning, Kit didn't find Ramsay waiting downstairs as she expected. The earplugs that Amy had sold her from Gandiegow's store had helped considerably. Or she had been so exhausted that a slew of bagpipers could've marched through her room and she wouldn't have noticed. She didn't even remember aligning her shoes under her bed, but she must have.

She went back upstairs and knocked on Ramsay's door. She heard a groan. She tried the door and it opened. She guessed a big guy like him didn't have to worry with locks. She peeked inside.

His naked chest registered with her first—chiseled with hard muscles. Next, she saw his feet—hanging off the end of the bed. Then she noticed how the sheet rested low on his hips.

Oh, God, he's naked under there!

But she couldn't turn away. She liked hair on a man's chest and Ramsay had the perfect amount trailing downward to the edge of the sheet.

His eyes opened halfway. "Could you think a little quieter? I have a wee bit of a headache." He didn't pull the sheet up. Either his near-nudeness didn't embarrass him or he didn't know that he was giving her quite a show.

She stood there, feasting her eyes on the rest of him. Even the angry scar on his arm was sexy. He really was a Scottish god.

He seemed to rouse more, studying her for a long moment. "Are ye wanting to join me? I can make room." He slid toward the wall and the sheet slipped farther south.

She put her hands up. "I was just wondering if you were up yet."

"I'm getting there," he drawled.

That's when she saw his growing interest poke at the sheet. Her cheeks burned.

"I'll be waiting downstairs for you." She backed out of the door quickly, but couldn't help taking one more peek. The man was beautiful, and infuriating, and laughing at her.

"Come back, lass," he called out. "I *need* yere assistance."

"Not on your life." She spun around and found she had an audience. One of the inn's guests was in their doorway, giving her a blurry-eyed stare. "Sorry about the noise," she mumbled, and headed downstairs, rattled that she'd been caught lusting over her driver.

Too soon Ramsay joined her. She was afraid to look at him, afraid she might be visualizing that chest of his all over again.

She sipped her tea and grabbed an oatcake from the

container set out for the inn's guests. She couldn't help herself. "Isn't the day half over to you fishermen?"

Ramsay went to the coffee carafe and poured himself a mug—no sugar, no cream, no response to her jab. He gulped it down.

She opened her day planner and pulled out the image of her grandmother's quilt, laying her hand over it while she studied her itinerary on the other side. Then she looked up at him. "You don't look well."

"I'll be grand. Why are ye so perky this morning?" His eyes dropped to her chest.

He was goading her and she was going to give it right back to him.

She stood and spun in a circle with her arms wide. "So?" She waited for the compliment, testing him. She knew her navy shorts and cute sandals were very feminine—fun and flirty. But it was her fitted striped sailor's top that should have been sexy as hell to a fisherman.

Ramsay shook his head, apparently not taking the bait. He motioned to the computer in the corner. "I glanced at yere website last night."

"Really? What did you learn?"

"You know where ye give tips to yere clients? You should add something about how *unattractive* it is for women to fish for compliments."

"Very funny." She would've lobbed her oatcake at his head, but he'd probably tell her to add *throwing food* to her Must Not Do list. "So did you find any of my suggestions helpful?"

"It's not ladylike to hound a man when he's a little under the weather." He seemed to be perplexed. "It was loud in here last night. Really loud—how can you be so painfully chipper this morning?"

"I feel renewed and rejuvenated. I'm confident we're going to sign up three bachelors today."

"*We're* not," he groused.

"Okay, but *I* am." She looked in his eyes. "Are you sure you feel up to driving today?"

"Was that an offer to go back to bed?" He held her gaze as he took another drink of his coffee before placing the mug on the counter.

Her cheeks felt on fire. "No, that wasn't an offer." But Ramsay flustered her in ways he shouldn't. "I'm only concerned for your well-being."

"I'm right as rain," he said. "Be ready to leave in five minutes."

She was ready in three but Ramsay was already waiting for her. On the road, she studied her list of potential bachelors. She wondered how she was going to make up for yesterday's strikeout and the fact that Art MacKay wouldn't be back in time for Deydie's deadline for the mandated quilt retreat and Kit's mixer. Six women would be coming to Scotland, and time was running out. Kit peeked over at Ramsay. Should she ask him to be one of her bachelors? She shook her head.

Ramsay glanced at her and then his gaze went back to the road. "What's going on in that pretty little head of yours?"

"*Now* you give me a compliment," she deflected.

"Spill it, lass."

"I'm going to have to set up more appointments."

"But why were you shaking your head at me?" he said.

"No reason." She turned back to her window. She wasn't desperate. Not yet. Ramsay wouldn't do at all for any of her clients. He was too obstinate. Too arrogant. And perhaps, *too observant*.

The rest of the trip to their first stop was made in silence as she studied the printout on Davey McBain, the successful whisky-maker and owner of the family's distillery. When they arrived at the compound, it wasn't at all what she'd imagined. She'd thought there'd be a large sterile-looking building, but instead there was a group of massive stone cottages, some with beautiful arched windows, others with tall steeples.

"Well, this is impressive."

Ramsay only grunted.

As he parked the SUV, Davey came out to meet them. Kit recognized him from an article in *Forbes* magazine. She'd scored big just getting Davey to meet with her. Looking at him, she couldn't imagine why he was thirty and still unattached. He was nearly as tall as Ramsay with basically the same build. For a moment her thoughts streaked back to Ramsay lying under the sheet with his essentials barely covered.

Good grief! She needed to focus.

She put her sights back on Davey, cataloging him. He was sporting jeans, a tailored navy shirt—casually untucked—and a pair of dimples to die for.

When she introduced herself, Ramsay stood close, as if Davey might accost her. In truth, the famous distiller did look at her with interest, which was always flattering from an influential man. But he just didn't do it for her.

Ramsay grumbled his greeting.

"I've blocked out the rest of the morning and the afternoon for you, Ms. Woodhouse." Davey glanced down at the wellies in her hand. "I don't think you'll need those, but you can bring them along if you like."

She was still processing that he would give her so much of his time. *Time that she didn't have.* Well, if they left in the early afternoon, she'd still get in one more appointment today—maybe.

Ramsay nudged her to answer.

Kit looked at her feet. "Yes. I was worried I'd ruin my shoes."

Davey gave her his dimpled grin. "No worries. Come this way." He put his hand to her back and guided her to the closest building.

His touch felt too intimate, but what could she say?

Kit turned to make sure Ramsay was following. What she saw was her chauffeur glowering at Davey's hand. Ramsay immediately schooled his features into an expression of indifference.

Davey was talking and she'd missed part of what he was saying. "Even though I grew up here with whisky making in my blood—my family has been making it for two hundred years—I rarely, if ever, drink it."

"Why?" she asked without thinking first.

Davey stopped and faced both of them. "It's no secret my father was an alcoholic. Because of his recklessness with his personal life and with the business, he nearly bankrupted the distillery and our family. I took over when I was just seventeen."

She knew this, feeling stupid for asking. She recovered quickly. "From what I've read, you've built back your family's empire and then some."

Davey seemed to approve of her comment and studied her closely. "It's taken thirteen years, but I think I can finally do something for myself." He put his hand on the small of her back again and started walking them toward the house. "It's past time I found a partner with whom to share my life."

Ramsay caught up to them again and shot her an eye

roll. "This is some property ye have here. How goes the fishing and the hunting?"

Davey stopped and looked wistfully off to the nearest mountain. "I have a ghillie who acts as gamekeeper. He's the one who has the pleasure."

"You can't mean to tell me that you have access to this bountiful land and yet ye don't enjoy it!"

"Whisky making is a twenty-four/seven endeavor." Davey said it as if it pained him.

Ramsay clamped a hand on his shoulder. "What say we keep the distillery talk to a minimum and ye show me what your trout look like over at yonder loch?"

Excitement lit up Davey's eyes. But then he glanced at his buildings, looking worried to leave his operation even for a few hours.

"You only live once," Ramsay said. "Seize the day, man."

"Right." Davey pointed off to a small cottage. "Let's get some gear." The two men headed off.

Kit stood there, forgotten, confused, and irritated.

Only a minute ago, Davey had given her too much attention. Now, it was as if Kit had faded away, and there she was, left holding her damned wellies.

She ran after them. Maybe she could use this outing to her advantage, as she'd done in Alaska. She'd gone fly-fishing, taken a harrowing flight on a bush plane during a storm, and even gone moose hunting in the name of getting bachelors to sign up. Besides, how bad could it be to spend a few hours with a couple of good-looking men who were trying to conquer the beasts of the land and water?

"Wait up." She followed them to the ghillie's cottage. Once there, she changed into her wellies while the men gathered what they needed for fishing. As they headed to the loch in the jeep, she tried to come up with an opening or at least an angle to use on Davey to get him to sign on as one of her clients. At the top of the steep hill, the view was breathtaking, with miles of water glistening below.

As the Scots unloaded their gear, Kit trekked down the near-perpendicular hill to get a closer look. Unfortunately, she didn't make it very far before one of her boots lodged in a hole and she lost her balance. With breakneck speed, she rolled and tumbled, shrieking all the way, until she hit the loch with a splash. Frigid water went up her nose. The cold took her breath away.

Her feet found the bottom but she was shaking too hard to stand. Strong arms fished her out and held her close.

Ramsay moved her hair out of her face. "I've got ye." Gently he laid her head on his shoulder. "I've never seen a more graceful fall. Are ye all right?"

"G-grand," she said, clinging to his neck and shivering.

As he long-stepped it back up the hill, he rubbed his chin on her hair. "Though entertaining, the Highlands are too cold for a wet T-shirt contest."

She looked down and groaned. Sure enough, her shirt was plastered to her breasts and her nipples were drawn tight as a tack. She slapped a hand over her chest.

Davey came up beside them. "She's got to get out of those clothes right away."

"You drive," Ramsay said.

Surely, he didn't mean to strip her on the way back to Davey's.

Jostling her, Ramsay maneuvered open the back door of the jeep and slid inside. Now she wasn't only in his arms but was sitting on his lap as well.

Davey got in the front and turned on the car.

"Do you have a flask in here?"

Davey produced a metal container from the glove box and handed it back.

Ramsay undid the lid and held it to her lips. She was really trembling now.

"Drink." His voice sounded husky. "To warm yere bones."

She took a shaky draw of the liquid fire. It did indeed warm her. She laid her head back on Ramsay's chest and snuggled in.

He held her tight. "For God's sake, man, get the heat going."

She placed a hand on his chest and gazed into his eyes, waiting until he looked down at her. "I'll be o-o-kay. It's summer, for h-heaven's sakes."

"You don't understand. It's Scotland. She can be cold and unforgiving. You could catch yere death."

She laid her head back on his shoulder. "Have a little faith."

Davey turned the heat on high and put the jeep in gear.

The ride was bumpy. The way her backside bounced around on Ramsay's man parts, she became aware that he was getting aroused. She was embarrassed, flattered, and intrigued. And in no way was she going to acknowledge what was going on between them.

Soon Davey was pulling up to the house.

"Bring her bag in from the SUV." Ramsay was getting out before the jeep had fully stopped.

Toting her, he carried her over the threshold like he owned the place, opening doors until he found a powder room. He set her down and reached for the hem of her shirt.

Shakily, she tried to swat him away. "What are you doing?"

"We're getting those clothes off you." He reached for her again.

"I c-can do it." But she couldn't, she was shaking so hard. Frustrated tears came to her eyes.

He laid a gentle hand on her shoulder. "What if I promise not to look?"

"Okay."

He yanked her shirt over her head—with his eyes wide-open!

He gave a low whistle. "Ye're a stunner. Now turn around."

Too shocked, or too cold to complain, she grabbed a towel from the rack and covered her chest. With her back turned to him, he unsnapped her bra.

Davey knocked on the door. "I have the bag."

"Leave it outside the door." He glanced over at Kit. "Are ye covered?"

She nodded, relieved he hadn't exposed her nakedness to the household.

He opened the door, pulled it inside, and unzipped it. He pulled out an NYU sweatshirt and jeans. "Let's get your shorts off next."

"No way, mister. Give me my top. And I won't put it on until you turn around." For a second, she wondered if he was going to be stubborn and ogle her while she dressed.

He turned, facing the wall. "Let me know if I can help. I know my way around brassieres."

"So you've demonstrated." She pulled the warm top over her head, deciding that was the most she could handle on her own. A bra could wait until she was warmer. "And for heaven's sakes, who says *brassieres*?"

He chuckled. "I'm an old-fashioned man."

"Well, how about you give me some old-fashioned privacy so I can dress the rest of the way without an audience?"

He turned around and gave her a brazen stare. "If I say *no*, does that mean I can stay?"

"Out." She tossed her wet shirt at him.

He picked up her soaked wellies from the floor. "Give me your shorts and skivvies and I'll make sure they make it in the dryer, too."

"You're not touching my . . ." She faltered for a second. "My underthings."

That cocky eyebrow of his lifted. "Wanna bet?" He took a step toward her.

She put her hand on his chest, stopping him. "Fine. Wait outside. I can manage now. I'm warming up."

He surprised her by reaching for the doorknob.

"Ramsay?"

He looked back over his shoulder. "Yeah?"

"Thanks."

Hurriedly she removed her remaining wet clothing and put on dry underwear, jeans, and her hiking boots. Not very attractive. But look what happened when she'd taken pride in her sailor outfit. *Pride goeth before a fall.* Literally. She looked down at her androgynous clothing. So much for proving to Ramsay that she was a woman and not a *wee laddie*, as he'd put it.

She wadded her panties up and buried them in the folds of her wet shorts before opening the door. Ramsay waited with his hand out. She begrudgingly transferred her things to him. He had the audacity to shoot her an arrogant look, as if he'd known it was only a matter of time before she stripped for him and forked over her clothes.

"You, sir, have a dirty mind."

"Aye. I do." He wasn't apologetic in the least as he scanned down the length of her, undressing her again.

What a teasing rogue. She knew he was messing with her, but her insides zinged with heat as his gaze slid down her body.

"Go find the laundry," she ordered, laughing. She intended to locate her messenger bag with the contracts tucked inside next.

As she went to the jeep, warmth settled into her chest. Ramsay could've given her a much worse time about being a klutz and tumbling into the loch. He could've laughed at her and called her a sad, wet selkie, or some such name. But instead, he'd been—she hated to admit it—kind of *gallant*. Convention said Davey should've been the one to fish her out of the loch; it had been his property, after all. But she was glad it had been Ramsay, more glad than she wanted to admit.

She pulled her bag from the jeep, banishing the knight-in-shining-armor image from her mind. When she went back inside, Davey was waiting for her with a cup of hot tea.

"Come sit in the parlor in front of the fire," he offered.

She glanced around for Ramsay but didn't see him. She followed Davey into a beautiful room with a huge fireplace, large paintings, ornate drapery, antique sofas, and a tall cocktail table in the corner with a dry bar nearby.

Davey ushered her closer to the fire with his hand once again pressed to the small of her back.

Ramsay cleared his throat at the door.

She turned around and tried to read his expression. He didn't look nearly as playful as he had back in the powder room.

"I gave your things to one of the household staff," he said. "Are ye feeling better?"

She felt her cheeks flush at his concern. "I've almost stopped shivering." She inched closer to the fire.

Ramsay sauntered into the room and stood by Davey. "It's a shame ye didn't get to actually cast in a line and fish. Maybe we should leave ye to it and we should get back on the road."

Kit wanted to launch the fireplace poker at Ramsay's head. "But we haven't had a chance yet to talk business." She directed her comment to Davey.

"Aye," Davey said. "Ye haven't even had a tour of the distillery."

She would much rather stay here in this cozy room and discuss what she could do for Davey in the relationship department. But the best way to get on the good side of a man was to let him talk about his work.

She stood, leaving the bachelor agreement lying on top of her messenger bag. "Sounds great." Her forced cheerfulness got lodged between her fake smile and her teeth.

They walked around the compound, stopping in all the buildings, while Davey explained the process of forming the liquid gold. They would've been done in half the time, but Ramsay asked a million questions about everything from making the maltings, to the mashing, to the fermentation. He'd been pleasant, but she wanted to mash his time-consuming extraneous questions under his heavy black boots. As they were leaving the final building, Ramsay winked at her.

"Davey, I think our little matchmaker would like to have a taste. I doubt if she's had any real whisky in her life. *Real* single malt."

She started to protest that she'd had a drink from the flask in the jeep, but Ramsay gave her a pointed look. She got his meaning—he meant to help her convince Davey to sign a contract. *Finally a little cooperation!*

Davey gave her a dazzling smile. "I think I can accommodate that request."

When they walked into the big house, Kit saw her dry clothes sitting on her suitcase. Unfortunately, her pink panties were displayed prominently like the cherry on top of a sundae.

"Excuse me." She rushed to the bag to stow her things while the men went down the hall, deep in whisky conversation.

When she got back to the parlor, Davey and Ramsay were in the corner with their heads together, seated at the tall cocktail table. Three nose glasses—special whisky-tasting snifters, curved in at the top—and a thick glass bottle with amber liquid inside sat in front of them.

"Come, lass, sit." Davey patted the tall barstool closest to him.

She ignored Ramsay's raised eyebrow and tried to do as Davey bid. In the end, she needed a hand up from Davey to plant herself on the tall wooden stool.

Ramsay shoved her nose glass toward her. "Davey here is going to show us how to be official taste testers."

"Aye." Davey went into a lengthy discourse while pouring them each a whisky. When he was done, he showed them how to smell the whisky before tasting it. But he didn't even take a sip.

Kit did, though. It was smoky and smooth. Davey had

explained that since it was top-quality whisky and properly aged, it wouldn't burn. It could be sipped and *not* knocked back like other whiskies.

"Very nice," she said.

Ramsay gave Davey an exaggerated frown and put his glass down before taking a drink. "I won't drink alone."

Alone? Was she invisible?

Ramsay continued on, ignoring her pout. "Davey, man, ye're sacrificing the finer things in life. You don't fish. You don't hunt. You don't drink. Only moments ago, ye declared you're going to turn over a new leaf, enjoy life more. Ye said you're not going to get bogged down in business and let it suck the life out of ye. Not drinking yere own whisky is nearly as bad, if not worse, than having all this land and not using it."

Davey seemed to mull over his words. "Perhaps ye're right."

This was the first time that Davey's brogue had shined through, Kit realized. Up until now, he seemed to have tamed it into submission.

Smiling, Ramsay raised his glass. "To good living. Good times. And to good whisky."

"Aye." Davey clinked his glass and drank his Scotch.

Ramsay gave a low whistle. "Aw, now that's good." He clunked his glass down.

"Should be. It's the best in the house." Davey poured all three of them another. Even though the first drink had been very good, she didn't have more. She wouldn't break her two-drink rule. The slug of whisky in the jeep counted.

But the men didn't notice her lack of imbibing. They drank and told fish stories, acting like they were at a men's-only club. When the talk turned to hunting, Davey marched them off to his gun room to view his ancient weaponry. She followed but wasn't needed. The round room was more of a museum than an arsenal. It was filled with swords, shields, and crossbows. Pretty soon, they were back in the parlor with a bottle of fifty-year-old Scotch on the coffee table now, the two men having a grand time.

Ramsay and Davey were old buds now, exchanging one story after another. A maid brought in a tray with sandwiches, which would've been useful three drinks ago, but now the men were too far gone. Kit checked her phone for the time and sighed heavily.

"Davey?" She tried again to get his attention. "Can we talk business now?" At this point, she didn't care if she got his signature while he was drunk or not. The day was wasting away and her anger with Ramsay was growing. She thought he'd meant to help her.

Ramsay pounded the whisky-maker on the back. "Tell her, mate."

Davey gave her a wobbly grin. "I don't think I need a woman right now. I need to spend some time doing the things that I want to do first. I have to make up for lost time. When I'm done hunting and fishing and doing what a man damn well pleases, *then* maybe I'll get a wife." He nodded, looking as if those words had hit the spot. Both he and Ramsay collapsed into laughter.

Kit jammed her stack of contracts back into her messenger bag. "I see." She glared at Ramsay. He grinned back. It wouldn't do any good to say they should leave because her chauffeur was too stinking drunk to take her anywhere. "I'll find a bedroom to settle into for the night."

"Make sure there's a double bed in it," Ramsay hollered.

"In your dreams." She stood and put her hands on her

hips. "I expect you to be ready first thing in the morning. Hangover or not. Good night, gentlemen." She marched out the door. It was only six o'clock.

The men broke into song; the tune followed her into the hallway. The maid gave her an understanding glance as she helped Kit carry her things upstairs and settle her into a luxurious bedroom for the night. The bed was a double, so Kit locked the door. She set up her laptop. Instead of working, though, she laid her head in her hands. What had she gotten herself into?

Chapter Five

Half asleep, Ramsay rolled onto his back as his wadded-up shirt hit his face.

"Get up," Kit hissed. "If you think you're sleeping the livelong day, well, think again."

Something heavier hit him. His jeans. He opened his eyes. "Is this a habit of yours, kitten—coming into a man's bedroom uninvited? Not that I'm complaining or anything."

"Don't flatter yourself, Ramsay. You're not that bodacious. Besides, *real men* don't get drunk on the job."

Oomph. His boots landed on his stomach. One bounced and almost took out his stones.

"Careful there, lass. My privates are sacred."

"Get a shower. You reek of alcohol." She picked up his backpack.

"Want to join me?" he offered.

She hefted his backpack at his chest. "I don't shower with *boys*. A *real man* . . . maybe."

"Gawd, ye're a saucy wench." And he liked it.

He sat up and saw her check him out. He liked that, too. "I need help in the shower, though. There's this place, ye see, on my back that I can't reach." He shifted, pretending to show her, and the sheet fell enough that it should've had her bolting for the door.

Instead, she froze. He loved that her eyes grew to the size of a captain's wheel. Large. Turned on.

"Aye, ye're curious, aren't you?" he challenged.

"I only have business on my mind."

"Don't kid yereself. Ye're interested."

"Yeah, I'm *interested*. Interested in getting on the road."

"Where are we headed?" In other words, what could he do today to thwart her plan?

"North. Way north." She spoke more to herself than to him. "I will get this one signed today. I have to."

Not if I have anything to say about it.

He dared her with a raised eyebrow. "I suggest, if you don't want to see more than you bargained for, that you skedaddle."

She put her hands on her hips. "I don't like being told what to do." *The typical sassy American woman.* Then she licked her lips.

"Aw, gawd." Either she was one hell of a tease or the bravest woman he'd ever met. He swung his legs over the side of the bed and stood. Before the sheet hit the floor, she was gone.

He did as Kit said—showered and generally got ready. He hadn't gotten drunk yesterday as she thought. He'd only pretended. He'd needed to keep his wits about him to control Sir Davey. And, aye, he had controlled him. Ramsay hoped his winning streak would continue until Kit was gone, so he could get back to his life. His boat. His plan.

He pulled out his smartphone and checked the list. Into the wee hours of the morning, he'd downloaded every bagpipe tune he could find. Most outsiders couldn't stand the wail of Scotland's national instrument. Hell, even some Scots found it annoying. Ramsay would test both her eardrums and her patience today, hopefully to the breaking point.

Downstairs, he scribbled Davey a note, as the man was still abed. When he gave it to the cook, he noticed Kit's note lying on the table as well.

She waited at the front door. "Ready?"

He grabbed her suitcase and headed out. In the vehicle, he cued up the music.

Kit turned it off. "I think we should talk."

He reached over to turn it back on, but she blocked his hand.

"What is it, lass?" He gave her a disarmingly patient smile, but when he looked into her eyes, he saw only pain. "Are ye okay?"

"It's about yesterday. The drinking."

He gave an exasperated sigh. "Now ye're going to lecture me. Don't I look like a grown man to ye?"

She pursed her lips together and looked over his person. "I'm not questioning your manhood." Her cheeks turned ruddy red. "I'm questioning your judgment."

"Can't a man have a drink or two without being nagged?" But the pain in her eyes told him that more lay beneath her puritanical stance. "Sorry. Tell me what you have against whisky."

"Not just whisky, but alcohol in general. It just brings back a lot of bad memories when someone, anyone, overdoes it." She chewed her lower lip as if the memory were fresh.

"Who was it, lass?" he said quietly. "Who overdid it in your life?"

"Start the car. I'll tell you while you drive." She stared out the window.

He turned the key and pulled down the driveway, waiting for her to continue.

She didn't speak again until he'd turned onto the main road.

"It was my father." She spoke in a whisper, looking as serious as the clergy at a funeral.

"Go on, lass. I'm listening."

"He didn't always drink, but when we hit a rough patch as a family, he began to drink a lot."

"Does he still hit the bottle?"

"He's dead."

That felt like ice water to the chest. *Dead* was a harsh word when said about a loved one. "Do you want to talk about it?" He sounded exactly like Emma, Gandiegow's psychologist. But dammit, Kit looked to be in physical pain, the way she had her arms wrapped around her waist so tight.

"No. I don't want to talk. I just thought you should know." She reached over and turned on the music. *And then turned it up.*

He hated to see her upset. But as the music wailed on, it surprisingly seemed to fix what ailed her. However, after a few hours of the bagpipes blaring through the speakers, he thought his ears would start bleeding. Kit, on the other hand, was swaying like she loved the bloody noise.

He punched the off button.

"No." She reached to turn it back on. "I adore that song."

He glanced over at her, incredulous. "Nay. You can't know it."

"I can. I own this CD." She named three more tracks

from the album and all but one of the group members' names.

He shook his head. "I'm officially impressed." He grinned while keeping his eyes on the road. "Are you one of those Americans who wishes they were Scottish?"

She gave him a coy shrug. "I have a little Scottish blood in me. My grandmother was from Pittenweem."

He laughed. "Well, that explains a lot."

"What?"

"Ye have the ire of a Scot."

She put her hands on her hips, which looked funny, the one elbow jutted forward because of the confines of the vehicle.

"See?" He nodded toward her semicramped stance. "A typical Scottish lass. Do ye look like yere gran as well?"

She shook her head as her expression changed to sadness. "She passed away nine years ago."

"Sorry."

"It's okay. But I miss her." She patted her day planner.

Even though she had Scottish blood in her, he couldn't let it change the fact that he needed her gone. But in some small way, it did.

He turned the music back on, to a tolerable level this time, and they went the rest of the way in companionable silence.

Kit stared at the map. It showed they had arrived at the premier potato provider of the U.K., but there was no outward proof that they had. No ostentatious signage. No castle. No stone cottage compound. Only a dirt road bisecting the green fields of potato plants. "Turn here."

Ramsay stopped the vehicle. "Are you sure? It doesn't look like this road is used much."

"I'm fairly certain." But she was beginning to doubt her information.

He turned onto the dirt path and drove between the fields. About a mile down the road, dilapidated greenhouses began to pop up, and that sinking feeling washed over Kit, like she'd been tossed in the ocean with concrete wellies. Then the old stone house appeared and her stomach sank further.

Half of the roof was missing shingles. The other half was hidden by a downed tree, never removed, its green leaves looking as if they'd been painted there. The window panes were either broken or missing, cardboard filling in spots. The metal fence around the house was mangled— kind of like Kit's emotions.

Ramsay laughed. "I see yere standards are a bit stricter than I thought. I dare not aspire to such heights."

"Not another word from you, mister."

A man dressed in filthy overalls came out of the equally dilapidated outbuilding next to the house, holding a shovel in his hand.

"Ah, this must be the lord of the manor himself." Mirth spilled out with Ramsay's words.

"It can't be." Kit held up the picture he'd sent her. "We must have the wrong place. Hurry, back away now."

"Nay." Ramsay pulled the keys from the ignition. "Let's ask directions."

Kit stared at him, incredulous. "You must be the first man to ever utter those words." She undid her seat belt and opened her door.

The man walked up to her, letting go with a low whistle. "Aren't ye the prettiest thing I've seen? I hope all the young misses ye have for me have the face of an angel like you. And stacked like you, too." He eyed her hungrily.

Ramsay came around her side of the car and stood close.

Crap! Crap! Crap! "You're Morven Kerr?"

"Yes, ma'am." He pounded the handle end of his shovel into the ground with one hand and slicked back his greasy hair with the other. "I've been waiting for ye."

She took a step back, wanting to make a run for it.

Ramsay stilled her with a hand on her shoulder. "Ye must need help with the potatoes. You got another shovel?"

"Right inside the doorway there. I appreciate the offer." Morven smiled, showing off one missing bottom front tooth.

Ramsay sauntered the few steps into the outbuilding and came back with the shovel. "Here." He thrust it at Kit.

She glared at her chauffeur. She could put the shovel to good use and whack Ramsay in the head to wipe that grin off his face.

"We've an old Scottish proverb." Ramsay put his free hand over his heart and looked heavenward. "When ye know a man's potatoes, ye'll know the man." He looked the picture of sincerity.

Old Scottish proverb, my ass. She latched on to the handle begrudgingly.

Morven smiled and revealed another missing tooth — up top, on the right. "I hadn't heard that proverb before, but I like it. It's so true. Come on, missy. Come see my potatoes."

Ramsay winked at her. "Aye. Go see his potatoes."

She glared at her driver a second longer and then followed Morven into the field.

"Ye know," Morven said, speaking over his shoulder, "ye're the first woman I've seen in months."

That didn't surprise her. She expected he hadn't seen a mirror or a comb lately, either.

Morven stopped in front of a row. "We need to see how the potatoes are coming along." He thrust the shovel deep into the rich ground and exposed the roots. He squatted down and rubbed the dirt off the tubers. "Not ready yet. Why don't ye check that patch behind you?"

"You know, don't you," Ramsay said, "I've heard potatoes aren't really good for you."

Morven stood to his five-foot-six height, turning red in the face. "Potatoes are too good for you. They have fiber."

"Or is it the sour cream on top that does?" Ramsay countered innocently.

"Potatoes have important nutrients."

"But the bacon bits ye have to eat with them have too much sodium."

"Potatoes are delicious." Morven looked ready to put up his puny dukes.

"Now, there's a point we both can agree on."

But Morven had worked himself into a dither and went into a long speech about the various attributes of the twenty different varieties of potatoes he grew on his farm. Kit stood nearby, wondering at Ramsay's mastery. He'd agitated the farmer with only a few well-placed words. But she had to hand it to him, Morven had forgotten she was supposed to be digging for the potatoes.

Finally, poor Morven ran out of steam. "Let's go into the house and have our tea now." He glared at Ramsay for a moment. "You can come, too." On the way into the house, he told them about the new fertilizer he'd bought and how it was supposed to increase his crops.

"He's a keeper," Ramsay whispered, taking her shovel and leaning it against the house on their way in.

Kit was careful not to touch the front door, as it hung precariously on its hinges. She probably should've prepared herself for the chaos inside, and actually had to pause in the entryway to keep herself from bowing out of the invitation for tea.

Morven was part hoarder and part zookeeper. Livestock — two pigs, three chickens, and a lamb — freely roamed throughout what little space was in the packed front room. Stacks of farm journals, four feet high or so, were scattered about. The farmer scooped up a chicken and held him like a football. "Watch this." He grabbed a pellet and stuck it between his lips. The chicken pecked it out of his mouth. "That's something, isn't it?"

Gross, is what it is.

She pulled out the picture he'd sent her and held it up. "Whose picture is this?" She figured it wasn't rude to ask since he'd misrepresented himself.

Morven gave her his dentistry-free smile. "Some bloke off the Internet. From what I hear, everyone stretches the truth online."

In the future, she'd triple-check her potential clients for honesty and accuracy. But for now, she'd seen more than enough. "Sorry. I think we need to be going." Appearance and manners could be fixed. But lying outright had ruined the deal for her.

"But, but . . ." Morven faltered. "Will I at least see you at the Highland games tomorrow in Crossmere?"

"Ye're participating in the games?" Ramsay asked with a heavy dose of doubt.

Morven chuckled. "No. I have a hot-potato booth. Can't have the games without steaming potatoes. So will ye be there?"

"No," she answered.

At the same time Ramsay said, "Yes."

She shot her chauffeur a searing glance as he ushered her out the door.

After they were safely inside the SUV, she turned to Ramsay. "Why would I want to see that man at the Highland games? I hope to never see him again. I can't believe we drove all the way here for nothing. *Nothing!*"

Ramsay *tsk*ed. "Think about it. Wouldn't the games be a good place to find ye some males to sell to yere rich friends? All the clan chieftains in the area will be attending."

"Well . . ."

"All in one place for the picking. Check them out in person. Make sure they're up to yere standards before ye even have to talk to them." Ramsay shot her a killer smile, and she kind of melted. "Ye could make sure they have all their teeth, too."

"You have a point." She could rearrange her schedule once again.

"Miss," Morven called, running toward them with a burlap sack.

She worried he had some critter in there for her. "Yes?"

"Some of my best potatoes for ye." He put the sack into her hands. "I'll see ye tomorrow, right?"

"We'll see."

As Morven made his way back to the house, Ramsay grinned at her. "Aw, he's such a fine man."

"Then you marry him," she offered.

Ramsay didn't miss a beat. "Not my type. Not enough curves." And then the devil had the nerve to check her out. "Want to take another dip in the loch? I'll be happy to help ye get your clothes off again."

"Drive." She turned toward her window, hiding her smile as she looked out.

"Off to Crossmere, then?"

Her smile fell away. "Hopefully they'll have a couple of rooms for us."

Ten minutes down the road, they found the medieval-looking village made up of narrow streets and old stone buildings. The town itself was small, but it was hopping with anticipation of the Highland games. A large sign declared that the B-and-Bs were fully booked. A few RVs were parked about but it looked like the majority of the people had set up tents in an open field.

She pointed to the gathering. "You didn't happen to pack us some camping equipment, did you?"

Ramsay gestured to a sign. "There's a boardinghouse that way."

"But the B-and-Bs are full," she argued.

"We'll check anyway."

He parked the car along the road and they walked the rest of the way to the two-story stone house. She hoped they had a pair of rooms for rent.

The parlor inside the front door had been converted into a lobby. An old woman sat in a rocking chair like she was guarding the stairs leading up. She listened to what Kit had to say, then pointed to the Vacancy sign hanging above her head. "There was a cancellation five minutes ago. I'll let you have it if you pay up front." She stuck her hand out as if to take their bills.

Kit turned toward Ramsay. "Can you sleep in the SUV?"

But instead of answering her, he pulled out his billfold and handed the old woman his money. "We'll take it."

Kit wanted to stomp on his foot. "But—"

"We'll get our things and come back." Ramsay took Kit's elbow and guided her toward the door.

She was surprised her glare didn't burn a hole in that thick skull of his.

Ramsay stopped and faced her as he opened the door. "I'm sure a lady such as yereself can be mature and share a room with an honorable man such as myself. But if you can't"—he dug in his pocket and produced the keys to the SUV—"then you can sleep in the auto."

"Oh. You—"

Grinning, he turned her toward the door and shoved her through. "I'll be outside in a second to help you with the bags."

She trudged to the SUV, worrying over things she normally had no need to worry over.

A naked man under the sheets, for one.

She'd seen enough of his bare chest and imagined enough of the rest of him to make her drool. No, yearn to run her hands over his hard chest. She put her hand on the SUV and shook her head.

"Here." His warm breath played with the hair on her neck. He handed her the room key over her shoulder. "I need to take care of something. I'll meet you back at *our* room later."

She turned around just in time to see him walk off. "If you think I'm lugging your bags up the stairs for you, you have another think coming, mister."

He waved to her without a backward glance.

Ramsay walked away, needing a break from Kit. What the hell had he been thinking? Sharing a room with the American lass was dangerous. Not to mention counterproductive to getting his boat. He was too damned impulsive for his own good. He should've slept in the car as she'd suggested.

He headed down the street to the crowd forming outside the mercantile. Men were signing up at a table, registering for the Highland games.

He needed to burn off some steam. A lot of steam. The matchmaker made his blood hot. He got in line.

She didn't know it yet, but he'd stayed behind and booked the room for two nights with the old woman, instead of one. It shouldn't be too hard to convince Kit to stay an extra day with the lure of all the strapping Scots in their kilts. But he would make sure none of the lads here would sign on with her, either.

He smiled to himself. Today had been a bust for her and he hadn't even had to lift a finger. The potato farmer had bungled it nicely just by being himself.

When it was Ramsay's turn, he filled out the form and laid out his money—money well spent. Anything to bring himself back to normal. *To neutral.* Since he'd met Kit, she'd been on his mind too often. He never let just one woman dominate his thoughts. Keeping it loose had always been his style. But Kit had a way of invading his every pore. The caber toss and the hammer throw should eradicate her from his mind.

As he walked back to the boardinghouse, he had a brilliant idea. So far, nothing had deterred the American lass from her plans. Maybe he needed to use his size and his manliness to scare the wits out of her—so much so, that she would take the first flight out of Scotland to get away from him.

He hurried back to the boardinghouse, eager to put his plan into action. Now, his impulsiveness didn't seem like a bad thing. They were going to be sequestered in the same room. He'd corner her, pour on the charm, and maybe even lean in for a kiss. That should be just enough to scare her back to the States.

Back inside the house, he took the steps two at a time and found their room. He didn't knock, but sauntered in, feeling cool and confident, in complete control.

Kit jumped when she saw him. *Good. She's already on the defensive.*

He walked toward her, soaking in her body, pouring on the heat, until her blush took over her face. She pushed that brown hair of hers back, even though it was barely long enough to do so. He frowned, thinking how he liked long hair. Long enough he could wrap his hands in.

"What's the matter?" Her voice was hoarse with emotion.

He shifted his gaze from her hair to her eyes. And along the way, he noticed her blush had kicked up another notch. *Aye.* He would throw her off guard by giving her a false sense of security. Keep the conversation light.

"Ye gotta tell me how old you are. I'm dying to know," he said nonchalantly. She was so young to have started a business on two different continents. A huge feat. The lass had moxie—he'd give her that.

Kit's eyes got wide. "What?"

He took a step toward her. "You look really young."

"Thanks. I guess." She took a step back.

He frowned. She'd probably been born with a trust fund, an offshore account, and a big flat in Manhattan. "I mean, ye're young for having your own business. You can't be what? Twenty-four? Twenty-five?"

The room was small, with only a twin bed. She took another step back. "Maybe we should go to another town, find a place with two rooms. Where are we both going to sleep?" Her hand motioned to the bed behind her, but her gaze stayed locked on his.

He gave her a smoldering grin and nodded toward the bed. He took a step closer. They were standing close together. *Verra close.*

She stepped back once more and when she did, her legs hit the bed and she lost her balance. She reached out to grab him. He could've stopped her fall, but he was just enough of a son-of-a-wanker to pretend to lose his balance, too. He fell forward on top of her, catching himself before he crushed her.

Perfect. It couldn't have worked out better if he'd planned it.

Her eyes were huge, shocked.

And green! He'd thought they were more brown than any other color before, but staring into them up close, they were *honest-to-gawd* green with brown flecks ringing the pupil. He could've stared into them forever. Which was possibly the most girly thought he'd ever had. Except . . .

She smells like lilacs, too. Aw, hell.

"I'm twenty-six." She was breathless. "You didn't have to fall on top of me to make me answer."

He grinned at her, then he moved his hand up and stroked her cheek. "I take it back; you don't look so young when you're up this close."

He meant to provoke her, keep her off-balance a bit longer, and pour on the charm. But her hair was fanned out around her head, and *she looked like a cranking angel.* His index finger strayed over and touched a silky strand. It was softer than monofilament fishing line. And thicker, richer. Blood rushed downward to his groin and he felt himself leaning in to kiss her. And if he pressed into her harder, she'd know the extent of his attraction. Her lips parted in invitation.

Aw, gawd! What am I doing? He shoved himself up and off of her.

"Sorry." Like a whupped laddie, he jammed his hands in his pockets.

She lay there, her cheeks bright red, looking up at him with innocent doe eyes. He took her hand and pulled her to her feet. *It's the least I can do.*

She let go of him quickly. "Um, thanks."

He barely heard the words as he rushed to the door.

He got out of there, using the closed door as a shield. Standing on the other side, he was still able to feel her underneath him. Various parts of his body warred against each other. His pecker wanted him to go back in there and give it another go. His hand wanted to wrap itself in her hair and hold her in place while he kissed the hell out of her. But it was his chest that he was most worried about. It pounded so hard, he was pretty sure he was going to have a damn heart attack.

"Dumbass," he said to the hall. He was so screwed. Kit the matchmaker had turned out to be a kind of kryptonite for him, a pain in the arse, and more trouble than he'd bargained for.

Chapter Six

Kit dropped back to the bed, staring at the door, not quite sure what had happened. One minute she'd been on her feet and in the next, her insides were a warm mess of hormones with Ramsay lying on top of her. It'd been thrilling and frightening and hot—oh, so very hot. His boyish charms had turned into rock-solid man in two seconds flat. She wondered if he was coming back. *No,* she worried he would. Although . . . she wouldn't lock the door.

She pushed herself up and off the bed. Duty called. At least ten text messages from the office in Alaska needed attention. Double that number in e-mails, too. Kit grabbed her phone, but instead of calling the office, she hit speed dial for Harper.

"It's night here," Kit said. The sisters had a long-standing, unspoken pact to always be there for each other. Harper could decipher the code.

"Do you want me to ask?" her sister said dutifully.

Kit sighed with relief. "Yes."

"Sleep, rest, talk, or play?" Harper said.

Kit smiled at her phone—the four words more comforting than her sister could know. Kit, Harper, and Bridget had played this game their whole lives. When they were young, each sister had had her own separate bedroom in their sprawling Connecticut mansion. But every night Kit and her sisters had pulled pink sleeping bags to their doorways, their heads in the hallway so they could be together. They had the opposite issue now. In their two-bedroom apartment in the Bronx, the three sisters shared one room. But in Connecticut, life had felt safe and secure. Now things were much more complicated than playing Barbies when the lights went out or talking about the first kisses of their youth.

"Are you there?" Harper asked.

"Yes."

"Sleep, rest, talk, or play?" she repeated.

For a second Kit thought about confiding in her sister, to tell her about the well-built, strangely dressed sheep farmer, Davey and his damned new priority, and Morven's missing teeth. She wanted to tell her how lonely she felt, how hard it was here. She thought about Ramsay's chest lying on top of hers and how *hard* it'd been. And distracting. But Kit was the strong one in the family. Everyone relied on her to keep it all together.

"Is everything all right?" Harper asked.

"It's going great." Trying to put a positive spin on it, Kit filled her in on the required quilting retreat. "It's a brilliant idea. It'll give my clients something to do while they get acclimated to the area, before they meet the bachelors." She tried to sound upbeat, but wasn't quite pulling it off.

Harper was silent for a second. "Make room for me at this retreat of yours. I'm coming. My passport is up-to-date."

"What? You are not coming. I thought you were taking graduate classes this summer."

"I took the summer off to do some fieldwork," Harper said. "But the site survey has been postponed."

"But what about the flight? It costs too much," Kit argued.

"Couldn't I use your miles? I think you need me. You sound stressed, and I'll help with your clients. I'll meet them at the airport. Be their traveling companion. Calm their nerves. Help their transition. Whatever you need me to do."

Kit chewed her lip. "That's actually a great idea."

"It would give me time to do some exploring in the North Sea, too." Harper sounded excited. "Several Viking ships and Spanish ships have been found along the east coast. While I'm in your little village, I could go diving and take a look for myself."

It wasn't Kit's *little village*; it was Ramsay's. "My sister the nautical archaeologist. I'm so proud."

"So can I come?"

Kit laughed, feeling calmer than she had since arriving in Scotland. "Yes, you can come. And yes, you can use my miles. How are things at home?"

Harper filled her in on their mother, Jacqueline, and how the art gallery where she worked had increased her hours. "And Sprout has taken a job as an aide at summer school."

"Bridget doesn't like it when you call her that. What if we went back to calling you *Pout*?"

"Fine. *Bridget* is all set for community college in the fall."

Their younger sister had always wanted to be an elementary school teacher. Kit would make sure her dream came true. No matter what. She just had to make Scotland work. She had to.

Hearing Harper's voice made Kit feel better. But at the same time, it reminded her of all her responsibilities. Bridget's tuition would be due mid-July. Harper hadn't told her when her grad school tuition was due, but it had to be coming up. And, of course, she would have to help her mother now that Bridget had aged out of survivor benefits. Part-time at the art gallery wouldn't pay the rent on the apartment, even with increased hours.

Harper finally got back to the original question. *"Sleep, rest, talk, or play?"*

"Play. Can you get Bridget online, too, so we can play Words with Friends?"

Harper laughed. "They should call it Words with Sisters."

They hung up and Kit had a few minutes to think before all three of them were online together. For the millionth time, she wondered what her father would think about how different their life was now. It wasn't a bad life by any stretch of the imagination . . . only different. But would he still have taken that bottle of champagne with him on his last spin in the yacht if he had known?

Kit and her sisters played for an hour and then she had to sign off to get some rest. She stretched out on the bed, but couldn't fall asleep. Instead she wondered about Ramsay. Where was he? And when was he coming back?

When he was around, he kept her from worrying. His constant teasing saved her from thinking nonstop about her all-encompassing responsibilities. But he'd given her something new to think about. *Now* she knew what it felt like to have him lying on top of her. She snuggled under the quilt and played out her fantasies in her mind.

Hours later, she woke up. It was dark out and the moon was high. Across the room, she saw Ramsay's shadow as he unrolled the sleeping bag on the floor. She held her breath and watched his silhouette as he pulled his shirt over his head. Would he drop his pants next? But instead, he lay down on the sleeping bag and stacked his hands behind his head.

"Good night, kitten." He said it so softly that a second after it had happened, she wondered if she hadn't dreamed it.

For a long time, she gazed upon his large figure on the floor, her playful guard dog.

But Kit reminded herself of the truth. She didn't need playful in her life. She shouldn't be distracted by him, either. She had too many responsibilities to lose focus now. She'd seen too many people get caught up in romance and forget to take care of themselves and their families. If Kit didn't take care of her family, no one else would. It was all on her. She turned away from Ramsay and toward the wall. After a long while, she finally fell asleep again.

Morning came and Kit didn't want to open her eyes. Her ears were getting a workout. Doors were slamming. Voices sounded in the hallway outside her room. People were knocking. *On her door?*

She opened one eye.

Ramsay came in. "Time to get up."

She squeezed her eyes shut. "No." She was more exhausted than when she'd gone to bed.

"I brought you breakfast before I have to leave."

"Leave? Where? You better not abandon me." She opened her eyes and sucked in a breath. The man certainly had a way of stealing the air from her lungs. She propped up on her elbows to get a better look.

His hair was wet and he was wearing a kilt!

This wasn't a khaki utility kilt either. The wool was a green-and-blue plaid with a red stripe in it. He wore a sleeveless black T-shirt that left nothing to the imagination about his brute strength. All Brawn was definitely *all brawn* today.

"Wow," slipped out before she could stop it. "Why are you all decked out?"

He handed her a small sack and a cup of coffee. "For the Highland games, lass. Get up and eat with me before I go." He winked at her. "For luck."

She narrowed her eyes at him. "Why luck? What's going on?"

"I'm competing." He grinned at her as he took a slug of his coffee; then he set his cup on the windowsill.

She sat all the way up and shook a finger at him. "You promised to help me today."

He frowned at her pointed finger and for a second she thought he might call her on it. Instead, he cocked his head to the side, narrowing his eyes playfully at her. "I made a promise to you?"

"Well, not exactly."

"You ought to know, lass, I'm not the promising type."

It was a telling statement. He was one of those men who couldn't be counted on. "But I paid you."

"Ye're paying me to drive you. Nothing else."

It was good they were going to have an argument. Because really, between what had transpired on the bed yesterday and how outrageously gorgeous he was this morning, fighting was her only salvation. She stood up and put her hands on her hips. "You have to help."

"The sprite is ordering me around." He laughed at her. "Aye, that'll work."

Desperate, she could only think of one way to convince him. *All Brawn could certainly be persuaded by All Woman.* She didn't think it through, but launched herself at him, knocking the breath from the both of them. She latched her arms around his neck and kissed him with everything she had. Certainly, this was the only way to get this Neanderthal to do what she wanted.

His arms automatically caught her, but he didn't kiss her back. He snarled as his fingers gripped her waist and he set her away from him. He took a deep breath as she held hers. He looked to be grounding himself.

"Sorry," she mumbled. Her cheeks were on fire and her lips tingled where she'd tried to persuade him.

"Don't fash yereself," he grunted. Then he cleared his throat. "It happens all the time—women throwing themselves at me. Ye couldn't help it."

She glanced up to read his expression. He didn't quite pull off the lightheartedness he was shooting for, but he was definitely in better shape than she was.

He grabbed his cup but then stopped, reaching a hand out to her. Did he mean to stroke her cheek, or some other tender gesture to make her feel better? She stood still in anticipation, terrified it would be some kind of intimate, romantic gesture and, at the same time, hoping it would be.

But then he chucked her lightly under the chin. "Hang in there, little sprite. You'll be okay." He turned and sauntered out the door, cocky as ever.

She stared after him. What had she been thinking,

making a pass at him? What kind of professional throws herself at a man, anyway? Prostitutes, maybe, to secure a client. But not a matchmaker! Kit could die of embarrassment. They'd bury her with red-hot cheeks, a frustrated body, and a stupid tombstone with only one word written on it — *Mortified*.

Chapter Seven

Kit finally got her nerve up for the Highland games. She was, after all, here to find bachelors—not to worry what her chauffeur thought of her ineptitude. Armed with her messenger bag for taking notes and cell phone for shooting pictures, she left the boardinghouse. Later, she would do background checks, so as not to encounter another Morven. Speaking of . . . She would steer clear of any booth that had a potato on it.

She followed the throng of people to the field and paid her eight pounds for access to the grounds.

It was a kilt-lover's paradise. *Real men* were everywhere, decked out in their clans' colors. Kit found herself inadvertently looking for the Armstrong tartan and made herself stop. She had a job to do. Today was not about Ramsay. She would put him from her mind. She had to forget how breathtakingly gorgeous he was in his tartan and remember that he was nothing more than a kid in a man's body. No woman could rely on a boy. Besides, today was solely about the business at hand. If she'd had some forewarning, maybe she could've rented one of the booth spaces and taken applications. She pulled out her notebook and jotted down that idea for the future.

Just as she was slipping her notebook back into her bag, people started forming a line. Two drum majors, fully dressed in their tartan uniforms, headed up the pack with the bagpipers and drummers lining up behind them. So this is what it looked like—the gathering of the clans.

Bagpipes rang out and the group began marching onto the field. Everyone, spectators included, followed the musicians. Kit was swept up into the crowd but felt out of place in her jeans without a stitch of plaid on her.

Once again she looked about for Ramsay, wondering if he'd gotten pulled along with the tide of the crowd. She found him walking along with a pack of beefy musclemen. Ramsay didn't have the meat and width of the others, but he had height and perfect proportion.

Automatically, her hand went up, but she stopped herself midwave.

He gave her a sideways grin, his eyes dancing as he nodded in the direction of the clan tents. She looked specifically where he wanted her to the Armstrong tent. Maybe she'd check it out after the parade; maybe she wouldn't. She had work to do. Unlike him, she did make promises. And she had a stack of them to keep!

Once on the field, the emcee proceeded with the roll call, shouting out each clan's name. In response, the flag-bearer raised his colors and shouted, "Aye" back. The pride of the clans was clear in the vibrato.

When it was done, she didn't immediately exit the field but waited to see where Ramsay was headed. She looked on her map and found he was going toward the heavy-athletics area. She knew enough about the Highland games to know that was where only the strongest competed, in the caber toss, the stone throw, the hammer throw, and others.

She scanned the whole of the area as she walked off the field, feeling overwhelmed. She should've asked Ramsay to point out the best place to look for bachelors. But since he was busy, she would just have to muddle through. There were so many to choose from—good-looking bagpipers and drummers, athletes, men walking dogs about—some of the dogs were even dressed in plaid.

Her eyes landed on the Armstrong tent again. Before she got too busy picking out men, she decided to see why Ramsay had pointed it out to her.

Under the Armstrong canopy, a tall, thin man stood behind the table and lit up when he saw her, acting as if he'd known her forever. "Ah, ye must be the American lass." He thrust a long, wide length of plaid at her, the same plaid that Ramsay wore.

"What makes you think I'm an American?" Was it stamped on her forehead?

The man held his hand above his head. "A bloke this tall, with shoulders this wide, said to give you this." He smiled and shoved the Armstrong plaid at her again.

"I'm not taking that."

"He said for ye to put it on." The man nodded his head up and down. "He said ye'd argue, but it was for yere own good."

"Thanks, but no, thanks." She backed away from the tent.

"But he already paid for it," the man called out.

She put her hands up. "I don't want it."

It just felt wrong to put on Ramsay's tartan. Especially when she knew that was how they distinguished which family you were from. She was fairly certain there wasn't a Woodhouse plaid.

She glanced over at the field where Ramsay stood

with his beefy posse. What had he been thinking—*she, wear his Armstrong plaid?* She headed in the opposite direction to where the bagpipers were hanging out. They were sexy, *real men*, weren't they? Surely there was a chieftain among them who was looking for a bride.

But along the way, she came across a group of drummers at one of the many performance tents, setting up for their gig. She tried her best to talk to them about her business, and about bringing the American girls to Gandiegow, but they weren't interested in what she was selling. They were, however, interested in *her*. The group of percussionists backed her into a corner.

She held her ground. "Gentlemen," she said calmly, but glanced from side to side, looking for an escape. "That's not why I'm here."

The burly bass drummer laughed, motioning to her attire. "But ye're not under the protection of any clan. Ye're free game under Scottish law."

She doubted that, but glanced down at her T-shirt and jeans anyway. "Explain."

He gave her a devilish grin. "Ye're not wearing any plaid."

"So?"

"If ye're not wearing plaid, then it means ye're looking for a mate. Ye're out searching for a man who'll give ye his plaid." He took a step forward, starting to unwind his own tartan from his shoulder.

She ducked under his arm. "I must've left my sash at the Armstrong tent." As she ran off, the men roared with laughter.

She muttered all the way to the Armstrong tent, "I don't need *his* protection. This is the twenty-first century, not the middle ages." But the scene at the performance tent had proved she at least needed the pretense of belonging to one of the clans. *Cave dwellers—all of them!*

Back at the tent, she put her hand out.

The thin man grinned. "I figured ye'd be back." He gave her the sash along with an Armstrong crest pin.

Kit stomped toward the athletic field. From a distance, she saw Ramsay take his spot with a stone cradled to his chin. Like a shot-putter, he spun in a circle and hefted the stone. The crowd gasped and roared as the stone landed a long ways off, men running with a tape measure to mark the divot. Something inside Kit hitched at the sight of his rippling muscles, his brawny body in action. He took her breath away and she didn't understand why. She'd planned the kind of life she wanted and what type of man was for her. Wall Street trader. Provider. Four-bedroom home. The right schools. Dinners out. Stability.

Ramsay walked to the fence line, wiping his brow. As she moved closer, he turned to her, as if he could feel her nearing.

"I see ye got my present." He grinned like the drummer had. But Ramsay's gaze felt different from the Burly Bass's. Ramsay's eyes on her felt more like a caress than a jeer.

She felt hot. She slammed her hands on her hips to cover up what he'd done to her. "A little warning about what would happen if I didn't accept the present might've been nice." She tied the sash around her waist and held out the pin. "Here. I don't need this."

"It's tied all wrong," Ramsay scolded. "Ye're not a pirate, lass. Come." He grabbed her wrist and yanked her to him, the fence between them.

The modern woman in her hated that his little yank

had turned her on. They stood so close together that she felt the heat as it rolled off him. It was intoxicating. She wanted to close the distance between them. But instead, she let her gaze move up his massive chest until her eyes met his.

"Here." He undid the knot at her waist, pulling the sash free. "Lift your arms. It goes like this."

He looped it under her arm and up to her shoulder in a way that felt intimate. She was a little dizzy having him so close. Catcalls and whistles broke out from the men on the field and in the stands.

"Give me the pin, lass." He stuck out his hand. "I'm not used to dressing a full-grown woman. Undressing? Yes." Ramsay pushed her hair back, clearing a spot. "But for you, I'll make an exception." He secured the sash in place with the Armstrong crest. "There." He placed his hands on both of her shoulders to look at his handiwork, holding her there as if she wasn't already paralyzed.

The fog cleared from her brain. She tried to wiggle from his grasp, if for no other reason than her sanity.

"Now, off with ye." He spun her around and swatted her bottom, laughing, and the crowd roared along with him.

She stomped off the way that she'd come, in the opposite direction from him.

She made several attempts to talk to men who were watching the dance competitions. But most of them had daughters who were competing, or they weren't interested. She finally found the group of bagpipers at a table eating lunch, but then was rejected by them as well. Feeling defeated, she trudged back to the athletic field, planning to snag Ramsay and beg him to find her a few men.

He stood at the fence again, but his back was to it this time, while he watched the caber toss—where the Highlanders hefted what looked like a telephone pole across the field.

"Ramsay?" She touched his arm; he felt warm.

He spun around. "What is it, lass? Have you come to watch me crush these chaps?"

One of the chaps spoke up. "In your dreams, pretty boy."

She pulled Ramsay away from the eavesdroppers. "I need to talk to you. I need your help."

Ramsay smiled at her. "Ye look nice in my clan's colors." He adjusted the sash as if he couldn't keep from touching her.

She grabbed his arm, biceps actually, and was struck by its solidness. "Concentrate, will you?" She could've possibly been directing those words at herself, but she stared at him. "Can you talk to them for me? I'll pay you extra." She motioned to the men competing in the heavy athletics with him. "I haven't had any luck on my own." She felt so off her game.

His eyes twinkled. "I want to hear ye say that *ye need me*."

"You're impossible." But she did need him.

"Say it."

She chewed her lip for a moment. "Fine. I need you." She patted his biceps for good measure. "Will you talk to them now?"

He grinned. "Nay."

"But you promised." She shook his rock-solid arm.

"No. I told you before that I don't make promises."

He was an infuriating man! She had firsthand experience with men and their promises. Her father had promised to come back and he never had.

The loudspeaker crackled and the announcer came back on with his thick burr. "And the last one, number seventy-four. Ye're up."

"That's me." Ramsay sauntered away. "Don't worry, lass. I'll talk to them."

Kit stood there, watching. He was pure beauty to gaze upon, but exasperating to talk to. She leaned over the fence to see how he would do.

Ramsay approached the tall pole lying on the ground. Two men lifted one end of the pole and walked toward Ramsay until the pole was standing straight up. Ramsay hugged the pole and then scooted his hands down until he lifted it straight in the air. With control, he walked forward and hefted the pole. It flew, landed on one end and fell over.

The loudspeaker rang out. "Och, that was a grand throw by seventy-four. But was it good enough to win?"

The men measuring gave the judges the thumbs-up, one of them signaling the length.

As the announcer praised seventy-four, Ramsay threw his head back and roared. He made his way toward her purposefully. When he got to the fence, he jumped over and pulled her into his arms. She gasped as he leaned down and kissed the breath out of her.

The crowd shouted their encouragement. But Ramsay's assaulting lips were doing fine on their own. He urged her mouth open with his tongue and thrust deep inside, claiming her. It was more than electrifying. In the back of her mind, she knew kissing him wasn't a good idea, but for the life of her she couldn't fathom why. Kissing Ramsay was breathtaking, making her legs feel as sturdy as the fabric of his shirtfront that she clutched. He held her tighter, lifting her feet off the ground.

When he finally set her away, she wobbled, but he was right there to steady her.

He grinned. "Gawd, ye're a passionate sprite." He turned, jumped the fence again, and sprinted back onto the field with his arms raised, victorious over her and the caber toss. As the three judges met him in the middle and presented him a medal, Kit turned, touched her fingers to her swollen lips, and slunk away.

Ramsay felt like the frigging king of the world with the other men slapping him on the back. He looked around for Kit, but he didn't see her anywhere. It was no big deal; he'd see her back at the boardinghouse. Maybe even pick up where he'd left off with her right kissable lips.

But hell, he couldn't kiss her again. It'd been a hoot, surprising her like that, and he'd enjoyed it and all, but he had his agenda. He took the medal off his neck and shoved it in his pocket.

One of the locals whacked him on the back. "We're all going over to the whisky tent. Join us."

"Aye." It would do Ramsay good. He needed a little distraction and distance. All he could think about was his need to find the matchmaker and take her back to the boardinghouse for some *adult games*. He wanted nothing more than to kiss her again, take her clothes off, and love on her tempting little body.

Unfortunately, the whisky tent didn't fix the problem. Thirty minutes later, he was bored with the other athletes and the untouched drink in front of him. He headed back to the boardinghouse to shower. When he got there,

Kit wasn't in their room. He did notice that her messenger bag had been left behind, which was strange. He quickly cleaned up in the communal restroom down the hall, then went in search of the sprite.

He found her at the pub with a group of men buying her drinks, and she was well into her cups. Ramsay squeezed through, ignoring the grumbles. "Excuse me, chaps. I've come to speak to my sister."

One fellow frowned at him, circumspect. "Sister? Isn't she the lass you kissed earlier?"

Ramsay gave him a hard stare. "We're a close family." He sidled up to her and wrapped his arm around the back of her stool, keeping the others at bay. "I've been looking for you."

She gazed up at him with sad eyes. "Why?"

"We need to talk." He slid his arm around her waist and helped her to her feet.

"I'm not talking about what happened back there." She waved in the general direction of the door and the field beyond.

"That kiss 'twas nothing. I got overcome by yere beauty, that's all."

"You got overcome by your testostcrone." She poked him in the chest. "You need to know one thing about me. I *never* mix business with pleasure."

He guided her to an empty table. "So when you attacked me at the boardinghouse this morning, that was all business and no pleasure?"

"I tripped and fell."

"Aye. And accidentally ravished my mouth. Well, that's what happened to me, too. I won the caber toss and accidentally fell on your lips." And dammit, it was the hottest kiss he'd ever had.

"Don't let it happen again." Her eyes dropped to the floor. "I mean it."

"Okay, but on one condition." He helped her into a chair and sat across the table from her.

"What condition?" she said.

"You have to give me some business advice." This was as good a time as any to pick her brain. Since she was a little drunk, she'd probably tell him her secret to success. She had to have a heck of a business sense for her to have done so well at such a young age.

"I'm all ears."

He couldn't help but skim his eyes down her body. "Ye're not all ears, lass. Ye have a few curves in there that have nothing to do with hearing."

She rolled her eyes at him. "Get on with it, Ramsay."

He waved a waitress over. "Two coffees."

"What if I'm not done drinking?" She placed both elbows on the table and pouted.

"I need ye sober to hear my plan. After that, hell, I'll buy ye a bottle if you want it."

"Fine."

He leaned toward her. "Here's the deal. I need your opinion on a business idea."

She reached over and squeezed his arm. "Shoot."

For a second he got waylaid by her touch and lost his concentration. But thankfully, she pulled her hand away so he could continue. "I've always wanted my own boat and my own business. But it wasn't until the quilt retreat started up in Gandiegow that I knew what I wanted to do exactly. Tell me what you think. What if the quilters brought their husbands with them to town? While the women are sewing, I could take the lads to all my favorite fishing spots on guided tours."

She narrowed her eyes at him. "Did you come up with this idea all on your own?"

He frowned back. "Aye. But by the way ye're skewering me with your gaze, maybe I should rethink my plan."

She grabbed his hand across the table and squeezed it. "I think it's brilliant."

He was the one to narrow his eyes this time. "How do I know it's not just the whisky talking?"

She smiled and shook her head. "Ask me about it again in the morning. I promise it'll still be brilliant." Her expression went from smiling to serious. "So you're not all brawn." She still held his hand, but caressed it now. "Why in the world are you not married yet?" She gazed into his eyes. Even though her cheeks were getting red, she didn't look away.

As nice as it felt for her to be stroking him, he pulled his hand away. Her touch turned him on too easily. He sat back and concentrated on her question, crossing his arms over his chest. She looked serious as hell, so he gave her his standard smartass answer—the one he gave every damn busybody in Gandiegow who tried to set him up with their daughters, granddaughters, nieces, and acquaintances from out of town. "Hell, kitten, I've been doing a pretty good job of ruining my life all on my own. Why would I need a wife?"

She sat back, too, and crossed her arms over her chest, mirroring him. The place between her eyebrows pinched together. "Liar. You can't fool me. You don't believe that."

But how could she know? The truth was—he hadn't found anyone who could hold his interest and doubted he ever would.

"I don't have you figured out yet." She caught her bottom lip by her upper teeth, and chewed on it like she was balancing the books. "But mark my words; one day, I will."

Her mouth captivated him—it kind of made him stop breathing—but he shook it off. "I doubt you will, lass."

She gave him a dazzling smile. "Then tell me your biggest secret."

For a second, he considered telling her about how tough it'd been being the babe of the family. How everyone still treated him that way. How he feared he would never be able to break away and become the man he knew he was meant to be.

But he wouldn't tell her any of those things. The matchmaker was just a pretty little sprite who happened to have the brain of a tycoon.

He leaned in and rested his arms on the table, like he was going to divulge something deep and dark. "Tell me how you've been able to be so successful at business."

She reached out and patted his hand. "That's easy, big guy. *Because I had to*."

"Had to?"

She nodded. "Everyone is counting on me."

That's not what I expected. He pulled his hand away. "What do you mean?"

She scooted her chair closer to him. "Do you want to know why I got so upset when you and Davey got stinking drunk?"

"Sure." Which seemed an odd question since she'd been well on her way to getting stinking drunk herself when he'd arrived.

The waitress set their coffees down in front of them.

Kit took a sip. "I'm going to start from the beginning, okay?"

He nodded.

She spread her arms wide. "My family used to be wealthier than God."

He expected she was still pretty damn wealthy, given the business she'd started and expanded. *Alaska. Scotland.*

She smiled at him like she was letting her statement sink in. "We had a beautiful estate, several vacation homes, a yacht—you get the picture." Her smile faded as she wrapped her hands around her coffee cup. "But we lost it all in the real estate collapse. When I say *all*, I mean *all.*"

Okay, but *all* to some people wasn't the same as *all* to others.

"Go on," he encouraged. He needed to figure out how this woman ticked.

"Well, Daddy started drinking. He'd always been a social drinker, but then he began clearing out the bar, one bottle at a time. The night before the yacht was going to be repossessed, he took his last case of expensive champagne with him for one final spin around the bay." She paused for a second. "He must've drunk too much and fell over while he was saying goodbye to the yacht. They never found his body."

Oh, gawd. Ramsay reached out and cradled her hand in his. "Lass, I'm sorry."

She waved him off like it was nothing, but her voice cracked just a little. "I was a junior in college. My mother and sisters were torn up. I spent the summer getting them set up in a cheap apartment and organizing everything for them—getting the girls enrolled in public school, making a budget, teaching them how to grocery shop."

"I don't understand. If your mother is still alive, why didn't she do those things?"

Kit laughed derisively. "I love my mother, but she has

no practical skills. She had no way to deal with what had happened to our family. She's old money, had lived her life in the society pages. The only things Mother knew how to do were to attend charity functions, how to write checks for the poor, and how to distinguish between a van Gogh and a Degas. Unfortunately, we had turned into the people we used to help. You ought to see the neighborhood we live in now."

He rubbed her hands. "There's no shame in being poor."

"True. But there's no shame in having money, either. Money buys stability. I only want to make enough to buy back our old estate and get Mother and Harper and Bridget closer to our old life. I know that then they'll be happy."

"And what's going to make you happy?" He surprised himself with the question, but he really wanted to know.

She pulled away from him and placed her hands on the table. "Making a go of it here in Scotland. Everything's riding on this, big guy." She motioned to him like he was some kind of mountain she had to conquer. "I've invested every penny I've ever made into this venture. And it looks like my gamble isn't going to pay off." She slumped back into her chair. "Both Harper's and Bridget's fall tuitions are coming due. I have to pay Mother's rent for her as well." She sighed heavily and then whispered, "Don't tell anyone, but the pressure is crushing me."

Ramsay felt like a cranking prick.

His assumptions about Kit were all wrong. He'd figured her for a spoiled rich girl, but she was nothing more than a woman trying to do right by her family.

Aw, hell.

He exhaled. "Let's get you back to the boardinghouse." He rose from his chair and pulled her to her feet. He didn't stop there but tucked her under his arm for support. As he walked her to the door, he caressed her shoulder as if warming her.

"I'm okay." But she leaned into him as they went out into the night. "The coffee did the trick."

"I'm not taking any chances of something happening to you. John would shoot me if you didn't pay him for the work I'm doing."

In the field down the street, people sat in lawn chairs around campfires, laughing and singing.

Her glassy eyes gazed up at him. "I guess I didn't think about it before . . . but why is John getting all the checks instead of you?"

He glanced away. "We're a family business. We have some expensive boat maintenance coming up. Your money is going to help pay for that."

She stopped. "If you're not getting paid to drive me around, then how are you going to pay for the boat you need for your tourism business?"

"There's the rub." He wrapped his arm around her again and continued walking toward the boardinghouse.

She pulled him to a stop. "Tell me." She didn't let go of his arm.

"Let's just say my dream has been put off a ways."

"No." She sounded as disappointed as he felt. Somehow, her empathy made it seem not so bad.

He walked her inside and helped her up the stairs. When he opened the bedroom door and got her inside, she looked up at him sheepishly. He wanted to wrap her in his arms and keep her there. She'd had just as hard of a life as he'd had.

"Thanks." She went up on tiptoes, but apparently she wasn't tall enough to give him a kiss on the cheek.

He bent down to help her out, but when he did, she snaked her arms around his neck, maintaining eye contact.

"Don't tell the boss," she whispered. "I'm going to break the rules and mix a little pleasure with business." She slipped her hands into his hair and pulled him down, molding her lips perfectly to his.

"*Aw, gawd.*" The matchmaker was a gifted temptress, plain and simple. She maneuvered her tongue into his mouth, making him growl at the pleasing pain she was causing. She kept wriggling closer into him—with her body, her chest, her hips—and it was driving him mad.

She trailed kisses down his neck, making him pant like a lovesick dog.

"Take me to bed, Ramsay," she pleaded between kisses. "I've had a rotten couple of days."

Her words hit him like a bucket of North Sea water—cold, shocking—straight to the chest. He unlatched himself from her.

He was the one who'd made her life hell since she'd arrived. He would not *reap* the reward when he'd been the one trying to ruin it for her in Scotland.

She ran her hands over his chest. "I'm certain you can make it all better. You can put it on my tab."

And he wouldn't be paid for his services, either—*gawd!*

She giggled. "That was an awful thing to say. I must be drunker than I thought."

The other men at the bar came to mind. There was no way in hell he was letting them reap anything from her, either.

"Go to bed, Kit." He sounded angry and he hated that he did. He had a policy about letting his emotions get to him—*don't take things seriously enough to let it happen.* He schooled his anger to kidding. "I think the boss would hate herself in the morning if the chauffeur played the gigolo for her tonight."

She stood there, looking too foggy to comprehend what had just happened.

He snatched up the sleeping bag, not trusting his will-power to last. He wanted nothing more than to wipe that confused look off her face by loving her all night long. But he couldn't.

He left the room. He would sleep in the hall to keep watch over her, to make sure she didn't slip out and go back to the pub.

But then he heard her swearing and the bed springs creak loudly. Then something slammed against the door. It sounded like her messenger bag.

"I never should've come to Scotland." She sounded defeated on her side of the door.

Well, at least that he could change. "I'll make it right, lass," he said to himself.

Every cell in his body wanted him to go back in the room and show her that Scotland could be a right good place to be. He gazed at what separated them—a paltry oak door. Because it wasn't enough to keep him from her tonight, he took his sleeping bag and stalked away. He'd have to sleep in the SUV.

Kit woke up to an empty room and a hangover. She pulled her pillow over her pounding head and groaned— partly because her head felt like it'd been hurtled across the field like one of the heavy stones in the Highland games. And partly because she'd been an idiot. Adding insult to injury was that Ramsay had stayed out all night after he'd rejected her. He'd probably gone back to some Scottish girl's place and showed *her* a good time.

Embarrassment made her head throb more. *God, I propositioned my driver!* There was only one way to overcome such an awkward situation—amnesia.

Slowly she rose from the bed, trying to keep her head as still as possible. Her eyes focused on a piece of paper lying by the door. When she bent down to pick it up, her head hammered so much that she sank down against the wall.

She crawled back to the bed, taking the note with her, and lay down. The words were written in a thick scrawl.

> Boss,
>   Stay put. I have an errand to run. I'll be back tomorrow to get you.
>
>   Ramsay

She had to read it through maybe ten times before she could believe it. And every time she read it, the angrier she got.

She stomped to the small bedroom window and stared out. She didn't expect him to be standing out there in the pouring rain, but still. *He'd left her?*

Then it occurred to her that the Highland games were likely called off, as the fields were abandoned and the rain was coming down in sheets. Her prospects of finding new bachelors today slipped away as the rain lashed away at the window.

But she could at least get some work done while Ramsay was out gallivanting. She checked her phone but had no service. She went downstairs to see if she could get a couple of bars there. She still had nothing. She asked the old woman in the rocking chair.

"Och. The storm knocked out the tower. Ye'll have to wait for it to be fixed."

"When will that be?" Kit asked.

The old woman looked at the watch dangling on her frail arm. "I expect by mid-July."

Kit stomped up the stairs, imagining Ramsay's grinning face under each of her steps. Without cell service, she couldn't work. She retrieved her e-reader from her luggage and plopped on the bed. Seeking comfort food for her brain, she opened her favorite book. It soothed her like no other. But more importantly, it kept her from doing something stupid—like going out on foot to find her lazy, good-for-nothing chauffeur. She began reading from the beginning:

It is a truth universally acknowledged, that a single man in possession of a good fortune must be in want of a wife.

Chapter Eight

The next morning, Kit woke slowly, feeling more rested than she could remember feeling in a long time. The sun radiated warmth on her face from the small window. Yesterday had been her first day off in years. Since the day her father died, she'd been *on*. Always working, always going a million miles per hour, always looking for an angle to improve their family's situation. But yesterday, she just *was*.

She stretched, rolled over, and opened her eyes. And jumped, tumbling out of the twin bed. "Shit."

Ramsay grinned at her from the folding chair in the corner. "Is that how ye say *good morn* in America?"

She climbed back onto the bed. "Why didn't you wake me when you came in?"

"You looked peaceful. I thought you might be dead. I was only sitting here watching to make sure you were breathing." He grinned at her chest.

She threw her pillow at him. "I have a bone to pick with you, mister."

"Can we do it over breakfast?"

"Where were you yesterday?"

"Dress first. Talk later. A man can only take so much, lass." He gave her a sideways glance, his eyes feasting on her camisole.

Her nipples were pushing against the fabric as if they were trying to get a better look at him, too.

"Fine." She grabbed her suitcase and headed for the door and the bathroom down the hall.

"I'll be waiting right here," Ramsay called after her.

"I'm sure you will," she muttered.

When she got back, the bed was made, and the rest of her things were sitting by the door.

"What's going on?" The weather looked okay outside. Surely she could find a few men to talk to today on the last day of the Highland games.

"I have to get you back to Gandiegow." He took her suitcase from her and left the room.

"Hold on." She pulled him to a stop, not an easy task when the man was as solid as the caber he'd tossed the other day. When he turned to look at her, she slammed her hands on her hips. "I hired you to drive me all over Scotland."

"Which I've done."

"But I don't have the men I need."

An odd look crossed his face, but he recovered quickly. "You have every man you need."

"If you're speaking of yourself, you don't count," she said.

He gave her that cocky grin that she'd grown so very used to. "Aw, that's where ye're wrong, lass."

"What are you talking about?"

"The errand I ran yesterday was for you. I found your bachelors. Yere stables are full."

She frowned at him. "With a bunch of jackasses?"

"Don't look a gift mule in the mouth. Have a little faith."

"Who are these men?"

He sighed, clearly exasperated. "A man could die of hunger around you. Come. Feed me. And I'll tell ye everything you want to know. I promise."

"Have a little faith, indeed," she grumbled, grabbing her messenger bag and following him down the stairs.

They wrapped up a few scones and fixed a couple of coffees for the road. Ramsay refused to tell her anything until he'd eaten, which was after they were well on their way.

When he'd taken his last bite, she turned to him. "Spill it."

"Open the glove box and pull out the paper in there."

She did and found a list of names. "So?"

"Those are your bachelors."

"You only got names? No phone numbers? No addresses?"

"Aw, lass, beggars—"

She finished for him. "Beggars quite often get screwed?" She rolled her eyes. "I have to vet these people. I can't have my clients hooking up with men I know nothing about."

"Hooking up? I didn't realize you were running that kind of operation."

"Ha. Ha. You know exactly what I mean. They need to sign a contract. I'm a legitimate business." She looked at the paper more closely. "Davey, the whisky-maker, and Ewan, our sheep farmer, are on here?"

"Aye. They reconsidered."

She waited, but Ramsay didn't elaborate.

"But I don't know the rest of these men."

"Ye'll have to trust me. They're good blokes, every one. Besides," he said, "what choice do you have?"

Well, he had her there. "You better not screw me on this, Ramsay."

He shot her a wicked grin. "You certainly know how to turn a phrase."

"You've got a dirty mind, Mr. Armstrong." But kissing her chauffeur, basically jamming her tongue down his throat, and then propositioning him last night came back at her like gangbusters. She felt her cheeks burn red.

He glanced at her again and chuckled. "I'm not the only one with the dirty mind." For a second his gaze fell on her lips.

"Hush. And drive." She picked up the list again. Six names. This wasn't normally how she ran her business. But she was desperate. Deydie's unreasonable deadline and Kit's own unsuccessful attempts to find good Scottish men had backed Kit into a corner.

"Thanks," she said quietly.

He reached over and squeezed her hand, holding on a few seconds too long. "Ye'll pay me back."

"Yeah, right." But then she realized there was one way that she could return the favor. "Maybe I'll set you up with a nice American girl."

"Nay." He laughed. "Maybe ye'll ask me back to your bed when you're stone-cold sober."

Her cheeks burned again. Her hand tingled where he'd touched her. And the voice in her head answered for her.
Maybe I will.

Ramsay had had all night to consider what to do about getting ole man Martin's boat. He could no longer in good conscience put all his energy into running Kit out of Scotland. Hell, he was even helping her now. But he still had to get the rest of the money he needed to start his guided fishing business. He knew what had to be done, but it was the last thing in the world he wanted to do. So he just wouldn't think about it until he got back to Gandiegow.

He glanced over at Kit, who was busy scribbling in her notebook. "What's the first thing we have to do when we get home?"

She snapped her head in his direction and gave him a funny look. "We? Home?"

"You know what I mean." He didn't know why he'd put it that way, either.

"I'll probably need to talk to Deydie first to check out the quilting dorms." She looked over at him. "I assume you spoke with my new bachelors about Deydie's requirement? That old woman is pretty creative with *my money* when it comes to more revenue for the Kilts and Quilts retreat. Charging the bachelors room and board will cost me, you know."

"Aye."

"And did you tell the bachelors the correct date?" she questioned.

"Aye, again. Eleven a.m., on July first. I read your itinerary."

"Eleven a.m.? But the mixer doesn't start until seven. What am I supposed to do with them all day? I don't think Deydie will be willing to teach them how to sew."

He shrugged. "Hey, I did my job. I found them. You keep them occupied." But he frowned at his own words. He didn't want *her* to be the one keeping a group of horny bastards busy. "I mean, we'll think of something."

"We better." She went back to her list. "I have to find

out what my clients need for the quilting retreat. I have to check out the location for the mixer and plan refreshments." She held up her notebook. "There's basically a hundred things that should've been done yesterday."

"Then it's good we're going home," he said, seeing her nod in his peripheral vision.

An hour later, they drove down the hill to Gandiegow's parking lot.

She looked over at him with a puzzled look on her face. "No boat ride this time?"

"Nay. The road's finally finished."

She read the posted sign aloud. "Closed Community No Cars Past the Parking Lot."

"We'll have to hoof it from here."

He helped get her things to the room over the pub and then walked her to Quilting Central. He didn't intend on going in but at the last second decided it was only right to make sure she made it in safely.

Deydie came at them like a freight train, waving a book. "I've got yere pattern right here."

Kit looked at him like he knew what the hell Deydie was talking about. He backed away. When it came to Deydie, Kit was on her own.

"Excuse me?" Maybe Kit should've taken a few moments to readjust to life in Gandiegow before hurrying over here.

Deydie shoved the book at her, cracking it open to the page marked with a Post-it. She tapped a gnarled finger on the picture of a quilt. "This is the quilt I'm going to teach you how to make."

Kit shook her head. "Oh, thank you, but no. I won't have time." She looked at her wristwatch as if her schedule was right there. "You've given me a deadline, remember? I'm going to have a tough time as it is getting everything done."

"Rubbish." Deydie planted her hands on her hips. "There's plenty of time. Plenty of grace. Plenty of creativity. You remember that, missy."

Kit looked back to Ramsay as if he could convince Deydie.

He steadied one edge of the book, his eyes dancing with merriment. "Give it a go, lass. You don't need to sleep."

Kit peered at the page with the red, white, blue, yellow, and black quilt.

"See? They're nautical flags," Deydie explained. "The complete alphabet. A way for one ship to communicate with another."

It really was intriguing, bright and beautiful. "It looks complicated." It would probably take a year to complete, too. "Do you have something easier?"

Deydie shook her head, the bun at the back of her neck bouncing determinedly. "This is the one that ye're going to make."

Ramsay laughed. "Deydie is the town bully."

Kit had already figured that out for herself.

"Watch it, wee Ramsay," Deydie warned. "My broom bristles have yere name written all over them." She whooshed her arms as if whacking him good with her imaginary broom. She turned back to Kit. "I just know what's best for you, that's all. Come back this afternoon and we'll get you started. You can take Sophie's spot at the table. We're having a sew-in."

Ramsay nudged Kit. "The quilters come here to work on their projects."

She looked to him. "Who's Sophie?"

"One of our local lasses who married a few months back. She moved north with her new husband," he explained.

She closed the book with the pattern in it and held it to her chest. "I have tons to do, but I'll try."

"Do better than try," Deydie said stubbornly. "Learning to quilt's important."

Kit mentally rolled her eyes, but Ramsay was watching her so closely, he must've caught on.

Ramsay put his arm around Deydie's shoulders conspiratorially. "Kit has a lot of important business to take care of." He said it as if Kit were the secretary to the Queen. Or perhaps the Queen herself. "Ye should let her get to it."

"No," Deydie said. "First she has to meet my quilt ladies. Or at least those that are here." She motioned to a woman with gray braids wound around her head. "Rhona, git yere arse over here."

Rhona smiled and pushed away from the sewing machine. As she did, Deydie gave Kit the rundown.

"Rhona has been Gandiegow's schoolteacher for thirty-two years. A fine teacher at that. But she's leaving us to move to Dundee to help her daughter with the new babies. Twins." Deydie's voice cracked at the end, as if she was going to miss her longtime friend. But she cleared her throat to cover it.

Rhona reached them and filled in the rest. "The new teacher will be here by the end of the summer." She stuck her hand out to Kit. "It's lovely to finally meet you. I didn't get to welcome you before."

Kit shuddered, remembering her *warm* welcome here at Quilting Central days earlier.

Deydie pointed across the room. "And that's Moira over there."

A man and a woman had their backs to them, standing next to the coffeemaker. As soon as Kit had walked into the building, she'd noticed them—the man sandy-haired and tall, the woman in a plum-colored dress belted at the waist. Their body language spoke volumes; they had some kind of connection.

"Moira, come here," Deydie hollered.

When the couple turned around, Kit was surprised to see the white collar of the clergy on the young, nice-looking man.

Deydie smacked Kit on the back. "That's Father Andrew, the pastor of the kirk. We've only the one church in town. If ye're not Episcopalian yet, ye will be by the time that ye leave."

Moira approached, her gaze lowered. *Very telling.* Moira was shy, but *shy* usually covered up tons of character. She had a nice face and long hair fashioned into a braid, which was slung over her shoulder. Father Andrew followed behind her with a pleasant, confident smile with intelligence showing in his eyes.

Kit got a pretty good read from the pastor's body language. He was both a little complacent and somewhat oblivious to how he felt about the bashful woman. As Deydie did the introductions, Kit made a decision. She would make Moira and the Episcopal priest her pro bono project. These two were a perfect match if ever there was one. She'd set these two up for free. It would spread some goodwill, plus be a way for her to give back to the community.

She shook hands with the couple and wondered when she could block out time to speak with them individually and begin working on their setup.

"Dammit, George," Deydie hollered, making Kit jump. The old woman pointed to the elderly gentleman in the corner working on the longarm quilting machine. "I told you to wait until I was over there before ye started it up." She waddled off at a fast clip.

"If you'll excuse us, too," Andrew said. "Moira and I were just now heading over to her cottage to take some refreshments to her father and to sit with him for a while." He lifted the sack and the to-go cup in his hand.

They said goodbye, and as they left, a new group of people walked in. Ramsay quietly groaned. She saw it was his brothers, though she hadn't been introduced. The two acknowledged her and Ramsay with a wink and a nod. They kept on, going directly to the back of the room to join Deydie and George. Kit recognized the three women who came in with them from her lynching right here in this very building. It was Maggie, with her sisters in tow.

They came directly to them. It might've been Kit's imagination, but Ramsay seemed to scoot closer to her instead of his sister-in-law.

Begrudgingly, he made the introductions. "Kit Woodhouse, this is Maggie, Rowena, and Sinnie."

Despite cultural differences, some things were universal. The three Scottish women sized Kit up and Ramsay's relations-in-law weren't thrilled to make her acquaintance, either. She suspected the introduction had less to do with wanting to know her and more to do with wanting to keep their enemy close. A tactical move.

Rowena and Sinnie stood behind Maggie, making it clear who was the alpha female in the pack.

Ramsay hovered, jamming his hands in his pockets. He glanced around as if torn between staying and making a run for it.

Maggie held Kit's gaze. "Come to dinner tonight." The statement wasn't even close to being a request.

Ramsay took a step back. "What?"

Maggie tilted her head toward Kit. "She heard me."

"She's busy," Ramsay said defiantly.

Kit looked up at him. "I am?"

He made a general wave to the room. "Ye said you have to prepare for the retreat."

"She has to eat," Maggie argued.

Before Ramsay could interject anything else on Kit's behalf, and because she was feeling ornery, she made a rash decision. "I'd be delighted to come to dinner."

"Aw, hell," Ramsay muttered. He gave her a hard glare that said she didn't know what she was in for. "Then don't set a place for me. I'll be out."

Did he have a date? Or was he chicken?

Maggie narrowed her eyes at him. "Ye'll not pass up my shepherd's pie."

His face showed the struggle between his brain and his stomach. "As I said, I've plans."

Kit's insides dropped. But why should she feel downcast because he had a date? Or was it that she'd be alone with his less than friendly sister-in-law?

Maggie put her hands on her hips and barked at Ramsay. "But ye'll make sure to burn the trash before you leave. John also expects ye to help with the nets in the morn. So don't be out too late."

His eyes turned heavenward. "Aye, I'll take care of the trash before I go. And I'll help with the damned nets in the morning." He stalked away to the far side of the room.

Maggie hollered after him. "Ye'll need to bring the matchmaker to the house."

"Nay," he grumbled. "I'll send someone to pick her up and bring her to the cottage."

Kit didn't know whether to be pissed to be seen as an inconvenience or to feel sorry for the guy. She couldn't blame him for being grumpy. He'd been publicly nagged and put in his place by his sister-in-law. Kit watched as he joined the two other men in the corner with some back pounding and posturing among the three.

"The Armstrong boys," Maggie explained, nodding territorially. "The redhead there is my John. The other one is Ross, the middle brother." She gave Kit a hard stare. "He's promised to Pippa."

"Which one is Pippa?" Kit gave the room a cursory glance.

"Och, Pippa lives in Edinburgh. She's an engineer."

"I see." Kit wondered if she would be warned off all the men in the town. She changed the subject fast. "Ramsay said you have a son."

Maggie's face softened, an expression Kit hadn't seen from her. "Aye, Dand. He's a handful." By the way she cooed the word *handful*, she made it sound like the highest praise for a Scottish lad. "Ye'll meet him tonight."

"I can't wait." But Kit could. She had a lot of work to do between now and then. Plus it wouldn't be the most pleasant of evenings sitting across the table from one of her adversaries. Kit wished Ramsay would reconsider so she'd have at least one friendly face to look at.

It hit her how quickly she'd grown used to Ramsay. But maybe that's what happened when you were in a foreign country—you formed attachments quickly.

"If you'll excuse me," Kit said to Maggie. "I really need to get to the restaurant and see what arrangements need to be made for the mixer."

"Sure," Maggie said. "Go on now."

Deydie hollered to Kit before she could make her getaway. "Remember. This afternoon—the sew-in."

For the rest of the day, she worked on preparing Gandiegow for her clients. She spoke with Claire and Dominic, the restaurant owners, about the menus for the mixer and the retreat, and the dietary restrictions of her clients. Then Cait Buchanan stopped by, and they discussed the supplies needed for the quilting workshops over a quick cup of tea at Pastas & Pastries.

Cait stood. "Let me give you a tour of the quilting dorms. You can set up yere U.S. clients in Thistle Glen Lodge and put the bachelors in Duncan's Den." She showed Kit both cottages that had been converted into the retreats' lodgings with plenty of beds to go around.

It all looked great, and Cait was being as nice as could be, but Kit still had her reservations. How would her clients feel about attending a quilt retreat? *Forced into it really.* They were quiet, unassuming girls. Although they'd agreed to the quilting retreat over the phone, it might be a different story when Deydie was barking orders at them.

They said goodbye. On her way back to the pub, Kit quickly stopped in the General Store and bought a scented candle to give to Maggie as a hostess gift. She hurried as she didn't have much time to get ready for her dinner at the Armstrongs'. Once again she wished Ramsay would be there tonight, or at the least he'd be the one to take her to his house.

When she opened the door to the pub, it was like she'd conjured him. Ramsay sat at the bar, talking to a man on the other side.

When Ramsay saw her, he stood. "It's about time you got here. Maggie will have your hide and mine if we're late." He motioned to the barkeep. "This is Coll. He does all the cooking for the pub."

"And throws rowdy Scots out on their arses if they get out of control." Coll gave Ramsay a pointed glance.

Ramsay laughed, but then turned his attention back to Kit. "Ready?"

She had about fifteen questions for him, but changing into something more appropriate for dinner was first and foremost. "I need a minute."

"Women," Ramsay complained. "Ye can't live with them—"

"Ye're not married. What do you know?" Coll laughed. "You won't know a thing until you are, and have wee bairns of your own. Stop yere bellyaching. Give the lass all the time she needs to get gussied up."

"Get up those steps, sprite," Ramsay urged. "The shepherd's pie is in the oven. And wear one of yere boy outfits."

She smiled and ran up the stairs. First she tucked the scented candle in her purse along with a short note for Maggie. Then she quickly put on a skirt and blouse that hugged her. At the last second, she grabbed her sweater. Ramsay was right; it was rather nippy here in the Highlands in summer.

When she got downstairs, she caught the series of expressions that passed over her chauffeur's face—first surprise, which turned to smolder, then to a deliberate blank slate—before he donned his typical grin. "Ye're taking the blame if Maggie rails on me," he said as he held open the door for her.

"Does that mean you're staying for dinner? Did she

make you? Or was it one of your brothers?" Kit asked, launching into the first of her numerous questions.

"I'm a free agent," he said defiantly.

"Oh, really? How did the trash burning go?" she asked.

"Okay. It was actually the smell of the shepherd's pie that has me staying for dinner."

"What about your date?" she inquired.

He grinned at her. "Rescheduled it. Besides, I couldn't wrangle anyone else to fetch ye to the house. Ye're not liked very well in these parts." He put his hand on her back and hurried her along.

"Yes. Thanks. Just what I needed to hear before I face the firing squad." She tried to ignore his touch. "So how do you get along with your brothers? Well?"

"Not at all," Ramsay said. "We can't stand the sight of each other."

"That's not what I saw at Quilting Central today."

"An anomaly," he quipped back.

"Yeah." But she recognized their close family ties, boisterous as they were.

She thought about the apartment back home that she shared with her mother and two sisters. It was as quiet as a library. Harper was very studious, and Bridget spent a lot of time out with friends. Her mother was either working at the art gallery or volunteering at the museum. It was as if when her father had died, the joy in their household had been extinguished as well, drowned into silence. And in Alaska. Kit had lived a pretty quiet existence all on her own.

Maggie met them at the door with a basket of silverware, which she promptly shoved at Ramsay. "You're late. You and the matchmaker set the table." She turned on her heel and marched away.

Kit sighed. The rocky start between them continued. She slipped the candle for Maggie on the end table with the small note of thanks that she'd written for her to find later.

The cottage opened up into a fairly large room as if it had been remodeled into an open concept; the living room, dining area, and kitchen were all together. The house was a hodgepodge of personal things scattered about—several quilts slung over the back of the couch, a child's drawing held on the refrigerator with a magnet, a couple of oars propped by the front door. *A home.*

A real family lived here.

The apartment in the Bronx was clutter-free, sterile, as if her mother and sisters had to make up for the chaotic neighborhood they lived in—the chaotic life they'd been forced to inhabit.

"Aye, Swab, ye get right on to setting the table," said the red-haired eldest brother. He stuck his hand out at Kit. "We didn't get a chance to meet earlier. John Armstrong."

Kit could see why Maggie had fallen for him. He was all brawn and all charm. Then again, so was Ramsay.

The other brother elbowed John out of the way and grabbed Kit's hand. "I'm Ross. The good-looking one in the family."

What a brood of gifted flirts.

Maggie cleared her throat in the kitchen. Kit would've sworn she heard the word *Pippa* amongst her throat clearing.

Kit took the silverware from Ramsay. "I'll take care of this." The plates were stacked on the table, ready to be set, too.

Maggie glanced over at her but didn't comment.

A small boy came running into the room and threw himself into Ramsay's arms. "Uncle Swab!"

Ramsay tossed him in the air a couple of times and then planted him on the couch safely.

Two teenage boys rumbled into the room with heavy footsteps.

"Robert and Samuel. My cousins," Maggie said be-grudgingly, as if explaining anything to Kit was as bad as enduring a boil. "They're here for dinner."

The noise really began then. The slightly taller cousin, who looked about fourteen, tackled the other, pinning him to the ground. Little Dand jumped on top.

The men, settled into the sofa and easy chair, laughed at the commotion.

Kit didn't see anything funny here. She finished placing the last fork and hurried into the kitchen as Dand hurtled himself again at the boys rolling around on the floor.

"Aren't you worried about them breaking things?" Kit said to Maggie, thinking of Dand's precious bones.

The men pushed the teenagers away from their feet, the open concept in full-on testosterone overload.

Maggie *tsk*ed, giving Kit a hard stare, as if Yankees didn't understand a whit about family life. "It's normal rambunctious behavior. They're burning off excess en-ergy. It's best to stand back and let them finish."

And pray no one gets maimed, Kit thought.

Playful rude comments from the men flew around the living room like the family flag in a strong wind.

Maggie brought Kit back to the work at hand by push-ing a basket of fresh bread at her. "Put that on the table."

"But what about Dand?" Kit inquired, not budging. "Aren't you worried he'll get hurt?"

Frowning, Maggie shoved a bowl at her, too. "He can handle himself."

The boy was seven at best. Kit thought Maggie's view was pretty callous or maybe irresponsible.

Maggie shooed her to the table with the food, talking over the noise of the wrestling match. "The lads actually take it easier on each other with Dand in the room."

"That's taking it easy?" The teenagers were grunting and tackling as Dand repeatedly threw himself into the mix.

"Aye," Maggie said, giving her crew that soft grin again. "Boys and men are like dogs. They need to burn off their energy or they'll start chewing on the furniture. You should've seen Robert and Samuel when they were younger. Little savages."

"No, thank you." Kit could barely take her eyes off them now.

"The lot of them should be carted off to a zoo." Maggie barked at them, "Boys, go wash up. And Ross, stand that lamp back up."

It might have been a zoo, but Kit had to admit that the house had life in it, a loving, unruly energy within its walls.

"Come on, Swab." John put his hand out and hauled Ramsay to his feet. "You, too, First Mate." He pulled Ross up next. The men and the teenagers headed off down the hall with Dand clinging to Ramsay's leg. The love among the crew was evident.

Maggie passed a couple of trivets to Kit. "Put them on either end."

Kit smiled at her, hoping for some friendly chitchat. "It smells great."

But Maggie only grunted, letting Kit know that she'd

made her mind up beforehand ... *They would not be friends*.

Ramsay sauntered back in, grinning, and came to stand close to Kit.

Since Maggie's back was turned, Kit nudged him. "Yeah, it's a shame you all don't get along."

"Swab, it's your turn to say grace," John said, carrying Dand under his arm like a football and dropping him onto a chair at the table.

Everyone stood at their places. Ramsay pointed to where Kit should stand—next to him. They folded their hands and Ramsay gave thanks for the good weather and good fishing and good food. He peeked over at her when he was done. He didn't look at all embarrassed to be singled out to pray in front of everyone. If Kit had been asked, she would've shrunk into the corner. And she never shrank away from anything. Ramsay, she thought once again, was more than she'd given him credit for in the beginning. He had a strength in him that she didn't have. Not just brute strength. He had character.

Dinner was delicious and entertaining, despite Maggie keeping her eye on Kit as if she might shove the silverware into her pockets. Soon Dand was regaling them all with the story of how Robert and Samuel had chased him into Mr. Menzie's garden.

"Robbie and Sam hid behind the cottage as Mr. Menzie yelled at me for trampling his turnips," Dand complained with a grin.

"He should've taken the rake handle to yere backside," Maggie said firmly.

The men laughed, but Maggie stared them down one by one.

"And you, Robert and Samuel. Ye were in charge of

Dand. You all need to learn to be respectful of others' property. Tomorrow ye'll all go to Mr. Menzie's and offer your weeding services for the rest of the season in exchange for his forgiveness."

The three boys hung their heads, muttering *aye*.

Kit saw the look that John gave his wife—fondness and gratefulness—and it hit her once again how much love this small cottage held. A lump formed in her throat.

After dinner, Maggie picked up the empty shepherd's pie pan, but John snatched it from her hands. "You go put your feet up." He dropped the pan in front of Ramsay. "Swab's doing the dishes."

Ramsay stood, stretched, and tapped the back of Kit's chair. "Come on, Woodhouse, it's time to earn yere keep."

John's head popped up with a start, but he said nothing to Ramsay. Maggie frowned and made her way to the sofa.

Kit followed her chauffeur into the kitchen and spoke quietly to him. "I thought I'd earned *my* dinner by setting the table. Who sat on the sofa and egged the children on while they rolled around on the floor like a pack of bear cubs?"

"Ye're a cheeky lass." Ramsay nudged her toward the sink, pushing up his sleeves. "You wash. I'll dry."

At the sink, they stood side by side, like the knife and the spoon had been next to each other on the table. Pretty cozy, she thought. Too cozy. The kisses they'd shared while on the road came to mind. Those hadn't been cozy at all. Hot. Steamy. Consuming.

She glanced over as Ramsay reached for a dish to dry. She saw the scar on his forearm and touched a soapy finger to it. "From what battle did you get this? Please don't tell me it's from something boring, like a bar fight."

She slid her finger down the scar for a moment before she realized what she was doing. She brought her eyes up to meet his and decided not to apologize for her brazen action.

His gaze was hooded for only a second, but when he spoke, he was all tease. "Nay, no bar fight. I got into a tussle with a conveyor at the North Sea Valve Company."

She pulled his towel from his hands and wiped her soapy caress from his arm as if it'd never happened. "The conveyor won?"

"Aye. She had me from the get-go."

His words seemed to hold a hidden meaning, or maybe Kit just wanted to think so. She really needed to start dating again. And as soon as she got the Real Men of Scotland off the ground and she was home, she would. She tossed the towel back to him. "Your dishes are piling up."

He motioned toward her face. "Yere cheeks are red."

"It's the hot water. I always blush when I wash the dishes."

"Liar," Ramsay mumbled.

Kit chose to ignore the accusation. They continued on without any further touching, or conversation. There was enough noise going on in the living room area for several cottages.

"I don't need a bath, Mum," Dand argued.

Maggie laughed. "You're a filthy mess. You look like ye've been playing in the pen with Dominic's pig."

"But I took a bath yesterday," he whined.

Kit glanced over her shoulder as John hefted the boy into his arms and began tickling him.

"You choose, lad. It's either the tub *or the ocean.*"

The boy giggled. "The tub! The tub!"

"Make sure you wash his hair," Maggie hollered. "Pouring a wee bit of water on it doesn't count, John. Use soap!" She leaned back and sighed.

"I'll be right back." Ramsay slung the dish towel over Kit's shoulder. "Finish up."

"Your dishes will be waiting for you," she said.

Ramsay went down the hall after John and Dand.

She could hear their hushed voices from the sink but not their actual words.

Ross joined her in the kitchen. "I'll take Swab's place." He took the towel from her. "So, how goes the manhunt?"

Should she rat Ramsay out and tell Ross she felt certain his brother had sabotaged her? But then he'd helped her by finding her bachelors. It still remained to be seen if he'd saved the day.

"It hasn't gone as I had hoped," she said truthfully. "But I'm remaining optimistic."

Ramsay came back in the kitchen and pulled Kit away from the sink. "Ross'll finish the rest. I need to get you back to the pub."

Normally, Kit hated being bossed around. But she let it go. Ramsay's bossiness felt like a layer of protection.

Kit turned to the Armstrongs. "Thank you so much for dinner." She didn't have a chance to register their response as Ramsay was ushering her toward the door.

John stepped into the room. "Maggie, I'll have a word."

The door had barely shut behind them when Maggie's voice rang out through the open window.

"What? No! Not under my roof!"

Chapter Nine

As they walked, Ramsay glanced over at Kit, but her gaze was fixed on the water lapping against the boardwalk. She didn't ask about Maggie's outburst, but after a few more steps he decided it was better to just get it over with. "I need to talk to you about something."

"Yeah. I already know. Maggie wishes I was gone."

Before he could set her straight, Deydie bustled out of Quilting Central and waved them over. "Get in here, lass. You, too, Ramsay." She met them halfway and grabbed an arm of each, pulling them into the building.

His proposal to the matchmaker would have to wait.

"What is it?" Kit asked.

Deydie waved a stack of fabric at her. "I want ye to see what I've picked out for yere Nautical Flag quilt."

Bethia, Deydie's oldest friend, came over to introduce herself to Kit and warmly shake her hand. Bethia was as kind and lovable as Deydie was crotchety.

"We cut out part of your quilt for you." Bethia pointed to the table where scraps of fabric were piled.

Kit frowned at the pieces and then at Bethia. "I can't imagine I can make those triangles, squares, and rectangles into the quilt that Deydie showed me."

"Sure you can," Bethia encouraged.

"Ye've got all of us to help you." Deydie motioned to the table. "We've set your machine up over there. Go on now and get started."

Ramsay still had to tell Kit the news. "She can't right now, ladies. She has to get to the pub."

Kit pinned him with a look.

Unfortunately, Deydie stepped closer, examining him as if her eyeglass prescription was out-of-date.

"What are ye about, wee Ramsay?" Deydie asked. Which was funny because she had to crank her head back to see him way up there.

"She's had a long day." He put a hand on Kit's lower back and ushered her to the door.

Kit kept glancing up at him, but he kept moving her along.

As soon as they were outside, she yanked his arm, pulling him to a stop. "Why *are* you walking me to the pub? It's not like the town is big enough for me to lose my way."

"I'm heading in that direction is all," he lied.

"For a drink." Her eyebrows pinched together.

He'd let her think that. For now. In fact, a dram of liquid courage might be called for.

They finished the last few steps in silence. At the pub door, the noise spilled outside, confirming his wisdom in doing what he'd done.

They went inside the pub. She turned to him, bid him good night, and went behind the bar and up the stairs.

Bonnie shot one glare at him and another at Kit's disappearing backside.

He stepped to the bar and pulled out his money. "Whisky."

"Ye look sick, Ramsay," Bonnie said as she fixed his drink. "I think ye've got the Yankee flu."

"Very funny." He downed the drink and ignored Bonnie's outrage as he stepped behind the bar to take the stairs, too.

Outside Kit's door, he hesitated. He could just walk away now and tell John that Kit had declined. Ramsay wasn't even sure why he'd done it. But then Thomas's hoot of laughter from down below ricocheted off the walls of the stairwell. Here was the reason why. Ramsay finally knocked.

Kit opened the door, cinching her bathrobe around her waist. Her skirt peeked out from underneath.

Aw, gawd. The bathrobe, her sweet legs. Was she topless under there?

She frowned at him. "Are you lost? Your cottage is in the other direction." She pointed. "Downstairs. Across town."

He couldn't stop himself. He scooped her in his arms and kissed her smart mouth into silence. Before he did more than get a good taste, he set her away from him. "Hush now."

She looked stunned and he felt breathless. He was afraid he might do it again if he didn't get to the business at hand.

"Pack your things," he said.

"What are you talking about? I just got unpacked."

"I know. But you're going to come stay with us at the cottage. John thinks ye're not getting enough rest here at the pub."

At that moment, a chorus of "The Maid Gaed to the Mill" broke out downstairs.

She looked at Ramsay skeptically. "So this was John's

idea? And tell me . . . what does Maggie have to say about it? As if I don't already know."

He gave her a grin. "Och, she thinks it's a *grand idea*."

"Yeah. Right. I'll stay right here, thank you."

The noise from the pub got louder, as if he'd orchestrated it to make his point. She stared at the door somewhat dismayed.

He laid a hand on her shoulder, working very hard not to run his hand down her back and pull her perfect body to him again. "Do it as a favor to me then? And my brothers? We'll not let Maggie harp at you." He tried to convey that this was all about looking out for her, because no matter the words, he wasn't feeling protective of Kit at all.

"I have a different idea," she said.

"Of course you do. Let me hear it."

"You go talk to Deydie and ask if I can stay at one of the quilting dorms."

He shook his head. "A retreat is starting soon. Full up." He didn't know that for sure.

Drums broke out downstairs now.

Kit stared toward the noise. "You've got to be kidding me."

Ramsay leaned against the door, grinning at the dilemma on her face. "Get yere things. I'll hold yere robe while you pack."

She tugged the belt tighter. "I'll stay at your house, as long as I'm not sleeping on the couch. Wait in the hall for a second." She pushed him out and closed the door behind him. A minute later, the door opened and her tight top from earlier was back in place.

"I could've stayed if that was all you were doing," he said.

She rewarded him for his cheek with a daggered look. He did like to rile his sprite. It didn't take her long to re-pack. It was as if the cadence of the drums set the pace, hurrying her along. She rolled her luggage toward him and grabbed her messenger bag. "Put your brawn to work." She walked past him and out the door, leaving him to get her bags.

"Now I'm your bellhop? Do I get a tip?"

But she was halfway down the steps by then and he followed her like he was her ever faithful dog.

As he hit the bottom stair, Bonnie turned and gave him such a withering glower that he was sure she'd been taking glaring lessons from Deydie.

"Where are you taking that one?" Bonnie barked, point-ing to Kit, who was opening the pub's door.

He could've said something clever but he was getting tired of Bonnie's bluster. "I'm taking her home with me."

It was the wrong thing to say. Bonnie was a mountain compared to Kit. She took a step toward him with her hands on her hips, looking ready to give him a lecture.

"Leave it," he said. He was done with her opinions. He walked past her, ignoring her gaping mouth.

Kit waited outside the pub. "Is everything okay?"

"Aye." But he didn't feel like talking about it. He was doing what he knew to be right and to hell with what the town thought about it.

Back at the house, Ross was still up, grinning when they came through the door. He took Kit's bags. "John said we were going to have a houseguest." He shot Ram-say a *you devil* grin. "Where should I put these?"

"My room," Ramsay said.

Kit spun on him. "No."

"Don't worry. I won't be sharing it with ye. I'll take the sofa." Ramsay gave Ross the final answer. "My room."

Ross wandered off with her things.

Kit looked around. "Where's Maggie? She may not want me to, but I should thank her for opening up her home to me."

"I expect Maggie is off to bed." Ramsay was surprised that John wasn't banned to the other sofa for allowing Kit to stay. "Come. I'll show you where you'll be sleeping."

Ross said good night to them as he passed them in the hallway.

Ramsay pointed out the loo to Kit, across the hall from his room. He pushed open his door and let her pass in front of him; then he pulled the door closed behind them.

She spun around, looking panicked. "What are you doing?"

"Shh," he said. "Thin walls. I shut the door so as not to wake up Dand."

"Oh."

Ross had left Kit's two bags by the far wall. It hit Ramsay kind of funny in the middle of his chest that it was both strange and right to have her in his room.

"There's the bed," Ramsay said stupidly. He went to the dresser and opened the top drawer, scooping out his socks. "You can have this for yere things."

"No, I couldn't."

He dropped his socks in the wicker basket by the closet. "You have to. The drawer's already cleared." He should probably have changed the sheets, but then he noticed that it had already been done. The bed looked perfect as only Maggie could make it. He'd get an earful when he thanked her for it, too.

Kit frowned at the bed. "But I don't want to put you out. I've changed my mind; the pub is fine."

Ramsay laid his hands on her shoulders and turned her to face him. "You need yere rest." He was only doing this because of his guilty conscience. He didn't give a damn about her well-being. He reached out to tuck a stray lock of hair behind her ear—but jerked his hand back at the last second. Her hair was too soft. He remembered how it had felt when it had been all fanned out on the bed at the boardinghouse.

"Get some sleep," he said gruffly. He headed for the door but turned back to her. "Maggie won't tolerate a crabby matchmaker in the house."

"As if she'd tolerate a noncrabby one better?" Kit cocked an eyebrow at him.

As an afterthought, he stopped and pulled open the bottom drawer, yanking out a pair of pajama pants. "Try to keep from going through my things." He was working at being his old self, the town teaser, but he didn't quite pull it off. He couldn't look into her green eyes, so he reached for the doorknob. He never should've shut the door with them in here all alone. The room was too small to breathe in.

"Good night, Ramsay," Kit said softly.

Aw, hell. Why'd she have to go and use his name? He didn't reply but closed the door quietly behind him, going to the living room.

Ross waited, stretched out on the couch and grinning broadly. "Did ye get her all tucked in then?"

"Sod off." Ramsay pushed Ross's legs off his new bed. He wasn't going to explain to his brother that it wasn't like that between him and the matchmaker. Although he wouldn't have minded kissing her good night with her hair twisted up in his hands. But hell, if he'd done that, he wouldn't have been able to stop.

"I'll be damned if she isn't a pretty little thing." Ross unfolded himself and stood. "I believe I'll have a go at her. Give her a real man to remember dear ole Scotland by."

Ramsay stepped in front of him, blocking the path to his bedroom. "Touch her and you'll be short an appendage." He pointed to the other side of the cottage. "Go to bed."

"All right," Ross said. "But only because I'm tired. I'll chat her up at breakfast and see if she wants to carry on with the likes of me while she's here." He raised his eyebrow as if he'd chunked the ball into Ramsay's court.

"Leave the matchmaker alone."

"We'll see." Ross laughed as he went to his room.

Hell. It had been a while since he'd punched Ross and meant it. Normally, they just horsed around. But if he meant to mess with Kit, Ramsay would have to kick his arse. She was here on business, just trying to do right by her family. And no one in his family or in this town would bother her again.

He spread out the large earth-tone quilt over the sofa—Maggie must've left it there for him—and he collapsed, stretching out. Immediately, a thought consumed him—Kit lying in *his* bed with only her tank top covering those perky little breasts. She was there between *his* sheets, with her hair fanned out on *his* pillow.

Aw, gawd. He went instantly hard.

Leave the matchmaker alone rang in his ears. His own damn words. It was sound advice. Come hell or high water, he'd better listen to it or he could be drowning in a world of trouble.

Kit lay down on the bed. *His bed.* Dang it, she couldn't stop herself from thinking about Ramsay stretched out here beside her. She'd bet the couch was uncomfortable. She rolled over on her side.

He was a good guy ... and you couldn't argue with his rugged good looks. But, she reminded herself, men like him weren't for her. He didn't have a serious bone in his body. *Just like my father.* If Daddy had been a little more serious, a little more responsible, maybe he would've seen the recession coming. That, or had the business sense not to put all their eggs into one basket.

But wasn't that what Kit had done? Every penny she'd saved had gone into the Real Men of Scotland.

But she was different from her father. Her father only liked to have a good time. He was a kidder, the life of the party. But Kit was all business, twenty-four/seven.

Ramsay ... he did nothing but tease.

Although she had to admit that he did have a fabulous idea—running a guided fishing business for the husbands of the quilters—brilliant! Now, that was a business she would like to invest in. A sure thing.

Every time she inhaled she could smell Ramsay in the room—the outdoors, his aftershave. At this rate, she wouldn't be getting any sleep. She sat up. Maybe if she got a drink of water that would help her relax.

She climbed out of his bed and went to the door, leaning her ear against it. She didn't hear a peep. Maybe she could sneak into the kitchen and get a drink without rousing anyone. She cracked open the door and stepped into the hall . . . just as the bathroom door opened to reveal the naked-chested, pajama-bottomed Ramsay.

Considering how seriously he was gazing upon her lips, he didn't look like the wisecracker now. He reached behind him, turned out the bathroom light, and pulled her into his arms, her palms landing on his solid chest. He kissed her breathless. Senseless. Numbing her to the fact that she shouldn't be kissing him in the hallway of his family home.

His lips eased off and he rested his forehead on hers. "Were you lost?" he whispered.

She shook her head *no*, not entirely sure he hadn't kissed the words out of her, too.

"Lonely?" he tried.

She lied, shaking her head *no*.

"Can't sleep?"

She shrugged. "Can I sit in the living room for a while?"

He frowned at her, seeming undecided. "What about my beauty sleep?"

She patted his chest. "You've gotten enough already." If he got any better-looking, he'd have to carry around mace to keep her off him. "If I'm not welcome, I'll just go back to bed." *Your bed.* She tried to step away.

He kissed her again quickly, spun her around, and patted her on the bottom, apparently his way to prod her down the dark hall. She thought she heard him mutter *trouble* under his breath.

"Can I have a glass of water?"

"Ye're a high-maintenance lass, aren't ye?" But he went to the kitchen cabinet and retrieved a tumbler as she went into the shadowy living room.

She sat down in the easy chair next to the sofa and pulled his pillow into her lap. Her camisole and boy shorts weren't completely decent for sitting in the living room.

Ramsay brought the drink to her. "The elixir of life for milady." He presented it with a bow.

She took it. "We really should talk."

"Give me a second." He went down the hall and was back quickly.

In the moonlight, she watched as he pulled a T-shirt over his head. Disappointment walloped her in the chest. It was a crying shame to cover that masterpiece.

As he sat on the couch, he reached over and pulled her to him, settling them very close together on the sofa. She liked his strong body next to hers—the heat of it, the power of him, and how it made her all hot and bothered.

But she gently shoved him away. "You're going to have to stop kissing me." Kit's lips were unhappy with that declaration. They liked kissing him. A lot. But the madness of mixing business and pleasure had to stop. Now.

"Ye're right," he said into the darkened room.

She hadn't expected him to agree with her. At least not so readily. She frowned, trying to make out the magazines on the coffee table in front of her.

"Aye," he continued as if she'd made some response. "We have to stop. There's no chemistry between us at all."

She heard the teasing in his voice and turned her body toward him. "Can't you be serious for one minute?"

"No, lass, not when it comes to things between a man and woman. I'm never serious."

"Just stop kissing me," she said, not sure how to take his statement. She shifted her body again so her head rested back on the couch.

"I'll try." He moved closer. "Here." He tucked his arm around her shoulders.

"But you are easy to talk to," she said more to herself than to him. She rested up against his T-shirted chest, wishing for the bare, naked one. "Do you know how unusual it is for me to open up? I've told you more about myself than I've ever told anyone else." Including her sisters. But Kit had been a little tipsy when she'd shared all about her family and the pressure she was under.

"Ye're easy to talk to, too," he said in his rich Scottish burr.

His words blanketed and warmed her. *Comforting her*. Sitting here in the dark like this, she felt like she could share everything with this man, and she'd be safe.

"Go ahead and tell me something else about yereself." He caressed her arm. "And make sure it's an embarrassing story." A little echo from their car trip.

"I could never top your story. *Pretty in pink*." She gave a quiet bark of laughter. "No one ever dressed me up like a boy."

He laid his head over on hers. "Ah, that's where ye're wrong. You dress yereself up as a lad all the time."

"Very funny." She relaxed against him and began her tale. "Once upon a time there were three sisters . . ."

Kit yawned. The nights were indeed chilly in the Highlands. She snuggled into Ramsay's chest for warmth and continued with her story. She should have gone back to his bed, but she'd take one minute more, indulge herself, and stay in his strong, capable arms.

When Ramsay woke, it was still dark . . . and his arm was painfully asleep. Not to mention he had the hard-on of a lifetime.

He was about to shift Kit to regain some feeling in his dead appendage when she stirred and shifted toward him.

She snaked her arm around his neck and pulled him down to her mouth.

Oh, gawd, she was hot, and his body roared to life even more than before. She kissed him as if she had all the time in the world. Languorously. Sensually. But hell, she was kissing him in her sleep. She could be kissing anyone in her dreams. But it felt so good that he continued to let her carry him away.

Kit pulled away too soon. She sighed contentedly and wrapped her arms around his waist, cuddling closer, burrowing into him.

The sprite was killing him! He wanted to go back in for another kiss, but he couldn't. It wouldn't exactly be right with her asleep. With his nondead hand, he caressed her arm, holding her close. Soon, he'd have to get up to check the nets with his brothers. He pulled the extra quilt from the back of the couch over them.

After this night of the two of them acting like a couple of lovesick idiots, he'd really have to keep his distance from her. He had plans. He needed to get his mind back in the game. But for right now, he'd give himself one more minute to hold *his sprite*.

He must've fallen asleep. He jolted awake when something kicked his leg. He opened his eyes to find Ross standing over him.

Chapter Ten

"What?" Ramsay hissed.

"You better get *yere matchmaker* outta here," Ross whispered. "Maggie'll be in any second to start the breakfast." He turned and headed for the kitchen.

"Aw, hell," Ramsay muttered. He gently prodded his sleeping companion awake. "Kitten. Ye've got to get up."

She snuggled closer.

"The house is coming awake."

She sat up and looked around wildly.

"Morning," Ross said.

She cranked her head around, red quickly creeping into her cheeks. She stood and glared down at Ramsay, like it was his fault that she'd been wrapped in his arms. "Why did you let me fall asleep?"

Instead of answering, he gave her a lazy grin. "Toddle off to my room. I'll be in shortly to get my things for the day. Just so ye're forewarned."

"The door will be locked." She huffed off.

No sooner had his door shut than he heard John's bedroom door open.

"You owe me," Ross said, filling the kettle.

Ramsay stood and stretched, not feeling too bad for

sleeping sitting up the whole night. He folded both of the quilts and sauntered down the hall, meeting up with Maggie at the bathroom door.

"Is *she* going to get up with the rest of us? Or sleep all day?" Maggie said.

"I expect she'll lie in for a while. She didn't get much rest when we were on the road," Ramsay answered truthfully.

"You watch yourself with her. She's not for the likes of us. Remember that, Ramsay."

"Aye." It was true. Kit wasn't for him. She seemed like the kind of woman who came preinstalled with a ball and chain. He usually picked up his female companionship in Lios or Fairge, or any other town but Gandiegow. He made sure he chose wisely—birds who didn't want to get involved, who only wanted to have a little fun. He wasn't the marrying type. Hell, he wasn't even the relationship type. He had too much to do in his life to be worried about that forever kind of crap that had John jumping whenever Maggie rattled his chain.

But Ramsay had liked holding Kit in his arms last night. And he'd certainly liked kissing her. "I'm going to sneak in and get my clothes," he said by way of explanation to Maggie.

"Make sure that's all ye do in there," she said.

Aw, gawd, Maggie was a bossy one.

Ramsay stole inside his room, shutting the door behind him.

Kit sat up. "I locked that door."

"I forgot to tell ye the lock's broken."

She dropped back on his pillow and crossed her arms over her chest.

He gazed at her, liking how she looked in his double

bed. Beautiful. Ticked-off. Kissable. As he walked over to her, her eyes got big.

She put up roadblock hands.

"Relax. I just don't want you to get cold." He pulled the quilt up and tucked it under her chin.

"Thanks," she said, chagrined.

And because he could, he leaned down and brushed his lips over hers.

She pushed at his chest. "I *said* no more kissing."

"I'm hard of hearing." He sat on the bed and leaned in again, but this time it was no light brush; he plundered her mouth.

She clutched the front of his T-shirt and plundered back. He heard a moan, and to his astonishment, he realized it was him.

"Aw, hell," he said as he pulled away.

The sprite patted his chest and had a gleam in her eyes, as if she was quite pleased with herself for bringing Ramsay to his knees.

He growled and stood, trying to ignore the instant hard-on she'd given him, and the fact that she'd won this round. He didn't meet her eyes as he grabbed his things out of his dresser. But he could certainly feel her eyes on him.

"Oh, Ramsay?" she purred.

"What?" he said roughly.

"Shut the door on the way out."

He could hear the sprite laugh as he walked into the hallway.

In the bathroom, he dressed quickly, knowing he had to hurry or his brothers would leave without him. Back in the kitchen, his family waited.

John jabbed a thumb toward the hallway. "Are ye keeping *her* happy?"

Ross sputtered into his coffee.

Ramsay glared at him and then spoke to John. "Aye. She's got her damned bachelors all lined up for her social."

"Good. I want you at her beck and call. I figure if she's happy, this could turn into a lucrative long-term relationship. The matchmaker could be our safety net. We could drive her all over Scotland and have some steady cash flowing in even when the fishing is slow."

"*We*, nothing," Maggie piped in. "You, John Armstrong, aren't driving anyone anywhere, unless it's yere wife. And, Ross, well, you're promised to Pippa." She glared at Ramsay. "You're welcome to keep her happy as long as she doesn't get her hooks into ye. She's a Yank. She's not meant for you or Gandiegow."

Ramsay wished Maggie would leave off telling him how to live his life. But she was right. He would leave Kit alone. And he meant it this time. Kissing her was fun, maybe even a little habit-forming, but he wasn't interested in anything long-term. Or even short-term. Settling down was the last thing on his mind. Having a wife and kids was for the likes of John and Ross. Ramsay liked being single too much—being his own man—to saddle himself with a woman.

"Let's get going, lads," John said, grabbing his cooler from the counter and pecking his wife on the cheek.

Ramsay and Ross picked up their coolers and coffee, too, and followed their older brother out.

At the dock, as if synchronized and choreographed, they each went aboard the *Indwaller* and touched the wooden cross before they went to their jobs. The cross had been carved by their great-grandfather for the boat he'd built with the help of his own father. Not all the boats in the Armstrong family had survived the sea, but the cross had, and was passed down from one generation to the next. Ramsay knew that an outsider would think it was superstitious to touch the cross when boarding . . . but fishermen understood. It was only right to remember and show respect to the one who ran the ocean and their boat—the Almighty—the true captain of their ship.

It didn't take long to get on the open water. Ramsay loved it out here—the sea was a part of him. He was like John and Ross in that way. He just wanted to be his own boss. He was going to have to talk to his brothers; he was running out of time.

He went in the wheelhouse and stood beside John near the captain's chair. Ramsay was quiet for a long moment. The three brothers could go days without talking and still be comfortable as hell. And they could spend hours talking bullshit just as well. But right now, Ramsay needed to ask his brothers for a favor and it wasn't going to be easy.

As if he'd been called, Ross joined them, pounding Ramsay on the back. "I know you were only gone for a few days, but it's good to have you back, Swab." He jabbed a finger in John's direction. "This one isn't much of a conversationalist."

John didn't even glance in his direction. "What is it ye want to say, Ramsay?"

Brothers were a funny breed. Ramsay should've been surprised that John knew he needed to talk to them, but he wasn't.

"Ole man Martin's boat is for sale," Ramsay blurted out. That wasn't what he'd planned to say first.

"So?" John patted the wheel as if their boat was the

only one that mattered. "Why should we care whether his boat is for sale or not?"

"I have an idea," Ramsay started.

"It'll have to wait," John said. "Get down there and pull those nets."

Ramsay frowned at John, but his brother was right. The nets came first. Hopefully he'd get another chance later and wouldn't muddle it.

He and Ross jumped down and began hauling the filled nets aboard. For the next several hours, he was occupied using his muscles while he went over in his head how he would broach the subject with his brothers. Lunch should've been the perfect time to speak with them, but while John and Ross sat with their coolers in the wheelhouse, Ramsay had to fill the bait jars. The day got away from him and he couldn't find another opening. Ole man Martin's boat was slipping through his fingers once again.

Before he knew it, they were back at the dock, tying up. Ross stepped off with his gear.

"Wait up," John said. "Ramsay, go ahead and say what ye need to say."

Ross came back aboard. "Dammit, John, I need to get to North Sea Valve. I promised the McDonnell I'd get the high-pressure pump working. Today."

"It can wait." John leaned against the boom. "Ramsay, go on."

"I want to start my own business," he announced. Crap, that's not what he should've said, either.

"Ye don't want to fish with yere brothers? Ye want to go off on your own?" Ross crossed his arms over his chest. "Armstrong brothers have been working the fishing grounds together for generations."

"No. I don't want to start a fishing business." But Ramsay had to amend that. "Yes, I do, but not commercial fishing. Not like what we have." He told them about his plan to take the quilting husbands on fishing tours. He was aware that they would think it was a cream-puff endeavor—not manly like *real* fishing—and yet, Ramsay pushed on, telling them all the details.

"Ye're a fisherman," Ross complained. "Not some slick businessman."

Ramsay shoved his hands in his pockets, not sure how to respond to that.

"Leave off, Ross," John said.

Ramsay couldn't believe John was on his side. But then the other shoe dropped.

"If Ramsay wants to leave us and start his own business, he's welcome to do it."

Shit. "But here's the thing," Ramsay tried. He'd gone this far, he might as well go the rest of the way. "I'm a little short on the cash to buy the boat." Something stopped him from pointing out the sacrifice he'd made for the family by driving Kit around. *Lost cash, lost opportunity.* It just seemed petty. The family fishing boat had, after all, given him a living his whole life. "I was hoping that you two might want to invest in the business."

As soon as he said it, he wished he could take it back. He felt like he was five years old again and didn't have enough money to buy the bobber he wanted from the General Store. His brothers had made it clear then that you never asked for money—ever.

"Never mind," Ramsay said.

John spoke up. "The extra money we have, Maggie has set aside to take Dand to see her grandfather in the old folks' home in Edinburgh."

"Hell," Ross said. "I put what little I had in the North

Sea Valve Company. I wanted a piece of it. That company should make me a mint down the road."

"It never hurts to get on the right side of your future father-in-law," John added. "So how short are you, Ramsay? This sounds like a pretty half-baked idea. Do you even have half of what ye need?"

Ramsay refused to justify himself to his brothers. Even though they were turning him down, he'd been happily surprised at their hint that if they had the money, they'd give it to him. But John's last question betrayed their true feelings. Ramsay was the little brother. The coaster. The kidder. With no substantial ideas. His brothers would never see him for who he was. What did a guy have to do to get a little respect around here?

He could move away. He'd thought about it a million times. But Gandiegow was home. He didn't want to live anywhere else. But to stay here meant that he'd never be treated as his own man.

"Well?" John prodded.

"There's no point in talking about it anymore." In their eyes, he would never be seen as an equal. He wouldn't tell his brothers that he'd saved nearly every pound he'd ever made, the vast majority in CDs and bonds. All he needed to get ole man Martin's boat was an extra month's work. But the boat would be gone in two weeks, up for auction. Ramsay doubted, even if he stood with the rest of them, that his bid would make the grade.

Ross smiled. "Ye're always good for a laugh, Swab. That's for sure."

But John peered at Ramsay for a long moment, not saying another word. John had this way of acting more like their father than their brother, and right now Ramsay wished their old man was here instead. Maybe he'd climb up the bluff later today and visit his father in the cemetery. At least the old man would listen to him and not say that his idea was half-baked.

Kit had only meant to close her eyes for a minute. She'd been lying on her side in Ramsay's bed with her head facing the door, in case Sir Kisses-A-Lot decided to come back in and do it again. She'd heard the front door close, but she couldn't be a hundred percent certain that Ramsay was truly gone. She'd decided to wait a bit longer before getting up to face the day . . . and Maggie. But when Kit woke up, the sun was high in the sky and blaring on her face through Ramsay's window.

She rolled out of bed and listened. The cottage was quiet. She quickly made his bed and grabbed his robe from the hook on the back of the door. Sure, she could've dug out her own robe, but his smelled like Ramsay— fresh soap and man. She inhaled more deeply.

She opened the door slowly and padded into the hallway. Still no sound. In the big room, she found no one, just a note on the dining table, two oatcakes, and a mug.

Gone for the day

—Maggie

Kit tapped one of the oatcakes. Hard as a rock. She plugged in the electric kettle, put a tea bag in her cup, and threw a glance at the clock on the wall. She really must've been dead to the world to not have woken up with a small energetic boy in the house. But she hadn't. When the tea was ready, she dunked the oatcake in the hot liquid and took a bite. It wasn't terrible so she did it again. She was undecided about what to do first. She frowned at the clothes washer under the counter. She needed clean socks and underwear and doubted Gandiegow had a Laundromat. She wondered how pissed Maggie would get if Kit did some laundry. She looked at Maggie's note again. There was nothing on there that said she *shouldn't* make herself at home.

She took another bite. Clean undies were a necessity. If she was going to make herself at home, it was best to do it when no one else was here. She went to get her dirty clothes.

While her clothes washed, Kit made calls to her office in Alaska, answered e-mails, and talked to her sister Harper. Travel arrangements were coming along nicely for her socialite clients. Next, she took a shower and dressed. Finally, she was ready to go to Quilting Central. The number one question she'd been getting from her wealthy clients was what the heck was a quilting retreat? Kit would make sure that Deydie gave her some details and an itinerary. Calming nerves was one of Kit's many jobs, and as the time drew nearer, her clients were feeling plenty nervous about coming to Scotland to meet men.

As Kit walked to Quilting Central, Ramsay wandered into her mind for about the fiftieth time that morning. She looked out at the water lapping against the retaining wall and prayed for his safety. She also couldn't help but think about sleeping in his arms last night. It had been wrong to do it; she knew that. But knowing didn't stop her from wanting to be back in his arms again. She was halfway to the parking lot before she realized that she'd walked right past her destination, so she backtracked to Quilting Central.

Deydie and her quilting crew were there, bustling around the one-day workshop. The teacher at the front was holding up fabrics and explaining to the out-of-towners how to do something called a "whack and stack." Kit stood and listened for a minute, but then Deydie saw her and lumbered over.

"I've got you all set up over there. We did part of it for you, but Moira is going to show you how to cut the rest of the fabric," the old woman said.

"Oh, no. I'm not here to sew. I'm here to get more information on my retreat."

Deydie put her hands on her hips. "We won't tell ye nothing about that retreat until yere quilt is started. Ye're a lass who needs a hobby." She glanced pointedly at Kit's messenger bag. "I know what's good for ye. Now scoot yereself over there. Moira doesn't have all day."

"Fine. But for every piece of fabric I cut, you'll have to tell me something about what my clients will be doing while they're here."

Deydie gave her a snaggly-toothed smile. "Pretty cheeky for needing something from me, aren't ye?"

Kit didn't get to answer. Deydie saw something beyond her shoulder and hustled off, muttering, "Dammit," under her breath.

Kit smiled after her, then joined Moira at the cutting table. This would actually work out perfectly. She wanted to interview the quiet woman anyway and start the process of trying to match her with the Episcopal priest.

Moira gave her a shy smile and showed her how to press the fabric and line it up on the mat, then how to measure and cut the fabric with the rotary blade. She was a competent instructor and patient when Kit got it wrong.

Time flew by, and Kit was so focused, she almost missed it when Ramsay came sauntering in with a tall, gorgeous strawberry blonde. They were laughing and carrying on, the woman touching Ramsay's arm. Kit's stomach dropped and she sliced the fabric in the wrong place. She mentally kicked herself. Not for the fabric, but because she'd been so dumb. Not twelve hours ago, she'd been kissing Ramsay, making him groan, and here he was parading his beautiful Amazonian girlfriend in front of her. Kit looked at her rotary blade, seriously considering slicing him into little pieces like she'd done to her fabric.

Moira grabbed her wrist to still her. "That's only Pippa."

"Pippa? Ross's Pippa?"

Moira shrugged. "Or so they say."

But it looked like Pippa had a thing for *Ramsay*. Maybe Kit should take the rotary blade to her instead.

"Cut," Moira said softly. "I'll tell ye the story."

Because Moira's voice soothed her, Kit pulled over the next piece of pressed fabric and laid it out.

Moira began her tale. "Pippa's mama died when she was a wee thing. She grew up with the Armstrong boys, as her papa and their papa were best friends. The Mc-Donnell is the one who is starting up the North Sea Valve Company."

"*Were* friends?" Kit asked.

"Alistair Armstrong died three years ago. It was a sad day when those three carted their papa's casket up the hill to the cemetery. They refused help from the rest of the town, insisting they carry their papa all on their own."

Kit glanced up at Ramsay. She knew what it meant to be fatherless and felt his loss along with her own. With new eyes she looked at Pippa and Ramsay joking around across the room. Maybe it was brotherly-sisterly affection that passed between them. But she wasn't 100 percent convinced. "So what about Ross and Pippa? Why are you skeptical?"

"I don't see it," Moira said quietly. "The papas decided when they were wee ones that those two would marry one day, and the rest of the town says it's going to happen. But I don't think it's right that people get involved in other people's love lives."

Kit waited for Moira to remember whom she was talking to.

"Present company excluded," Moira said sheepishly.

Kit laughed. "It's okay. I'm just glad not everyone feels as you do, or else I'd be out of a job."

Moira's cheeks turned pink. "I'm sorry. I didn't mean to offend you."

"You didn't. You were only speaking your mind." Kit suspected that Moira didn't speak up often, and it made her feel good that the woman was comfortable talking to her. But clearly she was barking up the wrong tree if she was going to set Moira up with the town's pastor. She would just have to work on Father Andrew instead to get the ball rolling.

At that moment, the door to Quilting Central blew open and the Episcopal priest himself walked in.

"Speak of the devil," Kit muttered.

Moira stopped in midpress. It looked as if she was holding her breath. "What?" She shifted her gaze to Kit.

"Nothing," she said.

Ramsay took that moment to look over at Kit with laughter in his eyes. She couldn't tell if it was because she was stuck quilting or if the luscious Pippa had said something funny.

Kit turned on Moira. "I thought Pippa lived in Edinburgh." Her voice didn't sound calm and serene as she'd hoped it would. "Or was that just a fib?"

Moira patted her hand. "Don't worry yereself. I told

you there's nothing between them. Besides, she's only here for the weekend."

Then Ramsay did the meanest thing; he walked right past Kit without acknowledging her existence, and out the door with the strawberry blonde goddess by his side.

Kit felt like an idiot. As soon as the Real Men of Scotland was up and running, Kit was going to find herself a man. Not one of those rugged men who looked better than God, but some lawyer or banker. Someone more like herself—business-minded, serious. Someone with the same goals as she had.

But above all, if she was being honest with herself, her future date better know how to kiss. Ramsay at least had that going for him. Hopefully he hadn't ruined her for all other men because of those talented lips of his. Yes, Kit wanted a man who could kiss, the kind of kiss that made her see forever.

"I'm not worried," Kit said, remembering to answer Moira. "I was only curious."

Moira passed her the red print fabric. "This is your last piece to cut. After that, we should head home for dinner."

It struck Kit that Moira had given her a good chunk of her day. "Thank you for teaching me and staying beside me. I'm sure you had better things to do."

"I enjoyed it. Besides, I have dinner in the Crock-Pot so I don't have to cook when I get home." Moira's gaze wandered over to the pastor again.

"Is Father Andrew coming to dinner tonight at your house? Or have you not asked him yet?" Kit said.

"What?" Moira's cheeks turned really red now. "I c-couldn't," she sputtered.

Andrew was speaking with Bonnie by the front door,

and it looked as if Bonnie was doing some serious flirting.

Kit nudged Moira. "If I were you, I'd hustle over there and seal the deal, before he makes other plans for the evening."

Moira looked down at her hands. "Nay. Andrew sits often at our table, but my da does the asking."

Bonnie took that moment to let out a bawdy laugh and to rub Andrew's arm. Instead of Moira setting down her fabric and going over there determinedly, she dropped her eyes to her shoes, shaking her head as if reiterating one more time that she *couldn't*.

Andrew left with Bonnie trailing behind him. Moira glanced up as they went out the door together. She shook her head one more time.

"It'll be all right," Kit encouraged, laying a hand on her arm. She liked to see women come out of their shells, but Moira was planted firmly within hers. It would take some serious coaching from Kit to get this shy woman to make a stand for what she wanted.

She thought about her clients, all sweet, shy women like Moira. All determined in their own way. Hopefully, they'd find love here in Scotland.

They finished up and stored everything in the plastic bin that Rhona, the schoolteacher, had dropped by the cutting table. Kit told the remaining quilt ladies goodbye, but Deydie grabbed her arm before she could leave. "I'll expect ye back here in the morning so you can work on yere quilt."

Kit forced a smile for the old woman. "You're the one who gave me a hard deadline for the quilting retreat. I have a lot to do to pull it off, including getting the details you promised me." And she still needed more information on the men who were coming, the ones she didn't know. Trying to research them online this morning, she'd had little luck. "I won't have time tomorrow to sew. Tomorrow is off."

Deydie shook her arm. "Nay. Tomorrow is on. I'm going to teach you how to make half-square triangles for your Nautical Flag quilt. While I do, I promise to tell ye everything ye and yere girls need to know for the quilt retreat."

"I guess I could take a little time," Kit said.

"Damn straight ye'll take time. Quilting is important in life," Deydie declared. "As important as water is to the fish."

At this Kit finally made her getaway, walking quickly to Ramsay's cottage. She hated to admit that she was looking forward to seeing him and his easy smile. Even more, she hated to admit that their bantering back and forth relaxed her, and she always needed to relax after talking to Deydie.

At the door to the Armstrongs' cottage, though, she hesitated. She couldn't just walk in. It wasn't her house. So she knocked.

Maggie opened the door. "Oh, it's you." She walked away, leaving the door open and Kit still standing outside.

Kit went through and shut the door behind her. "Can I help?" She followed Maggie to the stove.

"You could get yere underthings off the table."

"What?" Kit's eyes flashed toward the dining area. And sure enough, two of her French-cut panties were folded neatly by her place setting. She snatched them up and slunk off to Ramsay's bedroom. While she was there—and because she was too embarrassed to go out and face Maggie—she checked her texts.

Minutes later the house reverberated with noise as the brothers came home. Kit opened the bedroom door and ran to the living room. But Ramsay wasn't in the crowd. It was John, Ross, Dand, and . . . Pippa.

No Ramsay.

"Pippa, this is Kit Woodhouse, the matchmaker," said Ross, pointing.

There was a guttural noise from the sink. Kit chose to think that Maggie was only clearing her throat and not commenting on Kit and her profession.

John guided his son toward the restroom. As he passed, he answered Kit's unasked question.

"Ramsay won't be joining us for dinner." John gave no more explanation.

Kit felt completely out of place. And trapped. It was too late to make her excuses and go back to Quilting Central, the only spot she could think to hide out. She'd just have to suffer through.

Pippa made herself at home by going to the refrigerator and grabbing a bottle of ale. She held it out to Kit. "Would you like one?"

"Yes." Kit wasn't a fan of ale, but she wouldn't turn down the offer from the only person who was making her feel welcome.

"Get me one, too," Ross said.

Pippa pulled out three, passing them around. She punched Ross in the arm. "Ye should've had manners enough to offer one to your guest."

Ross opened his mouth, but shut it. Kit knew what he was going to say—she was Ramsay's guest, not his.

The three of them set the table while Maggie finished up. Ross and Pippa sniped back and forth while Kit got a pretty good read on them. These two were nothing more than good friends to each other, like Moira had said. It would be asinine to think they would be a love match. But Kit knew friendship wasn't the worst foundation to build a marriage on.

"So you live in Edinburgh," Kit started.

"She's a mechanical engineer like her da, the McDonnell," Ross supplied.

"He's the one who started the North Sea Valve Company, just outside of town." Pippa beamed. "He's brilliant."

"So are you going to work with him at the factory when it opens?" Kit asked.

Pippa laughed. "Heavens, no. Gandiegow is too small for me."

Something crossed Ross's face. Kit didn't know if it was disappointment or relief. She felt sorry for him. And Pippa. It seemed everyone expected them to get married except them.

The family ate their dinner companionably, although Kit had nothing to offer to their conversation about the fishing boat and the valve company.

Maggie wouldn't let her help with the dishes tonight as Ross and Pippa were in charge, so Kit grabbed her jacket and went for a walk.

She walked all the way to the end of town. Right before the last cottage, she took the path leading uphill. She assumed by what Moira had said earlier that the cemetery would be at the pinnacle. Instead she found a mansion built by the ruins of a castle. She would have to ask Ramsay later who lived here. She continued on the path that ran along the ridge and finally came across the cemetery. She spent some time reading the old headstones until she realized it was getting dark. She made her way back down the path on the other side.

When she returned to the Armstrongs', the house was quiet. Ramsay still wasn't home yet. Downcast, Kit went in his room and read until it was time for bed. Brazenly, she rummaged through his drawers and pulled out a T-shirt that read SHUT UP AND FISH. She slipped off her clothes and put on his shirt. He'd never know . . . because he wasn't here!

She climbed into bed and shut her eyes. But she couldn't go to sleep.

She must've dozed, because she woke up to darkness and rain hitting the windowpanes. Had something woken her other than the weather? She stole out of bed, went down the hallway, and tiptoed into the living room.

The couch was empty. No all-brawn man stretched out there. The quilts were still folded neatly on the back of the couch, too. She shuffled back to his bedroom with disappointment. And worry. And jealousy. *Whose bed had he climbed into?*

But why should she care anyway?

She lay in his bed for a long time with her arms wrapped around his T-shirt, willing herself to go to sleep. Her last thought before her body succumbed . . . Where's Ramsay?

Chapter Eleven

K it's first thought on waking was again of her chauffeur. She wondered when he'd made it home last night. *Or if he had.* She checked her phone for the time. By fishing standards, she'd slept in again. She climbed out of bed and slipped on Ramsay's robe to peek at the couch for evidence. The creases in the quilts didn't lie. Nothing had been moved. Everything was exactly as it had been when she'd gone to bed last night. He hadn't come home.

The same mean-spirited and sour taste of jealousy hit her stomach, as it had in the middle of the night. He must've found a willing woman to share her bed. Kit's awkward drunken proposition from the night at the boardinghouse came back to her with blunt force to the gut. He'd turned her down cold. Yet last night, he apparently hadn't had any problem telling another woman yes. A vision of Bonnie and her ginormous boobs flashed in Kit's brain, heating her insides. Those double D's would make a soft place for Ramsay to land. She stomped into the kitchen for coffee, pissed at him and with herself for getting so worked up. He wasn't worth it. She was here to do a job, not to hook up.

Near the coffee mugs, she found another note from Maggie. She was out again today. Kit filled her cup, refusing to look toward the sofa. She touched the crayon drawing of a boat hanging on the refrigerator and signed by Dand.

Dand was at school. Kit had learned that schools in Scotland didn't let out for summer until the first week in July. But where was Maggie? If Kit was running Maggie out of her own house, she ought to pack up and move back to the pub. Sure, she'd miss sleeping in Ramsay's bed, near Ramsay's possessions. But she'd sure like to talk to him before she cleared out. Where the hell was he?

A covered pan of porridge sat on the stove, a much better breakfast than yesterday. While Kit ate, she examined the schedule posted on the refrigerator beside Dand's picture. It was a list of chores for each member of the family, each day of the week. Well, if Kit really had run Maggie from her home, then Kit should do Maggie's chores for her. She found a mop and a bucket. As she scrubbed the floor, she hoped to high heaven she was doing the right thing and not offending Maggie further.

After the floor sparkled, she grabbed a pen, and checked it off the list just like the other completed chores had been checked. Next, she took a quick shower and then hurried off to Quilting Central, trying not to think about Ramsay. *Damn him.*

She rushed down the boardwalk, and noticed that the sea was choppy and unforgiving. As she passed the church with the large white steeple, she offered up a quick prayer for Ramsay's safety and safety for all the fishermen out today.

When she arrived at Quilting Central, old Deydie zoned in on her and lumbered her way. "Are ye ready to get back to work on the quilt?"

"I have a few phone calls to make first." She'd gotten two text messages on the walk over.

"Stop making excuses. It's time to get yereself behind that machine," Deydie ordered.

The old woman should have understood that the closer it came to an event, the busier Kit got with questions and problems. Making travel arrangements for so many at once was indeed a pain, but at least Harper would be there to corral the women and put them at ease.

"Maybe later," Kit said.

"There's no maybe about it." Deydie gave her a look that said she was close to handing out a serious lecture. "Working on it every day is the only way to get it done."

"Soon then." Kit smiled at her, but just then, the door to Quilting Central opened. Father Andrew walked in. "If you'll excuse me." Kit needed to have that chat with the Episcopal priest before things got any busier.

Deydie called after her, "Remember what I said."

Kit caught up to Father Andrew, who was pouring himself a cup of coffee at the counter. "Good morning, Father."

"Call me Andrew." He gave her a brilliant smile.

"Andrew, then." She pointed to one of the small café tables. "May I have a minute?"

"Sure." He followed her and they sat. But before Kit could get to the point, Andrew turned the tables on her.

"I hope the townsfolk are treating you well." He nodded toward Deydie as if he understood her bossy ways. "Gandiegow doesn't welcome newcomers easily."

Kit wanted to correct him, to tell him she wasn't really a newcomer, only passing through, but he continued on.

"If you ever need someone to talk to, I'm available." His eyes held genuine concern and reassurance. It was easy to understand why he'd become a pastor he had a sixth sense when it came to people and their problems.

Kit shook her head. "I'm fine. *Really*. But what I wanted to speak with you about is marriage. What are your thoughts on it?"

Andrew chuckled deeply and pointed at his white cleric's collar. "I'm pro-marriage. In fact, you might say I'm in the business of providing happily-ever-afters."

Kit gave him a thoughtful grin. "Yes, but what I'm getting at is how do you feel about marriage for you in particular?"

He jerked back a couple of inches as if she'd lit a torch in his face. "Marriage? Me? I'm in no rush." His gaze shifted to somewhere over Kit's shoulder.

She looked to where his attention had gone. Moira was gliding across the room to the cutting tables. Kit wanted to tell him that his actions spoke louder than words, that the way he gazed at Moira wasn't any ordinary look. But she held her tongue. "Moira's a pretty woman and smart, too."

"Aye." He snapped his eyes back to Kit. "She's a good person. Well-loved by the community."

"Really?" Kit only said it to make him elaborate.

As expected, he came to Moira's defense. "She's kind. She has a big heart. She's always willing to help those in need."

"Hmm," Kit said. "Like feeding the Episcopal priest when he's hungry?" She was going to be hard on him, because she felt the pastor needed a wake-up call.

Andrew got a perplexed look on his face. "Aye. She occasionally has me to dinner, but only because she's a good Christian woman."

"I know she is. But I'd like to give you some advice."

He didn't nod his head eagerly, but shifted to the side, giving her what could only be described as a wary glance.

Kit took it as his consent. "I have observed what's been going on. You and I both know Moira's not the type of woman to make demands. But that doesn't mean she should be taken for granted." *Like you've been doing.* "I think it's important for you to understand that well-loved woman could be snatched up at any time by someone who recognizes her value better than you do." Kit knew she might be crossing the line by being direct, but she went on. "Moira deserves to be taken care of, too, don't you think? I'm afraid that if you don't act, you might be left out in the cold while someone else takes your place at her table."

He schooled his frown into a forgiving smile. "Thank you for yere concern." He nodded in Moira's direction. "But we're doing fine. We're great friends."

Kit stood. "Well, remember, I'm here if you need my services."

"Thank you." Andrew rose, kept a smile frozen on his face as he headed out the door without glancing again at Moira.

"That boy's a blockhead," Deydie said.

Kit jumped. "Don't you know it's not nice to sneak up on people?"

"Moira pines after that lad like a seal after a bucket of fish. I heard you trying to talk some sense into him."

Kit shrugged. "He listened to what I had to say." But she doubted that he really heard her. *Oh, well.* Many a complacent man had missed out on the love of his life because he'd dragged his feet. "I did all I could do." *For now*.

"About that quilt," Deydie started.

"After I make my phone calls."

"Then git to it. The day's a-wasting," the old woman cackled.

Kit sat back down and settled in at the café table, again. She pulled out the picture of her grandmother's quilt, laid her hand on it, and made the first phone call.

The rest of the day flew by. People roamed in and out of Quilting Central—even a few fishermen in the afternoon, but none of them was Ramsay. Maggie and her sisters took up residence behind a row of sewing machines and worked for several hours. Kit didn't miss the glances from the three of them. Maggie and Rowena were disapproving, but Sinnie's glances seemed shy and curious.

After Maggie cleared up her area, she came over to Kit. "Dinner will be ready in an hour."

"Thank you." Kit put her phone down. "Is there anything I can do to help?"

Maggie's eyebrows lifted. "Be on time." She turned and left.

Kit hadn't had a minute to think about what she was going to say to the Armstrong family about moving back to the pub. But she'd had a vague thought to stay out of Maggie's hair by going to the restaurant for dinner. Well, that plan was shot. Kit only hoped Ramsay would be home tonight, sitting across the table and acting as her buffer.

Her hopes were dashed. Back at the cottage, it was just John, Maggie, Dand, and herself. Not even Ross was there. But Maggie seemed slightly less hostile toward Kit as she dished out the dinner of baked chicken and mashed potatoes, or "tatties" as they called them. As the conversation swirled around her, Kit remained quiet, trying to think of a nonchalant way to ask about Ramsay and his absence.

When Dand finished and excused himself to go play in his room, Kit decided to start by asking about Ross.

"So where is everyone tonight? Where's Ross?" Her voice was the epitome of casualness.

John picked up a piece of bread. "He's having dinner with the McDonnell. They're discussing how to put a new hydraulic tester in at the factory." He took a bite.

"And Ramsay?" Kit asked, willing her cheeks not to blush.

John put down the bread and gave her a strange look, as if he was deciding what bait to put on his hook. "Ramsay is working at the Spalding Farm in the evenings, building stalls in the barn."

"Oh." She felt kind of stupid for being jealous and thinking about Ramsay cheating on her.

Cheating? They weren't a couple by any stretch of the imagination. They were barely friends. Then she had a dreadful thought. What if the Spalding Farm was owned by a woman? Kit frowned at her plate.

John broke into her thoughts. "Ramsay and Colin, who owns the farm, have been friends since university. Colin picked up the farm for a pence and has turned it profitable."

"Ramsay went to college?" she blurted.

"One of us had to," John said as if an old memory plagued him.

Maggie laid her hand on John's. "Alistair, the boys' father, insisted that one of them go."

John glanced over at Maggie and gave her a loving smile. "Luv, ye look beat. Go lie down. Kit and I will straighten the kitchen."

"Absolutely," Kit piped in.

Maggie did look pale. "That would be grand." She

stood and walked toward the hallway, but then stopped. She didn't turn to Kit, but spoke to her over her shoulder. "Thank ye for the floor."

It took a second to register what she was talking about; by then, Maggie was gone.

John nodded. "It was a nice thing you did. I thank ye, too. Let me go start Dand in his bath and then I'll be back to help."

"Don't worry. I've got it." Besides, Kit wanted time alone to think.

While she cleared the table and started the water in the sink, she realized things had shifted. She no longer felt the need to pack her luggage and go back to the pub. She'd found a small place in the Armstrong household, helping out where she could. They needed her.

Her thoughts had shifted about Ramsay, too. Why had she assumed he hadn't gone to college? Ramsay had proved over and over to her how smart he was. But it was how he used his brain that was so damned attractive. She'd figured out pretty quickly that he wasn't all brawn; he was brain, too. One sexy combination.

John and Dand made a two-second appearance, saying good night, and then she was left alone. Kit changed into Ramsay's T-shirt, but instead of plugging in her laptop and getting some work done like she should've, she grabbed her e-reader and lay back on *his* pillow. An hour later, when the front door opened, she hurried to the bedroom door, hoping it was Ramsay. But when she peeked out, it was only Ross getting home. She sighed heavily and went back to her book.

In the wee hours of the morning, she woke up with her e-reader stuck to her cheek. No one else was up yet, not even the sun. As she wandered into the kitchen, she glanced at the empty couch and thought about how the heart really does grow fonder with absence. She pulled out the eggs, bacon, and cheese she'd seen in the refrigerator last night, and found potatoes under the counter in a basket, then set to work on making breakfast for the early risers. If she couldn't sleep, at least she could be useful.

Thirty minutes later, the breakfast casserole was in the oven, the dishes washed up, and the coffee brewing. Maggie wandered into the kitchen, sleepy-eyed.

For a long moment, she looked from Kit to the coffee to the stack of plates on the counter, then back to Kit.

"Why are you up?" Suspicion once again laced Maggie's voice.

"I couldn't sleep. I hope it's all right that I made breakfast."

John came up behind Maggie. "Gawd, that smells good."

Kit hurried to explain what else she'd done. "At dinner, you mentioned making chicken-salad sandwiches for the men for lunch." She swung open the refrigerator door. "I did that, too," she said sheepishly. She braced herself for Maggie's outrage.

John squeezed his wife. "Doll, go on back to bed. The babe needs its sleep."

Kit looked from John's adoring face to Maggie's small bump of a stomach. "You're pregnant?"

"Aye." Maggie frowned at her husband, but a smile lingered just below her disapproval. "We're going to be blessed again. We just haven't told anyone, 'tis all." Her gaze fell on Kit. "If you don't mind, I will go have a lie-in."

John gave his wife a sound kiss on the mouth and a swat on the bottom as she sashayed away.

"Congratulations." Kit grabbed a mug and poured him some coffee.

"I'm worried about her doing too much," John confessed. "She's had trouble carrying a bairn to full-term since Dand." He stopped abruptly as Ross came into the room.

Ross sniffed the air like a hungry canine. "What is that?"

"Breakfast casserole. I'll make you a plate," Kit said, glancing back at John, thinking about what he'd just told her.

"Make mine a double."

This would be the perfect time to bring up their absent brother without looking like she had some sort of crush or something. She dished up Ross's food. "I wasn't sure if I should make sandwiches for Ramsay, too. Will he be helping on the boat today?"

John grinned at her. "Aye. Ramsay will be on the boat with us. Ye best not forget him."

How can I? She'd tried every possible way to put him out of her mind. Without making eye contact, Kit stuck her red face in the refrigerator to cool off while pulling out the rest of the chicken salad for his sandwich.

The next two days ran together as Kit worked herself to the bone. In the early hours of the morning, she made massive breakfasts for John and Ross—Alabama biscuits and sausage one morning and her version of the Egg Mc-Muffin, the next. Before Maggie could get up and grumble at her, Kit would do as many of the chores on the list as she could. Whatever she could do to help out. Maggie took her husband's advice and stayed in bed, eating Kit's leftovers with Dand when she got up to ready him for school. Maggie's protests about the extra help turned into half-remonstrations, her feelings toward Kit softening a little more each day.

The rest of Kit's waking hours revolved around Quilting Central while she organized the social for her clients, and the occasional quilt block that Deydie insisted she make. Everyone seemed to have embraced her while she prepared for the quilt retreat. Cait and Deydie made lists while Rhona worked on lesson plans for the novice quilters. Moira and Gandiegow's matronly twins, Ailsa and Aileen, readied the tables, outfitting each sewing area with the tools of the trade—scissors, pins, and a small pail to dispose of clipped threads. And through it all, Kit was included in all the town gossip as if she were one of them. It turned out Emma and Doc weren't the only ones expecting; Claire and Dominic were, too. Emma had taken the time to sit with Kit a few times and helped her with her nautical quilt. When Claire and Emma weren't there, the townswomen talked of the baby quilts they were making for the mothers-to-be. Yes, the days passed well enough, but in the middle of the night, Kit was up, checking the vacant couch, hoping the lout had made it home, before making a hearty breakfast for the Armstrong brothers in residence.

Kit didn't inquire anymore after Ramsay. She'd made a fool enough of herself already with John. She was beginning to wonder if Ramsay was ever coming home, or if maybe he'd fallen off the end of Scotland, into the ocean, never to be seen again. But she was too busy to worry over him. Kit's clients would be flying in today with Harper and they should be in Gandiegow by supper tonight.

At the end of a long afternoon at Quilting Central, Kit

sat next to her sewing machine and pulled out the picture of her grandmother's quilt. For a moment she was lost in thought, but looked up as Maggie and her sisters made their way over to her.

"Can we have a moment of your time?" Maggie asked. "The lasses and I were wondering if there was anything we might help with to make your mixer easier."

"Aye," Rowena added. Sinnie only nodded.

The bachelors were due in a few days. "There's loads to do. I could use a few extra hands on the day of, to get the tables arranged." Kit looked at Maggie and then at her belly. "Rowena and Sinnie can help with that. Maybe you and I could work on some centerpieces tomorrow while my clients are quilting?"

"It's a plan." Maggie gave Kit her first genuine smile since she'd gotten here. "What's that a picture of?"

"It's my grandmother's quilt." Kit handed it to her, explaining as neutrally as she could why she didn't own the quilt anymore.

"'Tis beautiful." Maggie handed the picture back and Kit stored it in its spot.

Just then Cait Buchanan called out to Kit from across the room. "Can you come here and look at these fabrics I've cut up for your girls?"

"Excuse me." Kit left Maggie and her sisters sitting beside her things.

Twenty minutes later, when she made it back to her portfolio, Maggie was gone. And so was the picture of her grandmother's quilt.

In the wee hours of the morning, Ramsay drove maybe a little too fast in the pouring rain. He'd promised John he'd be back in time for the boat. But it had also been important to deposit the check in the night slot on his way back to Gandiegow. For the past four days, after fishing, he'd driven to Spalding Farm to help with the new barn stalls. Each night he'd slept for a few hours at Colin's and then hurried back to the fishing boat once more.

He was damned happy to have the work. It wasn't going to give him the money he needed to buy ole man Martin's boat in time, but it was always good to build up his bank account. More importantly, it kept him away from Kit—even if it hadn't kept him from thinking about her in his bed. He'd like to peel the clothes off the sprite slowly and get to what lay beneath. He wouldn't stop there. He'd like to kiss her senseless and make her moan. He'd like to . . .

He swerved, barely making the curve. He better keep his blasted thoughts on the road instead of how he'd like to make love to Kit. He wondered if she'd missed him. He hoped so. It would be payback for driving him crazy. There was nothing he could do about the guilty feeling he had for abandoning her in Gandiegow without even telling her where he was going. He was as spineless as a jellyfish.

He knew what day it was—the day Deydie had said the retreat should start. He wondered if her clients had made it in from the States. Or if she was ready for the bachelors to come to Gandiegow. Actually, he felt like he'd missed out on a lot. But that was the price he had to pay to keep his distance from her.

Kit was a beautiful, interesting woman, but he didn't need someone like her in his life. He had plans for himself. And getting tangled up with a woman would only hold him back.

Ramsay made it to the boat just as Ross was untying the line. "Was that the last night of it?"

Ramsay stepped aboard. "Aye." *Unfortunately.* It would be his last chance in a while to dig up an odd job for the season.

John nodded at him as he touched his hand to the cross. Over the last four days, he'd made a point not to ask after Kit. He didn't want his brothers to get the wrong idea. So instead, Ramsay kept his thoughts to himself.

They had a short day of it on the boat. Ross was in a hurry to get to the North Sea Valve Company, and John had made plans to take Maggie to Inverness for their anniversary.

The house was empty when they arrived home. John and Ross took turns in the bathroom, insisting they clean up first. After working two jobs with little sleep, Ramsay could barely keep his eyes open until it was his turn. When they finally left he cursed them to high heaven for leaving him no hot water. After his cold shower, he threw on boxers, shut his door, and collapsed into bed.

But as soon as his head hit the pillow, he felt another presence in the room. *Her.* She wasn't physically there, but his bed, his whole room, smelled of Kit. If he was a wuss, which he wasn't, he'd think her scent was irresistible. He sighed, shut his eyes, and was asleep instantly.

He came awake to a gentle touch to his face. He kept his eyes closed because he wasn't quite sure whether he was dreaming it or not. But there was the touch again, moving his hair off his forehead. He relished it for a second, then opened his eyes to a vision. "Hey, kitten."

Her cheeks blushed red. "Hey. You're not quite Goldilocks that I found sleeping in my bed."

He cocked an eyebrow. "*Yere* bed?"

She didn't answer but grabbed his T-shirt off the hook behind his bedroom door. "Put a shirt on." She tossed it at him.

"Is my manly chest getting to you?" He flexed his muscles as she rolled her eyes. He held the shirt to his nose. "Have you been wearing my clothes?"

She shook her head.

"Kitten, tell the truth. I know how you like to dress like a lad." He skimmed his gaze down her chambray shirt and jeans, lingering on the places he liked the most—her breasts, her hips. He held his shirt out to her. "But why'd you need *my* shirt? I bet this swam on you." He placed a hand over his heart, acting like the truth had just hit him square in the chest. "You missed me, didn't you?"

She huffed. "I haven't missed you. I've barely had time to breathe. Deydie kept me hopping. Where have you been for the last four days?"

He didn't answer. "What time is it?"

"Three. I barely escaped Deydie's clutches to run back here. I need to change before my clients get to town. And I needed to get my notebook." She canted her head to the side table.

"So we're here all alone," he drawled, glancing over at the shut door.

She nodded, looking more than a little unsure.

"In that case . . ." He grabbed her wrist and tugged. She fell on top of him. "Ye're a clumsy little sprite." And he kissed her. Tasted every last fiery morsel of her surprised mouth. He shouldn't have done it, especially since he'd done a helluva job staying away from her the last few days. But he loved the challenge of getting to her.

At first Kit didn't participate fully, but he was a determined man, especially when he had a goal in mind. He teased those lips of hers until she gave it right back to him.

He growled as he rolled on top of her. She dug her nails into him, clutching him, pulling him close, never breaking the kiss. And wasn't his pecker ever so happy they were finally going to do this? He felt like he was going to burst if he didn't get inside her soon. Not that it would mean that they were going steady or anything like that. It was just two adults having a bit of fun. He rolled off her and reached for his pants, needing the condom in his wallet.

She rolled in the other direction and got off the bed. The kitten was panting. "I've got to run."

"Run?" Ramsay said huskily, thinking the chase was on. "It was just starting to get interesting."

"But my sister. My clients. Here soon." She seemed to be having a hard time putting two words together. She put her hands up in front of her and backed away.

He felt like the dog that'd been told to stay.

He walked toward her anyway. "Answer me one question before ye go."

She stopped and put her arms down. "Okay. One."

"If ye were in such a hurry, what were you doing in here?"

"I told you. I came back to change."

"But you weren't changing. You were touching me, like you were . . ." He couldn't use the words that came to mind. He couldn't tell her that her touch felt like butterfly wings. Or that the way she moved his hair away from his face made it feel like the two of them were lovers. "And don't say you weren't toying with me." He grabbed her hand and hauled her up against his chest, using his finger to tip her chin up. "Look me in the eye and tell me the truth."

She brought her eyes up and once again he was hit with how green they were. And vulnerable. He saw some piece of the truth there and it scared the holy hell out of him.

Determination shuttered her emotions. Her gaze fell and she patted him on the chest. "Och, I couldn't keep me hands off ye." She'd put on a Scottish brogue like it was his damned T-shirt!

He planted both feet and cupped her face between his hands, searching her eyes again for the truth she wouldn't give him. When he bent down, he found it. In their kiss. He kissed her so tenderly that he nearly wept for the sissy that he was. In return, she wrapped her arms around his waist and mewed under his loving assault. Maybe he should've reached for the condom again—she felt so pliable that he could've done whatever the hell he wanted. But the game had changed—no longer a bit of fun, but something serious. He set her away from him and had to steady her as she wobbled.

"Ye've work to do," he said gruffly. "Now off with ye." He spun her around and shoved her toward the door.

He grabbed her notebook. "Wait."

She stopped and turned. She still looked as dazed as he felt.

He settled the notebook in her hands, the fog clearing a bit. "Be careful, my little sprite. Coming into a man's bedroom alone can be dangerous." *Especially if that man has a hankering to get a certain American lass naked.* "For the next time you wake me from a sleep with the gentle touch of yere soft hands, I won't be so honorable as to stop what I'm doing and let you make a run for it."

She clutched the notebook to her chest and stood her ground for a second to give him a hard glare. Then she grabbed her outfit hanging on the back of the door, too, and hightailed it out of there, slamming the door behind her.

He laughed heartily, knowing she'd hear him. But then he stopped as the gravity of the situation fell over him. He scrubbed his hand over his face, a conflicted man. For as much as he'd wanted to frighten her with his promise, she was turning out to be a bigger threat to him and the person he wanted to be. His own man. Who needed no one. But somehow, that last kiss had changed . . . everything.

Chapter Twelve

K it hurried and readied for the retreat, well aware that she was stripping naked only ten feet away from Ramsay—albeit with two doors and a hallway between them. She was unable to put that last kiss from her mind.

What had she been thinking? She shouldn't have been running her hands through his hair, pushing it off his forehead, enjoying the feel of his dark waves beneath her fingers. She'd just been so glad to see him again! But Ramsay wasn't some tame pet. He was wild in every sense of the word. Unlike a buttoned-up, controlled Wall Street suit, he was as unpredictable as a mountain lion.

But she had too much riding on this to lose focus now. Her clients needed her. Her family needed her more. She had the chance to undo the past, make up for what her father had done to them, if only she could be successful one more time.

Kit felt jumpy, wishing now that she'd been the one to go to the airport. But Harper insisted she could handle everything with the clients when they landed. Deydie insisted they needed help at Quilting Central, so that's where Kit headed.

But what Deydie really expected was for Kit to work

on her quilt. Why did Kit need a nautical quilt anyway? She banished the one sailor who came to mind. The one who kissed her with precision, skill . . . and passion.

Every time Kit tried to get up from her sewing machine, Deydie would bark another order at her to stitch another seam. The only reason Kit did as she was told—besides Deydie being scary—was because everything was under control. *Everything.*

Out of habit, Kit opened her planner. She gasped. The picture of her grandmother's quilt was back. She'd questioned everyone in Quilting Central twice about it, had asked everyone in Gandiegow if they'd seen it. But no one knew anything. But now it was back! Kit pulled it out and laid her hand on the picture for strength. Immediately, she felt calmer.

Right on time, her clients arrived with Harper, who ran to Kit. They hugged like they hadn't seen each other in years.

"We dropped our purses at the quilting dorm and came straight over," Harper said, squeezing her back. "The men are going to get our things to the dorm for us."

"I missed you so much!" Kit whispered into Harper's hair. "We'll talk in a bit, but first I better make the others feel welcome."

But it seemed that each Gandiegow quilter had adopted one of Kit's clients and was introducing themselves to her. Like a well-rehearsed dance, the quilting ladies got the girls settled at the long tables.

Cait Buchanan stood at the front of the room. "Welcome, everyone." While she gave the group an overview of the workshop, Deydie and Bethia directed Claire and Dominic as they settled the food on a table, banquet-style. "So after we eat, we'll show you your supplies. But we won't start anything until the morning. Tonight is all about fun and getting to know one another."

As Cait finished, the door to Quilting Central opened again, and a sea of men flowed into the room.

Bethia came over and laid a hand on Kit's arm. "After our menfolk get the luggage settled into the dorm, we reward them by filling their bellies."

But it was one fisherman in particular who caught Kit's eye. *Ramsay*. Apparently, she hadn't gotten her fill of watching him this afternoon while he slept, for she couldn't stop looking at him now. *And him at her*.

Harper nudged Kit; she hadn't even noticed that her sister had sidled up next to her.

"Been fraternizing with the locals?" Harper teased.

"No. Not hardly." *A few kisses didn't count.* "You know guys like him aren't my type."

Harper gave her a smile full of wisdom. "It never hurts to try something new off the menu."

"Always with the food analogies."

"I'm always hungry." Harper's eyes danced. She ate like a horse but stayed as slim as a supermodel.

"Go get something to eat." Kit nodded to where the other quilters were lining up her clients at the food table.

"I will because I'm famished, but then I want to hear all about Hunk-a-Burning-Love over there."

"His name's Ramsay Armstrong. He's not hunk-a-burning anything."

"And you're blind."

Kit gave her sister the older-sister *you'd better do as I say* glare.

Harper put her hands up in surrender. "I'm going, I'm going."

As her sister walked away, Kit noticed the local fish-

ermen eyeing her clients, the new meat in town. *Oh, crap.*
She'd screwed up. She'd brought her clients in a few days
early to help them get used to their surroundings and to
adjust to the time difference. It never occurred to her
that this wasn't a good idea. Kit was dangling her socialites in front of the local fishermen and they were itching
to take the bait — each one trying to get a closer look at
the catch of the day. Their posturing said they were staking a claim. She'd have to come up with some plan to
keep them separated until her bachelors arrived. Her
socialites were not fair game!

The bachelors. For the last few days, she'd been rolling
over in her mind what to do with the out-of-town Scots
before the mixer started. Kit thought about Maggie's
analogy — *Men are like dogs. They need to burn off their
energy or they'll start chewing on the furniture.* Kit was
afraid that the high-energy Scots would start throwing
punches at one another for sport if she didn't keep them
occupied.

She looked at Ramsay. He'd said he'd help her figure it
out, but then he'd gone missing. She should ask him now
if he had any bright ideas. But before she could take a step,
the answer came to her. *Ramsay.* He was her solution —
well, he and his idea of a fishing tourism business. He
could take her bachelors fishing for the day.

Kit grabbed her checkbook from her messenger bag and
made a beeline for her chauffeur. On her way, she looked
to Deydic to scc if she could run interference between her
clients and the fishermen, perhaps toss the wellies-wearers
from the building. But Deydie was just heading out the
door herself. One problem at a time, Kit thought. Her cli-
ent-fishermen problem could wait a minute or two. She
needed to square things away with Ramsay first.

She wove through the crowd to him. "Do you have a minute?" Before she could say any more, Ross came over and joined them.

He plopped a hand on her shoulder but spoke to Ramsay. "Oh, my gawd, ye've got to marry this one."

"What?" Kit whipped around and stared at Ross, but he held her shoulder in place.

"Aye. And ye both have to live with us." Ross grinned from ear to handsome ear.

Ramsay's mouth turned to a hard, flat line, his whole face going dark red, and his hands balling into fists.

Kit was already embarrassed by Ross's words, but to have Ramsay so visibly upset made her want to crawl under one of the sewing tables and die. "Stop it, Ross." She shrugged his hand off her shoulder.

"Seriously, she's a genius when it comes to satisfying a man." Ross eyed Ramsay closely for a moment, and Ramsay seemed to turn even angrier, ready to pounce. Ross took that moment to rub his belly. "She cooks breakfast like a son-of-a-witch. You missed it, brother." He let out a hearty laugh.

Ramsay's stance relaxed. "What's he talking about?" He kept his gaze on Ross, but apparently was speaking to her.

She shrugged. "I helped out. It was no big deal. I can cook a few things." Her face felt like it'd been stuck in the oven instead of the breakfast casserole she'd made.

"Maggie is even warming to yere matchmaker, brother. I'm serious. *Marry her*," Ross repeated, sighing, "and I'll be a happy man."

"Go away." Kit had had enough of his silliness. "I have business to discuss with your brother."

Ross gave her one last brilliant grin. "Only if ye'll

promise to make breakfast for the lot of us *until death do us part.*"

Ramsay elbowed him out of Kit's line of sight. "Speak," he said to her.

Ross made no move to leave, so Kit grabbed her chauffeur's arm and pulled him over to the corner for privacy. But then she made the mistake of gazing up into his expectant eyes, and for a second she forgot what she wanted to say. But the checkbook clutched in her other hand reminded her.

"Hear me out before you say anything. But I have a proposition for you."

"Hell's bells." Ramsay boldly ran his eyes down her. "It's not even Christmas and I'm getting exactly what I want." He was only half teasing. He reached out and ran a hand down her arm because looking at her wasn't enough. "I'm glad ye're stone-cold sober this time."

She took a step back. "What?"

Because he was a devil, he took a step closer. "Yere place or mine, little sprite?" Which was funny because they both resided under the same roof.

She got a clue and shook her checkbook at him. "This is not that kind of proposition." The red in her cheeks hitched up a notch. "This is a business proposition and nothing else."

"Call it whatever you like. *I'm yeres.*" He knew he was frustrating her and pissing her off at the same time, but he was enjoying the hell out of himself.

She positioned herself in front of him, apparently trying to block the view from the rest of the room, and punched him in the arm discreetly.

"Ouch." Her *punch* felt like a fly had landed on him,

but he rubbed his arm anyway. "I'm going to tell Deydie what you did."

Kit looked over her shoulder as if Deydie had appeared. "Why can't you ever be serious?"

Ramsay put his finger under her chin and moved her head back to face him. "What is it, kitten? What do you need?"

She exhaled heavily. "I need your help with the bachelors." She opened her checkbook and began scribbling while she talked. "You know they'll be here for eight hours before the mixer. They'll have nothing to do." She finished writing and looked up to him. "I love your idea of a guided fishing business and I want to be your first customer. Keep those men busy for me, get them cleaned up for the mixer, deliver them on time to the restaurant, and I'll be eternally grateful." She tore out the check and held it up to him.

He stared at her, trying to process what he had heard. She'd said the word *love* in there somewhere and it had gotten jammed up in his psyche, and he was having trouble getting past it. But then her offer sank in and he saw it for what it was. *Charity.*

"I don't want your handout," he growled. He would achieve his dreams on his own, or not at all.

She looked confused at first. But then understanding flowed across her face. Then anger. "You're a pigheaded man!" she hissed.

"Guilty," he agreed.

"Fine." She folded the check over. "I'll just get one of your brothers to do it for me. I'm sure they'd be happy to make some extra cash. Where did Ross go?" She turned around, searching for his brother. "Oh, there he is."

She took one step away, but Ramsay caught her arm

and spun her back around. "Give me the damn check."
But she held on to it. He sounded gruff and mean, not at
all like himself. Other emotions were prepared to spill
over, too. "Bathroom. Now." He pointed. They needed to
have this conversation in private.

She marched the few steps to the restroom and he
followed. He didn't care if everyone was watching or not,
but he didn't think they were; the quilters were busy with
the retreatgoers.

Once inside, she took his hand and slapped the check
into his palm. He pulled the door shut behind them, blocking the doorway. There were a million things he wanted to
say to her, the least of which was to stay away from his
brother, or anyone else for that matter. He didn't want
another man doing things for her that he could do himself.
But instead he reached out, grasped her, and in the process crushed the check. He kissed her fiercely, putting his
anger behind the kiss, and then set her away.

"I hope I've made myself clear." He turned and walked
out.

He kept walking, straight to the General Store, where
he checked out one of the town's shared vehicles. He drove
on to Fairge, his anger not easing up in the least. He'd keep
the cranking bachelors occupied for her if he had to. He'd
do this for her, but he was still pissed.

He parked in front of the bank. It wasn't until he got
inside and laid the check on the counter for deposit that
he saw the amount.

Motherducker! It's exactly what I need to buy the boat.

Good grief. Ramsay had made nothing clear, nothing at
all. Kit sighed and stared out the window, gazing at the
storm rolling in from the sea. Big black clouds were com-

ing. She'd been sitting here while Quilting Central buzzed around her for the last hour, and she still couldn't figure out what he meant. *Clear*, he'd said? The waters were muddier than ever.

Deydie came over to Kit. "I see now why yere American girls need ye. They're as shy as they come. Shy as our Moira."

Kit nodded. Over the years, she'd narrowed her client base, had specialized. Her clients were women who were more interested in reading novels or spending time with their horses than attending society balls. "I'm passionate about helping smart, quiet women. I try to find them men who can appreciate their inner qualities and not expect them to be social butterflies. They just need to meet some good men."

"Ye're doing a right nice thing for them. I approve." Deydie patted her hand and headed off, barreling toward the front of the room and her granddaughter, Cait.

Kit looked up as Moira sat down. She gave Kit a fortifying smile. Moira wasn't just shy. She had an inner strength that oozed from every pore. From what Kit had learned, Moira had been taking care of her ill father for many years, never complaining, and always willing to help others.

Moira motioned to the commotion—dinner—everyone getting to know one another. "It's going well."

Kit smiled back. They chatted quietly for a while about her quilt. But inside, Kit was still reeling over Ramsay.

Now that Harper and her clients were here, it only made sense that Kit should move in with them at the quilting dorm. She felt sad about it. She'd gotten used to the Armstrongs' noisy household, and she was just starting to build a rapport with Maggie. Also Kit very much liked sleeping in Ramsay's room, in his bed, surrounded by his things. Staying there made her feel safe and secure. Which was a strange sensation for her.

Maggie arrived at Quilting Central and walked straight to Kit. "Can you come back to the house with me now?" Her face was glowing, her eyes bright. "I have something to show you."

Moira touched Kit's arm and whispered, "Go on. All's going well. We've got yere girls."

At that moment, Rhona gathered Kit's clients around her own sewing machine and gave them a preliminary lesson on how to thread the machine and how to use the pedal.

"Don't be afraid. You won't hurt your machine," the schoolteacher instructed the group.

"Okay." Kit followed Maggie to the door, Rhona's words echoing in her head. *Don't be afraid.*

As soon as they set foot in the cottage, Kit saw that the dining table was filled with beautiful centerpieces: quart-sized Mason jars filled with shells, greenery, and long twigs. They were naturally elegant, a miniature depiction of life by the sea.

Kit turned to Maggie. "These are amazing."

Rowena and Sinnie came up behind them. "We helped," said the older of the two sisters.

Maggie picked up the closest jar. "I figured I would play around with a design and, well, the three of us got carried away."

Kit smiled at the sisters. "They're perfect."

Sinnie scooted two of them closer together. "We thought that right before yere gathering, we'd add a few fresh flowers."

"Thistles?"

"Aye."

"Perfect," Kit said again.

The door to the cottage opened and Ramsay stepped in, holding flowers and a box of chocolates in his hands. His eyes landed on her and her breath caught. If she'd been a dreamer instead of a feet-planted-firmly-on-the-ground sort of girl, she might have even said that his eyes were smoldering for her.

Ramsay handed the flowers and chocolates to Maggie. "For you."

Maggie gaped at him. "Why?"

"For all you do. For putting up with us." He leaned down and gave her a sisterly kiss on the cheek.

Kit's heart warmed . . . then squeezed in as if it had been hugged.

Rowena and Sinnie actually sighed.

Yeah, Kit knew how they felt. You just didn't expect a big brawny man like Ramsay to be so sweet and tender.

He winked at Maggie. "Does that get me off of trash-burning duty for a while?"

Maggie brought the flowers to her nose and inhaled. "Nay. But maybe tonight I'll make Ross do it for ye."

Ramsay walked to the kitchen, brushing Kit's arm as he passed.

He went straight to the trash can and pulled out the garbage bag. "I'll be back in a bit."

As he walked out, Rowena and Sinnie looked after him as if they might swoon. Poor Ramsay. He had no idea the effect he had on women. Kit made a decision. For Ramsay's sake, she better find a couple of men for Maggie's sisters. Those girls were carrying a serious torch for him.

Maggie handed the flowers off to Rowena. "Mama's

crystal vase is in the china hutch." She set the box of chocolates on the table and pulled the ribbon. "How about one piece before dinner?"

The four of them devoured some chocolates and had the box stored high in the cabinet before Ramsay made it back from the burn barrel.

"Kit, have you a minute?" Ramsay stood in the doorway. "There's something I want to show you."

Kit looked to Maggie.

"We were just headed back to Quilting Central anyway," she said. "Take your time."

Kit gestured toward the table. "Thank you again for the centerpieces. They're absolutely lovely."

"Och. 'Twas nothing."

Ramsay waited just outside. As Kit walked past, she could feel the energy rolling off him. She leaned in his direction, but as she did, she realized she was as bad as Rowena and Sinnie when it came to Ramsay.

When the door shut, Ramsay laid his hand on her lower back. It was a small courteous gesture, perhaps guiding her, and he couldn't know its effect. Warmth pooled low in her, and she had the need to lean into his hand to better feel the pressure of his touch. She pulled away instead and started walking down the boardwalk.

"So what do you want to show me?" She sounded way too perky, forced, maybe even a little shrill.

"Ye'll have to wait and see."

Kit glanced up. There was a twinkle in his eyes that she'd come to expect.

"Smile, sprite," Ramsay cajoled. "I'm afraid ye've been spending too much time with Deydie."

There was something contagious about his good nature that made her want to be near him. Kit bit her lower lip, trying to stop the smile he'd elicited. The more time she spent with him, the more she enjoyed his teasing.

Yes, Ramsay was as entertaining as he was gorgeous to look at, and he had nearly kissed the panties off of her.

But since her father's death, she'd shied away from fun-loving people. She'd surrounded herself with those who understood how hard the day-to-day could be, that every moment had to be wrangled into submission. Her kind of people understood that in an instant everything could change and all could be lost. Her people were serious businesspeople . . .

It hit her like a wrecking ball. She had no business kissing Ramsay, even if it was only for fun. She must hold true to her convictions. She glanced longingly at him and his talented lips, feeling sad.

As they approached the dock, he stopped and studied her closely, his eyebrows squinching together. "What's wrong?"

"Nothing." She forced a smile to her face. "Why do you ask?"

"Ye look like ye're lost."

In a way, she was.

He stepped up on the dock and she followed, wondering what this was all about. If he was forcing her onto another vessel, he'd better have her life vest ready.

He stopped in front of a boat and took her hand. "Here she is."

"Who?" She didn't recognize the boat, which definitely hadn't been there before. It was an older pleasure boat, large enough to hold a dozen people.

He pulled her into his arms and hugged her. "I was angry at you, lass. A man just doesn't take money from a woman. But I realized I could do an honest job of earning it. The amount you paid me was the last I needed to buy the boat for my guided fishing business."

For a second, she reveled at being in his arms once again. But she'd made her decision. She couldn't get her heart involved with this man. She patted his back platonically and then pushed him away.

"Good for you," she said.

He gave her a deep frown, not looking very Ramsaylike at all. He looked more like the pissed-off warrior she'd glimpsed yesterday when he'd abused her lips so thoroughly.

"And good for me," she added. "Now my bachelors will be occupied."

"It's always business with you," he said accusingly.

"Yes. It is." She stood tall as if he was challenging her. "It's who I am. But I'm still very happy for you."

He studied her for a moment. He seemed resigned as he climbed onto the boat. "Will you come aboard so I can show you around?" He put his hand out to her.

"Do you have any protection for me?"

He gave her a wicked grin and reached for his wallet, pulling out a small packet. It took a second for her brain to catch up with what her mouth had said.

"No! Not that. A life jacket. To keep me safe." She couldn't stop the heat from radiating in her cheeks.

"It's yere loss, kitten." He shoved the condom back in and returned his wallet to his pocket. "It could've been fun."

"I can't afford fun," Kit muttered. She stuck her hand out. "Life jacket?"

"We're not going anywhere. Ye'll be perfectly safe here at the dock," he assured her.

"Most sinkings happen at the dock." She'd read that.

"But we could just step off if she takes on water," he said.

"Humor me."

He reached under the seat, pulled out a life vest, and handed it over. "Better?"

"Better." She donned it.

He took her hand and helped her aboard, but seemed to lose his balance on purpose just so he could pull her to him again. He gazed into her eyes with his arms still around her. "You need my help, kitten."

Being this close kept her off-balance. "Oh?" She was a little mesmerized with the depths in his eyes. She saw wisdom there and it intrigued her.

"Aye. I need to teach ye to have a little fun." His voice was rough with emotion.

With one arm still clamped around her waist, he reached up and smoothed back her hair. The boat rocked her repeatedly against him. And because the life vest was bulky, her chest was pushed back while her hips pressed into him intimately. Images of the two of them together, what it might be like, washed over her, as the currents under the boat brought them together in an age-old rhythm.

As he leaned down to kiss her, Kit felt right with the world. To hell with the lecture she'd given herself only moments ago. Maybe her convictions were wrong and the man was right. Maybe she should learn to have a little fun.

She leaned up, closed the distance between their lips, and captured his mouth.

"Gawd," Ramsay growled into their kiss. He clutched at her, trying to get closer, but the vest was in the way.

She enjoyed his frustration as she Frenched the hell out of him.

But he stopped kissing her and started undoing the zipper of her life jacket. Just then a wave broke over the edge and splashed her feet. And it all came flooding back, raw panic coming over her. Someplace in the back of her mind, she knew it was unreasonable. They were, after all, tied to the dock. But she slapped his hands anyway, as if she was flailing helplessly in the water, drowning. Like her father.

Ramsay grabbed her hands and crushed her to him, slushing her, whispering guttural foreign words, calming words, soothing her.

That's when she realized she was sobbing, clutching him as she buried her face in his chest.

"*Mo chridhe*. My heart." He rubbed her back, not letting her go.

Slowly she relaxed, letting the safety of Ramsay's embrace steady her.

But it took a while to get herself completely under control. Which was so strange. She was, after all, the one in her family who never lost it. She never cried. Not even at her father's funeral. There hadn't been room for it. She had had to take charge, take care of her family—there had been no time to grieve. But here she was, years later, crying for the father who'd let her down.

Ramsay stooped to look at her face while tucking her hair behind her ears. "There. Better?"

She stared at his chest. "You probably should change your shirt. Sorry."

"Och. It's of no matter. How about we get you off this boat?"

She squeezed his biceps. "No. I'd like to take a look around. Really." It was one thing to be in a dinghy on the open water. It was quite another to be on a larger boat, tied to the dock. Her fear would not control her.

Ramsay kissed her forehead and took her hand, holding it between them. "If you suddenly need off the boat, I'll understand."

"I think I'm fine now." She stared at her drying tears on his chest. *He's a good man.* She wondered what would have happened if she'd cried all over one of her Wall Street dates. They probably would've asked her to pay for dry cleaning.

Ramsay proudly gave her the tour, pointing out his favorite features and talking about how things would run. His excitement was palpable and she knew how he felt. To finally achieve your dream after visualizing it and working toward it for years—it was a magical experience, almost as if it was ordained, everything coming together to a singular point. In a way, they really weren't that different.

Time slipped away and the sun started to set.

"I can't believe I stayed away so long. I have to get back to Quilting Central. Or the dorm by now. What will my clients think?"

He laid steadying hands on her shoulders. "Let me make a call." He pulled his cell from his jeans pocket. Five seconds later, he was speaking. "Cait? Ramsay here." He was silent for a second. "That's why I'm calling. Okay. I'll put her on speaker."

"Kit?" Cait said through his cell. "Don't worry about a thing. Harper got everyone settled in. Right now Deydie and Bethia are telling your ladies stories. You're not needed here tonight."

"I'm not?" Kit said.

"Just be at Quilting Central at nine a.m. We'll get going about then."

"But I had planned to stay at the dorm with them," Kit said.

Ramsay shook his head no.

"Maggie says you're needed at her cottage. Something about a male rebellion if you're not there to cook breakfast." Cait laughed. "What have you been feeding them?"

"Nothing special."

"Well, I think ye're needed more there than you are here," Cait said. "See you in the morning."

Ramsay hung up the phone with a grin on his face. "There." He spun Kit around so she was facing the ocean. "Now watch yere sunset and let the worries of the day go." He pulled her into him so that her back rested against his strong chest, all her tension washing away.

Her emotions had been all over the place today, but right now, she felt anchored. That was a feeling she hadn't had in a long, long time.

After the sun went down, they headed slowly back to the cottage, where only a small light in the kitchen remained on. Everyone seemed to have gone to bed. The centerpieces had been moved into boxes near the door.

"You better go get on my T-shirt and head off to bed," Ramsay said with mirth in his eyes. "Ye have to be up early to make me some breakfast."

She raised an eyebrow at him. "If you boss me around too much, John and Ross will be the only ones who get any of my cooking." She sashayed from the room.

"Good night, kitten," he said.

She went into his room and closed the door. She pulled his T-shirt from the hook and held it to her chest. It felt so good just knowing that he was back in the house. She took her time stripping out of her clothes and putting on his shirt. She heard him in the shower across the hall. When he left the bathroom, she grabbed his robe and stepped across the hall to use the facilities and brush her teeth. When she was done, all the lights were off in the living room. She peeked down the hallway, but she didn't see signs of life.

She trudged off to bed. His bed. Alone. But once she lay down, sleep wouldn't come. She rolled on her side and wondered if Ramsay was asleep.

She stole out of bed, quietly opened the bedroom door, and padded down the hallway. Once in the living room, she tiptoed over to the couch. She stood over him, looking at him by the moonlight. He was bare chested, wearing nothing but pajama bottoms.

She didn't expect his hand to reach out and yank her down. But when it did, she fell on top of him with an *oomph*.

"Shh." He settled her on his chest. "I'm tired and I'm trying to sleep."

She nuzzled into him, inhaling the smell of soap, shampoo, and Ramsay. She wasn't oblivious to the erection that her knee touched. "Are you uncomfortable?"

"Aye. But ignore it and go to sleep."

She snuggled in deeper and accidentally brushed up against him once more.

"Aw, gawd," he growled. "Sprite, either lie still or we're going to my room. And not for shut-eye either."

A threat or a promise. She sizzled low in her abdomen and was more than a little tempted to rub herself up against him again. No one had ever made her feel this way before. "But what if I want to make out just a little?"

He sighed as if being tortured. "There would be no little about it."

"Not even one little, eensy-teensy kiss?" Oh, she was bad, very bad. They were on the couch where anyone could walk in and see them. If she thought the lynching at Quilting Central had been unpleasant, she'd probably be strung up by her toes if caught seducing Ramsay under Maggie's roof.

"Okay." He sighed heavily like he had no choice. "One kiss."

She smiled into his chest, feeling victorious. For once she'd been successful with her womanly wiles—and with a 100 percent Scottish warrior.

But in the next second, she found she was wrong.

He kissed her all right. Fiercely even. But it was on the forehead. "There. Now sleep." He planted his hand on her knee, holding it in place. Apparently, he was taking a stand against whatever other wiles she had in mind to use against him tonight.

Chapter Thirteen

Kit woke up at her normal time to make breakfast. She didn't immediately move from the cocoon of Ramsay's arms. It felt too nice. Too wonderful. But she also didn't want to get caught by the family while she was snuggled up with her chauffeur . . . wearing nothing but her undies and his T-shirt.

She tried to wiggle out of his arms without waking him, but he gave her a gentle squeeze in protest.

"Breakfast," she whispered. "I'm earning my keep, remember?"

"One more minute." He ran his hand down her back, cupping her bottom for a brief second before tracing one finger under the elastic of her panties.

She shivered. Oh, yes, her human mattress had moves. And if Ross's and John's doors weren't about to pop open, she would've tempted her mattress with a little grinding to see if he would show her more.

Ramsay's hand moved back up and rested on her bottom for a moment. Then he gave her a pat and a squeeze. "Up, sprite. I've had enough." He chuckled. "Unless you want to skip breakfast and go straight for dessert."

She stretched out and slid across him, copping a feel as she stood.

He groaned in agony. "Ye're a mean little thing." He yanked her hand, pulling her down for a smoldering kiss. "Now, away with ye." He swatted her bottom as she retreated.

She ran off to his room, once again realizing he was too much man for her. With him, she didn't feel like she was in control of herself at all. He had her feeling womanly—all soft and feminine—not the tough-as-nails businesswoman she normally had to be. She knew enough about this world and its hard knocks, that if you were soft and feminine, you were bound to get rolled over and trampled on.

She threw on a running suit and a bra before hurrying back into the kitchen. This morning she was making a skillet breakfast of hash browns, cheese, bacon, and eggs. After the guys ate, she could put the covered cast-iron pan into the oven for when Maggie and Dand woke up.

She focused on cooking the bacon in the skillet and grating the potatoes while her distraction dressed and readied for the day in the other room. When Ramsay made an appearance, he was outfitted in jeans and an old T-shirt, looking very rugged and handsome. But wasn't he always rugged and handsome?

He took the empty coffee press and filled it with boiling water. As she walked by, he grabbed her around the waist with his free hand and hugged her to him.

It wasn't a wimpy hug. It was possessive, primal, and exhilarating.

He let her go. "I never figured you for one who knew her way around the kitchen."

She tried to ignore the chain reaction he'd started in

her body with that hug. She finally pulled herself together to answer. "Just some basics. I'm no gourmet chef." She threw the shredded potatoes into the pan and they sizzled. "What did John and Ross think of your big purchase?"

"What big purchase?" John said, making Kit jump and drop the spatula.

How long had he been standing there?

Ramsay frowned at her as if she couldn't be trusted with state secrets. "I hadn't gotten around to telling them. I was busy with another matter." He cocked his head, still gazing at her.

The way John scowled at Ramsay made Kit want to race off to her room—Ramsay's room—but she had to stay until the food was done. She flipped the bacon, maneuvering away from the popping grease. If only she could escape the impending argument as readily.

John took an imposing step toward Ramsay. "What are you blowing yere cash on?"

Ramsay straightened, not backing down, more serious than Kit had ever seen him. "I explained about the guided fishing business."

"Aye. I remember you asking for money." John's hard stare and almost imperceptible nod delivered the blow.

If he'd aimed that stare at Kit, she would've doubled over. As it was, she desperately wanted to slink away.

But Ramsay remained tall. His face, however, darkened with an angry red, his eyes turning to black steel, and he heaved the next statement at John like a tidal wave. "I don't owe you an explanation, but I'll give ye one anyway, brother."

Kit hoped to never be on the receiving end of this pissed-off Ramsay.

"Those days at the farm gave me the last I needed to buy ole man Martin's boat."

She noticed he said nothing about the check she'd given him to occupy the bachelors. But she couldn't blame him for the omission. She was in the midst of two unyielding, old-fashioned warriors.

John arched his eyebrows with the unasked, obvious question.

Ramsay exhaled so bitterly that she was surprised flames didn't burst from him. "I haven't done anything illegal to get the money, if that's what that look is all about. I've been stashing money away my entire life. Never turned down a job offered to me." He exhaled again, but this time, he seemed a little defeated. "I've always wanted a business of my own."

Kit flipped the hash browns and kept her head down when she went for the cheddar in the refrigerator.

"I see." John sounded like Ramsay had abandoned him, the family, and their business.

She felt bad for Ramsay. Was it really so terrible that he wanted something of his own? But then again, maybe he was leaving the other two brothers high and dry to run the fishing boat alone.

Ross wandered into the kitchen and grabbed a mug. "What's the argument about this time?"

"It's just you and me pulling the nets today." John moved the lunch cooler from the floor to the counter with a bang. "Ramsay has more important things to do." That was the first time that she'd heard John call him something other than Swab.

Ross turned to his younger brother for an explanation.

"I'll be working on my own boat today—maintenance," Ramsay supplied.

Ross turned to Kit. "Where did he get his own boat?" He must've thought she'd be the safer one to ask.

"Do I really have to get in the middle of this?"

Ross said, "Yes," while Ramsay said, "No."

She shrugged. What the heck. She'd taken over the Armstrongs' kitchen; why not mediate their family feud, too? "Ramsay used the money he's been saving his whole life to start a fishing tour business by buying a boat. John feels betrayed that he'd leave the family business. We're not sure yet how you feel about it." She glanced at each one of the three brothers. "Did I cover everything?"

John harrumphed and busied himself with getting out the ice packs.

Ramsay put his head down to hide a slight grin while he shook his head. "I probably should've warned ye; the sprite doesn't mince words."

Ross grinned at her. "I see that." He turned to Ramsay and pounded him on the back. "I wish ye well with yere new business. And I'm sure John does, too."

John glowered at Ross. "Aye. I wish ye well, too."

As Kit spread the shredded cheese over the top, she thought about calling for a group hug. But that might have been asking for too much, too soon. She crumbled the bacon over the skillet casserole, put the lid on, and turned to the men. "No peeking and no filching from that pan. I'll be back in a minute to serve it up." She sounded as bossy as Deydie. Kit was getting a clue why the old woman might be the way she was. The men in this town were not completely civilized.

She hurried down the hall and shut herself in Ramsay's room. She told herself that it was just to give the three of them a moment to be alone together. But more accurately, it was to give her poor estrogen-riddled body a break from their excessive testosterone. She plunked herself down on the bed with a heavy sigh.

The bedroom door opened and Ramsay came in, shutting the door behind him. "Come here."

She could've fought his magnetism, but instead, she dropped her feet to the floor and took two steps into his arms. He bent down and kissed the biscuits out of her.

"Oh, damn," she said, pulling away.

"What?"

"I forgot to start the biscuits."

Ramsay grinned down at her. She was a funny little thing.

She swatted at his chest. "You guys got me all frazzled. Those two brothers of yours love my biscuits."

"I kinda like yere biscuits, too," he said with a pointed look at her breasts. Then he pulled her back into his arms, leaned against his door, and tucked her head under his chin with a sigh. He had the strange feeling that he wanted to be the only one that frazzled her. No other men. Not even his brothers. "You know, don't ye . . . you're not a bad lass."

She cuddled closer. "Ye're getting better with those compliments. Keep working on it. Practice makes perfect."

"Aye." He leaned down and kissed her again, tenderly this time.

A quiet knock reverberated from the door into his back.

"Can we eat now, Kit?" It was Ross. "I'm drooling all over myself."

Gawd. Couldn't he get one moment alone?

Kit stepped away from him, patting him on the chest. Ramsay smiled down at her hand; he'd gotten used to that little habit of hers.

She laid her hand on the door. "Don't touch that lid, Ross."

"But I'm hungry," Ross grumbled quietly.

"I'm sure I could improve my kissing with practice, too," Ramsay teased, pushing her hair out of her face. "If only you'd give me a chance."

She backed away. "No. That particular skill, you've mastered. You better go eat." She opened the door, stepped around him, and was gone.

Ramsay was left alone in his room.

With the scent of her still lingering in the air.

And, aw, gawd, a hard-on that would need more than a few minutes to go away.

After breakfast, Ramsay spent the morning with his boat. His boat! He still couldn't believe it. The first thing he did was a full maintenance check on the engine. Next he checked the bilge pumps, one of the most important pieces of equipment on the vessel. The pumps kept excess water out of the bottom of the boat. Kit was right that most boats did sink at dock. Many a fisherman had come to his boat in the morning only to find it had sunk overnight due to failed bilge pumps. Ole man Martin said he'd just replaced one of them and, indeed, one did look brand-new. The other one checked out fine.

Ramsay patted the side of the boat. He hadn't named her yet. But he already felt that she belonged to him.

His cell phone vibrated in his pocket. A text from Kit.

Can you break away this afternoon? I need a driver.

He started to type *anything for you*. But decided that

sounded way too much like a sissy. But he would have done anything for her. He told himself it was because he owed her. She'd given him the bachelors' job, the final amount that he'd needed. But somewhere inside his thick skull, he knew it was more. The truth of it rested in his chest.

Sure, he texted back.

He closed everything down and stepped off as John and Ross were pulling in on the family boat, done with the morning run.

Ross stepped on the dock, tying off, and hollered to Ramsay. "How about you give us the grand tour of yere new ship?"

Ramsay glanced in John's direction and his oldest brother nodded. John hadn't done a complete one-eighty from this morning—his leftover frown still remained. But at least he seemed to be trying.

He checked the time. "I have a few minutes to spare before I have to leave. Kit needs her driver." The three brothers climbed on the boat and Ramsay showed them around.

"What's left to do?" Ross asked.

Ramsay named off the few things he'd hoped to get done before the bachelors showed up tomorrow.

"We'll do it for you," Ross said. "Won't we, John?"

"Aye." John sounded a little like Dand when he was told to pick up his room.

"Thanks," Ramsay said. "Drinks will be on me next time at the pub. I better run."

"Yes, yere matchmaker is waiting." Ross grinned at him.

Ramsay didn't have time to correct his smartass brother. The matchmaker wasn't his. But he did like to kiss her. And liked her lying on top of him. The question was, would he get the chance to have her lying underneath him again?

Ross gave him a nudge. "Are ye going or not?"

"I'm going." He better get his head screwed on straight, not that it would be easy. He was going to be spending the rest of the day with the woman who distracted him beyond his ken.

Ramsay ran home and took a quick shower. He met her at the car.

She had her trusty messenger bag in hand. "Thanks for doing this. I hated taking you away from your new boat. I'm sure you have plenty to do."

He opened the door for her. "Considering how pressed you are with the retreat and yere social, I'm surprised you would take time out to go meet with this bloke."

"I admit the timing isn't great." She slid in her side of the car. "But we're meeting with Art MacKay. He can't be part of the mixer tomorrow, but he will be an important client in the future. Besides, I need to make the most of every minute I have left here in Scotland."

Ramsay felt like he'd taken an anchor to the chest. Kit would be leaving? Of course, he'd known that all along. He'd even tried to hurry her out of the country with his schemes. But now the reality felt too real, too harsh. He stared out the front window. "When are you scheduled to go back?" His voice sounded strained to his ears.

"It all depends on how it goes at the mixer."

Ramsay struggled to identify what he was feeling. Was he sad? Angry? All he knew was that he didn't want her to leave.

"Are you okay?" she asked.

He started the car. *Kit is leaving*, his blasted brain said again.

She must've misunderstood his silence and said apologetically, "I could've asked someone else, but I didn't want anyone driving me but you."

The anchor on his chest lightened.

Ramsay would reassure her, but they wouldn't discuss her leaving again. "Ross and John have offered to do the rest of the prep on the boat for me while I'm gone today." Without thinking it through, Ramsay reached over and took her hand, squeezing it. "I don't want anyone else driving you, either."

He glanced over. Her gaze was fixed straight ahead and her cheeks were bright pink. He could've kidded her about it, but he cut her some slack. "What were you up to this morning?" Once again, he thought about her lying on top of him. "I mean after you left the house."

"I spent time at Quilting Central with Harper and my clients." She turned toward him in the seat. "Believe it or not, some of my women are very good at sewing. I don't know if their nannies taught them, but a few of them sure know their way around a machine."

"I bet Deydie was pleased," he said. It was strange how the old woman had taken to Kit. And the other quilters had taken to her, too. Outsiders weren't easily welcomed into Gandiegow.

"Deydie started them on a special project."

"What project?"

"I don't know. When I asked, she told me it was none of my damn business."

"Sounds like Deydie. How's yere sister?"

"It was hard to leave her today."

"So meeting this bloke is that important?" It irked him that she'd drop everything for another man, which his tone must have made clear.

"Yes, that important." She pulled her hand away. "It's not just him that I'm interested in. It's his connections as well."

It struck Ramsay, not for the first time, that this woman was all wrong for him. She came from the same country-club world as the rich bachelors she sought. She might not be wealthy now, but she sure was comfortable with it. Ramsay, on the other hand, didn't give a crank about the rich and famous. He only cared about being his own man and making a living.

Within the hour, they reached a very large manor house with a reflecting pond, making the estate look more English than Scottish. The lawns were pristine, the foliage trimmed. Ramsay hated the man already.

He shut off the car. Kit didn't move, though. She just sat there, watching as a man exited the tall, ornately carved double oak doors and gave them a little wave.

"What's wrong?" Ramsay asked.

"I think I made a mistake."

"What kind of mistake?"

"That's not who I thought I was meeting. All this time, I thought I had been e-mailing and texting the younger Art MacKay. But apparently, it's been the senior."

"He's definitely not one of the young bucks ye've set your sights on for yere stables. He looks at least fifty. I see by that look on yere face that his age is a problem."

"It's just that all my clients are in their late twenties and early thirties."

"Do you want me to turn the car around and leave?" he asked.

"No. We'll stay."

Art was at her door and opened it.

She gave Ramsay one more glance and he squeezed her hand to fortify her.

"It's lovely to finally meet you, Miss Woodhouse." Art took her other hand and helped her from the car.

Ramsay rushed around to her side to break contact between Kit and the old bachelor. And perhaps to break a few of Art's fingers in the process.

"You're just in time for tea," the older gentleman said. "I hope you're hungry."

Ramsay stood close to Kit. "She's always hungry." He stuck his hand out to Art to take his measure. "Ramsay Armstrong. Kit's bodyguard."

She shot him a pair of green daggers.

Art laughed and took a step back. "I hope you're hungry, too, Mr. Armstrong."

Art led them inside to the massive dining room. At tea, Kit and Art talked about her business and her strategy for this expansion. Kit pulled Ramsay into the conversation, insisting he tell Art about his fishing tourism business. Art gave him several suggestions—all sound ideas—then the topic turned to the possibility of Kit finding him a match. His wife had died five years ago and he was ready for companionship.

That's when Ramsay saw it. Not that the old guy was hitting on Kit like all the other horny bastards they'd encountered. But he saw that Kit and Art would make the perfect couple. With Kit being as smart and astute as she was, she could surely see it, too. She and Art had so much in common. They both had a head for business, spoke the same language, and she seemed to soak up his every word.

It hit Ramsay in the chest. Younger women marry

older men all the time. He wanted to stand up and de-clare that Kit was taken.

Ramsay stopped breathing. *Taken*?

Did he really want to stake a claim on Kit Wood-house? He didn't know. He only knew that he wanted to get her out of here, wrap her in his arms and kiss her, and make her forget the likes of Art MacKay. And think only of him.

Ramsay stood. "We really should be heading back." He put his hand out to Kit.

She looked a little startled at first, but she laid her hand in his. "Ramsay's right. I have my clients waiting for me back in Gandiegow. I do hope we can work together," she said to Art. "We'll talk soon about lining up a few dates for you."

"That would be great." Art turned to him. "Ramsay, keep me apprised of how your business goes. I think you have a gem of an idea there."

Ramsay nodded, but he didn't give a shit what the guy thought about his fishing business. He only wanted to get Kit away from there and have her to himself.

Chapter Fourteen

Kit ran after Ramsay to the SUV as the sky let loose with a downpour of rain. Her driver seemed to have flipped a switch from being fun and charming to grim and determined. As soon as they were both in the car and heading down the driveway, she turned to him.

"What was that all about?"

He ignored her.

She frowned at him and touched his arm. "What's wrong?"

He looked in the rearview mirror, pulled the car to the side of the road, and threw it into park. He unsnapped his seat belt, and hers, and pulled her into his arms, kissing her.

She ignited. It was passionate and uncontrollable. Whatever had prompted this kind of kissing, she was all for it.

"He's too old for you," Ramsay growled into their kiss.

She pulled back. "Who's too old?" She knew he had to mean Art, but she couldn't imagine why Ramsay would bring him up at a time like this.

He brushed her hair away from her face and kissed her again. "You need someone closer to your own age."

"Who kisses like you, I suppose?" she dared to ask.

"Aye. A sonovabitch who can kiss ye into silence." He positioned her head the other way like he wanted to attack her mouth from every direction.

And he did.

She was vaguely aware that the storm outside was getting worse, the wind rocking the vehicle.

Ramsay growled again and pulled away. "I better get ye home." He put the car into gear and began driving, although he didn't look happy about it.

Her lips still tingled. If it were up to her and her lips, they would stop the car again.

They rode along in silence. She wasn't sure what this was between them, but from a purely business standpoint, Ramsay had been good for her. As a matchmaker, she needed to experience a little lust every now and then— and Ramsay definitely provoked her in that department. Luckily for Kit, however, she wasn't out hunting for The One. All she needed was the occasional outlet while remaining in control of herself at all times.

She smiled at the deluge pounding the windshield. Yes, she was lucky. She had no intention of marrying. She was already married to her career and her responsibilities, and that wouldn't change. A memory came back to her—the first time that she'd gotten a glimpse of her future and the life that lay ahead of her. It was picking out her father's casket. Alone. Her mother had been too distraught and fragile to go to the funeral home with her, and Kit had shouldered it all. She had made a thousand other decisions alone since then, and was the stronger for it.

She squared her shoulders. When her father died she had had to be strong enough for her whole family. She would continue to be strong for them for the rest of her life.

"Oh, shite!" Ramsay slammed on the brakes.

Kit gasped, peering through the windshield, but she only saw rain. "What is it?"

"The bridge is covered in water." He threw the car in reverse and did a three-point turn.

"What do we do now?" Kit asked. "Is there another way back to Gandiegow?"

"Not until the water goes down." He drove back up the hill. "I saw a side road up there. That's where we'll park and wait."

"But for how long?" Panic began to set in. "What about Harper and my clients? I can't just leave them for the night!"

Ramsay pulled into what was nothing more than a path and stopped the car. "You do realize that you left your kin and clients with the most capable women in all of Christendom. Deydie, Cait, and the other quilting ladies will take great care of yere girls."

Kit pulled out her phone, looking in vain for a signal. "But they'll worry about us."

"Nay." He covered her hand that held the phone. "They'll have a little faith and only think the obvious— that we got caught in the storm. Which we have." He kissed her fingers. "I promise, it'll be okay."

"How long will it take for the water to go down?" She knew he couldn't possibly know, but she needed assurances.

"Certainly by morning." He shut the SUV off. "There are blankets in the back. It'll get cool tonight. You won't mind helping me to conserve heat, now, will ye?" Laughter edged around his smooth voice as he teased her again.

She flushed as she thought about the times she'd cuddled up to him on his couch, but she wasn't going to make it easy on him now. "If I'm forced to."

Now he laughed outright. "Who forced you back at the house when you climbed into my arms night after night?"

"Sleepwalking." She made sure to keep a straight face. "It's a nasty habit."

"Well, I better hold you tight tonight. If you decide to do a little sleepwalking, you might end up down in the burn."

Kit thought about her theory—the one where Ramsay and the lust he inspired might be good for her and her career. Her veins sizzled with excitement and anticipation. But she wasn't kidding anyone, not even herself. If she went to bed with him, it wouldn't be for her career. It would be because she wanted him and nothing else.

She chewed her lower lip. "Can you make us a bed in the back?"

There. She'd said it. She hadn't been as direct as she had been when she'd been tipsy, but it was the most direct offer he was going to get from her tonight.

"Are ye sure?"

All Brawn was no dummy; he knew what she meant when she said "us." He had a heck of a brain at the top of that beautiful, sexy body of his.

"Yes, I'm sure," she said. "But there are some caveats."

He laughed. "Of course there are."

"One—you have to be able to make our bed without either one of us going outside and getting wet. That would dampen the mood." She didn't wait for his answer. "Two—do you have protection?"

"A life vest? Surely the water won't get that high," he teased.

"You know what I mean. Do you still have it in your wallet?"

"If ye're speaking of a prophylactic, I have several of them at the ready," he answered.

She held her hand up. "And three—we have to agree that what we're about to do doesn't mean anything. We're just two adults out to have a bit of fun."

"A bit of fun?" He was clearly irritated with her choice of words.

Thunder crashed, echoing his darkened mood. She saw the storm in his eyes.

"What's wrong?"

"Nothing," he rumbled. "I'll get to work on our bed."

Ramsay squeezed into the back and tamped down his anger while he spread out the blankets. Talk about dampening the mood. Aye, he wanted to roll around with Kit in the back of the SUV, but not under her stupid conditions. If he was any kind of businessman, he would be negotiating his own terms with her right now.

He wanted her naked and burning for him. And only him.

He wanted her crying out his name.

He wanted to ruin her for all others.

Aye. They could have a bit of fun, but he wasn't the type to leave his feelings at the door. Kit had come to mean something to him.

Maybe he'd give her a dose of her own medicine. Hold out on her. Sure, he'd make her come, but for his sake, not hers. And he definitely wouldn't leave a piece of his heart behind in the process. She was, after all, only passing through. She'd said so earlier.

"Get back here, sprite," he said more gruffly than he'd intended.

She crossed her arms over her chest and kept facing forward. "You have to tell me why you're in such a foul mood first."

"I'm cold. Come back here and warm me up. I get grumpy when my body temperature drops." He poured it on thick. "Brrr."

"I've changed my mind."

"Gawd, ye're a stubborn woman." He lay down, stretched out, and stacked his hands behind his head, staring up at the ceiling of the SUV. His hard-on had no problem with her wanting to use him for fun. What was wrong with the rest of him?

"You, sir, don't understand a thing about wooing a woman."

"I read yere website. Ye're the one who said that it goes both ways. That a woman has the same responsibilities as the man—that she has to be willing to put herself out there and woo him right back."

"Did you not see the part about how important it is for the man to be the man?" she grumbled.

That was all the encouragement he needed; he sprang into action, wedging himself between the two front seats, ready to be the man.

And he kissed her. He kissed her with enough passion to let her know that he didn't want her to think about the things she had in common with Art MacKay. He kissed her to let her know that he did care about her. He kissed her to let her know that he wanted to be with her for whatever time they had left together before she went back to America.

He kissed her . . . because he had to.

He heard it again. He heard himself groaning for her. There was nothing he could do about it, either. When he had her in his arms he wanted her so much that he wanted to howl at the moon.

She pulled away, breathless, but laughing. "I was wrong, Ramsay Armstrong. You know a helluva lot about wooing a woman."

He rubbed her arms. "Ye're cold. Get yere arse back there so I can warm you up proper."

"Such a charmer," she muttered.

He moved away, making room for her to climb through the bucket seats. But when she joined him in the cargo area of the SUV, she didn't lie down. He sat back up as well, pretty sure she was having second thoughts.

"Aw, hell." He put his arm around her. "We don't have to do anything, kitten. But for heaven's sake, let me hold you. John would skewer me for sure if you caught your death of cold. In the morning, I'll return you home—safe, sound, and unruffled."

"That's not the problem." She sighed heavily "I want to be ruffled."

His deflating pecker jumped to life. He rubbed her arms again. "What's the problem then?"

"I like you. You're a fine person." Her tone made it sound like it was a bad thing.

"Such high praise."

"But I can't get involved with you on an emotional level." Now she sounded as if she was trying to convince herself. "I mean it. I have too much on the line to get serious about anyone."

What the crank? How was he supposed to respond to that? He cared about her and he just wanted to show her. But what good would it do for him to get inside her pants if she kept her emotions all buttoned up and tucked away from him?

"Fine," he said, his pecker making the decision for him. "Sounds perfect to me." Also for his pecker. "What man doesn't want the kind of relationship ye're talking about?" His pecker was such a prick. "Give me a beautiful woman with no strings attached and I'm as happy as a clam." But he wasn't happy. He was angry. His pecker, though, wanted what it wanted.

"Fine," she echoed back. She didn't sound all that happy, either. "Let's get this over with then."

Aw, gawd! He was going to do something stupid and his pecker was going to be very, very disappointed.

She kicked off her shoes as she went to unzip her dress.

He stilled her hands. "Sorry, kitten. That's not going to work for me." He really wanted to see what lay beneath her clothes. But he forced himself to think with his head and not his groin. He put his arms around her and pulled her down, wrapping the quilts around them as he snuggled her to him.

He tucked her under his chin and whispered into the night. "Listen to me, sprite. I'm going to tell you how it is. When I make love to you—"

"Sex," she corrected.

"Sex, then." He started again. "When we're together, when we're being intimate, I'm going to take it slow and easy."

She shivered, letting him know that she felt every word he was saying.

He moved his head, rubbing his chin over her hair. "The magic that happens between a man and a woman is not something to get over with. It's to be savored."

And cherished, but he wouldn't voice that girly senti-ment out loud. He kissed the top of her head. "You've now heard my terms. When ye're ready to accept them, then I'll be happy to seal the deal."

She sighed in his arms. "Is that you being the man?"

"Yup." He chuckled. "On this, babe, it's either my way or the highway."

She rested her head back and looked him in the eye. "I guess I have no choice then but to accept your terms. Will you kiss me?"

He brushed her hair back from her eyes. He wished they were in his bed. With the lights on. He wanted to see the emeralds in her eyes as they sparkled for him. He wanted her to know that he meant what he said. He would savor this moment. Perhaps for his whole life.

He leaned in and kissed her. He meant it to be slow and tender, like the lovemaking that he'd promised. But his shy kitten of a moment ago turned into a hellcat, wrapping her legs around him and pulling him down on top of her as he tried not to crush her. She kissed his lips as if she'd been starving and he was the only real food she'd tasted in a long, long time. Then she kissed his eyes, his jaw, his neck. She pulled at his clothes.

He captured her wrists and held them over her head, growling at her. "I will keep my promise."

She laughed. "Like hell you will. I can't wait. You've teased me from the moment I set eyes on you and I'm ready to explode." She ground her hips into him. "I prom-ise we can do it slow the next time. Take me now, Ramsay."

"No." He nibbled at her ear.

"But you're killing me."

"Then a slow death it will be." He suckled at the pulse on her neck. "I'm the man, remember?"

"Oh, my, how could I forget?"

He chuckled, but he felt frantic to get at her, too. Down, boy, he told himself, and he kissed her tenderly. He must've done it right because his kitten mewed.

He switched places with her, rolling her on top of him, her hands still shackled by one of his. He made short work of the zipper of her dress, and slowly kissed the fabric away. To slip her arms out, he had to release her, and Kit started tugging at his clothes once more.

He *tsk*ed at her, maneuvering himself on top and confining her hands again. "Easy now, sprite. We're making love here—"

"Sex," she reminded him again.

He glazed right over it. She was being ridiculous. "We're making love. Not trying to get to the finish line. Play along and I'll make it worth your while."

To his surprise, she acquiesced—and turned the tables on him. Her tender kisses and caresses became his torture—the student schooling the teacher—as she kissed her way to freeing her hands and working his clothes from him.

The storm outside wailed, but it was of no consequence to them in their quilt cocoon as they explored each other's body. Her caresses and kisses were becoming too much for him. Judging by her short breaths, she was in need of release as well. Wildly, his free hand searched for his pants, his wallet, and ultimately a condom. He hit pay dirt. But before he could rip it open, she snatched it from his hand.

"Let me," she purred. She tore the package open slowly with the deliberate pace of one who wanted to torment.

He groaned. "Now ye're killing me."

She reached down and stroked him. "But we don't want to rush, now, do we?"

It took everything in him not to come. He gritted his teeth. "Ye're a saucy wench."

Painstakingly, she rolled the rubber over him. When she was done, she nipped at his shoulder.

He spread her legs wide and thrust into her, nothing slow and gentle about it.

She gasped, and he stilled completely—he should've been more restrained.

But she clutched his back and demanded, "Again."

He eased out excruciatingly slow, only to ease back in.

She grabbed his bum and ground her hips into him.

It was almost his undoing. "That's a dangerous game ye're playing, lass."

"Then stop messing around," she growled.

He kissed her. Hard. And began a rhythm that satisfied the hell out of them. As he plundered her mouth and her other parts, she plundered him back.

At the moment of her release she gasped his name over and over again, then cried so loudly it should've vanquished the raging storm outside.

He stopped to enjoy the feel of her spasming around him. And the thought of her giving him such a gift was his undoing. He thrust into her once more and he came. It was blinding, powerful, nearly overwhelming. The best cranking sex of his life. Bar none.

He could barely pull in enough air, and he knew his smile was wide enough to stretch from here to Glasgow. Until he realized that her arms had dropped away from his body. Her head was turned away from him, too, and she lay still under him. His hellcat had turned into stone.

*   *   *

Kit's body stiffened and she sucked in a breath, holding it. Her hands clenched. What had she done? Her body throbbing under his, just as she'd wanted, but her heart was throbbing, too. *Damn, damn, damn.* She pushed him off her. *This was a mistake.*

"What's wrong?" Ramsay said, reaching out to stop her from grabbing her dress.

What could she tell him? That it had been a long time since she'd allowed herself to be romanced? But that was exactly what Ramsay-*damn-him*-Armstrong had done. She'd thought that getting back in the saddle would be good for her. But to remember what it felt like to be desired had been . . . unexpected, and too much. She'd only wanted to mess around with her handsome driver. *Have sex.* But somewhere during the messing around, it had really turned into *making love,* like he'd said. *Oh, crap!* Caring for Ramsay wasn't part of her plan. She couldn't afford to. Literally.

It was a man's world. If she didn't act like one, then she would be chewed up and spit out. And then where would her family be? More destitute than they'd been before.

"Will ye at least tell me what's bugging ye?"

She slipped her dress over her head. "I'm tired." *And this was a mistake.* But her body still hummed with the magic he'd performed on her. "I need sleep."

He grabbed his boxers and slipped them on. "I'm going to hold you."

"I know." She had no choice but to endure his strong arms as they wrapped around her.

She was only being practical. They were in close quarters and the temperature was indeed dropping. But just because he made her feel soft and feminine and protected didn't mean that she had to enjoy it. Only tolerate it. Until the morning. When she got back to Gandiegow, she would forget he'd ever made her feel this way—something no other man had ever done.

He spooned her and kissed her hair. "I'm sorry ye're unhappy, but I refuse to be sorry for making love. Do ye hear me?"

She wanted to snap at him that it had been sex, not making love! But it would have done no good to try to explain. Besides, Ramsay never took anything seriously anyway. And feeling miserable was serious business.

She closed her eyes, certain sleep wouldn't come. But she was wrong.

She woke up disoriented. Was it time to make the Armstrong men their breakfast? But she wasn't in Ramsay's bed. She was in the back of the SUV—alone. She sat up and looked around. Ramsay really wasn't in the vehicle. She found her shoes and quickly put them on. Just as she was crawling back into the front seat, the driver's side door opened.

"Morning, sprite." He sounded as cheerful as the birds in the tree. *Stupid birds.*

"Where were you?" Her pitch was higher than she liked.

"Nature called." He reached past her, popped open the glove box, and pulled out a small bottle of hand sanitizer.

"What time is it?" She dug in her messenger bag.

"Go make a pit stop yereself and then we'll get on the road. We'll make it back before yere bachelors arrive," he said.

She didn't like how he called them *hers.* But instead

of raising hell with him, she opened her door and went looking for a tree.

When she got back in the car, he handed her the hand sanitizer like they were an old married couple who had performed this particular act a million times. But they'd only *done it* once. Her body wanted to keep doing it to see if she would ever tire of the magic, but for her business's sake, once was more than enough.

She buckled her seat belt, determined to never mention what had happened in the back of the SUV. But out of the corner of her eye, she saw that the quilts had been folded and stacked.

He started the car and nodded in her direction. "There's a bottled water for ye in the holder."

She hated him being so thoughtful. Where was the tease when she needed him?

She took the water and opened it. "Do you have a plan for the bachelors today? Where you're going to take them?" She frowned at her water. "What about lunch for them?"

"Aye. I have a plan." He glanced at her, smiling as if he'd known her forever. "As far as food, the restaurant is catering my boat."

Catering? He sounded like such a businessman! Then she remembered him using the word *prophylactic*. Would he ever cease to amaze her?

It hit her again. That from the beginning, he'd surprised her. First, because she couldn't get a good read on him and then because she'd gotten him all wrong. But just because he was an interesting man didn't mean that she wanted him for herself. Far from it. It was best to stick with the kind of men she'd known. Men who were serious, not relaxed and carefree. *Men who didn't scare her.*

The silence between them felt awkward. But it was best. She didn't want to ride along companionably anymore. She didn't want to cuddle up with him at night on the couch, either. She definitely didn't want to make love with him again.

As incredible as it was.

An hour later, they pulled into Gandiegow's parking lot. She grabbed her messenger bag and hopped from the SUV, not looking back, not saying a word. She needed to escape. Shower. Get to Quilting Central.

She'd only made it a couple of feet, before Ramsay started laughing.

"Sprite?" he called to her.

She spun around with her hands on her hips. "What?"

He walked toward her. "I appreciate the show and all, but I'm not sure the rest of Gandiegow will feel as I do."

"What are you talking about?" Her pitch had definitely risen through the roof now. Didn't he understand that she was in a hurry? That she had responsibilities?

He put his hands on her shoulders and spun her around so her back was to him.

"It's yere panties. Yere dress is caught." He gave her garments a yank, straightening out her backside. "There. Ye're decent now." He patted her on the rump, at the same time he gave her a shove toward town. "Get on with ye now. No doubt ye've got more important things to do today than to flash me yere goodies and bits."

Chapter Fifteen

Ramsay leaned against the SUV, smiling as she huffed off. He'd give her time to shower before he headed home. But on second thought—wouldn't it be nice to surprise her and join her there?

No. His sprite was already in a snit about something. And he refused to let it rile him.

Last night she'd been perfect. Hell, he'd been perfect, too. They were explosive—pure dynamite together. It couldn't have gone better. Unless of course, she'd cuddled him back. But she did let him hold her as they slept in the back of the auto.

He whistled as he walked toward the dock and his boat. Hopefully, Ross and John had found him plenty of fishing gear. As he got near the dock, he slowed.

"That's strange." The boat was bobbing in the water right where it was supposed to be, but a tarp was hanging over the stern.

Ross popped out of the cabin, and in his hand was a paintbrush. He saw Ramsay and tucked the brush behind his back.

A sinking feeling swam over Ramsay. "Ross, what did you do?"

Ross looked around as if there was another *Ross* hanging out on his boat. "John and I got all the fishing gear loaded for you. Life vests and rafts are loaded, too." He pointed to the storage cubbies under the benches with his free hand.

"That's not what I'm speaking of," Ramsay growled. "Why is there a tarp over the stern?" He took the last steps and came aboard, going straight for the tarp.

"We were only helping." Ross shifted from one foot to the other. "Ye can't take her out without a proper name."

Ramsay pulled the tarp up and groaned. *"Lil Sister?"*

Ross shrugged. "John and I thought you might see the humor in it." He patted the gunwales. "She's a fine boat, Ramsay."

"But *Lil Sister*? Can't I have one thing in this world that's mine and not tainted by the two of you?"

Ross pounded him on the back. "It's better than the name we first came up with."

"I don't want to know," Ramsay said.

"*Pretty in Pink*," Ross supplied.

"Off my boat. Now!" It was too late to change the name. He had to shower. He had to fetch the bachelors. Later, though, he'd kick his brothers' arses.

Kit stood in the shower, realizing too late she had washed her hair three times. She didn't have enough bandwidth to deal with this right now—feeling vulnerable. It was all Ramsay's fault. His lovemaking had unraveled her. Her hands, buried in her sudsy hair, froze. That was the problem. He hadn't kept his side of the deal. It was supposed to be just sex, but he'd made love to her. *The bastard.* Now she was nothing more than a pile of shredded nerves.

No amount of shampoo could wash away how wonderful it had been with Ramsay . . . how he'd changed her. Kit quickly rinsed and stumbled from the shower.

She had the terrible feeling that if she didn't hurry and get out of the Armstrong household, Ramsay would find her. Peel her. And take her back to his bed. Kit knew that if he showed up, he'd use his power of persuasion on her. She was defenseless against him and what her own body wanted. Him. Again and again.

I have to get out of this town.

Kit threw on a bright summer dress—contradictory to her bad mood—and rushed out the door with her hair still wet, but at least it was combed. She resisted the urge to rush over to Duncan's Den, the quilting dorm, to see if any of the bachelors had arrived yet. She really wanted to get a glimpse of the men, but Ramsay would be collecting them soon, and she couldn't chance running into *him*. Especially with how exposed she felt. She would meet them tonight before the mixer and have each one sign a contract. She'd also explain what was expected of them.

As she arrived at Quilting Central, so did the rest of the crew—Harper and the girls. Kit held the door open for them, but Harper didn't go inside. When all her clients had entered, Harper shut the door and faced her.

"You look like hell." Harper brushed at the frown between her eyebrows. "What's wrong? And where were you last night? Deydie told us not to worry, that sometimes the storms can get people stuck. Is that what happened?"

Kit batted her sister's hand away from her face. "Yes. That's what happened. A flash flood and no signal to call and tell you."

"But why the frown?"

"A bad night's sleep. Nothing else." A lie. She'd slept great in Ramsay's arms. But she felt branded and tagged as one of Ramsay's possessions. She was afraid everyone could see that she belonged to him. Which wasn't true. "There's a lot riding on tonight, is all," Kit explained. Now, that was an understatement. *Everything* was riding on tonight. But Kit wouldn't burden her sister with the details of how this mixer could make or break their family.

Kit glanced away from Harper's analytical eyes and opened the door for her sister.

"Yeah. A bad night's sleep. That's it." Harper rolled her eyes and went in with Kit following.

She plastered a smile on her face for her clients. She was certain their nerves were getting to them. Or at least they should have been. As Kit went for a cup of coffee, Harper followed her.

"We have a problem," Harper said. She tilted her head toward Gretchen. "She didn't get to the dorm until after midnight."

Kit swiveled around to look at the woman. She stared at her scone with a secretive smile on her face. "Crap. Who is she seeing?"

"I think his name is Thomas, one of the fishermen. When you didn't come back last night, Kathleen snuck out, too. I waited up until she made it back safely, but I didn't think it was my place to question her."

"Hell." Kit set her coffee cup down without filling it.

It seemed that one by one, the fishermen were picking off her girls. Kit should've kept her eye on the ball and taken care of her fishermen problem. What if it was too late for her bachelors when they got here? But Kit had one thing going for her. The fishermen weren't invited to the mixer tonight. Out of sight, out of mind, she hoped. She'd have to give the bachelors a pep talk about making a good show of it for her clients. And Kit could always mention to the girls that their parents were not going to approve of them marrying fishermen. These girls were pleasers and would ultimately do what their families wanted them to do.

"Ladies, how about we get started?" Bethia stood at the front with Moira beside her. Everyone made her way to her chair and sat down to her project. "We'll be milling around. Just holler at one of us if you have a question or need some help."

Harper squeezed Kit's arm. "It's all going to work out. I promise."

"I hope so," Kit said. But Harper really shouldn't be making promises she knew nothing about.

An hour later, Ramsay made his way across town to pick up Kit's bachelors. *No. Kit's male clients.*

He glanced down at the release forms in his hand. He probably should've had the men sign Kit's contract when he'd gotten them to agree to come here. But heck, he didn't know the ins and outs of the matchmaking business. The release forms he had were another matter. He was damn well going to protect his boat and his own arse from any lawsuits, should one of the bachelors get a fish hook stuck in his hand.

He thought about Kit and how grateful he was to her for this opportunity to start his own business. As soon as he could get her alone today, he'd show her how grateful he could be. With his lips. His hands. And all the other parts that the two of them had fit together last night.

And because he was a guy, and he'd thought about her

at least a thousand times since waking, he imagined making love to her again. And again. Logistically, though, it would be tough to find a place for them to be alone. He'd never had to worry about this before; he'd always dated outside the village gaggle. At times like these, he wished he didn't live with his family. While he was on the ocean today, he'd give some serious thought to finding a private place.

Outside Duncan's Den, one of the two quilting dorms, Ramsay found Davey, Ewan, and Colin standing under the metal quilt block sign, discussing the seasonable summer weather.

Ramsay clapped Colin on the back. "Thanks for doing this, friend. It seems you've been doing me all kinds of favors these days."

"Don't worry. I'm keeping track." It had only taken a phone call and a few words to get Colin to come to Kit's rescue for the mixer tonight.

Davey frowned at Ramsay. "Why am I doing this again? I thought I was supposed to be focusing on myself for the first time in my life."

Ramsay shook his hand. "Ye're doing this to meet some bonny American lasses. Sometimes it's nice to stop and smell the roses."

"*Are* they bonny lasses?" Davey said.

"Aye." The fishermen of the village had taken quite a shine to them, but Ramsay kept that thought to himself. "They're refined women, too. Any one of them would make an excellent addition to the distillery," he said, thinking to appeal to the collector in Davey. "Where are the rest of the lads?"

Colin thumbed at the dorm. "Putting their things away. Mac only just arrived."

Ramsay had also called in a favor from his friend Mac,

a clerk at the bank in Fairge. Not exactly a landowner, but a decent fellow with a steady job. How could Kit argue with that?

Ramsay straightened. "We better hurry if we're to catch anything and get back in time for the mixer."

The men grumbled, and Ramsay understood where they were coming from. Fishing sounded a hell of a lot more fun than a blind date.

"I'll get the rest." Colin made for the door.

"Here." Ramsay handed him the papers. "Everyone needs to sign one before we get under way."

Colin took them and went inside.

After the formalities were done, they walked to the dock together. At the first sight of his boat, Ramsay's chest swelled. He'd finally done it. He was finally living his dream. Once aboard, he pointed out all the safety equipment, handed out the fishing gear, and then showed them where the refreshments were in the cooler. After that was done, he went to the wheelhouse to start the boat while Mac and Colin manned the lines.

It didn't take long to get to Ramsay's favorite fishing grounds. Once anchored, he found that all of the men knew their way around a tackle box—being Scots, they bluidy well should have known. They soon had their lines in the water. It occurred to Ramsay that he might have trouble when the Kilts and Quilts retreat had customers who weren't Scots and avid fishermen. He'd have to have extra help aboard to bait and perhaps babysit those who weren't born with a fishing rod in their hand. Ramsay thought of Maggie's cousins, Robert and Samuel. The teenagers would probably like to earn some coin while hanging out on his boat. He felt it again. Everything was coming together for him.

The day flew by and Ramsay enjoyed the hell out of himself. As they pulled back into Gandiegow's dock, he could tell his customers had enjoyed themselves, too, their fishing baskets full. He led them to the restaurant, where he'd arranged with Dominic to cook up their bounty for a premixer feast.

When they stepped into the restaurant, Bonnie, Moira, and Sinnie were there, settling food into boxes. Ramsay couldn't stop grinning over the amazing day that he'd had. And the only one he wanted to share the feeling with . . . was Kit.

Ramsay stopped them. "What's all this?"

Bonnie, the alpha of the three, stepped forward. "We're taking food to the dorm for the out-of-town women." Her tone suggested that she might be tempted to slip a bit of arsenic in their dinner. But then she seemed to notice the men crowding in around Ramsay. "Hey, fellas."

Some of the bachelors' taste seemed to have changed from fish to something more fleshy. Several of the men stared at Bonnie's cleavage.

Moira nudged Bonnie's arm. "The lasses' dinner is getting cold."

Davey rushed over to Moira. "Here. Let me help you with that." He hefted the last box to his shoulder. "Where can I put it for ye?" It looked like he was flexing his muscles for her.

Moira must've noticed, too, because her face turned pink and a slight smile spread across her lips as her eyes dropped to the floor. "The wagon outside would be grand. Thank ye."

Bonnie looked pointedly at several of the bachelors. "I hope to see you men later."

That's when Ramsay noticed that not all of the bachelors were ogling Bonnie's exposed breasts. A few of them were staring pointedly at Moira and Sinnie as well, like they were staking their claim, too.

Perfect, just perfect, thought Kit, sarcastically, as she watched the fishermen roll in that afternoon, bringing a heavy dose of testosterone and charm. One by one they lured her clients away from their quilt blocks, baiting them with Real Men magnetism. Kit searched her brain for an excuse to run the men out of Quilting Central and lock the doors behind them.

Unfortunately, Deydie took that moment to bring the retreat to an early close, as she'd promised Kit she would. Her clients needed time to change for the mixer. But when the old matriarch said the word, half of Kit's clients scattered with the fishermen.

Kit called for reinforcements. "Cait, can you take Harper to find Gretchen and Beatrice? And, Moira, can you help me find Morgan?"

Amy bounced her baby boy on her hip. "I'll keep the others corralled at the quilting dorm until you get back. I'll get Coll to help me."

"Thank you." Kit headed for the door, noticing that Andrew was right behind her and Moira.

"We should try the dock," Andrew said.

"Aye." Moira nodded at him. "Lochie probably took Morgan to his boat."

As Kit and her crew headed for the dock, Kit decided she'd have to move to the quilting dorm for the duration of her stay, in order to keep an eye on her clients. Maggie would have to understand. It was for the best, anyway. Moving out of the Armstrongs' house was the only way to keep from crawling back into Ramsay's arms.

Now that they'd had sex, it was as if Kit was hooked on Ramsay. If she stayed at his house any longer, not even the rest of his family under the same roof would keep her from being with him and giving his bed a workout. And that just couldn't happen.

Up ahead they saw Morgan stepping aboard Lochie's boat, the one he shared with his brother. Kit felt panicked. If they cast off and she wasn't there for the mixer, Kit would have to deal with the fallout from an unattached bachelor.

"I've got this." Andrew picked up the pace, leaving the women, and calling out, "Lochie. Hold up."

Kit relaxed when Lochie stopped. She and Moira stood and watched as Andrew talked the two out of making a getaway. When Andrew pointed to Kit, Lochie nodded, and Morgan came back with Andrew. God, she hoped Harper had had the same luck with the other runaways.

"Sorry," her client said, keeping her head down.

"It's okay." Kit wrapped her arm around her. She understood—the heart wanted what the heart wanted. "Just meet the bachelors tonight. You're under no obligation."

Morgan looked up at her with earnest eyes. "Then I can see Lochie again?"

Kit had backed herself into a corner. "We'll talk about it after the mixer, okay?"

Morgan's mouth turned downward and her shoulders slumped.

"Come on. Let's get ready for our social." Kit worried whether Morgan's deflated spirits were an omen for the evening.

*   *   *

Two hours later Kit stood in the center of Thistle Glen Lodge's living room. She had started her day being frazzled because of Ramsay, and had stayed frazzled because of the local fishermen. But lucky for her, all her clients had been found. Though some looked well kissed. *Damn the fishermen. The charming devils.* Kit felt as if the universe was out to get her.

She tried to look on the bright side. The evening was young. It could still turn out okay. Harper stood guard at the doorway of the dorm with a cricket bat in hand.

"Hey." Kit took a sip of her tea, trying not to think about all the other things that could go wrong tonight. "I've got a favor."

"Anything." Harper patted the bat like some tough guy. "I haven't had this much fun in a long time."

"Playing bodyguard to a bunch of heiresses is fun?"

Harper laughed. "Yeah. Weird, huh?"

"About that favor . . ." Kit hesitated. "I think a few of our bachelors are going to be left out in the cold."

"I'm afraid the pairing off is over and done with," Harper agreed. "I'm pretty sure your clients won't be interested in the men you brought in for them."

"About that . . ." Kit averted her eyes. "I wondered if you'd be willing to be one of my clients tonight. Help entertain the bachelors. I'm going to have a tough enough time charming the men so they don't feel like they came to Gandiegow for nothing."

Harper laughed. "First, you're crazy if you think Ramsay will stand for you flirting with anyone else."

Kit chewed her lip until she realized Harper was watching her closely. "But he won't know because he won't be there." *Unless he crashes the party.*

Harper shook her head. "You forget you're in a small town. Ramsay will find out, one way or another. Back to your favor . . . I can't be one of your clients because I have no interest in dating right now. Do you know how many times I've had to threaten the local fishermen with this bat since I've been here? When I tell them that I'm studying to be a nautical archaeologist, fistfights have broken out to see who gets to take me diving. You're going to have to do something about them if you plan to make Gandiegow your base."

"I know. But right now I have to worry about tonight." Kit was glad she hadn't signed Ramsay on as one of her clients. Harper was right—Ramsay would drag her from the mixer if he caught her flirting . . . which made her stomach do a little flip. She took a deep breath and plowed forward. "Do you have it all under control here?"

Harper hoisted her bat onto her shoulder. "Aye, aye, Captain."

"I have to go pack my things. I'm moving in here with you."

"Really?" Harper eyed her carefully. "Did you and Ramsay have a fight?"

Kit put her hands on her hips. "What makes you think this has anything to do with Ramsay? I just think we need another set of eyes on my clients, and perhaps another cricket bat at the ready for the fishermen."

"But have you told Ramsay what you're doing?"

"You're exasperating."

"I assume that's a *no*." Harper shrugged. "I think you just added another to your list of fishermen who are going to be a problem."

Kit walked past her and out the door. This was her

opportunity to get her things while Ramsay was occupied with the bachelors. Yes, she was a coward. Yes, she was using her clients' attraction to the local fishermen to run away from Ramsay. But she had to do this. Her family needed her to stay focused on the end goal—make enough money to buy back the security their father had gambled away.

She hurried to Ramsay's cottage, keeping her gaze on the sea, imagining Ramsay on his new boat, proud and happy. At the cottage door, she walked right in, at home enough now to do so. No one was in the living room area, and Kit blew out a sigh of relief. But as she made her way down the hallway, Maggie's bedroom door opened. Her new friend looked tired and pale.

Kit went to her and touched her arm. "Is everything all right?"

"This bairn likes to sleep. I might've overdone it the last few days."

Guilt seeped into Kit. Could she really move out and leave Maggie, especially knowing that she had problems carrying a baby to full-term? Maggie needed her here to get up early and cook for the men, and needed help with the housework, too.

"How about you and the baby go lie back down? I'll make you a cup of herbal tea."

"That does sound lovely." Maggie hugged her tightly. "I don't know what I'm going to do when ye're gone. Maybe you could stay here permanently." She laid a hand on her abdomen. "I know I'm being ridiculous, but I'm going to miss you when you go."

Kit shooed her off to bed, realizing her plan to move out wouldn't work. She was needed here. But how was she going to stay out of Ramsay's arms now? Well, she didn't have time to think about it. First she had to get Maggie squared away. Next, she had to get herself ready. Then she had to throw the mixer of the century.

It took nearly an hour to dress, fix her hair, and do her makeup. When Dand came home from playing with Mattie, Cait's boy, Kit made him a snack and sat with him while he ate. Then they sang silly songs together as she towed the energetic boy to Rowena and Sinnie's so Maggie could get some rest.

As Kit left Dand with his aunts and stood on the stoop, she saw Ramsay coming her way, presumably heading home. He looked like a commercial for *Living Well*. His face glowed and his long hair was windblown. He looked happy, alive, and irresistible to a woman who was used to pressed suits, relationship games, and guardedness.

Like two ships passing, she slowed only a little, nodding her head in acknowledgment. "Ramsay."

"Kitten." His burr was intoxicating and his eyes danced.

She almost came to a screeching halt, for no other reason than to run her lips over his. But she let him pass and only glanced back twice to watch his swagger against the backdrop of the sea.

But she was on a mission. She patted her messenger bag. She was headed to the men's dorm to get every last one of them to sign a client agreement. Whether they wanted her to or not, she was fixing them up. They would get their happily-ever-afters or else.

There was a little pang in her chest. She wished Ramsay would be there tonight. But this feeling she had for her chauffeur would pass. He had been her shelter in the storm when she'd first come to Scotland. Once she was home again, she would be able to shake this feeling, wouldn't she? This growing ache inside her was beginning to feel like a full-blown attack . . . on her sensibilities.

She stopped at the women's dorm first and found that Harper had the socialites under control.

"I'm going next door to speak with the bachelors." Kit patted her messenger bag again. "We have business to attend to."

"Good luck," Harper said.

"Luck better have nothing to do with it." Because Kit's luck since she'd come to Scotland . . . sucked.

She walked next door to Duncan's Den and knocked. While waiting, she practiced her pitch—all the reasons they should sign up for the Real Men of Scotland.

Davey finally opened the door, wearing a McBain kilt. His eyes lit up. "Come in, lass. We've all been waiting for you."

Waiting for me? She put on a forced smile and followed him in, feeling confused.

"Have a seat. I'll get the rest of the lads."

One by one, the men marched in, wearing their respective clan's kilt. It was an impressive show of legs and manliness. But she was befuddled. Of course, she didn't mind that they all had dressed for the occasion, but how had they known that she wanted them to go all-out for the girls? Instead of questioning them, she accepted the gift with a smile. Some of the tension caused by the evening's uncertain outcome released just a little. She perched on the arm of the sofa.

They gathered around her, and Davey, who was apparently the acting leader of the Scottish warriors, pointed to her bag. "You have contracts for us to sign?"

Kit almost fell off the couch in surprise. "I— I . . ."

Davey laughed with a deep timbre. "Ramsay told us to be prepared for the paperwork."

"And said he'd kick our arses if we didn't pony up our signatures." The blond man with dimples and huge biceps was apparently one of Ramsay's recruits, as she didn't know him. He offered her his hand. "I'm Colin. I own the Spalding Farm. Ramsay and I met at university and I can attest to his arse-kicking capabilities. Why don't ye give me one of your papers to sign?"

She didn't open her messenger bag, but instead looked at each of their faces, still a little stunned that Ramsay had gone out on a limb for her. The tension inside her loosened even more. It felt good to know that she wasn't in this alone, that Ramsay had her back.

For a split second she remembered he'd had more of her than just her back. For a brief night, he'd had *all of her*.

Another of the men she didn't know cleared his throat, bringing her back to them.

"I'm Mac," he said. "I work at the bank at Fairge."

And the other two she didn't know introduced themselves as well.

"So did Ramsay also tell you what to expect?" she said.

Mac frowned. "He said to expect that you would have rules. Said if we don't follow them that that would be grounds for an arse-kicking, too." He chuckled. "How you managed to wrap him around your little finger, I'll never know."

Davey gazed over at Kit, scanning all her attributes. "I know how she did it."

Mac laughed heartily this time. "One can never underestimate the power of a beautiful woman."

"Aye," each of the men said.

"Since you brought it up, let's go over those rules." She pulled out the contracts, feeling renewed. Everything was going to be okay. She got down to business, listing her expectations for the men tonight.

Twenty minutes later they were finished and she knew these were all good guys. Ramsay had done well in selecting the other four, even if they didn't have the kind of wealth she had originally been targeting. She was very pleased with them just the same.

She wished she could say the same of her girls. Love had a way of making even the meekest woman a bit wild. Love also had a way of making the most mild-tempered person a depressed mess. Although the bachelors seemed to be on board, Kit feared it was going to be the bachelorettes who were going to be the problem tonight. She went next door to give them a rallying speech.

Kit stood by the empty fireplace. "I realize that most of you aren't thrilled about our social tonight. That you've found some interesting men on your own since coming to Scotland." *Found* wasn't the correct term. Those girls didn't have a chance once the fishermen had caught them in their nets and poured on their "real men" charm. Kit sighed. "But the bachelors that I've brought to Gandiegow for tonight's gathering have made sacrifices to be here. I hope each of you will give them a fair chance."

"Lochie is upset that I'm going tonight," Morgan complained.

"Thomas insisted I shouldn't go," Gretchen, one of her quietest women, said.

Mercedes, another of her clients, put her hand up like she was in a classroom.

"Yes?" Kit said.

"You say on your website that we should be true to ourselves and follow our hearts."

Kit exhaled deeply. "Absolutely. All I ask is that you keep an open mind. Agreed?"

None of them looked convinced, but almost all of them nodded their heads.

"How about we head over to the restaurant and the mixer?" Kit retrieved her bag. As her clients filed out, the knot in her stomach was back.

Harper gave her a hug. "It's all going to work out as it should."

"Of course it will." Kit twisted her hands. "That doesn't mean I'm going to like it."

Harper laughed. "Let's look at it as an adventure, like we're diving for treasure. Who knows what might be found?"

Kit rolled her eyes. "You're quite the philosopher."

They followed the girls across town to the restaurant. Once inside, she saw that everything had been arranged perfectly—Maggie's centerpieces on the scattered tables, the soft music in the background, and the low lighting. Everything was set for love. But the bachelors were standing awkwardly on one side of the room while the women huddled by the entrance as though they couldn't wait to leave.

"Everyone join me over here. I've got some great icebreakers," Kit said, even though she didn't think a pickaxe would loosen up this bunch.

Harper helped her with the dating games, but there seemed to be no chemistry between the bachelors and the socialites. Everyone genuinely seemed to be trying, but it was as if the two species were completely incompatible.

Harper tugged her over to the side. "This isn't working."

Kit wanted to swear like a sailor, but instead, she plastered on an all-is-well smile, in case anyone was watching. "I know."

"What's your Plan B?"

Kit chewed on her lip. "Maybe a little physical contact would help."

"What are you suggesting, Kitten Woodhouse?" Harper's voice had a squeak to it, exactly like their mother's when she was flummoxed.

Kit grabbed her arm and spun her away from the others. "Shh. Quiet on the name or I'll tell everyone that your middle name is Magpie." God, their parents were the worst when it came to names. She'd been shocked when Ramsay had started calling her *kitten*. "I'm not talking about dirty dancing or anything! I thought we could turn up the music and play Musical Bachelors. Give each partner a shot for about half a song and see what happens." Kit motioned to the table against the wall. "You go change the music to something slow and easy to dance to, and I'll speak with the crowd."

Kit explained the game to her guests and lined them up into couples for the first round. Harper started the music, and Kit stood back and waited. The girls from the country club all had years of ballroom dancing lessons, but they looked like a six-pack of broom handles out on the floor, trying to keep as much space as possible between them and the Real Men of Scotland. It was painful to watch. When they switched partners two minutes later, it wasn't any better. Kit's knotted stomach turned into spoiled liverwurst and she felt a debilitating migraine coming on.

At that moment, Ramsay sauntered into the restaurant. Relief swept through Kit as if the chords of "Unchained Melody" had been syphoned into her cells. He didn't stop for the pleasantries, but came straight to her. She was pulled into his arms for a brief second before her Scottish Fred Astaire twirled her onto the dance floor.

Her impending migraine fled as he held her close and tucked her under his chin.

"You shouldn't be here," she said into his chest.

"I know," he rumbled.

"But thank you for coming."

He kissed her hair. Kit refused to glance at Harper to see the expression on her sister's face. Or her clients' faces, either. It could wait until the end of the song. She kept her eyes shut and soaked up Ramsay's strength.

As the song came to a close, Harper yelled, "Switch partners."

Reluctantly, Kit started to pull away, but Ramsay held her tight.

"No. Yere sister has them under control."

Never looking up, Kit relaxed back into him, letting the outside world stay away for a while longer. With his arms surrounding her, she could almost fool herself into thinking that this evening would work out okay.

Several more times Harper called for them to switch and Kit didn't move, except to the music. She heard people talking, and thought it was a good sign that her couples were beginning to open up. But the noise took on an increasingly unfriendly tone.

"*Aw, hell*," Ramsay growled.

Kit's eyes popped open to find the local fishermen out on the dance floor, kilted in their finest, and holding her U.S. clients to their chests like prized fishing trophies.

"Holy shit," she hissed, and managed to pull free from Ramsay. "How did this happen?" She looked up at him accusingly. "Did you do this?"

"Now, lass —" He reached out for her.

She stepped back. "You sabotaged me again." But crucifying her chauffeur would have to wait.

Harper's squeaking panic could be heard above the music. "Stop this!" She stood between Lochie and Ewan the sheep farmer, ready to break up what looked like the beginnings of a fight. Morgan cowered a foot away from them. But the expression on her face said she was both enthralled and pleased that the males were arguing over her.

Kit glared at Ramsay.

"Fine." He sighed. "I'll take care of it."

He took Harper's place and began smoothing feathers with his stinking Ramsay charm.

Damn him for reeling her in over and over again. As if she were the easiest catch in the world.

She marched over to the near-brawl and tried to pull Morgan away. But her client stood fast.

While Ramsay cajoled Ewan and Lochie, the rest of the men were squaring off, looking ready to rumble. The fishermen were arguing that they had gotten to the American lasses first. It was all too much. Kit wanted to crawl under a table before the men in kilts started throwing punches and tossing one another about the room.

The door to the restaurant flew open and a crowd of women came in, Deydie leading the pack. The rest of the town quilters followed with casserole dishes and goodies in their arms.

"We're here," Deydie hollered.

Kit rushed over to her as the old woman and the others spread out the food.

"*Why?* Why are you here?" Kit asked none too kindly.

"We didn't want to miss out on the dance or the brawl," Deydie cackled. "We haven't had a *céilidh* since Valentine's Day."

A tide of people streamed in behind the quilting ladies, children included. A group of musicians were setting up in the corner. Kit noticed that the impending rumble had diminished to a small reverberation as most of the out-of-town bachelors became distracted by the local girls. Davey was even talking with Moira. Sinnie and Ewan were getting a glass of punch. And Rowena and Colin had begun dancing to the jig that had just started.

Harper slipped her arm through Kit's. The dance floor was filling up and everyone looked happy. Abraham Clacher, a crusty old fisherman, had even dragged Deydie onto the dance floor. "I didn't see *this* coming."

"Me, neither." Kit sighed, but she wasn't completely relieved. "I'm going to have to rethink my career choice." She glanced around for Ramsay.

"He's over there." Harper pointed to where Ramsay stood with Father Andrew.

Andrew frowned as he watched Moira dancing with Davey. That girl was light on her feet, a gifted dancer. Davey leaned over and spoke in her ear, and she laughed. Kit watched as Andrew's hands balled into fists. Ramsay stilled him with a hand on his shoulder.

The song ended, but what was going on between Davey and Moira didn't. It was like watching a movie. Moira went and got her sweater; Davey walked her out the door with his hand at the small of her back. Meanwhile at the side of the room, Andrew's face drained, then reddened to the color of sacramental wine.

Ramsay caught Kit staring. He said something to Andrew and made a beeline for her. She frowned at him until he reached her.

"Still mad at me?" He didn't give her a chance to answer but pulled her out on the dance floor once again, this time to an upbeat tune.

"I should go talk to Andrew. He looks like he might do something stupid."

Ramsay spun her in that direction. "Bethia and Deydie have it under control."

Sure enough, the two older women had Andrew cornered. Bethia gazed upon him with her kind angel face while Deydie, the pitbull, ripped Andrew apart.

"So what is it, sprite? Forgive me? Or not?" Ramsay took her hand and pulled her near, their faces close together.

She tried glaring at him. But his eyes held the magic to soften her. She glanced away. "This is not what I had planned."

"Aye. It's so much better."

The music changed to a slow ballad, a song of unrequited love. Ramsay wrapped her in his arms as if he were her favorite quilt. She wanted to hang on to her anger, but she couldn't help but snuggle in.

A small body slammed into them. "Uncle Swab! Aunt Kitten!"

She glared up at Ramsay. Her brawny man shrugged and then scooped up Dand, letting him dance along with them in his arms.

"What is it, Rat?" Ramsay asked him. "Did some lass ask ye to dance?"

"Ew, no!" Dand made a face like he'd eaten fish bait. "I'm having a little brother." He pointed to where his parents stood by the food table. "Thank gawd it's not a sister. Ew!"

Ramsay laughed, hugging the boy tight. "That's excellent news, laddie. What are we going to call him?"

Dand screwed up his face just like he did when doing his arithmetic homework. "Let's call him *Flea*."

"Perfect," Ramsay rumbled. He kissed the boy on his forehead.

"Ew, Uncle Swab. *Boys don't kiss boys*." Dand wiggled out of his arms and ran toward his parents.

The two of them were alone again. "Careful, sprite," Ramsay murmured in her ear. "Something must be in the water. Claire, from the restaurant, and Doc's wife, Emma, are both pregnant. Now Maggie." Ramsay glanced down at her. "You don't seem surprised by the news."

She cuddled closer. "Maggie's baby being a *boy* is news to me."

He laughed again and it warmed her as if she'd downed a shot of smooth Scottish whisky.

He ran a hand down her back. "How have ye done it, sprite? How have ye made everyone love you?"

As soon as the words were out, her world stopped.

Surely he hadn't meant to imply that *he* loved her. He kept swaying her to the music as if nothing was different from ten seconds ago, but she felt changed. *Ramsay* was not part of her plan.

"Let's get out of here." He took her hand and dragged her toward the door.

She tugged back. "I can't leave my clients."

He planted his hands on her shoulders and spun her around to look at the dance floor. "Ye're assuming too much responsibility. They're doing grand without ye."

Indeed. Morgan didn't need help cuddling up to Lochie. Davey hadn't needed any tips on how to woo the shyest woman in Scotland from the room. Not even Deydie needed any prodding to dance with Abraham Clacher.

"Fine." Apparently matchmaking wasn't Kit's calling, after all. She'd have to find another way to support her family.

Ramsay caressed her cheek. "Chin up, kitten. A match is a match, however it comes about."

That didn't make Kit feel any better. Still downcast, she let him lead her toward the door.

John and Ramsay nodded at each other as they passed, some unsaid message communicated between the two.

When Kit and Ramsay stepped outside and the door closed behind them, she stopped. "Where are we going? For a walk? It's a nice night for it."

"We have an hour." He took her hand. "I don't want to waste it on a stroll."

"Oh." It was perfectly clear what he was talking about. So they were going to do *that*.

Hadn't she decided that they weren't going to muddy the waters any more than they had already? On the other hand, it'd been such a crappy day that sex with Ramsay would be the perfect way to put it all behind her. Just the thing the matchmaker needed before she kissed her career goodbye. A nice send-off, as it were.

Kit was entitled to a little fling, wasn't she? Hell, the hand holding hers had pure electricity flowing through it. Yes, she could have a fling with this man with no regrets. It would give her something to think about in the years to come, after her late shift at Arby's or McDonald's.

Ramsay led her to his cottage. "One hour," he reminded her. "That's all the time you have to take advantage of me before John brings home the family."

"And Ross?" she said.

"He'll not be a problem." Ramsay's voice had gone husky. He opened the front door and pulled her inside. He didn't stop there but lifted her into his arms and carried her down the hallway toward his room.

Kit felt a little awkward about doing the deed under the Armstrongs' roof, but clearly Ramsay had no such compunction. "How many other women have you brought home to play when everyone else was out?" She knew she didn't have a right to ask such a thing. This was only a fling. But she had to know.

He gave her a hard kiss. He must've known she was ready to bolt. "Don't worry, lass. Ye're the first." He set her down and shut the door behind him, blocking it with his body. He stripped off his shirt and pushed away from the door, never taking his eyes from her, then sat on the bed and untied the laces of his army boots. "The truth is, until now there's not been another woman I wanted bad enough to risk life and limb. For surely, if Maggie caught us, she'd put my balls in the bait grinder." His boots hit the floor. "Come here, sprite."

There's not been another woman I wanted bad enough ...

"I thought ..." she said.

"You thought what?" He stood and dropped his kilt, displaying plaid boxers.

"Never mind." She stared at the outline of his erection.

"Time's a-wasting," he said. "If ye don't want to get thoroughly loved in the next fifty minutes, let me know now." He looked down at himself, peering at the sideways tent he'd made of his boxers. "Some of us are getting impatient."

She should've sauntered over to him all seductive-like. But she was feeling as impatient as he was. She threw herself at him, wrapping her legs around his waist, and went in for a kiss.

"Oh, gawd, I love . . ." He faltered and fell back on the bed, taking her with him.

Oh, God, what! What did he love?

Part of her wanted him to finish the sentence. But the rational part of her didn't want to know.

"I love . . ." he said again as if choosing his words carefully. Their faces were only an inch apart and she watched as dueling emotions played out on his rugged, beautiful face. His open, honest expression, hinting at something raw, was replaced by his typical flirtiness. He grinned, pushing one of her stray locks behind her ear. "I love it that ye're so clumsy." He delivered his best rogue smile, the one she'd seen a thousand times. "I think we'd better have a go of it before the family gets home." He looked at her cleavage playfully.

Her passion evaporated. She wanted him to be serious. *Wanted him to finish the sentence of a moment ago!* She pulled away, crawling off his chest, sitting up with her feet dangling over the side of the bed.

She was a mess! She obviously couldn't have it both ways—casual sex and a man who loved her. No. She was going home soon. Ramsay was just a distraction—a Scottish fling to make up for her less-than-successful business venture.

He sat up, too, and exhaled heavily. She didn't blame him. Her hormones and her emotions were at war, and it had to be tough on him trying to figure her out. Heck, she didn't have herself figured out, either.

"Come here." He wrapped his arm around her shoulders tenderly, turning her slowly, pulling her down to the mattress. But this time he was on top, trapping her, gazing into her eyes.

She smiled up at him sadly. "Sorry."

"There's nothing to be sorry for." He caressed her cheek. "Every once in a while, I can be an arse. It doesn't happen very often, mind you, but it does happen. I should've wooed ye instead of rushing ye. I'm the one who's sorry." He tapped her nose, trying for playfulness. But that serious expression came over him again. He frowned as if he was concentrating very hard. For a long moment he searched her face.

She waited, holding her breath.

Finally he spoke and she knew he spoke from his heart. "I love that your eyes are green. The kind of green that comes to the trees and the fields when winter fades away and summer's on the horizon. I've never seen anything like yere eyes. Lovely." He fanned out her hair and took a handful. "I love that your hair is soft. It's softer than anything these fisherman hands have ever held." He kissed the handful and then gave it a gentle tug. "But yere hair needs to be longer. A man needs something to hold on to when he's after making love."

"I'm growing it out," she offered, not wanting the moment to end, soaking up how he gazed at her, as if she were a treasured gift.

He gave her a light kiss on her lips, a taste really. "But most of all, I love kissing you. Kissing you, lass, is like the best day at sea. But I won't pressure you. If you want to just lie in the arms of this son-of-a-fisherman, I would be as happy as a North Sea clam."

She put her hands on both of his cheeks. "I like kissing you, too, Ramsay. But could you shut up now and have your way with me?" She looked at her watch. "We only have thirty-nine minutes left."

"Aw, lass, don't rush me."

Before she could argue, he captured her lips with his.

Chapter Sixteen

Ramsay peeled Kit's clothes off slowly, cherishing every bit of exposed flesh, kissing each inch of her that he could reach and going after some he couldn't. When he laid her bare, he sat back and marveled at how beautiful she was.

"Stop that." Her cheeks colored to an adorable pink before she covered her face with her hands.

"Ye're just ... Ye're just so ..." He wanted to say *damned beautiful*, but that would've revealed too much, and he'd already said enough. "Ye're just so *naked*."

She dropped her hands and rolled her eyes. "You'll never change, will you?"

"I don't think ye want me to." He ran a hand over her thigh.

She snatched his hand and tugged. "Fine. You're right. Now come on."

He didn't budge, not letting her pull him on top of her. "Ye can't rush this Scot." He didn't stop gazing, either.

"Weren't you ever told that it's not nice to stare?"

"Oh, it's nice all right." This time he ran his hand down her length, barely touching the side of her breast. "At least from this angle."

"Well, ogling doesn't get the job done," she complained. Or perhaps she meant to challenge. "I guess I could start without you."

Like a flash, he covered her body with his again. "Not on yere life," he growled. "It's my responsibility to make sure the job is done right. Do you hear?"

She laughed. "Now who's assuming too much responsibility?"

He loved that she nipped at his biceps, and he nibbled at her ear in retaliation, knowing it drove her crazy. He couldn't hold back anymore. He whispered his feelings, letting the words pour from him in Gaelic, knowing she wouldn't understand, so he didn't have to weigh and measure each word.

Then she pushed down his boxers. When her hands would no longer reach, she used her foot to free his feet from the fabric, all the while gazing into his eyes.

He was mesmerized. "Aw, lass." He started to drive himself into her, but she put a hand on his chest, halting him.

"Condom."

"Aye," he said hoarsely. At least one of them was thinking straight. It was hell being the more affected of the two of them. But so it was—he couldn't stop what he felt for her or change it. He leaned away and pulled open the night table drawer. He retrieved what he needed and slipped it on. Those couple of seconds gave him a little breathing room.

If his stupid heart kept on the way it was going, he would pronounce his undying love before he came inside her.

She lay on his pillow, one arm out, relaxed, one hand toying with her hair, a lady in waiting. So beautiful.

Gawd, I'm in trouble.

"Are we back in business?" she purred.

"Aye," he growled, positioning himself above her. She seriously had him by the balls and didn't have a clue as to the power she had over him. He could do nothing about it, either.

Except maybe kiss her. He did, deeply, doing his best to make her feel as he did. *Undone. Utterly and completely undone.*

Soon she was writhing underneath him, and he knew it was time. But he had to get one thing straight with her first.

He pulled away. "I have to know. Do ye want me, lass?" He had to hear her say it. He needed some kind of pledge. He wanted her to want him—body, heart . . . and soul. The way he wanted her.

"Yes," she said, breathlessly.

"Open yere eyes and tell me. I have to see that ye mean it." The waiting was killing him, but he would have her answer.

She opened her eyes slowly and gazed up at him. "I want you, Ramsay. You know I do. You can have all of me."

He heard the truth of it in her words and saw the certainty of it in her eyes. "I want you, too." He'd never been more serious in his whole life.

He gazed upon her as he slid inside, feeling relieved that his passion for his *darling sprite* could finally be unleashed.

And unleash he did. He loved her with his body as he'd done to no other. He made sure she felt cherished while in his arms and in his bed, kissing and caressing each perfect part of her. He had the desperate feeling that he had to do this right; he had to make her see the truth—that she belonged to him. In the back of his mind, he knew that in the throes of passion, one could think all sorts of crazy things, perhaps say things that you'd want to take back in the morning. But the truth of it was, he knew that what he felt for her wasn't going to change tomorrow. Or the day after that. Or the day after that.

He came undone inside her. He didn't mean to; he'd meant to make sure she'd had hers first. But then he realized that she was coming with him, moaning his name, and it pleased the hell out of him. He gazed down at her. Her eyes were still closed, ecstasy written all over her face. The way she looked when she was loving him was the most beautiful thing he'd ever seen. *His lass. His love.*

For the first time in his life, he could see it. He saw what millions of men before him had apparently seen and understood. *This was why men got married.*

The future loomed before him, every detail clear.

"Aw, gawd." He couldn't breathe.

"What's wrong?" Kit said. She got that sinking feeling that she'd had the ultimate lapse in judgment. She'd offered herself up to Ramsay and he was rejecting her.

He confirmed it—his brows knit together. She didn't understand. How could he have just given her the best sex of her life—even more mind-blowing than the first time— and then act like it was all a mistake?

"Nothing's wrong." He pulled out of her and rolled away. He scrubbed his hand over his face as he sat on the edge of the bed, then snatched up his boxers. "I'll be back," he said, and left the bedroom.

"Shit," she whispered to his empty room. An old feeling came back to her. *Regret.*

Clearly he felt it, too. Well, she couldn't be there when he came back. She hurriedly dressed, ran her fingers through her hair, and made it out of his bedroom and out of the cottage before she had to see that look on his face again. His regret was more than she could take right now.

Outside, the Highland night air helped to cool her cheeks. She felt altered, changed, even more so than last time. She was getting used to how Ramsay made her feel. So cherished, so feminine. With him, she felt safe to explore being a woman.

But damn him. Why had he acted so strange afterward?

She loved it that he'd lost control. His need for her was the biggest turn-on of all. And the Gaelic he'd whispered in her ear was so sexy.

Damn him again. She'd just decided that she could have a fling with him—her Scottish Highland fling—and then he had to go all moody on her. For once, she wished the old teasing Ramsay had been in bed with her instead of the one who made her feel all sorts of crazy emotions.

Well, whatever his problem was . . . it was his problem. *Not hers.* She had problems of her own. She realized she was standing outside the restaurant, the music reverberating through the walls, the sound mingling with the crashing of the waves against the containment wall. Her problems lay within the restaurant, twelve single people for whom she was responsible. No, ten. She remembered Moira and Davey had left. How many others had slipped out over the last hour while Ramsay was having his way with her?

She opened the door just as John, Maggie, and Dand were on their way out. *That was cutting it close,* Kit thought, remembering Ramsay walking naked from his room with nothing on but a condom.

Kit made a quick decision and nabbed Maggie's arm,

pulling her aside. "I'm going to stay the night with Harper. But I'll be back to make breakfast so you don't have to get up in the morning."

Maggie looked up at John as a concerned glance passed between the two of them. She laid her hand over Kit's. "Nay. Don't fash yereself about the morn. I'm fine to get up with the men."

John put his arm around his wife's shoulders but spoke to Kit. "Is everything all right?" He tilted his head as if to acknowledge the direction of their cottage, and there was a protective edge to his voice. His next words confirmed it. "Do I need to kick some arse for you?"

Maggie looked up at him with love in her eyes, like he had offered to kick someone's ass for *her*.

Kit mustered a genuine smile. "I'm fine. But thanks. Really." It was kind of nice to have a big brother.

"Let's go home," Maggie said. "We'll see you tomorrow, Kit." She had *I mean it* behind her Scottish lilt. "Dand?"

The boy ran over and hugged Kit's legs. "Are ye ready to go home, Auntie?"

John unlatched the boy and slung him up on his shoulders. "She's going to spend the night with her sister."

The boy leaned over his dad's head, trying to look him in the eye. "Ye mean I have another aunt besides Aunt Kitten?"

"Aye." John winked at her. "Now stop asking questions. It's time for yere bath."

Dand's complaining began as the family went down the walkway.

Kit couldn't help smiling. Even though she was extremely close to her sisters and was comfortable taking care of them, it was nice to have someone looking out for *her* for a change. And it wasn't just John; little Dand had weaseled his way into her heart, too. She could be an aunt to Dand if she wanted to, couldn't she?

Kit pushed her thoughts aside, went into the restaurant, and focused on the present. Her sister was being chatted up by two Gandiegow men whose names she couldn't remember. Only one of her socialites, Mercedes, remained, slow-dancing with Colin, Ramsay's friend, the one who owned the farm nearby. *Well, maybe at least one of my clients might end up with one of the bachelors.* Two other couples remained. Mac was chatting with Sinnie, and Kolby, the fisherman, was feeding Rowena a chip. They all seemed pretty damned cozy. And nothing had turned out like Kit had imagined. She'd lost her touch.

She trudged over to rescue Harper from the local men. "Excuse us, fellows. I need a word with my sister."

Harper let herself be led away. She glanced over Kit's shoulder. "These Highlanders are a persistent lot."

"Persistent and hardheaded." *Sexy and confusing.*

"Where did you run off to?" Harper's voice was laced with laughter. "As if I didn't know."

"We're not going to talk about it." Kit gave her a sad smile. "Please."

"Talk about what?" Harper wrapped her arm through hers. "Should we start cleaning up?"

The music had stopped but Colin and Mercedes kept dancing. Ailsa and Aileen, two of the matronly quilters, started picking up dirty glasses.

Deydie lumbered toward Kit, smiling. But when she got close, she frowned. "What happened to you?"

Kit panicked. Did Deydie know that she and Ramsay had slipped off together?

"It's that damned Ramsay, isn't it? I'll take my broom

to him." Deydie snorted as she lumbered away, determined.

Kit was afraid she'd go back to the cottage to get him, but Deydie only went back to the task of bossing the others around to pick up the restaurant.

Kit turned to Harper. "Is it that apparent?"

"I could say that it's written all over your face, but we're not talking about it, remember? Come on. Let's help clean up."

Kit picked up a centerpiece and clutched it to her chest. "I'm coming back to stay with you tonight. Can I borrow pajamas?" She couldn't go back to Ramsay's. Harper studied her face worriedly. But she kept her promise and didn't pry. "Of course you can."

It didn't take long for the restaurant to be put back to rights, especially with so many hands to help. Kit wished her life would so easily be put back together—her career, her confidence, and her beliefs. The mixer had dashed her hopes of making the Real Men of Scotland a success. And Ramsay had knocked her off balance.

Kit and Harper hurried back to the quilting dorm. They had the place to themselves because her socialites were busy elsewhere. In Harper's bedroom, Kit chose the twin across from her sister's full-sized bed. Kit only wished she had reminded her girls about the importance of contraception before the mixer. But they were grown women and would have to face the consequences, *and their families*, if one of the fishermen's swimmers took root.

"Here." Harper tossed her a nightshirt.

Kit took it and slipped it on, sighing heavily as she climbed into bed, exhausted.

Harper turned out the light. Kit heard her sister's bed squeak as she crawled into hers across the room.

Harper whispered into the night, "Sleep, rest, talk, or play?"

Kit smiled into the darkness, grateful to have at least one of her sisters here with her.

Harper cleared her throat. "I said, sleep, rest, talk, or play?"

As tired as she was, Kit was afraid sleep would be elusive. "Talk."

Kit had never talked to her sisters about her problems before, or even their mother. She'd always been the adult, her sisters' sounding board and confidante. When she was worried about paying for groceries, school clothes, or tuition, she'd kept it to herself. It occurred to her that the only person Kit had ever confided in about her overwhelming responsibilities . . . was Ramsay.

Boy, that was irony for you—he was the only person she could talk to, but now she needed someone to talk to about *him*. The man was too much for her to handle on her own.

For the first time, Kit was ready to open up to her sister. Maybe here in the dark she could share what had happened with Ramsay. Her sisters always told her everything about their relationships, right down to the nitty-gritty. Maybe she could at least give the abridged version of the fiasco with Ramsay to Harper now.

"I'm here," Harper encouraged.

Slowly, Kit told her sister everything that had happened since coming to Scotland. How Ramsay had sabotaged her, only to turn around and save the day. How attractive he was, not just physically but in the way he'd cared for her and comforted her . . . but couldn't be serious for two seconds in a row.

"And?" Harper prodded. "Did you go to bed together?"

Kit felt her face redden, glad for the darkness. She had always kept her sex life to herself, wanting to set a good example for her younger siblings.

"Well?" her sister said again.

"You're a nag." But they were both adults and there was nothing to be embarrassed about. Maybe she should start treating Harper like an adult, too. "Yes, we slept together. I was working so hard and feeling stressed and Ramsay's just so damn sexy." Kit sighed. "Now everything is so complicated."

Harper got out of bed and padded across the room. "Scoot over."

"Why?"

"I need to give you *the talk*," Harper said.

"What talk?" But Kit did as her sister commanded.

"You know what talk. The one you gave to me and Bridget. I'm sure no one ever gave it to you." Harper gave a little bark of laughter. "You were much too busy bossing the rest of us around to listen to a lecture."

"Not bossing," Kit corrected. "I was taking care of you."

"Potato, po-tâ-to."

"Your feet are cold," Kit complained.

"Shh. I want you to pay attention. It's about sex."

Kit groaned. "I know the speech. You don't have to tell me; I'm the one who invented it."

"Tough. You're going to hear it anyway." Harper cleared her throat. "Sex is much bigger and more important than how TV or the movies portray it. Sex is rich and deep and complicated."

Yes, Kit had said this. She shook her head. She'd been so self-righteous when she'd passed along this wisdom to her sisters. So full of herself in her overresponsibility.

Harper took her hand and squeezed. "When you have

sex with a boy, there's a built-in emotional commitment. God made it that way to bind two people together. To be there for each other. To help each other. Because *life is hard*. You can't escape that feeling even if you think you're only having a fling."

A fling. Tears threatened Kit's eyes, her composure near crumbling. "Enough."

Harper had no mercy. "You have to hear it all. You made Bridget and me listen to it, and you will, too." She took a deep breath. "When you have sex, a little piece of your heart is left behind. Whether you want to leave it or not. So I beg you to be careful." Harper squeezed her hand again. "There. How did I do?"

A tear slipped down Kit's cheek. "If only I'd been smart enough to remember this beforehand."

"So how much of your heart did he take?" Harper asked.

But that wasn't the question. Ramsay hadn't taken her heart. The way he'd shot from the bed and out the door after sex, he clearly didn't want it.

"He didn't take anything from me." Kit wiped the tears from her eyes.

"Are you sure?"

Yes, Kit was sure. A sob escaped from someplace deep inside and she curled into her sister. Harper held her tight.

"He didn't want me," Kit cried. But whether he wanted her or not, her heart had stayed behind.

Ramsay sat on his boat. Alone. He stared out at the darkened sea, barely tolerating the moon as his companion. It was for the best that Kit had been gone when he got back to his bedroom. He had nothing to say to her. Then, or now.

He wasn't going to get married. Ever. He'd been firm

on that point his whole life. And didn't all women want to get married, no matter what they said? This was *his time*—his time to finally be independent and build up his own business—and he wasn't going to give up his freedom to some hell-bent matchmaker!

But Kit had changed something inside him. She'd weaseled her way into his heart—and he resented the hell out of her. No matter how irresistible she was.

He lobbed one of the life vests across the deck.

She didn't even like the water! *Aw, hell!* How could she ever love a fisherman?

If his own da had died at sea, he might not love it, either.

He trudged into the wheelhouse and plopped down in the captain's chair. What was he going to do?

Hell, he really liked having sex with Kit—he was getting a hard-on just thinking about it—but he didn't want the rest. Those errant thoughts about forever were just plain daft. They could have a bit of fun together, like she'd suggested, as long as she was here in Gandiegow. They could go at it, and leave their emotions at the door. Marriage was not required to have a good time, right?

Besides, they were from different worlds. She was the country club, and he was the pub. While she dined on caviar, he ate carp. She'd lived in a mansion and he'd lived his whole life in a cottage. She deserved some rich guy. Someone who could shower her with everything she wanted.

All the things Ramsay didn't have.

The thought depressed him.

He couldn't sit here all night, though. He'd promised another excursion tomorrow for the out-of-town bachelors, and he needed to leave a note for them at the dorm with the details. He put the life vest away and stepped off his boat.

As he was passing Moira's house, he noticed something strange. Andrew was pacing back and forth on the porch, talking to himself. The Episcopal priest was usually so calm. But maybe this was the new Andrew—the one who'd looked ready to throw daggers at Davey for slipping away with Moira.

"Women," Ramsay muttered. They made a man crazy.

He had taken one step toward Andrew when he heard shuffling and huffing behind him. He turned and groaned inwardly. *Deydie*. He wasn't in the mood for her right now, but it was too late to turn and walk away. He kept on up the short walk to Moira's door and said, "What's going on, Andrew?" As if Ramsay didn't know. "Did you forget where the parsonage was?"

Andrew looked up, startled, as if Ramsay had snuck up on him.

Deydie joined them, holding a whisky bottle in her hand. "I've come to have a dram with Kenneth," she said. "What are you two doing here?"

"That's nice of ye. Kenneth will be pleased." Ramsay hoped Deydie would go in so he could have a word with Andrew alone. The priest seemed to be in worse shape than earlier.

Deydie stacked her hands on her hips, her bottle firmly in her grasp. "I asked what you two were doing here."

Ramsay opened his mouth to answer, but Andrew beat him to it.

"I'm here on business."

"What kind of business?" Deydie huffed.

Andrew stood tall. "Kenneth has given me permission to ask Moira to marry me."

"Aw, gawd," Ramsay hissed. "Are ye nuts? No need to jump into the frying pan. Good grief, man, she only danced with the chap."

"And left with him!" Andrew glared in a very un-priestlike fashion. "I never should've listened to you. I should've stopped her. Kit was right."

"Kit?" Ramsay practically yelled. "What does she have to do with this?" She might be making his life miserable, but why was she interfering in Andrew's?

"Kit warned me. She told me to get off my duff and start wooing Moira properly. I didn't listen. And look what it got me."

Deydie pounded Andrew on his back with her free hand. "It's about damned time you claimed that girl. You two have been mooning after each other for months."

Ramsay grabbed his arm. "Don't rush into anything you might regret."

Andrew shook him off. "I'm going to ask her. I'm going to make Moira mine."

It was as if his words had made her appear; up the walk she came with Davey beside her. Thank God for the proximity of the crashing waves. Ramsay doubted Moira and Davey had heard what they'd been talking about. Maybe Ramsay could drag Andrew away before it was too late.

He grabbed Andrew's arm. "Come away."

Andrew stood firm. "No. I'm doing this."

Moira and her date were practically on the doorstep before she looked up and noticed them.

Andrew, *the fool*, put one foot forward and dropped to his knee. He held up a small ring box.

Moira froze, looking as shocked as Ramsay felt. Davey

tried to take a step between them as if to intervene, but Deydie blocked the large Scot.

"Moira?" Andrew jutted the box closer to her, his voice a mixture of nervousness and desperation. "Will ye marry me?"

Petrified, Moira shifted her gaze to each of their faces as if they could explain Andrew's crazy behavior. As the seconds wore on, her eyes widened, until finally her stone stature cracked. Shy Moira cried out and ran for the door, knocking the ring box from Andrew's outstretched hand.

Andrew's head dropped, followed by his shoulders, and finally his empty hand. Ramsay wanted to shake the priest. If the man was going to be stupid enough to propose, he probably should've planned it out better, *and not have it be a part of her date with another man!* Second, and more important, why would he want to get married anyway?

But Ramsay was no better. Only a few short hours ago, the thought of wedding bells and a happily-ever-after with Kit had been first and foremost on his mind. At least he'd kept his wits about him—unlike Andrew.

Davey had the decency and the composure to help Andrew to his feet.

But suddenly Andrew came alive. "Moira's my girl," the pastor growled. Like the wrath of God, Andrew shot a left hook to Davey's jaw.

Davey staggered for a second, but regained his footing quickly. Ramsay moved to stop the next blow, but Davey didn't look as if he was going to retaliate.

He rubbed his injured jaw instead. "Ye might've sought Moira's opinion first on whether she was your girl or not, *Father*."

The emphasis on *Father* did the trick. Andrew tugged uncomfortably at his cleric's collar as a crumpled expression of shame crowded his face. "I'm sorry. I never should've . . ." The words fell away from the man. In the next moment, the old Andrew emerged. "What I did was inexcusable. I ask you for your forgiveness." Andrew stuck his hand out in offering.

Davey straightened and took it, *the decent bloke*. "That was a hell of a punch. Did you box in seminary?"

The two walked off the porch together, leaving Ramsay alone with Deydie.

"Bonehead," she cursed.

"Which one?" Ramsay knew which he'd choose.

"All of yees."

Ramsay frowned down at the fierce woman. "Why are you including me? I didn't do anything."

"Exactly. You didn't do anything." She stared at him hard. "But if ye didn't do anything, then why does the matchmaker look like someone's filleted her heart? She's a good girl—and a decent seamstress. I don't care if she is an outsider, wee Ramsay, ye never should've broken her heart."

Ramsay's insides roared. "I didn't break anything." He wanted to tell Deydie that it was *Kit's* idea to have a bit of fun. He wanted to tell Deydie that he'd fallen much harder for the matchmaker than she had for him. But he didn't explain himself . . . He couldn't. "Aw, hell."

He stomped off the porch, barely able to draw a breath, as he left Deydie behind.

Whether he wanted to or not, he'd have to go home tonight and talk to Kit—make sure she was okay. *Even though I'm not.* Probably wouldn't be ever again. She'd changed everything. His life had gotten so confusing. But first he had to go to the men's dorm and tell them what time to be at the boat in the morning.

He tramped the rest of the way through town, Deydie's words pounding his brain like a series of rogue waves. Outside Duncan's Den, he heard a muffled conversation— two familiar voices—coming from the open window of Thistle Glen Lodge next door. He went nearer and listened.

"He didn't want me," rang out, a cry in the night.

What? But I do want you.

His chest ached. He'd hurt *his sprite* and that was the last thing he'd wanted to do. Hell, he'd take a thousand harpoons to the chest to make her stop crying. He'd sail to the ends of the earth for her to smile. He'd die for that woman.

A warm feeling spread through him and settled into his heart. Suddenly his whole world shifted and he knew what he had to do.

Chapter Seventeen

The next morning Kit stood in the bathroom at the quilting dorm, staring into the blasted mirror, examining herself in Harper's borrowed clothes. She was more than glad Maggie had given her a pass on making breakfast today. Heck, if Kit had shown up at the Armstrongs' looking as she did, she might have frightened the bejeebers out of them. Her face was puffed up like a muskrat's, even worse than when she'd gotten poison ivy as a kid; she was highly allergic.

But no allergy had caused these puffy eyes. She couldn't even blame Ramsay in the light of day. It was her own stupid fault. One of those lessons in life she never wanted to repeat. Ever. If she did decide to date again, it would be with her own species, not with some highly testosteroned Scot. Until she got back to the U.S., *shields were up.* Thank God she was leaving soon.

The girls had two days left of the retreat—today and tomorrow, and then they were flying home. Her bachelors were supposed to spend one more night. The plan had been to have everyone paired up by now, with these two days scheduled to give them more time to get to know one another better. But that plan was history. She sighed. She would have to double down on her efforts in Alaska to recoup what she'd lost by trying to make a go of it here in Scotland.

Kit applied Harper's makeup to her poor face. Maybe if she drank a gallon of water, it would wash away the evidence of last night's tears. But makeup and hydrating wouldn't help her pathetic heart. But she wouldn't think on it again. Ramsay was ancient history as far as she was concerned.

There was a quiet knock on the door and Harper's gentle voice. "Are you ready to go?"

"I'm coming." Kit gave herself one more look and plastered a smile on her face.

Only two of her clients had made it home last night. They trooped with her and Harper to Quilting Central. The others would hopefully be along soon. Kit wasn't looking forward to explaining the missing American girls to the quilters of Gandiegow. Deydie would probably blame Kit for corrupting the fishermen.

By the front door of Quilting Central, Lochie was in a full-on lip-lock with Morgan.

"Break it up, you two," Harper said. "I don't want to have to turn the fire hose on you."

Lochie pulled away. "I'll be back for lunch, lass." He gave her a quick kiss and was gone.

"I hope that wasn't code," Kit said pointedly.

Morgan didn't answer in words, only gave her a shy grin as she opened the door and went inside.

Kit stopped Harper. "Do I look okay?"

Harper put an arm around her shoulders. "Just remember that you're a force to be reckoned with and you'll be fine."

Kit leaned her head on her sister's shoulder. "I was hoping that my reflection had lied."

"You're my big sister and I love you." Harper squeezed her. "But you look like the devil this morning. Get in there and show them what true grit is. It's a woman rising up from the ashes and becoming stronger."

"You sound like a Hallmark movie. But thanks for the effort."

Kit didn't need to worry how she looked because she was barely noticed. A going-away party for Rhona, their retired teacher, was in full swing when they went inside. But Rhona's send-off to Dundee wasn't the only thing going on.

The building was abuzz with what had happened last night between Moira and Andrew. Amy gave Kit and Harper the heads-up as soon as they were inside. Even her clients were talking about it. Half of them thought it was terribly romantic of Andrew to propose like he did. The other half were in Moira's camp, agreeing they would be taken aback, too.

Moira was nowhere to be seen. She must've understood what kind of stir this would cause in their small community. *Poor Moira. And poor Andrew.*

The door to Quilting Central opened and the whole room went quiet. Kit glanced back over her shoulder to see the reason. *Poor Andrew* stood awkwardly in the doorway, until his eyes landed on her. With each step toward her, his pained face relaxed a little more.

Andrew sat down next to her. "We need to talk."

The whole room seemed to lean in closer so they wouldn't miss a word.

Kit turned off her machine. "Let's go to the restaurant for a scone and a cup of tea." She tilted her head toward the room, indicating the prying eyes and eavesdropping ears.

As soon as they were on the other side of the door away from the quilters, Andrew started. "You were right."

Kit kept quiet; it wouldn't do any good to rub it in.

"I should've listened to you."

"Why don't you tell me your version of what happened? Everyone has a slightly different story," she said kindly.

He told her about talking to Kenneth, Moira's father, and waiting around on the porch for Moira to show up. Kit almost stumbled when he mentioned Ramsay was there, too.

"Oh?" She stared straight ahead. Her cheeks, though, were on fire. "What did he say?"

"He tried to talk me out of proposing."

Of course he did.

Andrew stopped just inside the restaurant's door and ran a hand through his hair. "I've ruined it with Moira. I don't know what I'm going to do."

Kit laid a hand on his arm. "All is not lost. Let's sit down and talk."

He gave her a weak smile. "I wish I'd listened to you."

She tried to fortify him with a nod.

After Claire brought them their tea and scones, Andrew seemed to have no appetite.

"What am I going to do?" he said. "I've lost her."

"You haven't lost anything. You just scared her."

He shook his head.

"I know you care about Moira or else you wouldn't have done what you did. But what I need to know is if you're really the right kind of man for her. I understand shy women. They need someone to appreciate them for who they are. They don't want to be changed or pushed past their comfort zone." Moira was one of the shyest women Kit had ever met and that was saying something.

Andrew scooted his chair closer. "Finding Moira a man who can appreciate her isn't the problem. I'm that man! How do we make her love me back?"

Kit crossed her arms and studied Andrew. He truly was a man in love. Where there was love, there was hope. "Are you willing to try something different?"

"Anything."

"Forget the current screwed-up dating scene. Have you thought about courting her? I could facilitate."

She knew she'd just complicated things for herself. She was leaving soon. But in this day and age, there were ways to be present without her physically being here in Gandiegow.

Andrew's eyebrows were pinched together. "Courting?"

"I know. People don't use the word very often anymore." Text-messaged hookups were in vogue and the thought of them turned Kit's stomach. Her generation was confused about what real dating was. Real dating involved face-to-face communication, standing strong, showing your feelings even with the possibility of rejection.

A painful lesson I learned last night. She had given herself to Ramsay—body and soul—but he had rejected her. This experience would make her stronger and she would not be sorry for it. At least she'd tried.

She shook off her own heartache. She was going to take Andrew and Moira back to a simpler time—when there were constructs to dating, when things were clearer.

"But I have a feeling that Moira, if she isn't too gun-shy now, will be interested in the idea of a real courtship."

Andrew scooted his chair toward Kit. "What would I have to do?" For the first time since last night, he looked hopeful.

"To begin with, you're going to have to cool your jets." Kit patted his hand kindly. "Next, you're going to have to write Moira a letter of apology."

"For being an unmitigated arse?"

Kit laughed. "Exactly." She got serious quickly, though. "Be mindful in your letter not to scare her off any further. Do not spout your undying love."

"I understand."

"If she accepts your apology, then I'll speak with Moira about a proper courtship. No more proposals on the porch. You will have to take it slow. One step at a time. No getting overzealous again, skipping the holding hands phase and going straight to a handfasting. My hope is that you'll be able to woo her to the place where she can hear your feelings without being overwhelmed." Kit wouldn't tell him that she was pretty certain that Moira loved him, too. But like a graceful doe, she had to be coaxed out into the open to be comfortable exploring those feelings.

Andrew took Kit's hand, squeezing it. "Thank you. I'll do whatever you say, whatever I have to do to win Moira."

Out of the corner of her eye, Kit saw three people wander into the restaurant. Three wellies-wearing some-ones she knew well. The brothers Armstrong.

She couldn't breathe. She couldn't move. As Ramsay barreled toward them, Andrew took his hand away.

Ramsay didn't look his playful self. He looked like a

pissed-off dog whose bone had been stolen by another. "Are ye out proposing to every woman in town, *Father*?"

Andrew stood. "Kit was just giving me some helpful advice."

Ramsay postured like he might do something foolish.

Kit stepped in his path. "Don't." But Ramsay wasn't her problem anymore. If he wanted to call out the local pastor, then fine. It had nothing to do with her.

She dropped her hand. "Never mind. Do what you want." She stepped around him and went for the door. Before she left, though, she turned back to Andrew. "Bring the letter to Quilting Central. I'll deliver it to Moira."

He nodded.

She tried not to look at Ramsay, but her worthless will-power glanced at him anyway, looking for signs of life — for signs that he pined after his lost kitten the way she pined after him.

But he was still glowering at the Episcopal priest. Just as she was turning away, Ramsay shifted and speared her with his gaze.

"We have things to discuss," he growled.

"I don't think so." She had a business to run. She didn't have time to be an emotional wreck.

She left without saying more. She would not cry over Ramsay again. She couldn't.

She lifted her head high and headed for Quilting Central, striding down the boardwalk at a clip. Life had been so much simpler when she was only worrying about other people's love lives . . . instead of her own.

Ramsay watched her go, the light inside him seeming to go with her. "Ye're lucky ye let go of her when ye did."

The pastor would've had a hard time turning his Bible pages with a broken hand come Sunday morning.

Ross slapped Ramsay on the back. "Stop threatening Andrew. And pick up the tab for his breakfast for being such an arse."

He snatched up the bill. "Sorry, Andrew."

"It's already forgotten." But Andrew had a look on his face that said he completely understood.

Ramsay needed to collect the bachelors for their boat ride. "Claire, can I have a box of scones to go?"

Claire nodded and loaded up his food.

Ramsay wouldn't bemoan the fact that he was living his dream of starting his own tourist business, but he really wanted to get things straightened out with Kit.

Andrew had been the perfect example of what could happen if a man let his emotions get the best of him—he could do something stupid. Ramsay wouldn't hurry off after Kit. He would take his time. He needed to plan it out to the last detail. If he did that, nothing could go wrong.

Ramsay stared at the door again. Gawd, he didn't deserve her. He'd tried to sabotage her and had teased her within an inch of her life. How he'd ever gotten her to look his way, let alone give him the honor of going to bed with him, heaven only knew. No, he didn't deserve her, but God willing, he'd spend the rest of his life trying to.

There were so many decisions to make. Where would they live? How soon could they book the church? Would he have time today to make it to Inverness to get a ring?

"I'll meet up with you later," John said. "There's something I need to do."

As John left, Ramsay noticed his other brother giving him a goofy grin. "What?" he said to Ross.

"Oh, I was just thinking what a close call it was for you. It's best you made nice with the priest," Ross said, as if he had wisdom beyond his years.

They were back to talking about Andrew? "Why's that?"

Ross laughed. "He could refuse to marry ye when you walk the matchmaker down the aisle."

"Shut up."

But Ross was right. Ramsay would have to watch himself. Things were finally falling into place, and he didn't want to mess it up. *Everything will have to be perfect to make Kit mine.*

John caught up to Kit as she reached for the door to Quilting Central. "Can I talk to ye for a minute?"

"Sure." Hopefully, he didn't want to talk about Ramsay. Kit didn't think she was up for that.

He pointed to the bench next to the door. "You were missed at breakfast this morning." He sat beside her.

She nodded, not willing to talk about why she couldn't stay at their house any longer.

John rested his arms on his legs, his hands clasped, and looked out at the sea. "I wanted to talk to you about your business. I'm hoping the Armstrongs are still in your good graces and we can continue to taxi you around for the rest of your trip."

Ugh, this was awkward for both of them, but Kit understood that he was looking out for his family, especially with another baby on the way. She laid a hand on his arm. "Unfortunately, I don't think I'll have any more business here in Scotland. It's been pretty much a disaster since day one." *On both a professional and a personal level.* "Things have not gone as planned. I'm going to have to cut my losses." *And run.*

John straightened and turned to her. "When are you leaving?"

"Day after tomorrow. I'll fly home with the girls."

John frowned. "Does my brother know ye're leaving so soon?"

He didn't have to explain which brother. She couldn't speak; she shook her head. *No.*

He stood and stared at her for a long moment.

The conversation seemed to be over, so she stood as well. "I'm sorry. I had hoped for a long and enduring partnership, one that would have been good for the community as well as my business."

He waved off her comment, and then rested a hand on her shoulder. "You've been like one of the family to us. We'll all be sorry to see you go." He dropped his hand and walked away.

The gravity of what he said hit her. They had been like family to her, too. It wasn't just her Scotland-based business that she'd lost. As the seconds wore on, she felt the weight of the losses piling up.

For the next hour, Kit sat behind her sewing machine, staring at Bethia, who was instructing, but not hearing a word and not sewing a single stitch. She was relieved when Andrew showed up. Better to think about his problems than her own.

He handed her an envelope. "Thank you for doing this."

"I'm not making any promises." She gave him a reassuring smile. "But I'll give it my best shot. I'll be in touch, one way or the other."

Andrew nodded stoically and walked her out, but then they parted ways. When Kit got to Moira's house, she knocked quietly, knowing her father was ill.

Moira answered the door, not looking much better than Kit had this morning.

"May I come in?"

Moira stepped aside. "Let's sit in the kitchen. My da's asleep in the parlor."

Kit followed her into a small kitchen with a tiny round table.

Without asking, Moira set a mug in front of Kit and poured from a Victorian teapot.

"How are you holding up?" Kit asked.

Moira inhaled. "Then you and everyone else knows—"

"That Andrew was an overzealous lunkhead? Yes, we know." Kit dropped a teaspoon of sugar in her teacup.

"I've never been more embarrassed in my life."

Kit handed her the letter. "Someone would like to apologize."

Moira gazed at it, and for a moment, Kit wondered if she would open it. She looked up at her expectantly.

"I have e-mails to check. Go ahead and read it. Afterward, I'd like to have a minute of your time." Kit pulled out her phone, turning away from Moira, giving her some privacy.

After a few minutes, Moira refolded the note, slipped it into its envelope, and set it in her lap, her hand still covering it.

Kit put her phone away. "Did the lunkhead bungle that, too? Or did he do a good enough job that you would be willing to hear what I propose?"

Propose was the wrong choice of words. Moira flinched.

Kit rubbed the handle of her teacup. "Or would you rather see Davey again? He likes you."

Another little flinch.

Kit leaned on the table. "Of course, in this day and age, a lot of women are choosing to remain single. There's absolutely nothing wrong with that." It's what Kit was going to do.

Moira shook her head. For a moment, Kit worried that Andrew might be out of luck.

But then Moira held the envelope to her chest, speaking quietly. "I'll hear what ye have to say. About Andrew, that is."

Kit explained to her about the possibility of Andrew courting her, and how Kit would oversee the process.

Moira listened quietly. "I would be comfortable with that."

"At any time, you can back out of the deal." None of Kit's clients would ever be coerced into a relationship. "I want to assure you that you have the power to walk and no one will say a word."

"I thank ye for that." Moira had a shy smile on her face. "But I doubt it will come to that."

Kit rose. "Normally I would say let's let things cool off for a couple of days. But if it's okay with you, I'd like to set up a mini-date—say, tea at the restaurant this afternoon. I need to put you on the fast track because I'm leaving soon."

Moira's face blanched. She reached out to Kit.

Kit touched her hand. "I'll be here every step of the way. We can Skype or FaceTime. I promise to keep Andrew in line until you feel comfortable enough to keep him in line yourself."

Moira looked relieved, a small grin emerging. "Deydie says that every woman needs to know how to handle a broom."

Kit gave her a hug. "That old quilter makes a lot of

sense. Maybe I should add that advice to my website. I better get back to Quilting Central, though. I'll leave it up to you to share with the town what we've devised. Or not. It's up to you."

Moira looked down at her shoes. "Would you tell them for me? I don't want to answer any questions. Surely they would be asking."

Kit patted her hand. "I'll take care of everything."

Moira gave her a brilliant smile. It was easy to see why Andrew loved her.

Ramsay was about to pull away with his boatload of bachelors when he saw John and Ross running down the dock. "Wait up," John hollered from the shore.

Ross jumped on the boat, out of breath. "John needs to see you. I'm yere relief captain."

Ramsay looked over at his expectant passengers. "Give me two minutes and we'll be on our way."

Ross grabbed a drink from the cooler and began entertaining the others with fish tales as Ramsay stepped off the boat.

John was just reaching him. "Ye'll need to leave yere paying customers with Ross." He had that *I'll brook no argument* tone that he'd perfected as a teenager.

"Leave them? Nay. They're my responsibility and this is *my* boat."

John gave him a stony expression, serious even for him. "Ye're needed back at the house."

"Is Maggie all right? The babe?" Surely God wouldn't let them lose another one.

John jammed his hands in his pocket. "It's Kit."

Ramsay felt his world falling apart. "What about Kit?"

"I'm afraid yere time to win her over is shorter than you think."

"What are ye talking about? She's all right, isn't she? She's not ill or something?"

John frowned at him. "She's leaving in two days."

"*Aw, hell*," Ramsay growled. He wanted to do this right.

"Send Ross out with Kit's bachelors and come with me," John commanded.

"I can't come with you. I have to get to Inverness now."

"No. You don't. I have what ye need back at the cottage." John gave him the *oldest brother knows best* look.

"You know what I have planned?" Ramsay asked.

"It's as clear on yere face as the sky is blue."

Ramsay turned back to the boat and hollered to his passengers. "Something's come up, fellows. I leave you in my brother's capable hands. Ross, take them to the honey hole."

Ross saluted. "Aye, aye, Skipper."

Ramsay gave the boat one more glance before he walked away with John. When they arrived home, the house was empty. It felt even emptier knowing Kit wanted to leave Scotland so soon . . . without giving him a chance to do it up right.

John went into his bedroom and came back with two boxes, setting them on the table. "These were our grandmothers' rings. Mum gave them to me to choose one for Maggie."

Ramsay looked at him, puzzled. "Then why are there still two?"

"I was young and stupid and thought Maggie needed

something new. Now I regret not giving her a family heirloom. Don't make the same mistake that I did."

One was an amethyst. The other was an emerald.

"You choose one for your matchmaker and the other one will be for Ross to give to Pippa one day." John pushed the opened boxes toward Ramsay.

The choice was easy. "Her eyes are green." Ramsay thought his voice sounded thick. And at this moment, he didn't care that he sounded like a dumb kid.

John clamped him on the shoulder. "Excellent choice. Now go tell her."

"Don't you mean *ask her*?"

John shook his head. "Go tell her that ye love her."

Ramsay couldn't. He wasn't going to do what Andrew had done. Kit deserved a romantic evening. He'd get a bottle of wine from the pub. Maybe they had champagne somewhere in the back. He'd take *his sprite* for a sunset ride on his boat. He'd woo her. He'd make love to her. Then when she was all relaxed, he'd seal the deal by giving her the ring.

He pulled the emerald from the box and slipped it on his little finger, smiling. "Nay. I'll ask her out on a date for tonight. Before the evening is over, she'll be mine."

John frowned at him, an expression Ramsay had gotten well used to over the years. "Don't put off what needs to be done."

"It's my affair. I'll handle it as I see fit." Ramsay knew it was all going to work out just as he planned. He'd never been more certain of anything in his whole life.

Chapter Eighteen

Kit stood in front of everyone at Quilting Central, just like her first time in the building. Except this time, she wasn't under fire. She was here now as Moira's advocate, and she meant to be firm in her words.

"I wanted to speak with everyone at once, so we're all on the same page." Hopefully, what she had to say wouldn't get misconstrued and twisted when they talked about it later. "I'm here on behalf of Moira and Father Andrew. I've been asked to step in as their go-between, their dating coach, if you will."

A buzz went up around the room.

Kit put her hand up. "The reason I'm telling you this is to ask that you all respect their privacy. Have a little compassion. Moira appreciates your support, but doesn't want to discuss her love life with you." Kit stared directly at Deydie. "*Any of you*. No matter how much you want to give advice." *And stick your nose in their business.* "Andrew isn't going to want your questions, either."

"So ye're going to crack the whip?" Deydie challenged.

The door opened. From where Kit stood, she had an eagle-eyed view of the all-brawn man as he came in, his presence filling the room. She snapped her gaze away from him and back to Deydie, not remembering the question.

Deydie put her hands on her wide hips, looking powerful. "Who is going to keep us in line, lassie? You?"

Kit put her hands on her hips, too, mirroring the tough old woman. "Yes, me. At least while I'm here."

Kit sensed more than saw Ramsay's annoyance.

"I'll have spies reporting to me." Kit would ask Maggie, Rowena, and Sinnie to help her. "If you all don't behave," Kit said, smiling, "I'll have to come back here and kick some Scottish butt."

"Not with a skinny little arse like yeres." Deydie cackled. "Ye're good for a laugh, matchmaker. I'll grant you that."

The whole room laughed.

Once more Kit motioned for them to be quiet. "But seriously, though, can I count on you to help me with Moira and Andrew by giving them some space?" Her eyes—the little traitors—shifted to take in Ramsay. "Love needs room to grow."

Many of the women nodded their head *yes*, and the others talked among themselves.

Deydie joined her at the front. This time, she was the one who held up her hand. "The matchmaker has my full support. Her heart is in the right place and it's past time that those two wised up. If any of yees cross the line with the good Father and Moira, you'll have to answer to me and my broom."

Nervous laughter twittered around the room, the women looking at one another. Everyone knew that Deydie meant business when it came to her broom.

Harper gave her that smile that said she was proud of her big sister. Kit stepped toward her, to join her at her sewing machine, but Ramsay caught up to her first, blocking her path. He wasn't his old teasing self, but looked as serious as high seas.

"A minute?" He tilted his head, gesturing toward the door.

It wouldn't do her resolve any good to be alone with him now. "I'm busy."

"Aye, you are." He took her hand and towed her to the door.

The whole room went silent, all eyes on them. Kit thought her cheeks would incinerate right off her face. He didn't drop her hand as he opened the door, or when he dragged her through it to the sidewalk outside, and slammed the door behind them.

She pulled free and crossed her arms over her chest. "That was quite a show you put on. Taking tips from Andrew?"

Ramsay looked heavenward and exhaled heavily. "Gawd, ye're a saucy one, always making it hard on me."

She showed him saucy. She dropped her eyes to his crotch. She had the upper hand here, thanks to her anger. And her resolve.

"Don't goad me, little sprite," he drawled, closing the space between them. "There are plenty of quiet, private places where I can have my way with you, places where no one will hear you begging for more."

Oh, shit. Her resolve melted. Her breath became shallow with want, need. She dropped her arms and hung her head. "What do you want, Ramsay?"

He tipped her chin up with a finger and took both of

her hands. He gazed into her eyes. "I want a chance to make everything up to you. I didn't mean to run out on you. I only needed a minute to pull myself together. Say ye'll go on one date with me. *One date*."

"Don't worry yourself over it. We were only having a bit of fun." It was a lie, but she wouldn't put herself out there again. "I don't see the point."

Her brain knew her emotions couldn't take much more. He was a good man with a big heart. He was smart, caring and fun. The complete package. Her hormones and her body were on board. Every place that he'd touched and loved shouted, *Hell, yeah, I'm in!*

He seemed stumped by her reply.

She filled in the blanks for him. "I'm leaving soon. It would be a waste of both our time."

He caressed her captured hands. "Have I ever asked for one thing from you? One favor?" He looked at her pointedly.

She'd requested a million things from him. And he'd given in to all of them. *Eventually*.

She felt the energy flowing from his hands to hers. He squeezed to put an exclamation point on the chemistry between them.

Rationalization invaded her brain. To be in his arms one more time would be . . .

Heavenly.

Total bliss.

A nice farewell.

He'd already broken her heart. *How much more damage can he do?*

"Sure. Why not?" she acquiesced. She would make love to him and that would be the end of it. "Where are we going to do this thing?"

He dropped her hands. "Ye're about as romantic as a lug nut, sprite."

"Fine. Tell me about this date you've planned."

She was surprised when he didn't hesitate.

"I'll pick you up at the Thistle Glen Lodge at eight for a late dinner. Wear that yellow dress I like so much. And bring yere wellies."

She frowned at him. "Where's this date going to take place?"

He grinned at her. "On my boat. We're going to have our *romantic* dinner at my favorite spot." He took her hand and squeezed it. "I promise to give you a perfect evening."

She stared at the hand holding hers—big and strong. "Okay," she finally said. "I'm going to hold you to it."

He chuckled and let go of her. "I have work to do."

Already, she missed him. But she wasn't going to let him see the desperation written all over her pathetic face. "Well . . . I have work to do, too."

He walked away, talking over his shoulder. "Tonight then. And bring your A-game."

"What the hell is that supposed to mean?" But he was out of earshot by then. It was just as well. She had a date to plan herself—the one between Moira and Father Andrew.

It was one fifty-nine p.m. Kit and Moira waited at the restaurant for Andrew. She had left her clients with Harper and the quilting ladies. She knew that by this evening most of her girls would be scattered to the wind with their fishermen. Gretchen and Thomas still hadn't shown up. Bethia had assured her that all was well and the couple would no doubt reappear and would likely be married. Kit pushed her own fisherman troubles out of her mind.

Moira stood near the door, twisting her hands. *Poor woman.* Kit was glad that she'd brought her here early. Moira was the type of client who needed to arrive first, so she could get her bearings. A sign that said the restaurant was closed for a private party hung on the door. Dominic and Claire had been more than happy to give the budding couple the dining room for their first date.

Claire had dressed up the table for two with a frilly tablecloth, turned napkins into pup tents, and filled a plate with petit fours. The Royal Albert Country Roses teapot had a cozy over it to keep their tea warm.

Moira shifted and gazed at the table. "It's very pretty."

The poor girl had repeated herself several times.

"Remember—you'll go as you start. This is your chance to make that fresh beginning." Kit had already talked to Moira about not letting Andrew fall into the old pattern of taking her for granted.

The door opened and the Episcopal priest walked in. He looked around hesitantly. But when his eyes fell on Moira, his face broke into an expression of relief, as if he hadn't dared to believe that she would actually come.

Kit stepped into his path, stopping him, and spoke quietly. "Don't scare her off."

Andrew nodded solemnly as if her words had come from the Almighty himself.

She didn't need to remind him of his manners—at least those were impeccable.

He gazed over at Moira and motioned to the table. "Shall we?" He pulled out her chair and waited.

Moira gracefully walked across the room, her eyes darting to Kit a couple of times for reassurance.

Kit gave her a nod as if to say, *I'll be over here if you need me.* She went to her table across the room with her laptop and notebook, ready to do the unavoidable bookkeeping. After last night's debacle, her finances were ruined. Kit had always requested half of her payment up front, with the rest due when the client found her match. This had worked for her in the past—but in the past, Kit had been successful. She couldn't expect these clients to pay the balance when she hadn't really matched them at all.

She sighed and began entering expenses into her spreadsheets. But all the while, she kept her eye on things at the date table across the room. She wasn't completely eavesdropping but she heard Andrew's *You got my note?* and saw Moira's answering nod.

Kit had given Andrew a few talking points, and she noticed approvingly that Moira was engaging in the conversation. She had quit working her hands into knots and the pinch between her eyebrows was gone. Andrew was taking charge . . . but in a good way. He poured Moira's tea and offered her food from the plate. Only the light shake of his normally steady hands gave away what he had at stake here. By the secret smile on Moira's face, she was enjoying being looked after—something that surely hadn't happened often as she was the sole caregiver of her ill father.

The rest of the date ran smoothly enough. After precisely one hour, Andrew stood, as Kit had instructed. There was an awkward moment when the pastor looked like he wanted to go in for a hug, but like a good student, he offered Moira his hand instead.

Tentatively, she took it.

"May I see you again for a second date?"

Moira shocked them both by going up on tiptoes and pecking Andrew on the cheek. "Aye."

He blushed as a goofy grin came over his face.

Kit popped up and stepped in. "That's lovely. Goodbye now." She shooed him toward the door and out of the restaurant before he did anything stupid—like throwing Moira over his shoulder and carrying her off to the altar.

After the door closed behind him, Kit turned to Moira. "Well?"

Moira looked at the floor and smiled. "He'll do." After a moment, she looked up at Kit with her eyebrows furrowed. "But now, what are we going to do about you?"

Kit didn't pretend not to know what she meant. "I'll be fine." She ushered Moira out the door and stayed behind to clean up the restaurant alone.

Afterward she rushed to the cottage. Two hours later, after primping more than she wanted to admit, and wearing the yellow dress that Ramsay liked so much, Kit walked across town to the dock. She wondered if it was fair to compare Andrew and Moira's date with what Ramsay had planned for them tonight. Moira, who had only dared to kiss Andrew's cheek, would be scandalized at the steamy evening about to occur between the matchmaker and the fisherman.

"*You'll go as you start,*" Kit said to herself. But the cold, hard fact was that after this, she would just *go*. Back to the U.S. Back to concentrating on her Alaskan business. Back to her comfort zone.

Fear slowed her steps as she walked down the dock toward Ramsay's boat. But she kept putting one foot in front of the other.

As if he could sense she was near, Ramsay popped his

head out from the wheelhouse with a life vest in his hand. "Ye're here." He looked down at her wellies. "And properly dressed, too." His eyes skimmed up her boots, to the hem of her yellow dress, up farther, lingering on the flare of her hips, then on up to her modestly covered breasts.

She expected one of his teasing comments when his eyes finally met hers.

"Ye take my breath away, lass." There was a yearning there, one that she'd seen in small flashes; but this time, he seemed in no hurry to ever look away.

She'd wanted him to be a more serious person, but now that she'd found it in him, it made her uncomfortable. Her face felt hot and her stomach churned deliciously, like a mixture of warm caramel and nerves. "Shouldn't we get going?"

He smiled at her and offered his free hand. "Come here."

She shook her head. "Not until I have that thing on."

"Aye. Right." He handed over the life jacket. "Yere mantle, milady."

As she slipped it on, he spoke to her in a very calming tone. "Anytime you start to feel anxious, I want you to tell me, so I can kiss you. That should help take yere mind off your worries." He grinned at her.

"And he's back," she said, without explaining what she meant. The teasing Ramsay had returned and she could take some comfort in that. But if she did as he suggested, and kissed him every time she was uneasy, then how would he be able to steer the boat? She stepped aboard, looking around. "Where's the life raft?"

"That question says ye're anxious. Come here, sprite, so I can plant one on ye for your ulcer's sake."

She put her hand up. "No. I'm being serious. I want to know where the life raft is."

He took her hand and led her to the bench under which the life raft was stored. He pulled out one of the bundled rafts and showed her the rope to yank if she needed to inflate it.

"Now can we go?" he asked.

She reached into the storage under the seat and pulled out another life vest. "Not until you suit up, sailor."

For gawd's sake! Ramsay snatched the life vest from her. *The things men did for love.* This wasn't his first boat ride. He was on the water every day of his blasted life.

He put his arms in the holes and zipped it up. "Satisfied?"

"Thank you," she said quietly.

He leaned in and kissed her soundly. "Okay."

He walked into the wheelhouse—his pants uncomfortably tight—and started up the boat. She came in and stood beside him.

Without looking at her, he reached over and tugged on her hair. "Over time, ye'll get used to the ocean, lass."

She leaned into his hand. "I already have. Thanks to you. I'm starting to remember how much I loved being on the water."

"Are ye trying to say that I'm good for you?"

She gave a noncommittal shrug.

He put his arm around her waist and pulled her to him. "Ye're going to love my favorite spot." It was a secluded cove, perfect for making love to his woman. Even though he'd bet good money that she'd make him keep on the life jacket, he'd do his best to relax her. Because once she was well and thoroughly loved, she wouldn't be able to resist his proposal.

As he put his free hand in his pocket and touched the ring box he'd gotten from John, he looked over at his sprite. He had never felt happier, or more grateful, in his whole entire life. The Almighty had a way of turning obstacles into highways. Never in a million years could Ramsay have foreseen Kit as his future. In fact, at first he'd only seen her as a roadblock to his dream. Now *she was* the dream. He kissed her hair. "Aw, Kit."

She put her arm around his waist, leaning into him. "Hmm?"

"Nothing." He could wait until they were around the small peninsula and anchored.

Five minutes later, they were there. Away from the prying eyes of Gandiegow. The hideout cove he'd claimed as his own when he was a boy. The place he planned to claim Kit for always.

Kit turned toward the outcropping of bluffs and her eyes softened. "Oh, Ramsay, it's stunning."

"I told you ye'd love it." He dropped the anchor and retrieved the picnic basket that Dominic and Claire had fixed up for him at the restaurant—seafood alfredo, roasted broccoli, and fresh bread. Dom had chosen the wine and Claire had wrapped up a couple of cannolis for dessert.

Together, Ramsay and Kit set the table—an over-turned crate placed near the side benches, covered with a crisp white cloth. After their plates and food were out, Ramsay stood back and admired the scene, especially his sprite. "Perfect."

She blushed, looking even lovelier.

She sat and he took his place beside her, wanting everything to go perfectly. He was a gentleman and she was everything he'd ever wanted in a woman. They talked and laughed during their meal—so completely in tune with each other, connected—and Ramsay had never been happier. When they were done, they worked together in perfect harmony, clearing their dishes and stacking them back in the basket.

When the last item was stowed, Kit wrapped her arms around his waist. "Thank you. That was a wonderful date." She leaned up and kissed him lightly on the lips.

He wanted to deepen the kiss, but it could wait for a more private setting. "The date isn't over yet, kitten. The night is young. Come with me. There's something I need to show you below."

She gave him a slight smile. "Am I going to like it?"

"Verra much." He could tell she knew exactly what was going to happen next. In the captain's cabin, he'd left a box of condoms and his iPod, loaded with every love song he could think of. Everything would be perfect.

He took her hand and walked the three steps down and into his quarters. The bed was small, but he didn't need a lot of room to show her how much he cared for her. He shut the door behind him.

But with the door closed, she seemed unsure.

He pushed her hair behind her ear. "What's wrong?" He couldn't help but kiss her neck.

"Will the boat be all right? I mean, we're not up there watching things."

"You saw me drop the anchor. We'll be fine." He pulled her to him, but it wasn't close enough because of the damned life vest. He tugged at her flotation. "Can we take these off now?"

She shook her head no.

"Okay. For you, I'll work around it." He kissed her and maneuvered her toward the bed. He nuzzled and caressed every part he could get at. Finally, he laid her back and pulled off her wellies and socks, kissing the tops of her feet. He worked his way up her calves and thighs. Just as he was about to slip his hands under her dress, she tugged him up to her.

"I'll make you a deal. If you promise to put your life jacket back on afterward—I mean immediately—then I guess we can take these off."

He held up his hand in a solemn oath. "I promise."

She reached for the zipper of his life vest and pulled it down. As he shrugged out of it, she unzipped hers. He didn't stop there, but pulled off his polo shirt. She didn't stop there, either. She stood, unzipped her dress as well, and stepped out of it, waiting in her lacy white bra and yellow-checked underwear. The sweetest gift he'd ever gotten.

"*Aw, gawd.* Ye may have to give me mouth-to-mouth resuscitation before this is all over."

She stepped toward him and laid her hands on his chest, caressing the area over his heart. He was so filled with emotion that he wanted to propose *now*. But he would wait so she didn't think it was his hormones doing the asking.

"You're a beautiful man, Ramsay." She moistened her lips with her tongue, and that was all the invitation he needed.

He dove in and kissed her until he was weak in the knees. Gawd, she had a way of taking it out of him. He pulled her down to the bed, this time so that she was on top. "Have yere way with me, lass. I'm all yours." He meant it.

She brushed back the hair from his face, gazing into his eyes. There was a softness there that he could get lost in, and perhaps already had. She helped him out of his clothes and shoes, and then leaned down and kissed him tenderly. The kiss deepened with her taking complete control. He was in heaven.

He ran his hands down her back, cupping her bum to him, loving how they fit together. "Gawd, sprite, ye're awfully good at this," he growled into their kiss.

"Only with you," she said back.

His heart swelled. If he got any more overcome with emotion, he might start reciting poetry.

She reached for a condom and had him suited up in no time. He had thought she would take it slow, but not *his sprite*. She sighed as she slid down on him. It took all his effort not to come in that instant.

"Hold still," he commanded as he tried to regain concentration.

Of course, she didn't listen, but laughed as she taunted him with her moving hips.

He growled again, clutching her, rolling her over so he was on top.

He looked down at her flushed face, smiling up at him.

He pulled back a little and watched her expression change to one of complete bliss. He pushed back into her, and this time she closed her eyes and moaned.

"That's it," he crooned. And did it again.

Soon they were rocking the boat and he was loving her with everything he had. He wanted it to last forever, and when they were married, it would. They fell apart together in the most perfect way—she was saying his name, again, but this time he could hear that she loved him, too.

When he thought he could speak, he gazed into her eyes. "Gawd, lass, ye're wonderful."

"So are you." But she sounded sad. "I think my foot is cramping. Can you get up?"

He kissed her forehead and eased off of her. "Always, my romantic lass."

She frowned and swung her legs over the side of the bed, pulling the sheet to her chest, covering herself.

He wanted everything to be perfect. And for a few minutes it had been. But something was trying to trouble her now. He'd better act before things got worse.

He took care of the condom and slipped on his boxers and polo. He grinned over at her as he grabbed his life vest. "For you. As promised." He slipped his arms in and zipped it up.

She gave him a smile. *Better.*

As an afterthought, he slipped on his dungarees. He didn't want her to look back on this moment and think of him as uncivilized.

As she pulled her clothes on, he pulled the ring box from his pants pocket.

She was having trouble with the zipper on her dress.

"Here. Turn around." He pulled the zipper up with the box in this hand, and kissed her beautiful neck while he was there.

When she had barely turned around, he dropped to one knee. There wasn't a lot of room in his quarters, but he would do this right.

He held the opened box out to her and poured his heart out like a tipped-over bucket of water. "I love ye,

Kit. I need you. I want you here with me in Gandiegow forever. Calm the storm inside me and tell me that ye'll be mine for all time." He'd said it perfectly.

But instead of accepting his proposal, she stared at him as if he were the Loch Ness Monster.

His heart fell, so hard and heavy it was a wonder it didn't bust the hull and hit the bottom of the ocean.

Chapter Nineteen

"I can't," Kit whispered.

This feeling of utter despair was more suffocating than her fear of the water had ever been. The one thing she wanted more than anything else was this man and his love. Here it was, a ring box away, and she couldn't reach out and take it.

"I can't," she repeated.

Ramsay snapped the box shut, jerked himself up from the floor, and shoved the box in his pocket. He was so big that he filled the room. She couldn't escape. She couldn't breathe.

"I'll be on deck." He yanked the door open and stomped up the stairs.

He didn't understand—she had responsibilities. Though it might be her one chance at happiness, it would be selfish of her to take the life that he offered. She had to take care of her mother and sisters. It would be different if she'd made a success of her expansion into Scotland, but right now all she had was the business in Alaska. It was the only thing keeping her family afloat. They all depended on her. She couldn't take the ring and be Ramsay's wife, no matter how tempting the offer. She had to go back to the U.S. Find more clients. Pay her mother's rent, her sisters' tuition. She was boxed in from all sides, responsibility sitting on top, keeping her trapped. Keeping her from her one true love.

The boat's engine roared to life. She sat on the bed for a long moment, her responsibilities anchoring her to the spot. But she couldn't sit here for the rest of her life. She reached down and retrieved her socks and wellies. After dressing she went back on deck. The sky had turned dark.

For a moment she watched Ramsay at the controls—staunch, stiff, staring out at the sea.

"I owe you an explanation," she started.

"Don't fash yereself."

She sighed heavily. "Maybe I want to *fash* myself."

There was a thump to the boat.

"Holy hell." The anger in his voice was gone. It had turned to alarm.

"What was that?"

He didn't answer, but geared down to idle.

He hurried past her and went below. Obscenities flew. "Kit, get down here."

She froze.

"Kit, dammit, I need you. Now!"

She ran down the stairs, stopped on the last step, and stared in the engine room, horrified at the hairline crack in the hull. Water shot out like a shower set on high.

"Hold this here while I make sure the bilge pump is going full out."

She couldn't move.

He seemed to have remembered her fear, because he shifted gears with her, as surely as he had done with the boat.

"Lass, we're not far from home. We'll make it back

fine. I just need ye to hold this for me while I get something to plug it." He looked at her earnestly.

It was that look that had her taking the last step. Her wellies splashed in the water. He gave her a rag to hold against the crack and left through the doorway.

"There's nothing to worry about. Ye know where all the safety equipment is. I showed you, remember?" he shouted from the other room. "We have the satellite phone, the flares, and the first-aid kit under the counter in the wheelhouse. Ye know where the life raft is. We're going to be fine."

But the boat was listing a little to one side. She couldn't speak. The water was gaining on her wellies.

"Motherducker!" he said.

That helped her find her voice. "What is it? What's wrong?" She didn't leave her post, but she wanted to.

"A bilge pump has failed," he yelled. He came back into her room. "The other one can't keep up."

"What are we going to do?"

He kissed her soundly. "We're not going to panic."

But it was almost as if his words had flipped a switch. The waves began pounding the boat.

"We're going to try to patch her so we can make it home," he said in a calming voice. He retrieved a bag from a shelf and pulled out a small hammer and pieces of wood that looked like oddly shaped pencils. "You and I are going to insert these into the hole. If we can slow the leak, we'll be fine."

"And if we can't slow the leak?" she squeaked.

He grinned at her. "We'll make a run for it."

They worked together—she held the pieces of wood while he hammered the tapered and conical-shaped plugs in place, filling up the crack.

"When we get this patched, we'll call John and tell him that we're on our way." He hammered what looked to be the last one that would fill the hole. It still leaked, but at least they'd slowed it down.

"Is that going to hold?" she asked.

"We'll keep our fingers crossed." He winked at her, took her hand, and pulled her toward the door.

A huge wave slammed against the side, and she saw their slow leak gush more water. "It's not working," she said.

He glanced back. "We'll put a call into John first. Then you and I will fix it again. We make a good team." He squeezed her hand and pulled her up the stairs.

She held on to the railing as she was in danger of being bounced off the walls. With him holding her other hand, she felt assured that everything was going to be okay.

But as Ramsay's foot hit the deck, a wave hit the side of the boat hard. In horrible slow motion, he lost his footing, pitched forward, and hit his head on the mast. He went down.

"No!" she screamed. Her ears buzzed. Her head pounded. *This cannot be happening. This cannot be happening.* For a moment she waited—hoped—he was teasing her. A bad joke. But he just lay there.

She climbed over him and made sure he was still breathing. He was.

She shook him. "Wake up! Wake up!" He didn't move. *But he's breathing.*

The waves were rocking the boat but at least water wasn't coming over the edges. *Yet.* But water was coming in below. She stood and looked around at the ocean for a fishing boat and then to the shore. They were so close. But yet so far.

She looked heavenward. "Please, God, help us!"

The answer came to her. She ran to the storage under the seating and pulled out the life raft. She braced her foot on the raft and tugged the rope that Ramsay had shown her. With a piercing squeal of air, the raft came to life, filling with air, expanding. She kicked it aside so it wouldn't cover his beautiful head.

The list! "The satellite phone. The flare gun. The first-aid kit." She repeated it back to him as if he hadn't been knocked unconscious. She hurried into the wheelhouse, holding on to anything sturdy so she didn't get knocked out, either. She gathered everything in her arms and threw them into the lifeboat.

"Aren't you glad now that I'm a nervous wreck about the water?" she yelled.

He had his life vest on, but she knew, from when she fell into the loch, that hypothermia could overtake a person quickly. He couldn't go in the water. He couldn't get wet. Neither of them could . . . and survive.

She knelt beside him. "Ramsay, *please*, wake up." When he didn't, she got angry. "You promised to keep me safe."

But suddenly she realized that the only one to keep them safe was her. "I don't care if you do have a hundred pounds on me, mister. I will get you into that damned lifeboat!" She grabbed the shoulders of his life vest and tugged. God must've been with her, because another wave tipped the boat in the same direction that she pulled, and Ramsay moved twelve inches toward the life raft.

That was when the first raindrop hit. And she knew it was urgent to get him in the boat with the canvas tarp over them before it really started to storm. This time when she tugged, she walked backward, and Ramsay came with her. *She. Would. Not. Stop. Until. He. Was. Safe.*

The boat tossed her sideways, but she held on to Ramsay. With superhuman strength, she dragged him to the life raft. "You're not drowning on my watch."

She pulled him over the edge of the raft. She ran around to the other side and tugged his feet, until he was completely inside.

She climbed inside with him. Pulled the canopy over them to keep out the rain, and laid his head in her lap. The next wave hit and washed them over the edge. She didn't even want to think what would've happened if she'd waited another ten seconds.

She grabbed the satellite phone and called John. He picked up on the first ring.

"Oh, God, thank you," she cried. "Come get us!"

"Kit? What's wrong?"

She looked out of the hole in the canvas top and saw the last wave wash Ramsay's boat under. "It sank, John. We're in the life raft. Ramsay's hurt."

"Where are you?" John was calm and reassuring.

"We were on our way back from Ramsay's cove. I have the flare gun."

"Wait five minutes, then use it. We won't be long." He hung up.

Kit started counting. She kissed Ramsay's head and realized she was crying all over him. She got to three hundred, pointed the flare gun outside the canopy, and fired it upward.

Ramsay groaned and moved.

She watched as his eyes fluttered open and never felt happier in her entire life. "You're awake."

Ramsay glanced from side to side, wincing. "Where am I?"

"We're in the lifeboat. John and Ross are on their way."

"What?" Ramsay tried to sit up, but she held him in her lap.

"Don't move."

"Where's my boat?" he growled.

"It's gone."

He began cussing worse than when he'd found the leak.

"What did you expect me to do?" She laughed, just so glad they hadn't gone down with the boat. "Did you expect me to pull your boat in the life raft with us?"

"What are you smiling at?" He swore again.

She shook her head. "No man who's about to die could swear with this much proficiency."

He squeezed his eyes shut. "But my boat."

"I know." She smoothed his hair back from his face. "You've got a hell of a bump going on there."

A horn blew. Kit unzipped the canopy and looked out. The Armstrong family boat was approaching.

"How is he?" Ross hollered, clearly upset.

"He's spitting mad."

Ross smiled. "He'll be fine. Can you catch this rope?"

"Yes." Kit made sure to grab onto the handhold and stretched her other arm out as far as she could. She missed it the first time, but got it on the second try.

After they were towed to the boat, John and Ross helped her on board. Ross climbed down into the raft and with John got Ramsay aboard, too.

"Get him covered up," John said.

"Aye." Ross pulled out a space blanket and wrapped it around Ramsay.

All the while Ramsay complained. "Holy hell. I only just got her."

"'Tis a shame," Ross consoled. "But you and I know the sea takes what she wants."

"But I only just got her," he repeated.

Before Kit knew it, they were back at the dock. Doc MacGregor was there waiting for them.

"Maggie called and said I was needed."

Doc checked out Ramsay and turned to John. "I think he should have a CT scan. Just to be safe."

"I'm fine." Ramsay shoved Ross as he tried to help him up.

"Stop arguing." John succeeded in pulling Ramsay to his feet. "Ye're as bad as Dand about his bath. Ye'll go to the hospital in Inverness and that's the end of it."

Harper came running down the dock. When she got to Kit, she pulled her in her arms. "Are you okay?"

"She's grand." Ross put his arm around the other side of Ramsay. "It's the Skipper who's the clumsy oaf. He's banged his head."

"You know as soon as I stop seeing two of you that I'm going to kick yere arse."

Ross laughed. "I'm counting on it, Skipper. I'm counting on it."

At the quilting dorm, practically all the women of Gandiegow, along with her clients, were waiting when Kit got out of the shower. They had packed themselves into the hallway.

Harper shooed their audience away as she ushered Kit into the bedroom. "Give her some privacy."

But Deydie pushed herself into the room anyway. "Is she hurt? I need to see for myself." She yanked on Kit's arm until the old woman could look her in the eyes.

Kit tugged Harper's robe tighter around her body. "I'm fine. Right as rain. Grand, even. Now if only I can put on some underwear."

Deydie reached up and brushed her cheek. "Aye. But I can see that yere heart is hurting." She had the decency to say these words quietly enough that only Kit and Harper heard.

Deydie spun around and walked out of the room. "She's fine all right. Now, everyone back to Quilting Central. Let's leave the matchmaker and her sister alone."

Kit appreciated it. Because now that the elation of being alive had worn off, she felt wrung out, almost unable to take another step.

"Here." Harper handed her a nightgown. "I'll pour you some hot tea." She headed toward the door.

"He proposed," Kit said quietly.

Harper stopped midstep and spun around. "He *what*?"

Kit hung her head. "Proposed. He had a ring. Was down on one knee. The whole nine yards."

"I hope to high heaven that you had the sense to say yes. No, I hope you said *hell, yes*."

Kit shook her head. "How could I? I'm responsible for you guys. Everyone is counting on me. I can't get married and live in *Scotland*. And this is home to Ramsay." Kit waved her arm around, motioning to the town outside the walls. "He'd never leave here. He told me so."

Harper's gaze zeroed in on her. "What do you mean you're *responsible* for us?"

Kit stared right back. "Who do you think pays the rent and keeps the lights on? What about your tuition?"

"You really should learn to check your messages," Harper snapped. "Where's your phone?"

"The bottom of the ocean," Kit said wryly.

"Mother texted yesterday to say she sold a Modigliani. The gallery is so impressed that they're making her manager."

"But what about fall tuition?" Kit said.

Harper grabbed her purse and pulled out a bill, shaking it at her. "I took care of this myself."

"You did?"

"Of course I did. You being overly responsible isn't helping anyone. If you do everything for everyone, you're cheating people of the opportunity to do things for themselves." She shoved the tuition bill back in her purse. "Bridget and I talked. We love you for taking care of us when we were younger, but we are no longer accepting anything from you. Except sisterly love. You're done. Retired from being our keeper. We're going to stand on our own two feet—well, four feet between the two of us. But you know what I mean. Bridget applied for about a hundred scholarships. She got a few and will take out loans for the rest. Our little sister is proud of herself. Would you deny her that feeling of self-reliance? Well, I won't let you take that away from her. And I won't tolerate you doing it to me or Mom any longer, either. Your job of mothering, *and fathering*, the three of us is over."

"Oh." Kit had been so busy trying to make enough money for them all, that she hadn't seen the changes in her family. It looked like her mother had become successful in her own right. Her sisters had grown up. Heck, Harper was teaching her a lesson or two. Maybe it was time for Kit to take a step back and relax.

Kit was astonished. "How did you get so smart?"

"That's easy. By watching my big sister." Harper hugged her. "Promise me that you'll stop being such a control freak and start enjoying your life."

"I'll try."

"Now we need to discuss something really important. What are you going to do about Ramsay?"

*   *   *

Ramsay cussed all the way to the hospital, the whole time he was being scanned, and all the way home in the car with his brothers. He'd never had a worse day in his whole life.

His boat! His *cranking* boat was gone. Sunk. But he was almost glad of it. It gave him something to focus on other than Kit. Her rejection was killing him. The future he could see so clearly was gone.

He'd finally said what was in his heart, and she'd stomped on it. The ring in his pocket felt like kryptonite. His love for her made him weak, and he would always be weak for her. No matter what. He hated that he couldn't hate her. But she had the right of it. She was too good for a fisherman. Too good for him.

John had been too chipper for Ramsay on the drive home. When his older brother pulled into Gandiegow's parking lot, he piped up, "We're here."

"Captain Obvious," Ramsay grumbled.

Ross opened his door and hopped out, but then turned back toward the opened window. "I'll run to Doc's and get a wheelchair."

"You do and I'll break yere legs." Ramsay opened his door. His head hurt like a son of a bitch, but he would walk home by his own devices.

John and Ross rushed to his side.

"Get off." Ramsay pushed them away.

John gave him that older-brother glower. "The hospital said to watch you. And watch you we will."

"Aye," Ross concurred. "It'd be too much trouble otherwise."

"What do you mean?" Ramsay said.

"Too much trouble to carry yere sorry arse up the bluff."

But suddenly it was as if the three brothers were having a simultaneous memory—carrying their father's coffin up the bluff to the cemetery. The grief was almost palpable.

"We'll not do that again." John's jaw was stiff, as if the words had jabbed him on the way out.

"Aye." Ramsay would do as the hospital said. He'd caused enough worries for his family tonight. "How's Maggie?"

"I called her from the hospital. She's fine."

"The babe?" Ramsay didn't want to be the cause of trouble for Maggie.

"The bairn's fine," John said.

As they walked through the village, Ramsay couldn't stop his thoughts from wandering back to Kit. How was she doing after the ordeal she'd been through? He wanted to find her. But given her refusal of his proposal, he would respect her space.

He turned to Ross. "Will ye check in on Kit for me? Make sure she's all right?"

Ross looked at him, concerned. "Do ye not want to do it yereself? We could stop on the way."

Ramsay didn't answer.

John gave Ross his *or else* tone. "Ross'll take care of it for you."

John's protectiveness was irritating, but Ramsay's pounding head kept him from saying so.

When Ramsay stepped into the cottage, Dand barreled toward him. John and Ross caught him by the arms and backed him up.

"But I want to hug Uncle Skipper," Dand complained.

"Uncle Skipper?" Ramsay headed for the sofa but wasn't quick enough.

Dand broke free and ran back to him, tugging on his hand. "Da said ye've graduated from Swab to Skipper."

Ramsay turned a questioning gaze on John.

"Aye. And not because ye got yere own boat."

Suddenly, everything came into focus for Ramsay. He'd had it wrong all along. He didn't need his brothers' approval to have his independence. He just needed to claim it. Live it. And he had. He would always be their little brother, but he was also their equal.

John stuck out his hand, but when Ramsay went to clasp it, John pulled him into a fierce hug. "I love ye. I don't know what we would've done if you'd been lost."

Dand tackled their legs with a fierce hug. too.

"Break up the lovefest." Ross pounded them both on the back. "Or ye'll make me cry."

"Are you hungry, Ramsay?" Maggie had appeared. She leaned up and kissed John. "Thanks for calling from the hospital. I let Harper know Ramsay's okay. Is it all right if he eats?"

Ramsay broke apart from his brothers and went to Maggie, giving her a quick hug. "I haven't had a chance to tell you how happy I am about the babe. Ross, John, and I are going to take over all your housekeeping duties. You've done a grand job of taking care of us, and now it's our turn to take care of you." She'd had such a rough go of it when she'd lost the other babes. Ramsay turned to the other men in the room. "Agreed?"

The other two nodded.

"Ye're one with the speeches," she said. "Tell me then, what are ye going to do about our matchmaker?"

That shut him up. "I'm not hungry. I'm going to bed."

John blocked the hallway.

"What are you about? Going to tuck me in?" Ramsay steadied himself with a hand on the back of the chair.

John didn't budge. "The hospital said you should stay up a few more hours."

Ross piped up from the other side of the room. "We'll both sit up with you."

"Gawd. I'm not a bairn."

"No. But yere brothers are going to sit with you anyway. Ross, make him some tea. Dand, get Skipper his fishing magazine over there." John turned to Maggie. "Wife, off to bed with ye. I'll get Dand settled."

"But—" Maggie started.

John took two steps and kissed her soundly on the mouth. Ramsay assumed it was to shut her up, but it was also a reminder of how much his brother loved his wife. The kind of love their parents had had. The love of a lifetime. Like the love he had for Kit. She belonged here with him. But she'd slipped through his hands.

After the kiss, Maggie waved to them all. "Good night then." She sauntered off to bed.

John threw Dand over his shoulder, tickling him. "And you, my little sea monster, it's off to bed with you, too." He carried him away as well.

Ramsay sat on the couch, willing his headache to go away. He wanted the thoughts of Kit to go away, too. But he wasn't getting what he wanted.

Ross set a mug down for him on the side table. "In all seriousness, what are you going to do about Kit? Ye're not going to let her go back to America, are ye?"

So much for not thinking about her. "What do you expect me to do?" He pulled out the ring box and held it up. "She said *no*."

Ross took the box and opened it up. "So you actually did it."

"I don't want to talk about it."

But Ross was a bastard and plowed ahead anyway. "In the old days, you would've just snatched your bride and run off with her. And keep her away until she accepts you as her husband."

"Aye. Now it's called kidnapping and punishable by law." Ramsay turned away from his brother's gaze. "Look, she's made up her mind. We all have to accept it. She's going back to America and that's the end of it."

Ross snapped the box shut. "Ye're giving up too easy."

But Ross didn't understand that when you loved someone, you would do anything to make her happy, even let her go. Kit didn't want him. Whether it killed him or not, he was letting her go home.

After Dand was in bed, John rejoined them. The three of them talked about fishing, but avoided the elephant in the room—Ramsay's sunk boat.

After a while, Ross and John both fell asleep, but Ramsay couldn't, his thoughts churning like a restless sea. He sat on the couch where he and Kit had held each other and slept. Before the sunrise, he stood and stretched.

John roused and stood also. "What are you doing?"

"I'm going to get ready for the day," Ramsay said.

John shook his head as if Ramsay was Dand with a harebrained idea. "Nay. You're staying home. You'll not be fishing with us today."

"But I'm fine," Ramsay lied. His head hurt like an anchor had fallen on it. But if he didn't go fishing, what would he do? "I won't sit here all day."

"What are you two girls bickering about?" Ross wiped a bit of drool from his mouth.

"Ye're staying home, Ramsay." John crossed his arms over his chest. "That's final. The hospital said for ye to take a few days off to rest."

"Ye're sounding like a broken record, brother." Ramsay exhaled, in no mood to do more than complain. "What do you expect me to do with my time?"

"Ross, go get Skipper's present," John said.

"Are ye sure this is the right time?" Ross questioned. "I mean, well, ye know . . ."

John raised an eyebrow and Ross went to the hall closet and pulled out a large paper bag.

John took it and handed the bag to Ramsay. "We had it made for you. We thought we'd give it to you at the christening."

"What is it?" Ramsay wasn't in the right frame of mind for a frigging gift, and he started to give it back.

"Open it," John said.

Ramsay looked inside and pulled out the wooden cross, which was nearly identical to the cross hanging on their family fishing boat. He stared at it for a long moment, not knowing how he was supposed to feel. He ran his hand over the wood. *John had given him his own cross?* Did this mean that he forgave him for starting his own business? Ramsay glanced up at his eldest brother. "Why?" *And why now?* Ramsay had nowhere to hang it. His wonder and amazement turned into anger. He glared at John. Was he just rubbing it in?

But Ross broke into his thoughts by taking the cross from Ramsay. "We went to Abraham Clacher and had him make it for ye in his woodshop."

John removed the cross from Ross's hands. "You want to know what ye're going to do with your time now, Skipper?" He passed the cross back to Ramsay. "Ye're going to figure out how to get yereself another boat."

Bastard. "So much for ignoring the elephant in the room," Ramsay grumbled and frowned at John. "My life savings are at the bottom of the Pirate's Cove. The insurance won't give me enough to get another boat like her."

John pierced him with that older brother glare that had been around since the day that Ramsay had been born. "You were smart enough to come up with this fishing business. Ye're smart enough to come up with another boat." John ran a hand through his hair. "You've got vision, Ramsay. And ambition. See your way out of this mess and move forward."

"Easy for you to say. Yere head isn't being crushed by a vise."

John laid a paternal hand on his shoulder, just like their father would have done if he'd been here. "I have confidence in you. We all do."

Ramsay expected Ross to make some smartass comment, but he only nodded solemnly in agreement.

"Fine. I'll think my way out. Don't you have some fishing to do?"

"That's the spirit, Swa— I mean, Skipper," Ross said.

Ramsay trudged off to his room, propped the cross up on his dresser, and shut the door. He stretched out on his bed, nearly overwrought with grief. To make it worse, *her* things were still here—her hairbrush on the dresser, her clothes in his closet, and the scent of her on his pillow. He didn't want any of it here. At the same time, he didn't want them gone, either.

He didn't want her gone.

But that was a done deal. He had no choice but to

accept it. He closed his eyes, and despite being cranking tired, he couldn't go to sleep. For a long while, random thoughts of Kit, his boat, and his family rattled around in his brain. He finally got frustrated and opened his eyes. He glanced over at the cross. And then, as if the Almighty had used the hammer himself, an idea hit him square on the head. A bluidy brilliant idea! He could get back into the fishing tourism game.

The only problem was he was going to have to speak with the matchmaker to make it happen.

Chapter Twenty

Kit had a terrible night's sleep—and she didn't need anyone to interpret the nightmare she'd had. She dreamed her sisters and mother were in a dinghy during a storm, being swept out to sea. Every time Kit tried to throw them a line, they insisted they didn't need her help. Kit woke up tired, confused, and feeling displaced in her own life.

But Ramsay was alive. Thank God! Though the thought of him made her want to fall apart again.

Today was the last day of the retreat. Tomorrow, all her clients were supposed to head home. She doubted they were all going, judging by the hormones bouncing around between them and their local fishermen. For these shy women to take a stand like they had, they must really have it bad for their men. Kit understood.

But what a failure she had turned out to be as a matchmaker. But at least her clients—correction, former clients—were happy. Most of them, anyway. Colin and Mercedes—the one match she could possibly claim— were talking of seeing each other again. But in truth, Kit couldn't even take credit for that one as Ramsay had chosen Colin for the mixer.

At Quilting Central everything was going along

smoothly. No one needed a thing from her. It seemed that everyone had grown beyond her help. It was damned uncomfortable not to feel needed. What was she supposed to do with her life now?

Well, at least she had one thing to look forward to today. Art McKay was coming. He'd decided he could use Kit's help to find a woman near his age. The Real Men of Scotland operation was kaput, but she could do this one last thing for Art and call it a day . . . or call it *forever* in Scotland.

When Ramsay woke up, the sun was high in the sky. He hadn't slept this late since . . . well, he couldn't remember when. His head still pounded, but he didn't have time to worry over it now. Quickly, he readied for the day, preparing himself to talk to Kit.

He'd get what he wanted from her and get out of there fast.

Ramsay went to Quilting Central first, sure Kit would be there. But when he walked in, he didn't see her.

Harper came over to him. "She's not here. And get that look off your face. She didn't steal away in the night. She's at the quilting dorm."

He hadn't realized that he'd been holding his breath. "Thanks."

He rushed to Thistle Glen Lodge. He was hurrying because he needed information from Kit, and maybe because he was anxious to see her and to make sure she was okay. But he would get the phone number from her and get the hell away before he was down on his knee, proposing again like some pathetic sap. He wouldn't beg, even though it might be the last time he'd ever see her.

The last time.

He slowed his pace, that thought jelling around in him, suffocating him. But he trudged on.

At the dorm, he walked right in, heading down the hallway, determined to get this over with. As he stepped into the living room, he made his presence known, in case any of the other women were still there. "Is everyone decent?"

He stopped short, trying hard to register what he was seeing. They both looked up at him. Kit sat at the small desk by the wall with a man leaning over her shoulder — way too close.

The man was Art MacKay. The reason Ramsay had wanted to see Kit.

Kit looked from him to Art, then back to him. Her cheeks turned pink. "I'm helping Art plan his trip to the States."

Aw, hell. It was exactly as he'd once suspected. Kit wasn't daft. She and Art were a perfect match. Their thirty years' age difference was no hindrance; they had loads in common.

Ramsay spun around. He didn't need this. He walked away.

"Wait!" Kit shouted.

"Why?" Ramsay said, still walking. "I give ye two my bleeding blessing." He made it outside and sucked in much-needed air, leaning a hand against the dorm's stone wall. He hoped to heaven that she would end up breaking Art's heart, too. Because right now, that was the only thing keeping him from breaking Art's jaw.

The door opened, and for a moment he thought it was Kit running after him. But it was the bluidy wealthy Scot.

"What do you want?" Ramsay said. Couldn't the guy leave him in peace to lick his wounds alone?

"We have business to discuss."

Ramsay had hoped so, at least when he'd *thought* he'd come up with a solution to get past his drowned boat. But the only business to be discussed now was whether it should be pistols or swords at dawn.

Ramsay put his hands up. "We've nothing to talk about." He couldn't partner with Art. Not now. He couldn't ask Art to finance a new boat for him.

"I heard about your vessel," Art said.

"Good news travels fast." *Bastard.* "Did Kit have you on speed dial?" Why would she tell him anyway? Guilt for turning his proposal down? Or to emasculate him further?

Art looked confused. "I don't know what you're speaking of, lad. I heard about your loss at the restaurant when I arrived this morning."

Now Ramsay was the one confused. "The restaurant? Why are you in town?" Did he really want to hear how he'd come to town to sweep the matchmaker off her feet?

"Kit and I had an appointment to meet today."

"An appointment?"

"Aye. I have business in Boston and thought I would use her services to meet a couple of eligible women."

"Then ye're not here for Kit?"

Art laughed. "Nay. I'm here *because* of Kit. She wanted to get everything arranged before she left."

There it was again—talk of Kit leaving. And once again, Ramsay couldn't breathe.

"About yere boat?" Art said.

"What about it? It's sitting at the bottom of Pirate's Cove."

"I've a proposition for you."

For a brief moment, Ramsay considered telling him to shove off, but he jammed his hands in his pockets. "I'm listening."

"I was intrigued by your guided fishing tour business. I'd like a piece of the action."

This was the reason Ramsay wanted Art's phone number to begin with. Ramsay's mood lightened infinitesimally. But had Kit told him that he needed Art's help? Charity? A handout?

"Did Kit put you up to this?" Ramsay asked roughly.

"Not at all. I've been thinking about it since your visit. I believe your idea is pure gold. I ran some numbers on the projected growth of the quilting retreats and I think you have a very viable business."

"Except that the *Lil Sister* sits on the ocean floor."

"Yes, 'tis a shame. But I would like to partner with you. I provide the boat . . . you do all the work." Art chuckled. "It sounds like it would lend itself to both of our strengths."

"But—"

"After you get the kinks worked out—schedules, pricing, maintenance—then we could expand. Maybe have a small fleet of boats, up and down the coast, and enlist some of the other fishermen in the area. Maybe some retired fishermen would be interested?"

Ramsay ran a hand through his hair. It was almost perfect. "I only have one problem with what ye're offering," he said. "I don't want to seem ungrateful . . . but I can't work with you holding the purse strings. That's the whole reason I went into business for myself."

"Nay. I've been thinking this through all morning. I'll finance the first boat, but over time, you'll acquire full ownership of it." Art held out the folder he was carrying.

"I brought a proposal with me. Of course, it'll have to be altered to include a new boat."

The fact that Art had understood that Ramsay would have to own the boat eventually spoke volumes. Only another Scot would know how important that point was.

Art stuck out his hand. "Do we have a deal?"

Ramsay took the folder and shook his hand. "If it all works out on paper."

"Good man. And it will. A good deal is where both parties walk away feeling like they won."

Was it completely nuts that Ramsay wanted to rush back in the door and tell Kit the good news? Would he always have this urge to share his life with her? Ramsay's dream had righted itself in the blink of an eye . . . or at least part of it. The most important piece still eluded him—Kit, becoming his wife.

Art motioned down the boardwalk. "I'm sure the pub isn't open yet, but let's go to the restaurant and discuss our deal over coffee and scones."

Ramsay looked one more time at the dorm longingly, but left with Art. Once at the restaurant and seated, the door blew open and Deydie rushed in, storming straight to their table.

"There you are!" she said. "What did ye do to the matchmaker?"

Hell.

Deydie slammed her hands on her hips. "She's upset about something. I saw her last night. Ye're the one who stole the light from her eyes." Deydie speared him with her glare. "I'll take my broom to ye, wee Ramsay."

Ramsay opened his mouth to tell the town's matriarch that it was none of her business, but decided the truth would be better instead. "Yere broom won't be needed,

Deydie. I proposed to the lass and she shut me out cold. So . . . no. I am not the one who *stole the light from her eyes.*" Ramsay hated to think of hurt settling into his sprite's green eyes, instead of the sparkle that he'd come to love. But she'd been clear that she didn't want any part of him.

But Kit had stroked his hair when they were in the life raft.

And she'd looked longingly at him only a while ago in the quilting dorm.

Deydie harrumphed. "Well, then, that damned lass needs her head examined."

Art cleared his throat. "If I'm not mistaken, I believe Kit has had time to rethink her position. She acts like a woman with regrets."

Ramsay pounded the table. "What the hell is that supposed to mean?"

"It means," Deydie barked, "that you should get off your arse and go ask her again."

Kit sat alone for a long time at the dorm before trudging back to Quilting Central. When she opened the door, it seemed as if the whole town was there again. The fishermen with her clients. The bachelors with the local girls. Her one match of Colin and Mercedes. And a multitude of other quilters.

The room went quiet as Deydie waddled toward her. "It's about damn time you showed up. We were going to start dredging the bay."

"Is this another lynching?" Kit asked lightheartedly, but half serious, too. What could she have done this time to make everyone gather like this?

Deydie took her arm and dragged her up front to a

lone chair. "Here. Sit. We've something for ye." The old woman pushed her into the seat. "Now don't move."

Kit's client Morgan came up to her with a plain white box wrapped with a single scrap of fabric, tied in a bow. The rest of her clients—Gretchen had finally shown up, too—came up also and gathered around her.

Kit took the box from Morgan. "What's all this?"

"Just open it and see."

Smiling, Kit pulled the bow and the tie fell away. "I don't know why you did this." She tugged off the top and set it on the ground beside her. She pushed the tissue paper away . . . and found her grandmother's quilt. Or its identical twin.

"Well?" Deydie groused.

"Omigod." Kit stood on shaky legs and unfolded the quilt. "How did you do this?"

"It was yere girls from America. They did it." Deydie cleared her throat. "With a little help from the rest of us. We're calling it the Gandiegow Matchmaker quilt."

Her clients-turned-friends smiled at her with sincerity. Kit stared at each one in disbelief. She finally found her voice.

"Come here." She gathered them in a group hug.

They all spoke at once. "You never gave up on us." "You were so sure we would find our soul mates." "We are so grateful." At the same time, they clamored to tell her what hand they'd each had in making her grandmother's look-alike quilt.

Deydie pushed Harper into the circle. "Yere sister here has a real knack with the longarm quilting machine. She manhandled that monster into submission."

Kit hugged Harper extra hard. "I love you, sweetie."

"I love you, too."

In the next second, Deydie was shooing everyone back to their places. "The party's over. Now everyone get back to work. Those projects aren't going to finish themselves."

Quilting Central went back to its normal activities. Harper and Kit went to her sewing machine. "I better get the rest of this stuff packed away." Her nautical quilt pieces would be going home with her. A reminder of her time in Gandiegow. She had more than the quilt pieces to take back with her. The thought of Ramsay lived in her heart.

But as she stacked the pieces together, another crowd formed around her—the bachelors and her American clients.

Davey held out a check. "We thought we should pay you now, as some of us have plans for the rest of the day." Sinnie stood beside him, looking up at him with a huge smile on her face.

Huh? She hadn't see that one coming, either.

Kit became even more speechless as a dozen checks were thrust at her, along with thanks for helping them.

"But it's undeserved." She'd gotten it all wrong in Scotland.

"No." Morgan stood beside Lochie, who wrapped an arm around her waist. "We think you handled it brilliantly." She gazed up at her fisherman.

Kit was so confused. Only ten minutes ago, she'd thought her business in Scotland was dead. Instead of dead, she now had double the revenue? "But—"

"Hold up there, missy." Deydie came at her, waving a spiral notebook. Kit was a little worried the old woman was going to give her quilting homework to take back with her to the States. "There's a little matter of business we need to handle."

Was that black notebook filled with more expenses for Kit to pay? She should probably just sign the backs of the checks and hand them over to Deydie now.

Deydie slammed the book down on the table and sat in front of it, then pulled a pencil from behind her ear. "Best to get yere dates written in now."

"What dates?"

"Yere matchmaking dates for the rest of year. Remember, you have to have a quilting retreat each time. Ye best do it now as we're filling up." Deydie flipped the notebook open with the efficiency of an executive secretary. "How's about the first week in August? Do ye think ye'll have enough lads and lassies gathered by then for the matching?"

Harper and Cait sat down, too, and helped negotiate two more retreats for this year and four for the following.

By the time it was done, Kit's head was spinning and she had to get out of there. "I'm going back to the Armstrongs' and pack up my things."

Harper stood, too, in a show of solidarity. "Do you want me to come with you?"

"No. I shouldn't be too long." Kit planned to get in and out before she was waylaid by any of the Armstrong clan.

When she got to the house, luck was with her and she breathed a sigh of relief. There was no one in the living room or kitchen and the house was silent. But when she went into Ramsay's room, she almost jumped out of her shoes.

"You scared me!"

He lay stretched out on the bed with his hands behind his head. He glanced for a second at her but then went back to staring at the ceiling.

She walked carefully into the room. "I'll be out of your hair soon. I just need to pack my things."

"Oh? Going somewhere?"

"You know I am. I have a flight out tomorrow with everyone else." She went to the closet, but her hanging clothes were gone. She spun around and saw that the two suitcases that had been by the window were gone, too.

"Missing something?"

She stomped over to him. "Ramsay Armstrong, I'm in no mood for your teasing."

He grabbed her hand and pulled her onto the bed. He didn't force her to stay there, but she felt befuddled about what to do next.

He gazed into her eyes. "You and I need to have a talk."

"About what?"

"About how you were wrong and want to reconsider yere answer."

"To what?" But she knew.

He *tsk*ed at her. "Now, kitten, are you going to play hard to get?"

"I'm not playing at anything."

"Aye, you are." He grinned at her with the same old grin that she'd fallen in love with. "Do you want me to show you how it's going to be, kitten, or tell you?"

She'd hurt him. How could he still want her? While she was trying to make up her mind how to answer him, he made it up for her.

"Kiss me." He didn't lay a hand on her, only looked at her with smolder and confidence in his eyes. And something else too. *Love*.

She leaned over and pressed her lips to his. After a moment, it wasn't enough and she deepened the kiss.

He wrapped his arms around her, cradling her like they would be together forever. Finally, he broke the kiss, but didn't let her go. "Reconsider. Say *yes*."

"But—"

He cut her off with a heavy sigh, but spoke patiently to her. "Ye're not going anywhere, sprite. I have your clothes—nice collection of panties, by the way. And I have yere messenger bag. Oh"—he paused for a second—"and yere passport. It's all tucked away for safekeeping."

She batted his chest. "You are the most maddening man I've ever met."

"Marry me so you can fix me." He gave her a grin that said that he knew he was perfect.

She rolled to her back and looked up at the ceiling. "You're exasperating."

He gave her a cocky smile. "It must count for something that I proposed to ye before I hit my head. Doesn't it?"

It was her turn to sigh heavily.

He gently rolled her back to face him, both of them on their sides. The teasing Ramsay was gone. Serious Ramsay was gazing into her eyes. He tucked her hair behind her ear—this gentle habit of his—and took both of her hands. "Choose love." He kissed her hands.

"But—"

"Shh." He rested his finger on her lips. "I love ye, lass, with every last bit of this fisherman's heart. You've landed me—hook, line, and sinker. Marry me."

She knew the truth of what he was saying. She could choose love. She gazed into his eyes and saw a future. It was bright, filled with laughter and love. Partnership and commitment. And it was hers for the taking.

"Here." He pulled the ring from his pocket and held

it out to her. "If you say ye'll marry me, I'll tell you where I've stashed yere things."

She took the ring and gazed at the emeralds. "And give me back my passport?"

"I'll not make any promises on that count." He held her hand with the ring cupped in her palm. "I will insist on your vow before you slip my ring on your finger. I can hear it plainly from your heart, but I need to hear the words from yere mouth."

"What about your vow to me?"

"Gawd, lass, ye're going to be the death of me. I'm begging here, for the luvagawd. Ye know I love ye more than the very air that I breathe. Ye're my sprite, my kitten, my lass, my everything."

She scooted closer to him and cupped his face. "I love you, too, Ramsay." And she kissed him.

Without breaking the kiss, he took her left hand and slipped on the ring.

She pulled away. "Where are my things?"

"At our place."

"Our place? We have a place?" she said.

"Well, we can't exactly live together until we stand before the priest. One of us will stay here, and one of us there. The family will probably want ye here to keep an eye on you. But yes, we have a place. We're renting Rhona's cottage."

She gazed at him in wonder. "When did you arrange all this?"

"Before I proposed. *The first time*," he said pointedly.

"I'm glad I came around to your way of thinking."

"Me, too." He kissed her.

"How much time do you think we have?" she said around the kiss.

"Time?" the big tease asked innocently.

"Time before the family gets home," she clarified, running a hand down his chest.

"Ye're a scamp. An insatiable scamp." Ramsay gazed into her eyes. "And I love ye for it."

"Then lock the door."

Epilogue

K it walked into their cottage and hung her messenger bag on the hook, the one Ramsay had put next to the door especially for her. They had been married the second week in August in front of her family and all of Gandiegow as they made a promise to themselves and to God to love each other for always.

She was starting to figure things out for the Real Men of Scotland, fine-tuning her strategies. First, she had to make sure to have her socials on the first night of the retreat so that her handpicked bachelors at least had a shot with her clients from America. And now she would include any locals who wanted to come, at no charge, and let the chips fall as they may.

The door opened and her husband walked in, all swagger, *and all hers*. She smiled at him. She still couldn't believe that she was Mrs. Ramsay Armstrong!

"Wife, what's for dinner?" He was so full of himself, but she loved him that way.

"Husband, whatever you're cooking is fine with me."

He reached outside the door. "Then the catch of the day it is." He produced a plastic container with a cleaned fish. "I thought I'd bake it."

She glanced at the bed, tempting him. "Could we hold off on dinner for a bit?"

He grinned at her and she knew the teasing was coming. "But I'm a big, strong man. I need sustenance."

She walked over and patted the quilt, the Gandiegow Matchmaker quilt. "Some things are more important than food."

"More important than food? I'm not sure I believe ye." He placed a hand over his heart in faked solemnity. "Perhaps ye'll have to show me. First, let me put this in the icebox."

"And wash up," she said.

He grinned. "Only if you'll join me."

She nodded and he took a step toward her, the fire in his eyes igniting.

She put her hand up, laughing. "Put the fish away first."

She watched as he stowed their dinner in the refrigerator and felt bone-deep contentment. Never in her wildest dreams had she seen herself living in a one-room cottage . . . and feeling so rich! After all was said and done, she didn't need to buy back her family's honor; she only needed to make room for love in her life.

Continue reading for a preview
of the next book in
Patience Griffin's Kilts and Quilts series,

The Accidental Scot

Coming from Signet Eclipse in December 2016.

A pang of guilt hit Pippa. She never should've left Gandiegow in the first place. She should've been here. Sure, she'd come back to visit, but she hadn't been here when the McDonnell had needed her most, when he'd almost killed himself doing something incredibly stupid. Who in his right mind put a pallet on a forklift, then a ladder on the pallet, then climbed to the top of the ladder to change a lightbulb? A pigheaded old Scot who wouldn't dream of asking for help, that's who.

But guilt and lecturing the McDonnell weren't going to fix the problem at hand. She needed to find a way to save the factory and afford private care for her da.

Only last year, MTech had made an offer for NSV, when they'd gotten wind of Da's new subsea shutoff-valve design. Da told them flat-out *No, the North Sea Valve Company is not for sale.* But whether her da liked it or not, she would let MTech, or any other outside investor, come in, and she'd listen to what they had to say. Scots weren't known for taking charity, but she'd entertain the foreigners as long as they brought an infusion of cash to the table.

She pulled out a pad of engineering paper and began jotting down ideas, just like when she was designing a piece of equipment.

Ross leaned into her office. "Can we talk to you a minute?"

Ross and his brother Ramsay stood outside her door. These two hulking Scots were close childhood friends who'd grown into a couple of tall, handsome fishermen.

She joined them outside her office. "Can you both take a look at conveyor three? There's something hanging it up."

They both frowned down at her, but it was Ross who spoke up first. "We want to know what the doctor had to say yesterday when ye were in Aberdeen. We're worried about the McDonnell."

Hell. Couldn't she have a little more time to process the news herself? "I really don't want to talk about it."

More of the workers made their way over and gathered around.

Ross motioned to the group. "We have a right to know."

Many of the men had invested not only their time into her father's vision, but what little money that they had, Ross included.

"He's not healing." Toag, her father's ancient machinist, seemed to have read her mind. "What a rotten herring. 'Tis bad enough the McDonnell took a spill."

"'Twas more than a spill," Murdoch interrupted, running his fingers through his beard. He was the other machinist. He and Toag were always together and, more times than not, were at each other's throat. "I saw the bone sticking out of his leg meself. Jagged, it was. Och, blood was everywhere."

"Quiet," Ramsay commanded.

"Don't worry, lass." Toag dug in his pocket and produced his wallet. "Somehow, we'll get him the medical treatment he needs. We'll pass around a bucket to collect for private care."

"Nay." She pointed at Toag. "Grab the notepad off my desk."

Toag lumbered past her to get it.

"But we want to help." Murdoch nodded his head, his beard bouncing.

"I know you do. And most of ye will." Pippa took the pad from Toag. "Here's how we're going to raise money." She thanked the Almighty for the ideas that He'd dropped in her lap today. "There's no need to call anyone. We have all we need right here." She looked around at the ruggedly handsome men of the village, the *single*, handsome men. "We'll have an auction. We're going to sell off our bachelors."

Ramsay's face clouded over, a storm coming. "And who's going to tell my wife about yere plan? It won't be me."

Pippa laughed, and it felt good after so much sadness. "No worries. It shouldn't interfere with Kit's matchmaking business. It's just a bit of fun for one evening."

Ramsay grinned. "Then I'm sure you can count on us to help you with it."

"Aye, ye'll all help and I'll not tolerate any of you crybabies whining about this auction, either. Do you hear me?"

"Aye, Pippa," they all agreed one by one.

She could get away with talking to them like this. The whole lot of them were like brothers to her. "Each of you will be shaved, showered, and kilted. And the stink of bluidy fish had better not be on any one of you. Do ye hear?"

"What'd'ya have in mind?" Toag, being an old married man, had nothing to worry about.

"Here's the plan," Pippa said. "We'll round up every rich, lonely female in Scotland. We'll even reach out to London if we have to. We'll entice them to come to Gandiegow with their purses stuffed with money. And after we've filled them with our best single-malt whisky, we'll sell off you lads for an evening of debauchery to the highest bidders."

Max McKinley was jarred awake from his nightmare as the plane touched down in Scotland. *The same damn dream every time.* The real, live nightmare he'd lived through at fifteen. He wiped the cold sweat from his forehead and tried to put the tragedy out of his mind. It always got worse this time of year. God, he hated Christmas.

He gathered his belongings and rushed off the plane. The first order of business was to call Mom and let her know he wouldn't be home for the holidays. She would have a cow. Maybe he should've called before he left. But hell, he'd barely had enough time to pack before MTech had pushed him out the door. It still puzzled him. Max was the new guy. The technical asset. Brand-new in the acquisitions department. Why send him?

Before he went in search of his rental car, he pulled out his phone and delivered the bad news.

"You're what?" His mom came close to blowing a gasket.

"Not coming home for the holidays," Max repeated.

"Or *won't*? How did you arrange it this time?" There was severity in her Mom-knows-all Texas twang.

He cringed at the truth in her words. But he was thirty-four, for chrissakes. He loved his mom and her heart was in the right place, but she was ruthless when it came to the holidays. He was tired from traveling and tired of the same old argument.

"Come for at least the day," she said.

Max released the second bombshell. "I can't. I'm in Scotland."

"You're where?"

"Scotland. For work. Please don't give me a guilt trip over it." Max sighed heavily into his cell, making sure his mother heard him all the way back in Houston.

She lit into him. "You volunteered for it, didn't you? Found the perfect excuse to get out of Christmas this year."

"Mom—"

"Your father would've wanted you to move past this. And your brother . . . Well, at least we bought him a wheelchair instead of a casket."

Max ran a hand through his hair. "I know."

"You blame yourself about Jake's accident, but—"

He cut her off. "Enough, okay? This trip has nothing to do with the past. It's work." But both nightmares still felt fresh. Fifteen-year-old boys should not be told their dad was dead on Christmas morning. The television had replayed the oil-rig explosion over and over for the whole day. Max had made it through some rough Christmases since. Then Jake's accident . . .

Mom was the one who sighed heavily this time. "Why couldn't they send someone else?" She could be such a pit bull when it came to family. And Christmas. "Why you?"

Exactly the question he'd asked himself. "I guess MTech wants me to cut my teeth on this deal." Even though he had no experience as yet in the acquisitions department. It must be trial by fire.

"Well, I hope at least you packed some warm clothes," Mom said begrudgingly.

"Love you, Mom." He made his tone let her know he meant it. "Tell Bitsy and Jake I'll call Christmas day."

After a few more good-byes, he hung up. He got his rental car and started the trek to Gandiegow. It was only four o'clock in the afternoon, but the sky was pitch-black, no moon in sight. The northeast coast of Scotland at the beginning of December would take some getting used to. With only the hum of the car to keep him company, the question niggled again. Why had MTech sent him?

Max understood the importance of the new technology he was to evaluate. He was also here to close the deal. Miranda and the rest of the acquisitions department must have had some pretty big Christmas plans to ship Max out alone. The whole thing was crazy, but he hadn't questioned his superiors. *Anything to get out of Christmas.*

Yes, this trip had come at exactly the right time. A nice cold visit to Scotland *alone* would be an excellent way to spend the holidays.

The drive took longer than expected to get to the small town—due to the curvy, icy pavement. And then there was the herd of languorous hairy cows dawdling in the road. When Max finally arrived in the village, he parked his rental car in the lot on the edge of town. No vehicles were allowed within the actual city limits. The walking paths were only wide enough for the small carts or wheelbarrows parked here and there in front of doorways. He'd read about this and the many other quirks of the community in the MTech file.

He pulled out his American Tourister, locked his rental car, and rolled his bag toward the sparse civilization of stone cottages. He wasn't in Texas anymore.

The small village of Gandiegow hugged the coastline in an arc with a smattering of houses and buildings. The town looked as if an artist had painted it there to add visual interest to the snow-dusted bluffs rising out of the North Sea.

Before the valve factory, Gandiegow was known for two things: its commercial fishing and most recently its international quilt retreats—Kilts and Quilts, they called it.

Max wheeled his bag over the snow-covered cobblestones until he reached the first building—his destination, the Fisherman. After getting a look at the town, he understood better why there was no hotel. It was a small community, and ancient. He should be happy there was at least a space for him to rent—the room over the pub.

For a moment, he stood peering down the narrow walkway that ran to the other end of town. This strip of concrete was the only thing separating the ocean from the village. He really should go inside the pub—he was freezing his ass off—but he couldn't get over it. One strong wave and the town could be washed away, the sixty-three houses and various establishments pulled out to sea. Who in their right minds would live near such danger looming outside their doors?

He stepped inside the mayhem of the crowded pub and made his way to the bar with his bag in tow. He'd considered staying in Lios or Fairge at one of their bed-and-breakfasts, but he needed to be close to the factory, and it wouldn't hurt to embed himself in this community. He had only a month to win these people over and convince Lachlan McDonnell and his son to make the deal with MTech.

It would be a hell of a partnership. NSV's new subsea shutoff valve had the capability of shutting down an oil-rig leak in seconds and preventing a catastrophic event. *Like the ones that killed my father and many others over the years.* If Max did his job right, the valve would be developed in MTech's sixty-million-dollar research facility and in full production by the end of next quarter.

As soon as he sat on the barstool, a strawberry blonde—

tall, lean, and tempting—materialized in front of him, glancing at his luggage, then peering at him.

"What can I get for ye, Yank?" She had a thick Scottish burr and the most incredible sea blue eyes.

Before he could answer, an inebriated lug pushed Max aside and got in the bartender's face.

"Give us a kiss, Pippa," the man slurred. "Just one kiss before I have to go home to me wife."

"Och, ye're stinking drunk, Coby. Back off with ye. Can't you see we have an important guest in our midst? An American."

"American?" Coby telescoped his head back and forth, trying to get Max in focus.

Max caught him as he fell forward.

"Don't muss the pretty Yank." She motioned to the group at the end of the bar. "Toag, Murdoch, get Coby home, will ye?"

Max transferred Coby to the others and waited until they were out of earshot. "So I'm pretty, huh?"

"Aye, and you damn well know it." She gave him a sardonic once-over as if real men were honed during barroom brawls and covered in scars from wrestling with sharks. She plunked a shot glass in front of him and filled it, though he hadn't ordered. "Here's yere drink, *sir*." She cocked a mocking eyebrow at him.

He didn't let her less than warm welcome bother him. He'd expected some resistance, especially since MTech had tried to buy NSV outright before. Instead, he smiled and reflected how her name, Pippa, suited her. He'd grown up around sassy women—his tough mother, grandmother, and firecracker of a little sister. He wasn't in the least put off by this Scottish lass and her sharp tongue. Actually it was quite the opposite. Her long, curly hair and perfect curves made this Texas-born man want to know more about—*Pippa*.

But he wasn't here to hook up with the local barmaid. He was here to make a deal for the lifesaving valve, which would prove himself to the higher-ups at MTech. Max needed to earn the trust of the Gandiegowans or he'd go home empty-handed.

"Thanks." He picked up the mystery drink and eyed the caramel-colored liquid before knocking it back. It didn't taste like the Scotch back in the States. It was smoky and burned smooth. He pulled out money for another, enjoying the shocked expression on Pippa's face.

She leaned on the bar, and he couldn't help but notice the tease of her cleavage in her tight green sweater.

"So ye can handle your whisky?" There was an air of respect in her tone and perhaps reverence shining in her sea blue eyes.

"Aye," he said teasingly.

"But here in Scotland, we sip our drinks." A reprimand as she poured him another one.

Before taking the dram, he stuck out his hand. "I'm Max McKinley."

She eyed his hand but didn't take it. "We know who you are." She motioned to the room, but no one else paid attention. "You may have been invited here, but beware. We know ye've come to rob us blind—take our factory and its jobs away from our town."

Her words doused him as if she'd thrown ice water in his face.

"Whoa there." He scooted back, putting his hands up. "I haven't come to steal anything."

"Are you not with the big American company who was sniffing around before?"

"Yes, but that doesn't mean—"

"Just because our factory needs a little help, you Yanks think it's a fine time to swoop in and swallow us whole, then spit out the leftover bits."

He frowned. He didn't agree with all of MTech's business practices. Yes, many times they bought a company for one of their products, only to dismantle the rest, letting thousands of employees go in the process. He had to keep telling himself, *Business is business. It isn't personal.* Besides, the deal he brought to the table was different. MTech wouldn't get run out of town with a proposal to buy this time; they were willing to do a partnership. *And I didn't come in here to discuss it at the local pub over a shot of whisky.* He was here to discuss it with Alistair McDonnell, the chief engineer, and his father, Lachlan McDonnell, the owner of the North Sea Valve Company.

"You needn't say a word. It's plainly written on your face." She gave him a dismissive glower.

Maybe it was the exhaustion, or the jet lag, or the Scotch. But he'd had enough.

"For a bartender," he snapped, "you certainly act like you have some say in the matter."

She didn't flinch but surprisingly backed down. "Aye, you're right. 'Tis not my fight. It's up to the McDonnell." She dropped her eyes with a submissive shake to her gorgeous head.

She wandered off and he downed his shot, regretting what he'd just done. He couldn't afford to get on the wrong side of even one villager. The stakes were too high.

"Miss?" he called out to her, motioning for her to come back. When she sauntered toward him, he saw the disguised shrewdness playing in her eyes. She wasn't the demure pussycat who'd backed down a moment ago. She was as cunning as a panther, ready to pounce.

She stopped in front of him and smiled sweetly. "Yes?"

"Sorry for how I acted. I hope you'll forgive my rudeness. Let me buy you a drink to make it up to you."

She *tsk*ed at him. "Papa says never to drink at the trough with the swine."

He winced. "Ouch."

"Besides, us working girls can't afford to drink on the job and get fired. How long are you planning on being here, Yank?"

"As long as it takes. The New Year? Maybe longer." Max knew these deals took time.

"That long, huh?" She looked at him as if taking his measurements; then she sashayed away.

She hadn't forgiven him and he hated being in this position — the perceived bad guy. He squeezed his empty glass. But he was the one who'd put in for the promotion, trying to stretch his skill set. He wasn't just an engineer anymore. He was a *closer*. And by God, he would close this deal if it was the last thing he did.

The next morning Max woke to a text message from Alistair McDonnell. He'd moved the appointment up, which was fine with Max. Over the last twenty-four hours, the two of them had exchanged many messages, and Alistair seemed like a decent, knowledgeable guy. Max knew Alistair was the one to be credited for calling MTech back to the table. From the project file, Max knew the McDonnell — as others referred to Lachlan McDonnell — would never have opened the door to another meeting with MTech.

Max stretched and gazed out the small window of his room. During the night, the snow had quietly tiptoed in. White covered everything, which was a real treat. Living in Houston, he'd only seen snow when traveling to Vale or Durango to ski.

After a quick shower, Max trudged to the parking lot in a business suit, tie, and dress shoes. By the time he arrived at his car, his dress shoes were soaked and his feet had turned into ice blocks. Thankfully, the steep road that led in and out of town had been scraped, but he wasn't taking any chances with any slick spots beneath the wheels. Slowly and carefully, he drove back up and over the rounded bluff to where NSV sat, about a mile away from Gandiegow. Just as the factory came into view, the sun peeked through the clouds, giving Max hope that all would go well here today with Alistair and the McDonnell.

NSV was made of ancient stone, without all the glitz or size of the megafactories in the U.S. But it did have character—an old warrior, worn-out from many years of battling time and the elements. From reports, he knew the building had stood empty for the last sixty years. Eighteen months ago, the McDonnell had reopened the factory doors. His son, Alistair, had recently joined him, stepping in as chief engineer.

Max pulled into the lot and turned off the car. No one was outside except a single worker, who shoveled snow from the sidewalk leading to the front entrance.

As he got closer, two things struck him at once. It wasn't a man clearing the sidewalk at all. It was a woman in men's coveralls. Secondly this wasn't any woman. It was the tall barmaid from last night. *Pippa*.

"Mornin'," she said as chipper as the sunlight above.

"Good morning to you, too." He was glad she'd let bygones be bygones from last night. He pointed to her shovel. "Your day job?"

She smiled brightly. "Aye. Here in Gandiegow, a lass needs to hold several positions to make ends meet. You'll never know where I might turn up."

"Where else do you work?" And because he was a guy, and hadn't had the bandwidth to date lately, when she'd said the word *positions*, it kind of got caught in his mind, rolling around. And not in an innocent way either.

Down, boy.

"You'll see me here and there." She smiled evasively and scraped the last bit of snow from the walk. "Come. I'll point you in the right direction." She leaned her shovel against the building and took the lead.

Inside, the lobby was the strangest he'd ever seen. No contemporary plush seating or end tables with trendy magazines. This place was bare-bones. Three kitchen chairs, one folding, and one dilapidated Queen Anne sat against the wall. A crest and a sword hung above the seating. In the corner sat the grand prize, a beautiful Douglas fir, decorated with loads of Christmas cheer. The over-the-top tree didn't fit with the other substandard decor.

A brunette came from behind a worn receptionist desk with a *hungry-for-men* smile and a mug in her hand. "I saw you pull up and poured you a cup of tea, in case you needed warming up. I'm Bonnie, by the way." She seemed to stick out her chest, flaunting her very large breasts in his direction.

But Max wasn't half as interested as he was in the strawberry blonde who'd put him in his place last night. He took his tea and thanked the receptionist just the same.

Pippa unzipped her coveralls and slipped her arms out,

letting the top half dangle down. He kind of quit breathing. Underneath, she wore an old formfitting Tau Beta Pi T-shirt, which befuddled the hell out of him.

Tau Beta Pi? The engineering honor society?

If he could've formed words, he might've asked why she wore it. Except he couldn't stop staring at her nipples. *God help him!* He jerked his eyes away and, in the process, spilled tea all over his suit, from his chest to his knees.

"Damn."

"Not to worry." Pippa leaned over the desk and whispered to the brunette, who had resumed her position behind it. The only word he made out from the exchange was *auction*. From the closet behind the desk, Bonnie retrieved two items—a kilt clipped to a hanger along with a brown paper bag. She handed them to Pippa.

Pippa presented the clothing to him. "Here, put this on. We'll take care of yere suit."

He frowned at the skirt. "Thank you, no. I'll be fine."

"It's company policy to wear a kilt." Amusement danced in her eyes, along with a fair dose of determination. "Everyone has to wear one for their company badge. For plant security."

That seemed highly unlikely. He glanced at her chest and she wore no badge.

He tore his eyes away. "Don't you have a guest badge?" *Like a normal factory?*

"A guest badge is for daily visitors. Ye said you plan to be here the month." She planted her hands on her hips. "It's company—"

"Policy?" he finished for her.

"You catch on quick, Mr. McKinley."

"That's what they tell me." He grimaced at the kilt again.

She spun him toward a small door. "I'll be the one taking yere picture when you come out."

"Another one of your jobs?"

"Aye. Now change in there."

He marched into the small water closet and closed the door behind him. The brown bag held a flowing white shirt, black hiking boots, and thick cream-colored knee-high socks.

"Don't be long, Yank," she hollered through the door. "I've work to do."

He quickly dressed, surprised the clothes and boots fit pretty well, considering. He left his wet things over the towel rack and went back out.

The brunette rose, giving him a low whistle. "Aye, Pippa, you were right about the Yank in a kilt."

Pippa nodded appreciatively at his legs. She grabbed a tartan and threw it over his shoulder. When she bent to fasten it by his hip, he couldn't help but let his mind wander to places it shouldn't. She smelled like fresh snow and woman. He felt both turned on and a little like Rob Roy.

She dragged him to the Christmas tree, positioning him in front of it.

"What are you doing?" he asked.

"Just smile for the birdie."

He didn't.

She snapped several photos anyway.

"Bonnie, pull the Queen Anne chair over to the tree and I'll take a few more."

He folded his arms across his chest. "What's really going on here?"

Pippa gave him an innocent *I've-no-idea-what-you're-talking-about* stare. "Are you sure ye're not Scottish, Mr. McKinley? You have the name for it. The stubborn attitude. A veritable Scottish warrior through and through."

"Stop buttering me up." He narrowed his eyes at her. "You're up to something."

"Don't be a prig, Mr. McKinley." Pippa readjusted the sash on his shoulder. "Americans love to claim to be Scottish."

"Can I change back into my clothes yet?"

"Nay. We have to make sure you look right. For the badge and all." Pippa snapped a few more shots. One with him standing by the Queen Anne chair. Another with him seated like the frigging king of Scotland or something. She even had the audacity to point the camera at his legs and take two more, mumbling, "Good, good," to his shins.

"So do all the employees have their legs on their badges?" he drawled.

"Oh, aye, absolutely." Pippa looked as if she could barely hold back from laughing. "Leg shots are imperative for security. *Especially if someone is running from the building with our top secret designs.*" She gave him a pointed look, as if that was why he was here. Her own words had a sobering effect. "I think we're done here." She brushed her long curls out of her face like being the photographer had worn her out. Or was that relief he saw on her face?

"Go change now, Mr. McKinley," Pippa ordered. Without a backward glance, she walked through the double doors leading into the plant with the camera swinging at her side.

He stood all alone in the lobby; Bonnie was gone too. Max looked again at the double doors Pippa had gone through. He wondered if her other jobs included sweeping the factory floor or cleaning the toilets. He forced her from his mind and went into the bathroom to put his clothes back on.

"What the hell?"

His tea-soaked pants weren't where he'd left them. Or his jacket. Or his dress shirt. He marched back out and found Bonnie had returned.

"Where are my clothes?"

Bonnie smiled helpfully. "Soaking in a bucket in the break room. Tea can be a bitch to get out."

He stared at her slack-jawed. "What am I supposed to wear?"

Bonnie eyed him like her favorite box of Christmas candy. "The kilt, of course."

"I can't go around like this."

"Och. It's Scotland. Ye'll be grand."

He peered down at his outfit, wishing to be anywhere else, and then tried to look at the bright side. At least the boots were warm. He approached her desk. "I assume Alistair McDonnell knows I'm here."

Bonnie stilled. For a moment, he wondered if maybe she'd misunderstood him. She seemed genuinely confused.

He tried again. "Alistair McDonnell? The reason I'm here? We have an appointment." He lifted his mug and drained the remaining dribbles of his now-cold tea.

She frowned at him, picked up the phone, and put it to her ear. "The American says to tell ye he's here." She glanced up at him as if he'd been shortchanged upstairs. "Go ahead and take a seat."

He wandered over to the coat of arms and studied it. After a few minutes, he chose a chair as far away from the Christmas tree as he could manage and checked his messages.

One from his mom. One from his sister. One from his brother.

And crap. Miranda wanted him to check in. He texted back quickly that he'd arrived, was staying in the room over the pub, and was about to meet with the NSV's chief engineer.

As he hit SEND, the doors swung open and a professionally dressed woman came through. He stood. She had on a well-fitted navy suit with a tantalizing slit up the left side of her calf-length skirt. The way her heels clicked as she walked toward him sounded like a command. Her loose braid from earlier had been stretched into a knot at the back of her head. However, it was her sea blue eyes that shocked him.

Pippa stuck out her hand to him. "Alistair Philippa McDonnell. It's nice to meet you." She gave him a firm handshake.

He fumbled with the mug. If there'd been any tea left in it, he would've doused his kilt and been forced to tour the factory buck naked.

She smiled, as innocent as the new snow outside, her professional aloofness daring him to acknowledge the switch-up. "Well, then," she finally said, "should we have a tour?"

He seldom backed down from a challenge. "But last night—" he started.

"Let's not ruin last night by talking about it," she purred.

Bonnie's head shot up.

Pippa—*no, Alistair*—gave a throaty laugh and sashayed away, not seeming to give a damn about her reputation.

Max trailed behind her through the double doors like her lowly servant. They went down a long corridor as a million questions rolled through his baffled brain. How had he not known that Alistair McDonnell was female? He certainly knew now by the shapely derriere in front of him.

He didn't let the subject drop. "Hold up. What am I to call you?"

She stopped and turned to him, the epitome of seriousness. "How about Yere Excellency?"

ALSO AVAILABLE FROM

PATIENCE GRIFFIN

TO SCOTLAND WITH LOVE

A Kilts and Quilts Novel

Caitriona Macleod reluctantly gave up her career as an investigative reporter for the role of perfect wife. But after her cheating husband passes away, a devastated Cait leaves Chicago for the birthplace she hasn't seen since she was a child...

Quilting with her gran and the other women of the village brings Cait a peace she hasn't known in years. But if she turns in a story about Graham Buchanan—a handsome movie star who stays in his hometown between films—Gandiegow will never forgive her for betraying one of its own. Should she suffer the consequences to resurrect her career? Or listen to her battered and bruised heart and give love another chance?

"[A] lyrical and moving debut."
—*Publishers Weekly* (Starred Review)

Available wherever books are sold or at
penguin.com